The Jewi
Iraq's lost past

A novel by

Judit Neurink

Translation by Pamela Williams

Original title in Dutch: De Joodse bruid

Published by Uitgeverij Jurgen Maas, 2014

www.uitgeverijjurgenmaas.nl

Cover English edition: Annet Stirling

Translation: Pamela Williams

The Jewish Bride, @2018

All rights reserved.

ISBN-13: 9781980257929

For my dad, who taught me to care for people and their stories

Her mother walks to the stove and lifts the lids off the pans. That enhances the smell of rice and meat in the kitchen. She tells Zara to spread out the sofra in the living room, and hands her a dish with tomato and cucumber salad.
"Himen and Kamran, are you staying for dinner?"
Zara's oldest brother says that his wife is waiting for him and leaves, while Kamran phones home to let them know he is staying to eat.
A few minutes later the family is sitting around the dishes with rice and warm sauce with meat. The television is on; men and women in Kurdish outfits are dancing through a spring meadow. Kamram hums along with the music, Zara laughs, moving her shoulders to the music in the way of traditional Kurdish dances.

Alone in her room, Zara stares at the book that she has just unpacked. The red cloth cover is faded and worn. She wanted it for herself, but why, remains a mystery to her. She strokes the cover. Curious about who it was that left the fingerprints, she opens the book.
There is a photo in the front. A crumpled, faded picture of a distinguished looking young woman next to a young man dressed in black. Her colourful dress is a striking contrast to his sober black clothing. Just like her abundance of gold: gold coins on her forehead, a belt with golden decorations, bracelets, rings and earrings.
Amazement makes way for astonishment when Zara recognized the belt. The coins on the forehead – is one of the chains on the kitchen table a headdress?

Who is this – the woman of the house? The one who wrote this book?

She turns the picture over. She cannot read the notation on the back. It is neither Arabic nor Kurdish. It only looks a bit like it.

On the flyleaf is a small silver hand that is decorated with blue and orange stones. A hand to ward off the evil eye. So much more beautiful and delicate than the ones made today.

Carefully she lays it to one side and then she sees a name and date on the flyleaf. In Arabic handwriting.

'Rahila Jozua's daughter. June 1, 1941.'

No title. No author. Only once again words in a language that she does not know.

Is Rahila the woman in the photograph?

She carefully turns the page. The paper is thin and vulnerable. Her eyes fly over the delicately formed Arabic letters and words.

My cousin Tova has been murdered, in her house in Baghdad. Along with Aunt Naima. I can barely believe it, but we received word this morning that Uncle Nasim is on the way to Penjwin with my nephews.

Breathlessly, Zara turns the pages. Words and names jump from the filled pages. Abba, ima – again: neither Arabic nor Kurdish. Did the Jews in Kurdistan have their own language? Just like the Christians? She wants to continue flipping through the pages until she can read the end, just like she often does with a novel, when she hears her name being called.

for her father, but also from frustration over his unwavering point of view.

Sometimes she wonders how he can be a leader – since he sees everything from his point of view as a fighter. His knowledge has been formed by war and conflicts. Just like most of the politicians in Iraqi Kurdistan who owe their job to their peshmerga past, he does not know how to function and operate in peace time.

Her father shakes his head. "You are a bright young lady, but you have no understanding of politics."

Zara's mother raises her hand in disagreement. "That is not a legitimate argument, Saman. She simply has another opinion."

Her mother surprises Zara. Usually she chooses the side of her father.

He lays down the remote control impatiently and stands up. "I cannot compete against a women's dispute."

The door slams shut.

"And he thinks that together they will be able to work out their differences in a Great Kurdistan!"

"Banu, that's enough," Zara's mother says sternly.

But Zara sees from the small smile on her lips that she silently agrees with Banu.

2 RAHILA'S JOURNAL

June 3, 1941

My cousin Tova has been murdered. The day before yesterday, in her house in Baghdad. Along with Aunt Naima. I can barely believe it, but we received the news this morning that Uncle Nasim is on his way to Penjwin with my nephews.

I think of Tova and how we played together, when they came to Kurdistan in the summer. Even though still very young, she is very smart. No: she was smart. She is no longer here – I can't believe it.

Their house has been emptied – just as it happened with the houses of many other Jews in Baghdad. Shops have been looted. Hundreds of people were murdered. Who is responsible for such a tragedy!

I am so shocked by all the reports. It is so difficult to believe what has happened.

Luckily, he and the boys were able to reach the home of a business acquaintance, who is a Muslim. They sent a few of their workers to auntie's house, to get her and Tova, but it was already very dangerous on the streets. When one of them became injured because someone thought that they were Jews, they had to return.

The rest of the day, the night and the following morning the bridges over the Tigris could hardly bear their burdens. Men ran empty handed in one direction, only to return loaded with goods and treasures.

The house of Uncle Nasim's friend looks out over the river, and he sat there watching for hours. He knew what was happening at home and wanted to go there, but his friend wouldn't let him. He would not have survived it.

On the second afternoon, the Kurdish troops arrived that the regent had called in to bring back the peace. A curfew was established, and the soldiers were given the orders to shoot anyone who was out on the streets. Uncle thinks that dozens were killed this way. Only at the end of the afternoon did it become calm once more and the flood of robbers over the bridge dried up. But uncle was still unable to return home.

Eventually he was able to go there with a group of soldiers. Everywhere you looked there were bodies, he says. He also saw rugs and furniture that had been left behind when looters had to flee to escape the soldiers.

The Jewish houses were marked with a red hand. Who had done that, uncle did not know. The looters knew exactly where to go.

The door of the house was open. The house was empty, on the bare shelves lay only the stuff no one wanted. Auntie and Tova were not downstairs. Uncle found them upstairs in the empty bedroom. When he said this, he started to cry.

A grown man who is crying, I had never seen that before. Men are not supposed to cry.

No one said a word. I felt relief when ima sent me to get him a glass of water. But when I came back she was crying too.

I don't dare ask the question, about how he found them. What the criminals had done to them. Actually, I don't really want to know.

Immediately after he had buried my auntie and Tova at the Jewish cemetery, uncle came to Penjwin. How long he will stay, I do not know. Neither does he, I think. Uncle now lives with my nephews in our guest room.

No one helps ima and me with the extra work. I am busy all day long carrying *stikan* tea inside, and baking the bread has now become my task solely as well. I hate it. The heavy work from kneading the dough, and the heat from the open oven.

And the way they give me orders! Ima tells me that I should not complain, as it is simply the duty of the women to look after the needs of the men.

But I want to go to school, to learn everything there is to learn. There is so much I want to know.

July 5, 1941

Abba has promised me that starting in September, I will be allowed to help him at school! Because ima wouldn't listen to me, I went to abba to complain about the work I have to do in the house. He told me that I am too impatient, since because of his lessons I already know more than most of the boys my age. But he did give me a stack of books to read until the school opens again.

He said that it is getting too busy for him at school, and that I know enough to help him out by taking over some of his work. In September I get to start!

Not that my life will change drastically, as I will remain to be the house slave. Abba's condition is that I continue helping ima.

Uncle Nasim still lives in the guest room. He wants to open a textile shop in Sulaymaniya, because he will not be returning to Baghdad. As calm has returned there, they have discussed this over and again. The fact that he barely speaks Kurdish, could pose a problem as he is planning on selling fabric to the Kurds. But he says that there are too many painful memories in Baghdad.

Every time that I am reminded of Tova, I start to cry. Along with her and auntie, some three hundred people were killed, we have heard. Amongst them are 170

Jews, and seventy looters that were shot by the Kurdish units.

There were Muslim deaths too, from those who tried to protect their Jewish neighbours in the mixed neighbourhoods. Good people, like the friend of Uncle Nasim, who could not save my uncle's family.

Over the past days, there have been stories flying around about attacks on Jews. There is talk about the murder of Jews and a bomb in a full synagogue that happily did not explode. When you hear about all of it, you might almost believe that the attacks on the Shavuot are not that special after all. What is this that is going on in our country?

Even here in Kurdistan, things have been happening. Uncle Masrour came up with the story about Abba Shanbraat, a Jewish merchant who was robbed while travelling, and murdered. That was thirty years ago, in 1914.

His family converted to the Islamic faith after his death, which shows how threatened they felt. The granddaughter is a friend of one of my girlfriends.

Suddenly, all is getting very close. Sometimes I wake up in the middle of the night, drenched in sweat. Then I wonder how safe we are here in Penjwin.

Imagine that the Penjwinians also turn against us. That they come to the *Jewlakan* to kill us. That they come to empty out our house, and that of the neighbours, and those of my uncles further up in the street. That the weaving mill of Uncle Salim is smashed to bits and that all his rugs and fabrics are stolen. And the same thing would happen to the silver forge of Uncle Masour. That they come to take abba's study books, and his maps.

Abba says that we are just talking ourselves into being afraid. Was Abba Shahbraat murdered because he was a Jew, or because someone wanted to steal his merchandise? Couldn't that have happened to a Kurdish merchant as well?

In Baghdad, a new government has restored the order, and I find comfort in the stories coming out of Sulaymaniya. There, a group of young men was planning on attacking the homes of Jews on the second day of Shavuot. They gathered at the synagogue. How the news could travel so quickly is a mystery to me, but the imam of Sulaymaniya heard about it and rushed to the Jewlakan.

He started a discussion with the looters.

"Who has given you the order to do this: Moses, Jesus or Mohammed?" he asked them.

The men answered that the Jews were infidels.

The imam lashed out at them saying: "The one who told you that is an infidel himself. The looters in Baghdad are criminals. They do not believe in God and his messenger. The Jews are under our protection. Whoever brings harm to an ally, will be punished in hell."

He sent the men home with the order to fast so that God would be able to forgive their sinful intentions. They kissed his hands and left.

I shudder to think how differently it could have ended if the imam had not heard the news in time, or did not react to it.

Now I understand why abba with the other men of our synagogue went to see the imam, when they heard the news from Baghdad. And to the agha, the wealthy Kurdish landowner to whom abba sends kilos of sugar on a regular basis. I understand now where those guards came from who stood for days in front of the synagogue. We are dependent on the protection of the imam and the agha. Without them we would be lost, abba says.

Uncle Nasim blames the Zionists as being the cause for the Farhud. And once again I learned a new word. Abba explained it to me. Zionists want their own Jewish state in Palestine. They want Arab land for the promised land of our people. And that is something that many Arabs are angry about.

Justly so, I think, it is their land. We here in Kurdistan would be angry if the Arabs tried to conquer our land too.

According to abba, the problem lies in Baghdad. He blames especially the Iraqi nationalists who think that all Jews are Zionists, and that we, the Jews in Iraq, also want our own Jewish state here. And that is why uncle will not return to Baghdad. He thinks that it can all happen again at any time.

The imam from the mosque just outside of the Jewlakan calls for the afternoon prayers. I have to get the oven lit, knead the dough and then bake the naan. I can smell ima frying onions. She is making the sauce for the rice. I must hurry up.

September 2, 1941

I was too excited to sleep these past nights.

This week the school has started once again. And it is really happening: I am helping abba with teaching! I am so excited, that in the morning I can barely wait until it is time to walk to school with abba.

My job is to teach the youngest boys how to write. We are with a group in a corner of the synagogue. Abba does the beginning, the explanation about the letters, and then I teach the boys to write them.

This way abba can focus on the older children. How did he manage this on his own, three groups of some 30 boys in all! We have the youngest aged around six and seven, a middle group and then the older boys of up to twelve. While he is busy with one group, the boys in the other groups must work on their own.

And it is fun when you see how a young boy recognizes a letter, and then manages to copy it! We teach them the Hebrew alphabet first and then the Arabic, because the government demands this, but the lessons are done in the Targum, our own language.

After that, the boys must learn the Torah from memory. Much differently than how I learned it; abba gave me everything in the translation from the beginning. I think that is why I was able to learn so quickly.

Our Benjamin is twelve and is in abba's oldest group, and he understands nothing from the meaning of the Torah. But because he has a good memory, he knows nearly all of it by heart. With his beautiful voice he can recite very well. He has started reciting verses from the Torah for a fee at weddings and funerals.

My brother will no doubt become a great businessman, but he has no idea what it is exactly that he is reciting. Thinking of this makes me laugh.

Uncle Nasim has left for Sulaymaniya. I am happy that he has gone, although I know that I shouldn't think that way.

He has asked ima if I couldn't go with him to look after the boys, but abba wouldn't have it. He needed me at school, he said. But I heard him talking to ima. The age difference is too big, he said. It was then that I understood that Uncle Nasim had wanted to marry me.

The thought made me giggle. The idea: Uncle Nasim as my husband! There are grey hairs in his beard. How old is he? Certainly, over thirty. That is twice my age.

I want someone like Azam, who is working at the vegetable shop. With those nice thick curls. And those dark-brown eyes like a mirror so you can see yourself.

How could Uncle Nasim even suggest such a thing! As if I could take the place of Aunt Naima. And I couldn't possibly be a mother to Moshe and Salim!

The boys stayed behind, when uncle left for Sulaymaniya. Moshe is now in my class, Salim is still too young. Ima looks after him. Now we have a house with seven men and two women.

But I am still the house slave. Ima demands that I help her in the evenings with the preparations for next-day's meal. I have to clean the rice, prepare the dough, wash the dishes and do the weekly laundry.

The laundry I don't mind so much, even though I miss a half day of school because of it. On Thursdays, we wash the clothes by the river so that we will have clean ones on the Sabbath. All the adult Jewish women gather there. While we soap, scrub and rinse, we chat, sing and gossip. All of Penjwin is talked about.

The women are talking a lot about the Farhud. These stories touch me deeply.

They say that the killing could go on for so long because the Baghdad police remained inactive. And even worse: that the British had not sent any help or assistance because they wanted the Iraqis to handle their own affairs. That the regent had only just returned, and was barely in control yet. So there was no intervention. Who is then to blame, you might wonder.

According to the women, there were far more deaths than the official number. A number of them have been buried in mass graves in a Muslim cemetery, because there was no one to identify them.

I listen to this with disgust. But at the same time, I wonder how much is really true. The people talk too much, and not everything is to be believed, abba often says.

The women surprise me. Everything that is discussed at home, is shared above the laundry. After two days of doing the washing I know more than I normally hear in an entire month.

March 22, 1942

Yesterday I danced in the street with Azam! He sees me!

I am so happy!

It is *Nowroz*, the Kurdish New Year, and that is celebrated more cheerfully with each year passing. This year, we had young men jumping over fires in the streets, and musicians trying to persuade the people to dance. Some families set a table outside with food and drinks. Children played games on the street, happy that the cold, boring months of winter have passed. And everyone was wearing their best clothes.

I stood there looking around, in my favourite purple dress with the matching black scarf with purple decorations. Then Azam suddenly took my hand and joined a group in a line dance. We had never spoken a word to one another before, except in the shop and that was only about how many kilos of carrots or onions I needed. And now we stood there together, shaking our shoulders to the music, along with the other youths in the line.

His hand was calloused and warm, and he used his thumb to caress the palm of my hand. And we smiled at one another while we made the dance moves. He has such beautiful eyes! Often, he took the lead, and waved the handkerchief. He is such a good dancer. And this beautiful boy chooses me.

I think we danced for hours. The women doing the washing on Thursday will now certainly have something to talk about.

This morning ima unexpectedly asked me about him. She must have heard something. She hardly comes into the shops or the market since she leaves that to me or abba, and so she didn't see much of him. But her excuse is a bit of nonsense since in Penjwin everybody knows one another.

I could hardly say that he has thick curls and beautiful brown eyes and that his mouth always seems to be smiling... I mumbled something in response and then quickly left with some excuse about the food.

I am so happy, that I don't even mind that Uncle Nasim is back this week. Moshe and Salim hang from his arms. And of course, they celebrated Nowroz yesterday too. Uncle Nasim taught the boys how to move their shoulders to the music, and which steps go along with it.

He has brought a guest along: Ezra Kadoori, who went to Palestine as a child and recently returned to Iraq. Uncle Nasim met him via a friend from Baghdad. Ezra is staying with him in Sulaymaniya.

When I enter the guest room with the tea and sweets, I keep hearing words like Zionism, armed struggle, our own state in Palestine. Only in the beginning, they would fall silent when I entered the room.

Didn't Uncle Nasim say that Zionism was to blame for the Farhud? Yes, he did say that, I have written it down. Now he seems to be a Zionist himself. I cannot stand that man.

What do we need with Palestine? Our land is here, in Iraq. How often have I heard abba tell us that we have lived here since an Assyrian king took us out of Samaria as the spoils of war? And that when the next king allowed us to return, we didn't even want to, since we enjoyed living here so much? That we had given up our Hebrew for the local language, the Aramaic, which we still speak today? Why would we now, after all these centuries, suddenly need a land of our own?

Today there was a call for tea from the guest room, and then Azam was sitting there too. I didn't know where to look, and realized that I wasn't wearing a headscarf. He looked at me, when I put the stikan down for him. I thought that I was going to faint.

Ezra was talking in Arabic about the role of young Jews in the establishment of our own Jewish state.

About the struggle that is needed to fulfil our rights, the British colonialism in our promised land, and about the Arabs who have no reason being there.

The Arabs have so many states, he said, why must they have the land that God has given to us?

The ash of his cigarettes was all over the carpet.

My brother Yesula asked, whether there could be no political solution. He sounded just like abba, serious and thoughtful.

Ezra answered patiently, that political solutions sometimes had to be forced. Then he looked at me and said that in Eretz, the women have equal rights. They are needed for more important things than making and serving tea, he said.

And who will then take care of the tea?

The question was out before I realized it. I felt the blood flush to my cheeks.

Ezra smiled. However it turns out, he said, anyone or all of them.

I stood by the door with the empty tray in my hands and felt that all eyes were on me. Yet I could not stop myself from asking about the children. Are they all going to look after them as well?

The boys laughed at my question, but Ezra remained serious. He said that if they are gathered, a number of the women can look after them, so the others will be free to do something else.

And the cooking? I wondered.

Uncle Nasim said that there are very good male cooks.

Why don't I ever see you in the kitchen then, I thought, as I bit on my tongue to keep myself from saying this out loud.

Erza offered that I could stay here if I liked. Just then, as if she was eavesdropping, I heard ima calling for me.

Here in the house the women still do the cooking, I said sharply, while I turned to open the door.

Then I guiltily remembered the rules of politeness that ima had invested in me. Once again, my face flushed with colour.

Would they need anything else now? I said with the doorknob in my hand.

Uncle Nasim said nicely that I could go, while he changed from Arabic to Targum, as if it was only between the two of us, that he heard my mother calling for me.

It is getting dark outside; I am almost unable to read what I have written. Happily, the days are becoming longer. Soon I will once again be able to write up on the roof.

Abba has asked Uncle Nasim to no longer bring any guests to the house. Uncle then left yesterday with Ezra. I do not understand this at all: abba's request goes against all the proper forms of hospitality.

This morning I came into the kitchen and found myself in the middle of a serious discussion.

He did not want Yesula to join the Khalutz, abba said, and those meetings about Zionism here in this house were far too dangerous.

Ima protested that Nasim and Ezra are our guests, and that we would get a bad name because of abba's actions.

She fell silent when she saw me. Abba looked sternly towards me.

I told him what Ezra has said, that women in Eretz Israel will get equal rights. And that men can cook food too, make tea and look after the children.

Do you see now how he is polluting their thoughts! abba exclaimed. He stormed outside.

Ima shook her head wearily. She pushed a broom into my hands and told me to go and clean the guest room.

Sighing, I got started on the unpleasant chore. It was dusty there, with fine sand from the street and the ash from Ezra's cigarettes. There were overflowing ashtrays everywhere. Even the water pipe had not been cleaned away.

To give myself some distraction, I tried to imagine the room as it was when I had found Azam there. I saw him leaning against the pillows. I touched the spot, but the warmth of his body was long gone. My hand bumped against something hard that was shoved under the cushion.

A thin book. "Our own state," was written in Arabic on the cover. Had Ezra forgotten this?

I paged through the book. "In order to be able to defend the new state against the many threats, we will need good, well-trained young soldiers," I read.

I pushed the book back under the pillow. Later, when the room was clean, I would put it under my dress and bring it to my secret place.

A song came to mind. I hummed it softly while I cleaned the room, and I saw Azam's dance moves before me. When would I see him again?

April 15, 1942

He looked around to make sure that no one was watching, and then quickly pushed a note into my hand. As if nothing had happened, he asked how many onions I needed, and offered the potatoes and radishes from Iran.

Then he reached under the counter. He had these first mountain daffodils especially for me. I should just smell how nice.

With a red head I stuck my nose in the fragrant bouquet of tiny flowers.

The note was burning in my hand. I could barely wait to read it. What could it be that Azam had to tell me? Maybe he wanted to declare his love for me... how romantic! For days now, all I can think about is him.

I had to wait until after dinner, before going to the outhouse where I could read the note.

The Arabic was written in a sloppy handwriting and I saw at least three mistakes right away. Written in a hurry? Or was writing simply not Azam's strongest feature?

I heard Shalom call from outside. My time was nearly up. Quickly my eyes fled over the words. "Bring the book to school with you tomorrow. I will come and get it," I was able to decipher from the note.

I was disappointed. No declaration of love, only a book about Zionism that he had forgotten in our guestroom. Angry with myself for having expected so much more from the note, I crumpled it up.

Shalom angrily shouted to hurry up.

I used the water pitcher to wash myself and flush away the poop through the hole in the ground. The crumpled piece of paper washed away too.

At school, I hid the book between the books for new readers.

I have read it, but was not that impressed. The writer uses many difficult words to say that the Jews must all live together, because there is a promised land for us. As if the existence of Eretz Israel should be enough of a reason to want to come and settle there.

Azam was standing outside the synagogue when we were finished. He greeted me with his smile. It warmed me inside, as if a warm glow was being pulled through me. I hoped that my burning cheeks wouldn't give me away.

Could he walk some way with me, he asked?

I told him I had his book.

He ignored that. What was wrong? We walked in silence.

Rahila, I want to ask for your hand, he said abruptly.

I thought that my heart had stopped. I looked at him, had I heard him correctly? He shyly smiled.

He would like to marry me and go to Palestine together, he said softly.

Was this real? Azam wanted to marry me? My tongue was stuck; I didn't know what to say.

I could only nod.

His smile returned.

I was his girl, he beamed. So, could he go and ask my father?

Suddenly I imagined it. Abba showing him the door: You are poisoning her mind!

No… I stuttered. I pushed an escaped curl back under the headscarf.

His smile had vanished.

Don't talk about Palestine, I blurted out. I told him Abba doesn't want to hear anything about it. He hates Zionism. He feels that Iraq is good to us.

The smile was back.

Did he understand? I insisted. Abba would send him away if he would so much as mention it.

I looked around to see whether anyone was looking at us, and then reached for the book. I warned him that it is dangerous, and he should not get caught with it.

He quickly tucked it away in his wide waistband. He said he would be careful.

Zara hesitates before she replies. If she tells her mother about the diary, she will most certainly have to hand it over. She is not ready to be separated from it. She wants to know what happens to Rahila.

"The Jewish treasure…," she just says vaguely.

Her mother looks at her inquiringly.

"Did you know that the Jews arrived in Kurdistan some 2,800 years ago, after having been deported by an Assyrian king?"

Her mother plops down next to her on the couch.

Zara reads from the screen: "A majority of the Ten Tribes of Israel, which were part of Samaria, the northern part Israel during the biblical period, were taken prisoner by the Assyrians during 721 and 715 BC. They were deported to Media, Assyria and Mesopotamia. This is roughly what is known today as Kurdistan."

"We know nothing about them," her mother says softly.

"A large part of our history has been stolen from us by the Arab nationalists."

"The Jews in Kurdistan came from Samaria?"

"Yes, and the ones from the rest of Iraq came from Judea, the other part of the modern state of Israel. Two different groups, at different times." Zara searches through the text on the screen. "An estimated hundred years after the first deportation actions, the Babylonian Nebuchadnezzar II inherited the Assyrian empire. He conquered Judea and deported a large group of the residents to Babylon."

"The Assyrians deported people from within their own empire? That reminds me of Saddam Hussein, who brought the Arabs to Kirkuk and the Kurds to Baghdad."

"In that way you can control people, and as they are strangers in that region you will know for sure that they will never be able to gain power. My studies are filled with these kinds of examples."

"Why the Jews didn't go back?"

"They settled, and even gained permission to practice their faith. As a result, the Kurdish Adiabene dynasty, which had Erbil as its capital, converted to Judaism in the first century BC. Ever heard of Queen Helena?"

"She converted?"

"With her husband, the king and her son. And a large number of Kurdish nationals."

"And the Jews in Babylon, what happened to them?"

"They were of a different category than the Kurdish Jews. Here we had farmers, merchants, textile workers and painters, and jewellers. But the Jews in Babylon wrote the Talmud, one of the most important Jewish religious books. They were the intellectuals."

"And after that they became the economic power of Baghdad," her mother adds.

"Yes, that's right. In Baghdad, the Jews were the bankers, the investors, the businessmen. But also, the singers and the poets. When they left in the fifties, Baghdad lost not only her soul and her voice, but also her financial power."

"You say that beautifully, *janakam*."

"Dayke, it is amazing, that in a ten-year period more than two thirds of the 150,000 Jews left Iraq. Why?"

"What do your teachers say?"

"Later this year we will be discussing the establishment of the state of Israel, and the departure of the Jews from the

Arabic lands. But I doubt that we will really go into it. This is a black page."

"What did the Iraqi government do at the time?"

"The British were in charge, together with the regent who was in power, since King Faisal was still too young to reign by himself. The monarchy and the British assigned Jews to important positions. That created a lot of tensions. But the real villain turned out to be Rashid al-Gaylani, an Arab nationalist who was prime minister briefly three times over. The second time in 1940, and then he was a close friend of the Germans."

"The Nazis?"

"Yes. The British sent him away, since they were at war with the Germans at the time. But in 1941 – let me check," as she searched through her notes, "yes, in March of 1941 he regained power after a coup. Then his regime was even more nationalist than before. And, with the excuse that the British were favouring the Jews, even more anti-Jewish. There were numerous anti-Jewish demonstrations and then in June of 1941 the Farhud took place."

Zara's mother looks at her inquiringly. "The Farhud? Looting, like after the American invasion in Baghdad and in the south?"

"They also called that a Farhud at the time? Interesting." Zara makes a note. "In 1941, it was a pogrom in Baghdad. Nearly two hundred Jews were murdered, but the death toll might have been closer to six hundred. Many people were so disfigured that they were buried in mass graves. Houses and shops were looted. Women and girls were raped; their breasts were even cut off. People walked through the city

and shouted *Kutal al yehud* – slaughter the Jews."
Zara has read many horrid things since she began her investigation, but this she finds to be the worst so far. Iraqis who murdered other Iraqis, only because they are different. Just like happens again in Baghdad, between the different Muslim groups and the Christians.

"How horrible. But the entire Farhud has disappeared from our collective memories."

"Yet it brought about a major turnaround. Jews no longer trusted the Arabs. In Baghdad, a third of the population was Jewish. Can you imagine what that level of distrust did to such a society?"

Zara's mother sighs. "I can. We Kurds have learned to distrust the Arabs, because under Saddam's regime, our lives were very uncertain."

"And we continue to distrust them."

Zara's mother gets up and sits down again.

"I should do the washing-up, but your stories are too interesting. Have you found out anything yet about the objects we found?"

Zara turns back towards the computer and opens one of the folders she has created for her investigations. Her mother bends down towards the screen.

"Ah, that silver tray, the cup, the candlestick and that small barrel belong together?"

"It is a set that is used to celebrate the Sabbath," Zara explains. "On Saturdays, the Jews are not allowed to work, it is their day of rest. The day would end with wine – in the cup, with light – from the candlestick, and with herbs – from the small barrel."

"Once that was a part of our society. And now it has completely vanished," her mother says.
She gets up. "Zara, sitting behind the computer all day is not good for your eyes. Why don't you help me to polish the Sabbath set? Then we can put it in the cupboard."
"You want to show the treasure to others?"
In the kitchen Zara's mother opens the cupboard and hands her the objects. She searches for the silver polish.
"Yes, why not? We inherited them from your grandma and grandpa, haven't we?"
Surprised, Zara looks at her mother's back as she is doing the dishes.
"How did they get it? From the Jews who left?"
"Yes, of course. How else? And you can tell your visitors the story that goes along with it."
Zara nods silently, picks up a candlestick and begins to polish.

The old man is standing at the gate to his house, waiting for Zara.
While they walk across the small courtyard, he tells her in great detail how he has known her father since he was a child. "He was a good student. Those are the children that I remember best."
She has asked her father if there were still people living in Penjwin who could remember how life was in the forties. People who perhaps even knew some of the Jews. He had remembered his old teacher, Omar Derwish.
"He is probably very old by now and I don't know how good his memory is," he had warned her.

THE JEWISH BRIDE

After she has left her shoes outside, Zara looks around the room. It is one of those traditional rooms with small mattresses along the walls, a lone picture and a clock on the wall.

This is the room of someone who must manage to live on a small pension. And who still lives by the ways that she has read about in Rahila's journal.

Omar Derwish rather formally tells her that he is open to answering all her questions. "I am grateful that the younger generation is interested in our past."

Zara takes out her notebook. His wife brings in some tea and joins them on the floor.

The old man tells her that he still remembers the old Penjwin well, the village of his early youth, when Jews and Muslims lived together as friends.

"Our neighbour was called Yesula. I often played with his four children. One time one of the daughters had fallen while playing, and had hurt herself. I can't remember if I had anything to do with it, but I was afraid I would be punished, and I hid myself."

He loudly slurps his tea, his eyes on her fast-writing hand.

"My father came looking for me, together with the neighbour. Who pleaded for me. He said: Don't punish the boy, otherwise I will leave this place."

He laughs a raspy laugh.

"And that happened?"

"Now, I didn't get punished. My father knew that the neighbour meant what he said."

The old man falls silent. His wife gets up to turn down the kerosene heater; it isn't so cold yet outside, she mentions when she sits down again.

"Did the Jews stand out in any way?"

Omar Derwish shakes his head. "They acted just like everyone else. We children visited one another's homes, eating together, there was no difference. Even their clothing wasn't much different: men wore the Kurdish turban, and women a headscarf. The Jewish women were often more covered up than the Muslim women."

Zara asks if the groups intermarried. The old man confirms this. But it was only possible if the woman converted to the religion of the man, he adds. "The Jews advised against such a marriage."

"Why?"

The old man thinks for a moment. "They wanted them to stay Jewish, I think."

Zara asks him what he knows about the Jewish families who lived in Penjwin.

"There were five, and eventually they all left because they were working on the establishment of their own Jewish state. There were ties with Jews in Palestine, and they were well aware of what was happening there."

Zara is reminded of Azam from Rahila's journal, and of Ezra who came by with his stories about Palestine. But Rahila writes nothing about how others in Penjwin reacted towards these Jewish efforts.

"Didn't that create problems?"

"Not with the normal people. But even then, there were radical Muslims. They stoned a Jewish merchant to death just outside Penjwin, whose name was Numa. The stoning of Jews was for them like throwing stones at the devil. They thought that they would get into heaven. His grave is still there, at the spot where he was murdered."

A long and heavy silence falls. Zara asks about the Farud, but the old man knows little about this. He was too young at the time.

Zara changes the subject and asks what set the Jews apart from the rest in the old Penjwin.

Omar Derwish needs to think about that. "They had their own doctor for the circumcisions," he then says, "and they had their own cemetery."

Zara looks up in surprise. "Where is it?"

The old man motions, to the mountains towards Iran. "There is nothing left of it. It was all cleared under Saddam." He also remembers a holy place with a well. "Women who wanted to bear children went there, and people in search of healing. On Wednesdays, it was especially busy there."

Funny how memory works, Zara thinks. Why would he remember the detail about the Wednesdays?

He tells her that this garden was sold when the Jews left in 1951, and that homes were built on the spot since a long time.

And the synagogue, that she read about in Rahila's journal, where was that?

"At the riverside," the man answers with certainty. "After the Jews had left, the building was used as a mosque. Up until the time of the war with Iran, when Saddam destroyed all of Penjwin. The stones were used to build new houses."

All of Penjwin in ruins - but her old house was left standing. Strange. She asks him about this. He thinks about it for quite some time; the silence only broken by the hissing of the kerosene heater.

"Maybe only the roof was gone," he eventually says hesitantly, "and the walls were left standing. That was the case with many homes, and perhaps also that of your parents."

She nods. Carefully she returns to the subject of the departure of the Jews from Penjwin.

"I was ten, maybe eleven. And I didn't understand anything about it. Suddenly my friends had to go."

In an effort to hide his emotions, the old man hands his tea glass to his wife. She sets the empty glasses obediently onto the tray.

When he remains silent, Zara carefully formulates a next question that is less personal.

"What did their departure mean for Penjwin?"

"It was a great loss." He says it with conviction. "I wanted that the Jews had stayed. It was better when we were living together. Their knowledge was an enrichment for everyone."

Zara listens and writes.

"At the time, for example, only about five percent of the people could read and write, particularly the Jews. And they shared their knowledge with others. They had small manual labour businesses for weaving and painting of fabrics. Four Muslim brothers in Penjwin learned the trade from them." Suddenly he starts to laugh. "They were smart businessmen too. Everyone bought their sugar at the Jewish grocer's. It was cheaper than elsewhere. The sugar came in big bags, that the other shopkeepers threw away. But the Jewish shopkeeper sold them. There was quite a demand for them as they were sturdy bags and the women cut them up to make many things out of them. And that way, he was able to make the sugar cheaper, and sell more than his neighbours."

Together they laugh.

"Have you heard about the buried treasures?" the old man asks, just as she is putting away her notebook getting ready to leave. She looks at him in surprise.

He gets up with some difficulty, and leans against his wife while slowly straightening his back. "We aren't getting any younger," he says, gasping somewhat from the exertion.

"That God may grant and give you many more years," she repeats one of the polite phrases that have been imprinted on her. Her thoughts flash to Rahila; politeness as a rule is still embedded in their culture.

The old man shakes his head. "That He will not do, but don't worry about that, janakam. Where were we? The treasures. When the Jews left, they were unable to take much of anything with them. First, they had thought of a trick in which gold jewellery was hidden in the bread they took along, but soon enough, that was discovered. Then neighbours helped them to keep these belongings safe. The Jews left their money with them, to get it back when they would return."

"And the neighbours buried it?"

"I think so. I remember a few years back, that a boy working in the shop of Rashe Rasul came running and yelling that he had found a treasure. Something had been dug up when they were building a house next to the shop. But the shopkeeper calmed him and said that he had buried it himself."

"The shopkeeper did that?"

"For his neighbours, from what I understand, but of course there is no way of knowing for sure if it is true."

Zara nods. It would be a logical explanation. Her grandparents had buried the treasure for the Jewish family that had to leave.

Gratefully she says goodbye, politely refusing the usual invitation to remain for lunch.

Outside, she notices the grey sky. Snow is on the way. Slowly she wanders through the town, to the place where the old man said the Jewish cemetery had been located. She passes the ruins of homes that have never been repaired after the war with Iran.

High against the hills are the triangular warning signs placed by the mine clearers. Here still are landmines, as there are throughout the mountains around Penjwin.

But of a cemetery, there is not a trace. Vanished, erased, just as most of the Jewish past of Penjwin.

The first snowflakes hit the ground. They quickly disappear, sucked up by the earth. But soon the snow will cover all the remaining lost tracks.

Zara turns around. It is time to go home, if she doesn't want to get soaked.

"Zara! Zara!"

Banu's clear voice sounds in the street where the snow absorbs most of the sound. Zara quickly puts on her coat, hat and gloves.

In the courtyard, she has to dig for the sleigh that she had

set out yesterday. It has disappeared under the thick layer of snow that fell during the night.
"Zara! What is keeping you?"
Banu's voice sounds cheerful. Zara opens the gate, pulling the sleigh along behind her.
"There you are, finally! We have to hurry, if we still want to find fresh snow!"
"*Bayani bash*, Banu," Zara greets, somewhat demonstrative.
"Yes, yes," she laughs, "a good morning to you too. Now hurry up!"
They make their way pulling their sleighs through the thick layer of fresh snow in the direction of the only hill that has been declared free of mines. With each step they sink into the snow. Huffing and sweating they arrive at the top.
"We are the first," Banu declares. She takes a seat on her sleigh. "Just catching my breath."
They look out over the town, pointing out to each other the many new buildings.
"This is our last year, janakam," Banu says.
Zara knows what she means: married women no longer ride on sleighs.
"What you do is up to you, but I am going to learn to ski. Just like them."
She points at two young men on skis who are coming up the mountain.
"Hey, that is something new," Banu laughs surprised. "Do you know them? They aren't from here, eh?"
Excitedly they wait until the men arrive at the top. Banu greets them warmly.
"What are you doing," she asks them innocently.

The men are both wearing ski coats. "We are going to try and see how good the snow is," one of them answers.
"Where are you from?" Zara asks them.
"I am from Sulaymaniya, he comes from Spain."
A Spanish person here, in isolated Penjwin? "You must be joking. What is he doing here?"
"Well, skiing!"
"But you can do that better in Europe, can't you? At least there they don't have any landmines!"
The man smiles. "We are going to set-up a ski school here."
The Spaniard interrupts, asking about their sleighs. Isn't that something for children?
That causes Zara and Banu to laugh out loud. Zara explains that this is an old tradition in Penjwin, and that this hill has been used for years by young and old alike to sleigh down. That before the war, they went even higher up the mountain, but now that isn't considered safe because of the mines.
Then Zara becomes impatient. She pulls at Banu's sleeve to attract her attention down the hill, to the others coming up in their footsteps. They must really hurry, if they want the pristine snow for themselves.
She is already lying on the sleigh. Banu follows her example.
"*Yallah dey*! Here we go!"
Beneath her the snow crunches, snowflakes fly up from beneath the irons of the sleigh. Zara pulls her legs up even further and clamps tightly onto the wood. The wind zooms past her ears. Her cheeks are red from the cold.
The two men ski past, and then in front of her. Snow sprays out from behind them while they zigzag down the hill. She

feels the flakes on her cheeks.
A sense of freedom gushes through her. The last time. Banu is crazy. This is not something that she will allow anyone to take away from her.
Her sleigh slows to a halt just clear of the two men on their skis.
"That was good!" she exclaims, getting off the sleigh.
The Spaniard gallantly offers her a hand to get up.
"Skiing is even better", he says in English.
"I'd love to try", Zara says longingly, dusting down her clothes from the snow.
"Why not?" He explains that with some assistance from the Spanish government, they want to open a school which will give skiing lessons.
"Cross country," he adds. "You don't need any ski lift for that. So much easier, and better for the environment."
"Why Penjwin?" Zara asks.
"Here the snows stays on the ground longer than anywhere else in Iraqi Kurdistan."
"You should talk to my father," she says. "He will find this very interesting and he might be able to help."
After Zara exchanges telephone numbers with the skiers, Banu and she retrace their steps up the mountain for one more ride. Next time she will go down on skies, Zara promises herself silently.

"Did you know that the name Penjwin actually means five Jews?"
Soran mumbles something. He steers the car carefully in the ever-increasing darkness through the narrow streets

blanketed with fresh snow.

"Originally, there were five Jewish families living here, and at the beginning of the last century about thirty. Roughly a few hundred people all together, when they left in 1951."

"Zara, we are on the way to our engagement ceremony. Is this really something that you need to discuss now?"

His outburst startles her. In the past weeks, she has been so busy with investigating the journal, that she has been able to think of little else.

"I am terrible, Soran. Sorry. Shall we rewind this tape?"

Their own personal joke, a result of the hours spent together as volunteers in the small local radio station, works as it always has. Soran laughs and makes the sound of a rewinding tape.

The car stops in front of her house.

"Listen," he says seriously.

She tries to hide her concern. Inside people are waiting for them.

"In a bit, the imam will inquire if you accept me as your husband. You know that we will then in fact be married, even though they refer to it as an engagement. Are you sure that this is what you want, *goshawistakam*?"

"Why do you ask such a thing?"

He sighs deeply. "You have been very distant lately, janakam. You are now all the time preoccupied with the Jewish treasure, with the history. I never hear you talking about our future, or our live together."

Warm blood is gushing to Zara's face. She lays her cold hands on her cheeks.

She knows that she has neglected him. He didn't complain,

as Banu did, who threatened to end the friendship. If only he had done that too.

She has been unable to share with either one of them what she was doing. After their initial excitement about the buried treasure, they were no longer interested. She was completely unable to talk about the journal. They didn't even know it existed.

"You have spent more time with that Spanish guy than with me in the past weeks."

He has every reason to be jealous, she silently admits. Because every chance she got, she has put on her skis and was on the slope that Carlos was able to carve out for practicing with her father's help.

What must she say? This is a dream, to be able to go down the mountain on skis. And it has nothing to do with her feelings for Soran.

Soran then breaks the silence. "I will not hold it against you if you say now that you have changed you mind. But I will, if you do that before or after the wedding."

"Soran, of course I want to marry you. But the subject I have stumbled across takes up so much of my time... you understand that, don't you?"

"No, I don't understand it at all, dear. Why? You aren't Jewish, are you?"

I wished I knew, Zara sighs. She shakes her head. "That is not something that I can explain in a few minutes, in the car outside of the house where the imam and our family and friends are waiting. That will have to wait until afterwards." She hears her agitated tone and lays a consolatory hand on Soran's arm.

"Tolerate me just a little longer, goshawistakam. It will be all right."
"When was the last time that you said that you loved me?"
"What kind of question is that, Soran?"
"Well, when?"
"Last week?"
"No dear, it was much longer ago. A month, more than that. That is why I wonder if you still want to go through with this."
Is he right? Suddenly doubt slithers in.
Do I love him enough? Perhaps we won't be able to get along so well together, once we are married. Maybe our interests are too different. Then it is better not to go through with it. The shame of cancelling the engagement now is less than it would be later. But is that what I want?
His eyes are wet, Zara notices suddenly. Has she caused this?
"Soran, I love you. I want to share my life with you. You must believe me."
He rubs over his eyes and leans towards her. "Kiss," he says softly.
"They see us, Soran. Everyone sees us here."
"Kiss," he repeats.
Why not? In a while, they will be engaged and then nobody will be able to say anything about it anymore. She answers his kiss just as she sees Banu shivering in the winter cold.
"You are too early," she says.
To regain her composure, Zara takes a deep breath and looks demonstratively at her watch.
"No, we aren't, rather too late."

"That kiss isn't allowed until after the imam," Banu says laughing. "Hurry up, everyone is waiting inside."
"Help me with one of the boxes," Soran says.
The moment is over. Relief flods through her.
She takes one of the heavy boxes from the back seat with presents for the guests. It is a Kurdish tradition: every guest will go home with a small memento. Instead of the usual sweets, Zara and Soran have chosen for a large pebble, specially painted for them by an artist friend in Sulaymaniya.
Inside, the living room is packed, as is the kitchen. Everyone is there, Zara sees. Their families, uncles, aunts, nephews and nieces. And of course, all their friends. In the back of the room she catches a glimpse of the imam's turban.
"Two seconds," she says to Soran, and runs to her room. The belt they found with the Jewish treasure is waiting for her. She steps out of her jeans and into a long skirt. A long white blouse is hanging on the closet door. Carefully she fastens the old belt. A quick glance in the mirror and then she is again at the door.
Abruptly, she stops, and walks back to the mirror.
Perhaps Soran is right. Is this what I want? Or am I doing it, because it is expected of me, as you are supposed to be married before you are twenty-four?
What has changed, since that September day when she got the journal? Before then, she had never asked herself that question. Soran and she are childhood friends, and that they were to marry has for many years been a well-known fact. She loves his sense of humour, his free-thinking mentality. She knows that she can trust him. How many

men like Soran would you be able to find? Why then, is she in doubt?

Yes, there is the way he always must get his own way. The way he tends to criticize her. How he tries to get her to do things his way. And everything is always about him.

A knock on the door, and her mother comes in. She sees Zara standing there, lays an arm around her shoulders and pulls her towards her.

"You are having doubts."

Zara looks at their reflection. Her mother is shorter than she is, she now notices. How long has that been the case? Slowly she nods.

"That is good, janakam. That is supposed to happen, today. You must be sure of what you are doing."

"I love him."

"But?"

She shrugs her shoulders. "There is so much that he doesn't understand."

"Your search into the history of the house."

Surprised she looks at her mother in the mirror. Is that so obvious? Does this mean she agrees with Soran?

"Zara, perhaps you should let it rest. You are almost obsessed. I don't know what you are looking for. Concentrate on your studies, on Soran, on the preparations for your wedding in the spring."

"But..." she searches for the words. "If we are going to share our lives, then must he not also be open for what occupies my mind?"

"Certainly, but why is it that you are so preoccupied with the Jewish treasure? Why should Soran be interested in that?"

Zara fidgets with the belt. How does she explain that she identifies with Rahila? With a Jewish woman that lived in her house more than sixty years ago? Her mother doesn't even know about the diary.

She sighs. But that is not what it is about now. It is about her and Soran. Her mother is right. For him, she must let the past rest for now.

She turns away from the mirror and kisses her mother.

"We cannot let them wait out there any longer."

Soran is in the hallway talking to Banu.

"Wow," he says when he sees her. She takes his hand.

He pulls her along to the room. Family members and friends greet, kiss, and step aside to let them pass. The imam turns towards them.

4 THE CALL OF PALESTINE

June 20, 1942

It was a long journey to Al Qosh.

Ima had decided that there, at Prophet Nahum's grave, we would ask for his blessings for Yesula's upcoming marriage. At the same time, we would pay tribute to Naima's and Tova's deaths of a year ago. The visit to the grave is a beautiful tradition during the Shavuot, which has also become known as the Festival of the Pilgrimage.

"He who has not made the pilgrimage to Nahum's tomb, has not yet known real pleasure," abba kept repeating. He was very happy about the prospect of the journey and of seeing old friends. He even had his beard trimmed and dyed.

Abba had arranged a horse and wagon. He sat next to coachman and Yesula. Ima, my other three brothers and I sat in the wagon, between the clothing, blankets, mattresses, the food, the pots and pans and the barrels with *ayran* to lessen our thirst. We took the best route, and that is not the shortest, via Sulaymaniya, Kirkuk, Erbil and Mosul, and in all of those cities we slept in the Jewlakan.

In Sulaymaniya we slept at Uncle Nasim's, who lives above his fabric shop. His business is going well. He sells much of Uncle Salim's fabrics, who just last month hired my brother Sasson as an apprentice weaver. In the shop, I found rolls of cotton from Iran, and beautifully thin silk from India. Ima has promised that she will use it to make me a dress for Yesula's wedding.

In Kirkuk, we passed the mosque with the grave of the Prophet Daniel. And everywhere we went, abba had stories about our history – he knows so much, how can I possibly ever remember it all?

After five days on the road in that hard wagon, I thought that I no longer had a bottom. But the landscapes we saw were so beautiful, even though the heat had devoured most of the green. The high mountains under the perfect blue June skies, alternated with gently sloping hills, and rivers that flowed swiftly to keep from being captured.

I love this country, why should I leave from here?

Azam has kept his word. He said nothing about Palestine, when he asked abba for my hand. The wonderful thing is that we now see one another on a regular basis. The only condition for this is, that someone must keep an eye on us, but that isn't very strict.

Often, we meet by the river behind the synagogue. We must get to know one another before we marry, don't we? Abba wants us to wait for another year. I am in no hurry – I have nearly all that I could possibly wish for. Why should I give up most of that for going to Palestine?

Here, thanks to abba, I have work – as one of the few women in our community. And as the daughter of the teacher I get looked up to. In Palestine I am no one.

Luckily, the journey to Al Qosh has also opened other possibilities. Al Qosh is a beautiful, centuries-old town nestled against the mountainside, with the high peaks of the Qandil Mountains in the distance. Christians and Jews live next to each other in the steep streets. There are some small churches, a monastery and there is the synagogue, guarding over the town. It is very old, built from sand stone and blocks of rock, and restored many times. In the middle is the grave of the prophet that is covered with green cloths, embroidered with gold trim.

We stayed in one of the guest rooms of the synagogue – because abba knows the *maloum*. There were thousands of pilgrims, and most of the families slept in tents on the grounds or in the fields outside. It was a lively chaos, with children running around, mothers who were cooking outside, and bread that was being baked non-stop in the open oven within the walls of the synagogue. And of course, there was a lot of sour milk and butter, as part of the Shavuot.

The Shavuot began early in the morning with a long walk of nearly three hours into the mountains. We all walked behind a group of men who were carrying the rolls of the Torah, to a mountain that they call the Sinai. There, the prayer was recited about the gift of the Ten Commandments to Moses. The sound of it was overwhelming; with all the voices echoing off of the mountainside.

The Nineveh plains at your feet are green and fertile, you see the water flowing. Villages become nearly invisible, as the mud houses have the colour of the earth. Far in the distance, Mosul can be seen. I had wanted to stay there for hours.

But soon, we started on the descent. We walked in a long line, to the beat of a drum. The men were part of a re-enactment of the battle between Gog and Magog – the battle that acknowledges the coming of the Messiah. They waved their swords, clouds of dust rose, and they were screaming as if the end of the world had come. It made me laugh, as they were such bad actors.

Afterwards, the men occupied the synagogue to read from the Book of Nahum. Singing and reciting, they circled the grave seven times. And on the last round, the women could join. The atmosphere changed, because we danced and sang.

I visited the synagogue at least ten times. In Penjwin, it is the domain of the men, but Nahum is known for giving infertile women children, so his grave is also their place. The fencing around it is covered with their wishing ribbons. It is very beautiful, with versus in Hebrew chiselled into the walls, beautiful decorations about the doorways and on the ceiling, and old oil lamps on the pillars.

I met a young female teacher from Mosul. That in itself was special, meeting another woman who also teaches. Her name was Asenath, and she told me that she was named after a famous Jewish woman who was a rabbi and even led the yeshivah in Mosul.

She said that her father called her Asenath because he wanted her to follow in his footsteps. Her father is the rabbi in Mosul, or the *hakham*, as they call it there.

The famous Asenath was the daughter of the rabbi Samuel Barzani, one of our most famous and superior rabbis in Kurdistan. She learned everything from him: the Torah, the secrets of the Kabbala, the Jewish stories in Iraq, the Talmud. When he died, she took his place.

Because he also had no sons, Asenath explained, just like her father.

What an exciting thought! A woman, who in the 17th century had amassed so much knowledge that she was called Assenath tanna'it, which is an honorary title for someone who knows a great deal about the Talmud. Someone who didn't busy herself with cooking and washing, but with reciting the Torah, reading prayers and leading the studies in the Talmud schools!

Men accepted her. And that was in the 17th century. Would they still do that today? Would my new friend get the same opportunities?

Not that she could fill his shoes, Asenath continued about her namesake. She was only allowed to fulfil part of his duties. She could not pass judgements, or slaughter animals.

But she led the prayers in the synagogue, she led the school. She became the best Torah teacher in Kurdistan. And all of this while, she also had a family, and eventually she got her son to take over her work. What a woman.

Her grave is in Amadiya, Asenath said. She suggested we would visit that together sometime. That seemed like a great idea, but how would we ever get the chance to visit a place that is so far away, without our fathers or brothers?

There is a legend about her in Amadiya. After her father's death, Asenath Barzani was said to have had regular visits from him in her sleep. That way, he passed along messages. That was the main reason why the community in Amadiya had decided to celebrate Rosh Hodesh outside. Then, when the celebration was going on, they saw flames coming out of the roof of the synagogue.

Asenath Barzani is said to have whispered a secret code, after which a swarm of angels landed on the roof of the synagogue and beat out the fire with their wings.

When it was extinguished, they flew towards the heavens as white doves.

The great miracle was, that the fire did not cause even the slightest of damage. The Torah rolls were still completely intact. It is a nonsense story but a beautiful one, don't you think? Asenath said.

Her comment made me grin. Asenath isn't afraid to say exactly what she thinks. When abba tells these stories, he is always very serious. For him, all the stories are true, however impossible they may seem.

Why isn't my father a hakham, like hers? she wanted to know.

I told her what abba told me, that he doesn't know enough Hebrew. She was not convinced, as she already is learning the language herself.

She was making me jealous. This skinny, cheerful woman was studying Hebrew, and everything else necessary to become a rabbi.

Why didn't I come and live with her in Mosul, so that we could study together? she then asked.

I thought of all the children I was teaching in Penjwin, and about Azam who I was to marry, and about his parents who we were going to live with.

Abba would never approve of that, I said, brushing aside the idea. It was too strange, too new. I could not imagine that my life would change so much.

Why didn't we ask him? she said cheerfully. She had already gotten up to go and look for him.

Why was I hesitating? If I wanted to gain more knowledge, then this was clearly a chance, wasn't it? If I no longer wanted to do all the work in the house?

Abba looked at me with some curiosity, when Asenath made her proposal. We had found him in a corner of the synagogue.

Asenath Barzani, he said thoughtfully, who would have guessed that.

Asenath and I looked at one another wondering. Was this a yes, or indeed a no?

Abba said he had always thought that I would one day take over from him. That I was the smartest of the lot. But that tanna'it Asenath Barzani would be my inspiration, he did not foresee.

Abba was only very proud. I glowed from happiness. And suddenly all the objections I had simply vanished.

The entire long journey back, it sang in me. Prophet Nahum had heard my wish. Asenath and I will become the most educated Jewish women of Kurdistan. Or even better: from all of Iraq.

Abba had asked me to bring him the arak bottle and the water pipe. He was alone in the guestroom, which is strange. Normally he drinks arak with his friends, and sometimes with Yesula or Sasson who both are over eighteen.

A bit later he called me in. We had to talk.

My heart was pounding in my throat when I sat down across from him.

He was silent as he replaced the charcoal of the water pipe. The air was already thick with the sweet smell of the apple tobacco.

He said he would support me, if I really wanted to go to Mosul to study with Asenath's father. It would be a great honour, to study with Yacoub Rahamin Tzemah. But did I realize what the consequences of this decision would be?

He looked seriously at me. Something in the way he spoke made me uneasy. Only now, looking back, I can put a finger on it. Abba was talking to me as I had heard him speak to Yesula and Sasson. With his adult sons.

If I go to Mosul, I won't be able to help ima anymore, I said.

He smiled and said we would find a solution for that. He asked me to look further: what did I want to do with my life?

I want to learn. I want to learn everything I can, I told him. Not only the Torah, also the Talmud and the secrets of the Kabbala. I want to be able to read and write Hebrew fluently. And then I want to share that knowledge with others.

Pensively, Abba stroked through his beard, and said that this would not be simple for a woman. That I would have to overcome many obstacles, and would meet with much opposition. That men would not like the fact that a woman is more educated than they are.

Problems are meant to be overcome, I said, using one of his own sayings. It resulted in a small smile.

I probably had wondered why he is not a maloum, he then said seriously. Not all problems can be overcome.

He fell silent and smoked. I waited impatiently for what was about to come.

His father was not Jewish, he then said. His mother had married a Muslim because she loved him, against the wishes of her parents and the community.

My grandmother was married to a non-Jew? What a scandalous secret!

Abba concentrated on sucking the pipe, as if he was unaware of my shock.

My grandmother loved the man because he was a poet and a writer, he said. He had taught her how to read and write. He had treated her as his equal. Abba said he saw many similarities when he looked at me. She knew what she wanted, and fought for it. Her life knew many setbacks, but she always stood tall. It was a pity that I had never known her.

I wasn't quite sure what to think. Abba thought that I was like a woman who had brought shame to her family. He said it, like it was a compliment.

The community never forgave my grandma, he said, her marriage was considered as a kind of betrayal. His father never converted to Judaism. If he had, perhaps things would have been different. Now his mother was an outsider. And her children were too, abba said.

I could keep quiet no longer. Children, plural? How many more secrets?

A new plume of smoke was blown into the room. Father continued his story as if he hadn't heard me, which made me feel that asking my question had been a mistake.

He said that after his mother's death, his two brothers went with his father to Baghdad. He stayed behind. He had managed to gain a teaching position in the yeshivah in Kirkuk and did not want to lose that. He said he felt Jewish, because Judaism is carried over by the mother. His brothers became Muslims.

The new knowledge tumbled through my mind. I had two uncles in Baghdad who had converted to Islam.

Abba took out a yellowed and crumpled picture. It showed a stately-looking young woman, next to a young man in a black suit. No Kurdish costume, I immediately noticed. His father's family did not originate from Kurdistan, but from Baghdad, abba then explained.

My eyes focussed on the woman in the picture. She smiled with her eyes. She was beautiful, especially with the golden coins hanging from the headpiece on her forehead. She wore a colourful silk dress with a short sleeveless silk vest over it. And much gold, around her waist, on her arms. A beautiful Jewish bride.

Abba said that I take after her. I took another look, but could not see it.

After their marriage, my grandparents had left for Sulaymaniya. That is where grandfather had worked and written his books, which were printed and sold in Baghdad. He travelled back and forth often. My grandmother did not want to move to Baghdad, she had not wanted to leave Kurdistan.

Grandmother had died when abba was eighteen, from a bad flu. Grandfather a few years later. Abba had kept his past hidden when he came to live in Penjwin, but he had kept in contact. Also with his younger brothers, who were successful businessmen in Baghdad.

That is how Nasim could escape the Farhud, said abba. His brother took him in.

So many lies, so many secrets. I could barely come to terms with it. But I suddenly understood much more about my father. Because his father was not Jewish, he could not become a maloum. There was no relation to his knowledge of the Hebrew.

Abba poured himself another arak and took a sip. He grimaced. He said he had tried to get a position in several communities. Eventually, they had wanted him here as a teacher in the synagogue. And that is what he had done.

The decision his mother made had a profound effect on his life! Suddenly, I realized: could this all possibly have an effect on my life too? The fact that my grandfather was not Jewish?

He told me this because I have a right to my past, abba said, while he flattened the picture before placing it in a book. But it would be a wise decision to keep this a secret. People jump to the wrong conclusions, he said.

Of course. If he was able to keep this secret for so long, how could I ever just blurt it out like that! But who else could know about this? Ima, surely. My brothers?

Abba pointed out that if I go to Mosul, my marriage would have to be postponed. I said that Azam would not be happy, because he wants to get married next summer and wants me to leave with him to Palestine.

Abba asked if I want to go there. He wasn't even surprised. Perhaps he had heard about it from others. Azam spoke to anyone and everyone willing to listen about it!

I shared my doubts. That I think my life is here. And that I am afraid in Palestine I will end up in the kitchens, or as a child minder.

Abba stood up, and pulled me into a strong hug. I smelled the odour of anise from the arak on his breath, his beard tickled my forehead. He said that as I had made my decision, in September, after Rosh Hashana, I would go to Mosul. And with his blessing.

December 7, 1942

I sat copying old Hebrew texts, when Asenath called me to say I had a visitor. Her voice sounded so loud in the quiet room, that she even startled me. My fellow students also looked up surprised.

Somewhat resentful, I got up. I pulled the thick shawl tighter around me. In my concentration, I had not even noticed the cold.

Muddy men's boots stood outside the guestroom. My visitor had travelled far, and through the rain. My heart skipped a beat. That could only be Azam.

He was alone in the room. The mud spatters were even on his face. Smiling he kissed my hands, before pulling me towards him. I drowned in his embrace, until I broke free with a start. What if someone were to see us?

I asked him why he was here. What had happened?

He quickly reassured me. Abba and ima sent their greetings and best wishes. He once again pulled me tightly towards him. His mouth tasted of sweet tea. I drowned again; then fought my way back to the surface.

When I pointed out to him that we were in a yeshivah, he laughed and suggested to go outside.

Teasingly his finger touched my lips. He could wait no longer, he said.

I looked in those smiling, delicious brown eyes and longed for another kiss. Kisses are dangerous, ima had drummed into me. Men always want more than kisses, and before you know it you have lost your honour.

A quick knock at the door gave me just enough time to step away from Azam before Asenath came in.

She was happy to see Azam, she said as she motioned towards the cushions for him to rest. It must have been a long journey, she said. Was there snow in Penjwin yet?

Azam gave an extensive report about his difficult journey, starting with the metres of snow which blanketed the valleys near Penjwin. He had to walk far, because wheels and horse hooves got stuck in the snow.

He told us the latest news from Penjwin, about the engagements, marriages and *bar mitzvah's* I had missed. And about the fire at the Jewlaken caused by an oil heater that had fallen over, and how the entire neighbourhood had helped fight the fire. It luckily had been limited to three homes, and the synagogue was spared. And about his sick father, who had come down with a bad flu and left him to run the shop on his own for weeks.

One of the students then brought in some fresh tea.

I realized that in the two months that I had been living with Asenath in Mosul, I had not missed Penjwin for a moment. Every day there was something new. And the other students, all of them boys between the ages of 15 and 20 from all over Iraq, each had their own stories to tell.

Much differently than I had originally anticipated, they said little when I joined them. I think that was caused by the fact that Asenath was already studying with them. What surprised me most, is that no one ever asked me anything when I stayed away whilst I was physically impure. Then I have to keep far from our holy books.

Asenath's father teaches our lessons, but for a portion of the day we must study on our own or the elder students are to share their knowledge. We learn words, copy scriptures, memorize text and read the Talmud. Part of the lessons are to teach us to discuss the laws in the Torah and their logic. I don't yet dare to participate in those, as I still have so much to learn before I can really take part of the heated debates.

Ustad Yacoub suggested that I also learn to recite the Torah, although that is typically something only reserved for men. I am honoured, but I find it to be difficult, because you have to move your body to the rhythm of the text you are reading.

Azam was clearly tired, and his curls were sticking to his head from the grime of the journey.

Seeing him confronted me with the fact that the moment I will return to Penjwin to marry Azam, still is very far away. I still have years of study in front of me.

All those years without him lie before me. It will be so long, before we will ever really be able to be together. Then I will no longer be young. I chose this for myself, and yet I did not realize this at the time.

He asked me if I was getting settled in, and I told him about my life in Mosul – until I saw that he wasn't really listening. I interrupted myself and told him that the boys could show him where he could get cleaned up.

He agreed that he could not go to see Ezra covered in mud. He was in Mosul too, and they had a meeting tonight.

Azam hadn't come for me at all. He came for a meeting with the Zionists. I stared at the worn rug.

He came to Mosul, because Ezra Kadoori and his propaganda for the Jewish state no longer were welcome in Penjwin. I knew that Azam had also travelled to Sulaymaniya and Kirkuk for similar meetings.

He suggested that I would come along. His invitation surprised me. But then I realized that he hoped that Ezra would be able to convince me to come with him to Palestine. And that is why I searched for an easy excuse, and said that Asenath's father would not likely approve.

Hearing her name, Asenath asked what we were talking about.

Azam told her with much passion that we Jews need our own place where we can be safe. That he and Ezra are working to achieve this, and tonight were having a meeting. In Europe the Jews are being murdered by the Germans, he said. Here explosives are thrown into a full synagogue.

When I reacted surprised, he asked me if I had locked myself away. The tea houses were buzzing with the news of what had happened in Baghdad. Luckily, the bomb didn't go off; otherwise there would have been many deaths, he said.

Asenath admitted that we don't go to the tea houses. She said she would like to join the meeting. That her father would surely approve.

A few hours later, we were the only women in a full, smoky room in the home of a wealthy merchant elsewhere in the Jewlakan. Ezra had greeted me as a long-lost daughter, and he politely kissed Asenath's hand.

Surprisingly enough he took the time to ask about our studies, and even said how much respect for it he had. He said that such educated women are needed in Eretz Israel.

The evening was less about Zionism and about the rights of Jews to their own state, than about the experiences of the first pioneers. About the problems with the British, who were occupying Palestine, and attempting to prevent the Jews from establishing homes there. While Eretz Israel is the birthplace of the Jewish people, as Ezra put it.

He spoke mainly about how the Zionists in Iraq can prepare for their lives there. By learning Hebrew, but also how to handle a weapon. Ezra announced that whoever wanted to do that could join one of the military trainings.

It was the first time that I heard about the plight of the Jews in Europe. Ezra talked about the people who had fled Nazi Germany and Poland, who had been witness to a continually worsening situation in the Jewish neighbourhoods, and about special work camps for

Jews from where no one ever returns. The Germans speak about a "final solution to the Jewish problem." As if we are no more but a problem for which you think up a final solution. It sounds unimaginable and horrible.

And then, there are stories about large-scale murders. This week the British minister of Foreign Affairs condemned the mass executions, the transportation of Jews to the camps and the emptying out of the Jewish neighbourhoods. In Kiev they say that in a two-day period, many thousands of Jews were shot to death. Men, women and children. There is only one possible conclusion: the Germans want to eradicate our people. And that is indeed shocking. How can this possibly be true?

These kinds of issues are never discussed at Asenath's house or in the yeshivah. There all talk is about knowledge, religion, and wisdom. Everything is based on the Jewish stories from the past, which also are about our persecution. What is happening, is no coincidence. The exodus from Egypt, the parting of the Red Sea so that Moses and our people could escape – all of these happened against the backdrop of the extermination of the Jews. And look at our own background in Iraq: we were transported here some 2,800 years ago as slaves. Our people have attracted this fate.

I understand Azam. His fierceness, his drive. It is all about our people.

But it is also about Europe, and not about us here in Iraq. Here, there are no Germans, here, there are no Jews being deported. Here in Mosul, we live together with the Muslims, the men visit the same tea houses, we meet each other at the market. Here, we bring one another the special dishes on each other's holidays. Here, Muslims light the fire on the Sabbath for their Jewish neighbours.

Ezra asked for help to get German and Polish refugees who are in Iran, smuggled out to Palestine. The men thrust themselves into coming up with the best smuggling routes. The evening ended with a request from Ezra to everyone, to report for the aliya to Eretz Israel, or "the return to the Jewish homeland." That sounds, as if we only yesterday arrived in Kurdistan. It completely denies our past here.

Ezra said that his group in 1935 already had sent 60,000 Jews to Palestine, but that their numbers had barely grown since the Arabic uprising and the measures taken by the British. He needs strong, young people like us, he said, telling us that we would be the base for our new state.

There was no real enthusiasm, I noticed. The men were only willing to talk about it, not to actually do it. Apart from Azam, hardly a soul signed up to discuss a departure for Palestine, or for the military training.

Just like me, Asenath spent the evening mainly listening and observing. She started to talk about it when we were waiting on our mattresses for sleep to come. What was I going to do, if Azam went to Palestine? The question had kept haunting me throughout the evening.

I told her how difficult it is for me. That I want to learn, and finish my studies. But I also want to marry Azam and have children. And how should I make this combination if Azam goes to Palestine?

I could feel Asenath looking at me in the dark. Thoughtfully, she said that according to her father, time answers all questions. And that perhaps I could only wait and see what happens.

And let Azam go? That was a thought that I kept pushing away.

She suggested that I should finish what I started, and then go to him later on.

I nodded in the dark, and realized that she couldn't see me and said that it might be a solution, even though a life in Palestine is not at all appealing to me, nor is leaving here.

She said she understood. Mosul is her city too. Iraq her home. Here our forefathers came to live thousands of years ago. They never left after that.

But I would go with the man I loved, she then said. That should turn all of the sour things sweet, shouldn't it?

I lay awake for a long time. Eventually, one thing was clear: I would have to let Azam go to Palestine on his own. I would ask him to wait for me there. If he said no, then I would once again have to reconsider.

March 20, 1943
Little Benjamin has really grown, in the six months since I last saw him. He is already almost taller than me, and ready for his Bar Mitzvah. Tomorrow in the synagogue, he will be reciting from the Torah – and I will be with ima in the courtyard listening and sharing in her pride. As her youngest son reaches adulthood.

Penjwin seemed much smaller when I returned – I have grown so used to the big city! I can see now how simple our houses are, with their thick stone walls and the flat roofs. In Mosul every house where Jews live, has the lion of Judea above the door. Most of the homes have a second floor, large basements, which are isolated to withstand the heat of summer and the cold of winter, and courtyards with running water and plenty of green. In Penjwin, you would be lucky to have a tree in the yard that offers a bit of shade on hot days.

In Mosul, we have a school for the small children, and there are numerous yeshivahs where the young people study. Penjwin only has abba's school in the synagogue. In Mosul, the brightest boys go from the yeshivah to a mixed school to continue their education, here is nothing for them but a job as an apprentice of the weaver, the painter or the blacksmith. Or they become farmers.

But Penjwin has *yapprach* and *kubba* from ima, and nothing else can top that!

The first thing that ima made me do after arriving, was to eat. Unasked, she set a plate with her delicious stuffed wine leaves down in front of me. She said that I have become too thin.

Even Sasson, my favourite brother, is home from Sulaymaniya. We spent the entire afternoon together in the spring sunshine of the courtyard, just talking. About Mosul and Sulaymaniya, about my studies, about his work, but also about the war in Europe, with the bombings on London and the many Jewish victims. And Sasson agrees with me: these are the problems of the European Jews. The war is there, not here. They need their own state, we do not.

It is a pleasant change, to be able to have a conversation with someone who is not continually trying to convince you that they are right, as Azam does. We talked about the Jewish state, and about the dangers of Zionism for us, here in Iraq. For example, the recent attempt to bomb the synagogue in Baghdad. The fact that the European Jews plan to build their home on Arabic ground, is turning against us, Sasson said. People blame us, since we are Jewish.

I added that we feel more Kurdish, or Iraqi, than Jewish.

He looked at me inquisitively. Did I still feel that way, even since I had gotten so knowledgeable about Jewish affairs?

That is the history of our people, our faith, our laws, I said. It has nothing to do with my country: that is Iraq. My roots are here.

I see that my mother is getting old. I feel guilty when I think about her having to do everything on her own these past months. Even the laundry, which in the winter is a cold and heavy job.

I found Azam in the vegetable shop, when I went to buy vegetables for ima.

No one had told him I was already here, he exclaimed offended.

He took off his apron. We walked to our spot on the river near the synagogue. That too I viewed with different eyes: I had never noticed before how simple and small our *kanishta* is.

There Azam pulled me firmly up against him. This time there were no immediate reasons to deny him, except that ima needed the vegetables. The sun added to the heat of Azam's kisses that I could but answer. I became warm and excited. From the pressure of his lower body against mine, and from the pleasure of his hands that were roaming over my body. Only when he tried to reach under my clothes, did I pull away, panting heavily. I stepped away from him, straightened my clothing, and went to sit on a rock on the river bank.

He begged me to marry him. He could wait no longer.

The sound of the babbling river calmed me down. Azam sat down next to me and took my hand. He said he missed me so. How could I admit that the studies took up so much of my time, that there was little left over for missing him?

Then he mentioned 'all those men who study with me.' Could they keep their hands off me? Horrified by his suggestion, I pulled my hand away. What does he think that a yeshivah is?

He asked me how much longer I was going to keep him waiting? This was the moment that I had been dreading for months. I told him that I wanted to finish my studies. That maybe he should go to Palestine on his own first, and I would join him later. With a throbbing heart and eyes cast downward, I waited for his reaction.

He was silent. Then his hand hit the wet rock next to him. He said that my 'damned studies' come before him. Why should he even bother waiting?

I swallowed, and tried to remember all those sentences that I had rehearsed during my sleepless nights. Not a single one came up. Because he was right, and I knew he was.

In the silence, the sound of river swelled once again. He stared at the water, and then turned to me. He said he was sorry, that he should not have become so angry with me. But did I even still want to marry him?

I took the hand that I had let go. Of course, I said, we will marry, but just a little later than we planned. And in a moment of inspiration I suggested he would come to Mosul, then we could get married there and live at ustad Yacoub's until I would be finished.

He stared at our hands, and said that he would go to Palestine this summer with a group from Iraq.

Why couldn't he change his plans for me? I begged him to consider it. Palestine can wait, then we can go together. He said he had made arrangements with Ezra.

You complain about my studies, but Palestine comes first, I thought. Your commitments are important, mine are not.

I stood up. Ima was waiting for me.

At the synagogue, I turned around. Azam was still sitting there, staring at the river. He suddenly looked so very lonely. I started towards him again, but stopped myself. It would solve nothing.

I no longer need to hide my journal above the oven. Everyone now finds it normal that I am reading and writing, so I can even sit openly in the courtyard and write. That is what I planned to do, sit in the sun and write about the past weeks before I return to Mosul, when Azam came running in, panicked and out of breath.

Had I heard the news? His uncle had been robbed that morning with all his goods, outside Penjwin. They had stoned him, he exclaimed, stoned him!

If we had not been in the courtyard I would have taken him in my arms. Instead I pulled him onto the mattress covering the stony bench.

Azam had become an angry waterfall of words. They had hit his uncle on the head, stolen everything, and finished off by stoning his unconscious body. He leaves behind a wife and five children.

For Azam, the message was clear, and written in blood. The hatred against Jews is here too, he said. They were going to kill us all. The Farhud had only been the beginning. He went on about the anti-Jewish publications and anti-Zionist politicians in Baghdad. I listened, nodded. He just had to deal with the shock, I thought.

He said his uncle never even hurt a fly. That he was a good man, and not even a Zionist.

They were after his money, I then said.

Azam reacted as if he had been stung by a bee. Why did they have to murder him? Stoning him? This was anti-Jewish hatred, he said. I should open my eyes!

I suggested that he had known his attackers. That they had been afraid that he would betray them.

And then you stone someone? As I read books, I should understand the symbolism.

But did they know this too? I asked. Without meaning to, we had started a heated discussion. I said the thieves only had stones at hand to use to kill him.

Azam looked at me impatiently, and said I was kidding myself. That we are living on a volcano. And he is leaving before it blows.

Our argument had brought ima out of the kitchen. She put her arms motherly around Azam when she heard the news. Abba and Sasson were called to join them, and here once again he repeated his story.

And that I could not see that this is anti-Jewish hatred, he said, looking at me angrily. An uneasy silence fell over the courtyard. No one wanted to contradict him, nor agree with him.

Now he knew for sure, Azam said. This summer he would leave for Palestine. He will help build a country, instead of standing by and watching one being destroyed.

Abba's calming words and the conversation that followed somewhat escaped me. That last sentence kept echoing in my mind. Our country is being destroyed. But my destiny is not his. I want to hold on to what we have.

Will I miss him? Of course. Perhaps more than I realize now.

July 30, 1944

Today a letter finally arrived from Palestine. It took more than a month to reach Mosul. Azam is doing well. He writes about the land of milk and honey, but also how he misses Iraq. And me. And about when I think that I will be able to join him.

The letter does not give many details. I think that Azam was afraid that it might have fallen into the wrong hands. So, I know nothing about his role in the battle between the Jewish resistance groups and the British army, which we hear about all the time.

"My tent looks out over the sea. Rahila, you cannot imagine it. It is the bluest surface looking different every day. Now it is a bright blue, but if there is wind or when it is cloudy, the blue can be different from day to day."

My fiancé will transform into a poet, if he stays there much longer! I look again at the handwriting, and suddenly remember the scribbling of his first note, that he passed to me in the vegetable shop. All the mistakes in the Arabic it had, while this letter is perfect.

Azam did not write this one himself. He asked someone to do it for him, who then added his own poetic sentences. Could he be ashamed about his imperfect Arabic? I would have preferred to read his own words, rather than those of another. What difference do a few mistakes make!

"I miss your eyes, your sweet face, your beautiful mouth. I even miss the discussions that you always started, and your talent for disagreeing with me..."

Through the beautiful Arabic of another I can still read and see Azam's loneliness. I wonder what he reads in my letters. The few I had written, were about the ongoing life in Mosul. How I can now recite just as well from the Torah as the boys.

More than ever before I follow the world news in which my people have begun to play a major role. In

Europe thousands of Jews have been murdered. The workcamps are death camps.

Many European cities have been bombed: Cologne, Hamburg, Berlin... Entire German armies have been killed in Russia. The Americans have come to the aid of the British. Roosevelt and Churchill have decided that the war will continue until Hitler surrenders. Their troops landed on the French coast last month, and are headed to Paris.

Last week, more of my fellow students left for Palestine. Other boys in the yeshivah also plan to join. They are encouraged by the stories of the pioneers and of fighters like Azam.

Ezra has come to the yeshivah telling them that the new country indeed needs the old knowledge, and that it must not only come from Europe. After all, the Talmud was written here in Iraq, this is the birth place of our knowledge. The boys are going to set up synagogues in Palestine, and teach children.

All this changed my role too; the younger students look up to me, and come to me with all kinds of questions.

Next week, I turn nineteen. In Penjwin, all the girls of my age are married. Some already have children. When I was there the last time for Newroz, Melka had just given birth to a daughter – the first grandchild for abba and ima. And Parwa's son was just starting to crawl when I visited her. We had little to talk about, this time. Parwa's entire life is comprised of her husband and child, care giving, cooking, washing – mine is made up of the yeshivah, the fellow students and Asenath, and learning, learning, learning. Whatever did Parwa and I talk about before?

Animated conversations I did have with Sasson and his childhood friend Kawa, who often joined us in the afternoon shade of the courtyard. Because he is a Muslim, our conversations are more about politics in general and less about the persecution of the Jews. About the war in Europe, and especially what will happen once it is over. With the coming of the Americans that shouldn't be much longer. Will Germany be split up, like the Americans and Russians have discussed? Is America the great world power or will that be the Soviet Union?

We discussed the arrival of the Arabs from Palestine to Iraq. That they are trickling in, is an unwanted result of the emigration of the Jews to Palestine, and their fight for a Jewish state. Unwanted, but unavoidable. Would I be willing to stay in my country, if it was being overrun by people who believe that they have more rights to it than I? I wonder.

I told Sasson and Kawa about the teacher from Palestine that is now working in one of the state schools in Mosul. I shared my concerns about his influence, and the hate that he is sowing. The propaganda he is pouring out over the youths! The Jews have stolen the Palestinian lands, and the Jews in

Iraq are helping them to do this, those kinds of statements.

Kawa said he has heard that this had angered an imam in Zakho. He had said during the Friday sermon that it is not about the Iraqi Jews, and that Jews and Muslims here in Iraq live together in peace. That not all Jews are Zionists.

I fiercely hope that this conciliatory message is spread elsewhere, and that it reaches the students of the Arab teacher in Mosul as well.

I really like Kawa, he is a smart guy. When he was studying in Sulaymaniya, he often played a game of *tawla* with Sasson in the teahouse. He is back in Penjwin to teach at the new government school, where all the boys must go now, the Jewish ones as well. As a result, Abba's lessons in the synagogue have been limited to the afternoons.

I know that the feeling is mutual, and that Kawa doesn't only come to visit Sasson. He makes no secret of this. But I am engaged, and he is a Muslim. So, we enjoy the good conversations, and do not mention it in any way. How else could it be, while Azam waits for me in Palestine!

That should not last too long, ima has warned me. Soon, I would be too old, and no one would want me anymore, she said. I reminded her that soon, I am going to marry Azam. She just looked at me.

5 THE OTHER'S TASK

May 10, 1945

The war in Europe is over! The German army has been defeated! Hitler is dead. Finally, the persecution of Jews in Europe has come to an end.

Many of the Jewish survivors want to go to Palestine. But will the British allow them entry now – as they failed to do during the time of the persecutions?

In his last letter, Azam asked me again when I was coming. But I keep thinking: When are you coming back, Azam? If the Jews are no longer being persecuted in Europe, then why do you need to fight for their Jewish state any longer?

He does not see it that way at all. The Jewish state is not there yet, he says. We still have to work hard to achieve it, by talking to the British, and looking for the support of the Americans and the Russians. What happened in Europe, just goes to prove that we need such a state, he feels.

He said that I could come to Palestine to teach, but how is that possible if there is continuous fighting and attacks on our settlements? Azam is not only fighting against the British, but also against the Arabs whose land he wants to take, and I am to teach there with the bullets flying around my ears?

Everything revolves around Palestine, even here in Mosul. Asenath got engaged yesterday. To the son of the wealthy businessman whose house Ezra always uses for his meetings. That is where she met David. Ustad Yacoub had his proposal under consideration for days, but he could not refuse. The father is the most important supporter of the yeshivah.

David wants her to go with him to Palestine. Him too. But Asenath is really going, while her father and mother both are against it. An important role is waiting for her there, she says. Here too, we keep telling her. Her mother tries it with tears, me with arguments. Because I don't want to lose her. How empty Mosul will be without her!

She says she could teach there. She has listened well to Ezra. I remind her that the kibbutzim and villages are being attacked. She answers that it does not mean that children must do without an education. I think that she must secretly have a romantic image of it all. Protecting the children and comforting them, while her brave husband is outside emptying his rifle against the attackers. I had not expected this from Asenath. But since the engagement, she has barely busied herself with our lessons anymore.

I am trying to understand her decision, which goes against everything on which our friendship is based. Like our admiration for Asenath Barzani. She says it is a childhood dream that she has outgrown. And our day and age are different from the seventeenth century when Asenath Barzani lived. What she is going to do wasn't possible at that time, was it?

I have to agree with her on that. Our great role model never left Kurdistan. Yet I cannot understand why she is in such a rush to leave. She has no good explanation for that either, except to say that David's plans were already made.

I miss Asenath, even before she is gone. How will things be, once she is in Palestine? I am a bit afraid of the void after her departure. And that causes me to wonder if it isn't time that I follow Azam too.

January 15, 1946

Azam has set an ultimatum. If I do not come to Palestine before Passover, in April, he will break the engagement.

"I do not want to wait for you any longer, dearest. Now that Asenath is also here, you have no reason to postpone your coming any longer. You cannot continue saying that after three years in Mosul, you have not yet garnered enough knowledge."

I stare at the words. He is right about that last point. The yeshivah has little more to teach me.

One thing the doubts of the past months have taught me: that I have many more reasons to not go to Palestine, than to go. The violence, the battle that is not mine, my country that I do not want to leave. Azam would be the only reason to go. And that reason is not strong enough. I miss him, but can do well without him too. That looks terrible; the letters seem to pound on the paper. But it is the truth. I would really like to marry Azam, but I can manage without him.

"Rahila, your task is here, at my side. So that we can raise our children together in this new country."

I admit that I find the tone irritating. Who is Azam to decide what my task is? I know that I have changed, over the time in Mosul. The unknowing, girly Rahila who fainted for the charms of Azam no longer exists. In the house of Asenath's father, I am regarded as an educated woman, someone you listen to. Not someone to order around.

And yet I can still effortlessly see his face before me. Feel the excitement of his kisses just by thinking about them. I still want to marry and have children with him. But not in this manner, in a strange country, where I can see no task for myself.

Breaking an engagement is a scandal for the woman, and Azam know this too. You are somehow viewed as damaged goods. A new engagement or marriage often does not happen, or it must be with a widower who needs someone to look after his children. That is not something that I am longing to do.

And on the other hand, I still want to study, but where can I go? There are few possibilities for women in Kurdistan. And my knowledge barely compares to what is being taught at universities. I know everything about the history of the Jews and our laws, but little about the contemporary world.

How many letters from Palestine have been lost along the way? If I do not answer this one, Azam will not know whether I received it or not. Then he will be forced to repeat his ultimatum, to make sure that the message is received. If I make this letter disappear, I will be able to postpone things for a few more months.

It only takes the flames half a minute to change the paper into ashes. Of course, I know that finding a solution will not be as easy. And that I will not be able to do that on my own. I suddenly feel very much alone without Asenath – who can I ask advice from now?

Sasson, perhaps. Or even better: Kawa. But this is not a subject which should be discussed by way of a letter. It is January, and the roads have become treacherous from the winter weather. Where can I find a chaperone that would be willing to take this unpleasant journey with me?

February 20, 1946

A reason had not presented itself in the past month. Until today, I thought at I would have to wait for Nowroz, the usual time to go to Penjwin.

Then, late in the afternoon Asenath's father called me to join him. The old man had a water pipe and a bottle of arak next to him. That took me back in time, to the discussion with abba, years ago, that would eventually change my life. Even the smell; ustad Yacoub uses the same tobacco blend as abba.

He said he had an urgent request for me. This made me a bit nervous.

He motioned for me to come and sit across from him, and started by explaining that he was happy that I had joined his daughter, three years ago. He was happy that we had become like sisters. That both he and his wife were always happy to have me around.

It almost sounded like a farewell.

He reminded me that he had other plans for Asenath, than the path she has chosen. He sighed: God did not grant him any sons, and yet someone must continue his work. I suggested carefully that perhaps one of the students could.

He stared at me, while blowing a plume of smoke into the room. He said he was getting old, that his eyes are getting bad and his back causes him a great deal of pain. He can no longer do it alone. He said that as the government has made new rules for the education system, we must change the way we teach. He is too old for that, he said.

I had not heard of new rules. He said that we must now also teach the youngest children mathematics, geography and history. The government wants to send us their own teachers for that. And the Arabic lessons must improve.

I nodded. The government was right. With only knowledge of Jewish history, our laws and wisdoms, one would not get far in this world. I was already jealous of the students who would get the new subjects. A world would open up for them.

Ustad Yacoub said that the rules only apply to the teaching of young children, and not at the Talmud school. There, nothing had to change.

The old man poured himself another arak. After he had added water, he handed it to me. I looked at him in amazement. Arak? For me, a woman? I would drink arak with the great master?

Smiling, he told me to take it. I shook my head. It would be impolite to refuse anything offered by the master, but this I could not accept. Women are not supposed to drink.

I was not to shame his hospitality, he said. Reluctantly I took the glass and set it down next to me, trying to understand why this was happening. It seemed to be a kind of initiation. But for what?

The hakham continued where he left off. If the teachers came from the outside, someone would have to oversee things. He could not, as he still has the Talmud students and his obligations in the synagogue. He said he needed someone to run the school, and give the Torah lessons - and Asenath is in Palestine.

Ustad Yacoub wanted me to lead the school? It made me flustered. Wasn't that far too great an assignment for me? He said I had taken the place of his daughter. Asenath could only go to Palestine, because she knew that I would stay here. And that is exactly the reason why he allowed her to go.

When I started protesting, he stopped me. He knew that I was now going to say that I cannot do it. He pulled on the pipe. I could do it ten times better than the best of the boys, he said. They can perhaps recite the Torah more beautifully, and maybe debate better on the Talmud. He called me a practical woman; he had seen how I handle and teach the young students. I know how to stimulate them, he said, how to connect with them.

I swallowed. But leading a school is something completely different, I protested. He eyed me from under his rough eyebrows, a look I know from our discussion sessions. Convince me, was the message. I searched for courage and arguments.

He pointed to the untouched glass next to me. Okay then, maybe it would help, I thought.

I carefully took a sip. The white substance tasted better than I had expected. It warmed my stomach. And with that came the words, and the courage to speak out.

How can a woman lead a school here in Mosul, I asked him. Would the people accept that?
The old man smiled. Was that my main issue? Of course, he would run the school in name. The authorities would deal with him if there was a problem. But in reality, I would be doing the work.
How could I oversee men who are more learned than me? Who says they are more learned? he asked. They had other knowledge, in other subjects. But he could guarantee me that my level of knowledge is not inferior in any way to theirs. Who would choose the teachers? He answered that the government comes with suggestions; he can either agree or refuse. He said the changes will take effect in the new school year. We have until September to get everything prepared.
When I asked how we will deal with the different age groups, the old man had a big grin on his face, and noted that we now had arrived at the practical problems. First, he wanted to know if I agreed about taking the position. I admitted that I was afraid how people would react. An unmarried woman, from a village, leading a Jewish school in Mosul with only male teachers and students… He promised me that all the gossiping would cease if I did my job well. And that he had not a single doubt that I would. And I had a fiancé in Palestine? That was a proper status, was it not?
I could not hide a smile. It suddenly occurred to me that ustad Yacoub was offering me a future in Iraq. A

definitive reason not to go to Palestine for the time being. And one which I need not feel guilty about.

The old man looked at me inquiringly. "Is that the sun I see in your eyes? Have you realized what your calling is?"

When I mentioned that I did not know if my fiancé would permit me to postpone our marriage any longer, the old men said Azam was right. It must be difficult to wait for one's bride for such a long time, but it was for a good cause. Then he offered to support my request to him. All the problems were suddenly solved. I was a bit lightheaded by this unexpected development.

The memory of abba was suddenly immense. I had all this thanks to him, and to the fact that he had broken with all the traditions by teaching me. He should be proud.

Ustad Yacoub seemed as relieved as I was. He pushed me to finish my glass. That was all part of the job, due to the regular meetings I would be having with my boss.

The paper lies in front of me. A blank, white sheet. On this, I must seem to find the words to explain to Azam that I will not be able to join him anytime soon.

The solution that I have prayed for, has presented itself. But how can I convince my fiancé that a school in Mosul is more important than one in Palestine? How can I ask him for more time, when he has already waited so long - and while I do not even know how long it will be?

What it comes down to, is that I do not love him enough to leave everything here that I am attached to, and go to him. That must also be Azam's conclusion. And he would be well within his right to break our engagement and to look for someone else. While I need the status of being an engaged woman as a means of protection against gossip and complaints in the new job. What else can I do, except to be honest? Or as honest as possible?

Azam, my heart and my life.
I have news that I can no longer keep from you. Ustad Yacoub has asked me to lead the new school that he is setting up for the younger children. Because Asenath is in Palestine, he wants me to take her place. He let her leave, because he believed that I would take over her work. He thinks that he is too old for all of the work, and therefore wants to leave a part of it to me.
It is an honourable assignment, and a difficult one. I feel I cannot refuse this. It is what I have studied for. Why my father first started teaching me.
That means that for the time being, I will not be able to come to Palestine, that I will not yet be able to become your wife. I am just as sad about this as you are, because we have waited for so long already. But I still must ask you once again for a postponement, and for your understanding. Ustad Yacoub has told me that he supports my request to you.

On the other hand, I would understand if you decide enough is enough, and should choose to break off our engagement. That would cause me much pain and heartbreak, because I love you and I long for you and our children. And I know that you long for this too.
Your loving fiancé, Rahila

April 25, 1946
Rahila, my life,
Passover has come and gone. We have just celebrated the exodus from Egypt, for me that was for the third time here in Palestine.
I had convinced myself that if you did not join me here quickly, this Passover would mean an end for us, as the Red Sea split before Moses' feet. Then your letter arrived with your request for a new postponement.
I understand the request from Ustad Yacoub is important for you. And that this is your answer to my question: why lead a school in Mosul, and not in Palestine? I realize that you find his proposal more important than mine. He is unquestionably a more important man than I, but he is not your fiancé and not the future father of your children.
What must I do, my love? You are leading me on. You are not prepared to come to me, here in Palestine, and yet you tell me how much you long for me and our children. My life is here, and returning to Iraq is not part of my plans. There is no way to combine the two.
It seems so strange to be talking to you in such a business-like manner, while my heart burns with desire for you. When I think of the men in Mosul who can enjoy your company, I

go mad. How long will you continue to torture me? I want to feel you in my arms, I want to start a life with you. I want to make you happy.

I cannot force you. And my heart does not want another. I will give you another year, my love. I want us to be able to spend the next Passover together, here in Palestine. So that together we can eat the matzes and bitter spice, to remind us of the exodus from before, and what we left behind.

And if you do not then come by yourself, I will come and get you.

Your loving fiancé, Azam

September 28, 1946

I am so tired, so very tired! But satisfied, and proud.

For two weeks now, the school has been operating in the new way. With the teachers Mustafa, Saman and Jalal who each fill a day with mathematics, geography and history. And while they are each working with one of the groups, I see to it that the others are kept busy. I give them lessons in reading, writing and Arabic, and on the two remaining days it is time for Torah-lessons and Jewish history.

It is hard work. Also for the children, much more so than with the old system. And I can clearly see that some need more repetition, must practice more and get the opportunity to learn dates from memory. I try to convince the teachers about this, but they say that their program does not allow any space for this.

So, I am left to do it. I have started reading through the books they use at night. A world has opened up for me. It is amazingly interesting to discover what was going on in the world at certain moments of our history. Now I know where Palestine is, and how far away Germany is. And of course, America too!

Ustad Yacoub only showed himself in the first days. Perhaps he wanted to show that he had every faith in me and my abilities, but it would have been nice if he could take over the Torah lessons from me. I am afraid to ask him. Perhaps it will become easier once I get used to it.

My fear that I would not be respected as a woman, proved to be untrue. I can calm the children down more quickly than the teachers. And the three men address me since the beginning as ustada Rahila, teacher Rahila, as if I am their superior. That is what I am, but I still find it difficult to accept that as a fact. They are all older than I am, and men.

Sasson had come from Sulaymaniya, to be at the opening of the school. I was very happy that he had made the long journey for me! He told everyone that would listen, that he came to deliver the pride of my father. He brought a stack of books along that abba had sent from Baghdad. I think that they were written by my grandfather, but I was afraid to ask Sasson – did he know about the family secret?

Could writing be hereditary in the family? I realize that I reach for this notebook whenever something happens in my life that I want to contemplate carefully, or when I feel I cannot share it with anyone. It is becoming a chronicle of my life, or about my search for knowledge, or perhaps even about the life of a Jewish woman.

Will there ever be offspring who will read my words, and will then know what the life of a Jewish woman was like in Iraqi Kurdistan in the Forties? I like that thought. Perhaps I can stimulate a granddaughter in this way, to choose for herself and to head down a path that leads to knowledge, respect and self-respect.

The war has been over for nearly a year now, and Palestine still dominates our image of the world. Of course, the horrible bombs on Japan have frightened us all, and the realization that knowledge can lead to these kinds of atrocities – but everything here revolves around Palestine. And with that, the fear of Zionism is abundant.

The Arab states have established a League to prevent Palestine from becoming the land of the Jews. They are calling for Arab troops to be sent to Palestine to beat the 'Zionistic enemy.' Poor Azam, poor Asenath – the struggle is becoming increasingly unfair. Before long they too might find themselves facing Arab soldiers.

At the end of last year, there were anti-Jewish riots in Cairo, and a synagogue and Jewish homes were destroyed. The government in Baghdad has forbidden similar demonstrations in Iraq. But it is obvious that anti-Semitism is seeping in everywhere none the less.

My job is even a direct result of this. The Muslim educators have been sent to us to prevent Zionism from spreading by way of our schools. We now can only give Torah lessons if we also give a translation or explanation in Arabic. I was already doing this, as I know from my own experience that children more easily remember words if they understand them.

It tells you something about the changes in the way we think in Iraq, that Jewish children would be indoctrinated with Zionism. As if Zionism is a dangerous disease which may ultimately deem to be fatal. The hate that is being generated hits us hard. I heard from ustad Yacoub that many Jews holding jobs in the governmental services have been fired, and Sasson tells me that continually fewer Jews are being accepted into the law and medical studies in Baghdad. Jewish businessmen are being forced to take a Muslim as a business partner.

Why can't people understand that being Jewish, and being a Zionist, are two different things? That a Jew does not have to be a Zionist? And certainly not in Iraq, where we all love our fatherland because it is also the crib of our knowledge of Judaism?

Sasson and Kawa have joined the Anti-Zionistic League that was established this spring in Baghdad. Sasson has told me that many prominent Jews became members: doctors, bankers, businessmen, lawyers. Their motto is "Zionism is colonialism", he said.

After the opening ceremony of the school, we sat in the courtyard of the house in Mosul, where Asenath's mother had provided us with tea and sweets. Sasson began to quote various League statements. That the absence of democracy in the Arab countries has resulted in fertile ground for Zionism. That the Arab masses and the institutions must become involved in the battle against the British colonization, because that is responsible for the creation of the Zionist movement in Palestine.

I asked him if he had become a communist. He denied. Members of the communist party are active in their League, but they are a minority, he said. I repeated his slogan about the Arab masses. What are they doing here in Iraq? He said that I have been very occupied by school matters. That I did not see how the people are being played. That the Arab League only exists to create a joint Arabic struggle – against Zionism. To keep the population occupied, so it does not realize how uninformed and poor it is being kept. The masses speak out with actions, he said, and that could be very dangerous for us Jews.

I was reminded of this summer's demonstrations, when someone had even died in front of the British embassy in Baghdad. 'Go away Brits' and 'Justice for the Palestinian people' were some of the slogans. Anti-British and anti-Zionist.

The fact that the Jews in Iraq have always supported the British, will turn against us, Sasson predicted. The British support those in power, and that is what the people are now turning against, he said. There has been unrest for months, and not just because the people have had enough of the British, their support for our dynasty and the presence of their troops. The prices have gone up, the wages have gone down and there is a shortage of work – while the landowners keep getting wealthier. Strikes in the oil industry for higher wages have led to riots, where the army had to intervene and left at least ten people dead.

Sasson told me about the British-American commission for Palestine that came to visit Iraq. It is looking for a solution for Palestine, but according to Sasson, it is in reality giving Palestine away to the Zionists. The call to boycott it had no effect, he said, and the commission wants to immediately allow a hundred thousand Jews from Europe to enter Palestine. As if that wouldn't lead to a Zionist state, he stated. And yet, the commission does not want Palestine to become either an Arab or Jewish state. He thinks that impossible. The Anti-Zionist League is demanding that the United Nations make an end to the British mandate in Palestine, Sasson said, so that the Arabs in Palestine can establish their own democracy where everyone can live in peace and equality.

I let his words sink in. Then I felt a cold hand gripping my heart. When did people like Azam, Asenath and David become our enemies? Sasson thinks that the turnaround came when Palestine became an Arab question. When it no longer only was about groups of people wanting to settle there against the will of the British. The world changed when the war was over. Arab governments needed something to maintain themselves against the movement from the West to allow civilians to take part in government, wealth, knowledge. And that something became Zionism.

I concluded that what started with the Farhud in 1941, has never really stopped, and he nodded sadly. It can only get worse, he feels. Unless we can remove Palestine from the political conflict, and it becomes a land not only for Jews, but also for Muslims and Christians, like Iraq has been for centuries.

I pointed out that Azam and his friends want a Jewish state, not one which must be shared. They absolutely do not want another Iraq. That is why they have become a threat to our safety, he said. That is why we must declare our loyalties. If we are for Zionism, then we are against Iraq. So, we are against it.

Sasson was right, no matter how painful it was. Yet I turned down his offer to become a member of his League. That would feel like a betrayal against Azam.

March 10, 1947

Tonight, Sasson appeared unexpectedly in the room. I saw on his weary face that he was the bearer of bad news.

Is it abba, ima? I asked.

He quickly reassured me.

It was about Azam, I could feel it with great certainty.

I no longer trusted my legs and dropped down unto the pillows.

Sasson told me that he was killed a few days ago in Palestine.

The ground disappeared under my feet. I looked at Sasson, begging that it not be true. Yet I knew that it was. My tongue was stuck. I was cold. And my heart was in so much pain that I could hardly bear it.

Ustad Yacoub had entered the room. Sasson told him that three days ago, Azam's parents in Penjwin had received a message. And that abba had asked him to come and tell me the news. His voice sounded very distant.

My Azam, my faithful, sweet Azam... How often had I not asked myself if he was in danger, only to then push those thoughts away? I hardly saw the room through the blur of my tears.

Ustad Yacoub asked the questions I could not, and for which I did not even want to know the answer. Sasson answered that not many details were available. Only that the group of fighters he was travelling with, stumbled across a British patrol. None of the five survived.

It was as if the conversation was taking place at the end of a tunnel. What the two men discussed further, I do not know any more. The images were bumping around in my head. Azam, at the vegetable shop, at my house, in the courtyard, by the river. His kisses, his grin, his delicious mouth. His hurried walk, his happy haste. I saw him at the river again, that last time we said goodbye. Disappointed. I had hurt him. And I felt guilty for not giving him more. Why had I not done that? What was I thinking of?

There will be no marriage. I will never be his wife. We will never share a life together. I have lost him.

Awkwardly, Sasson tried to dry my tears. I pushed his hand away. What are my tears compared to this loss?

And suddenly I had to know. What had happened, there in that far-away country that I now completely hated? How quickly had it happened? How quickly did something like that happen? I heard my voice, no more than a whisper. Did he suffer?

Sasson did not know. He brushed the wet hairs from my face and gave me his big handkerchief. Ustad Yacoub pushed a glass of water into my hand. I looked at it. How could I drink that?

When ustad Yacoub asked if his body is coming to Iraq, Sasson answered Azam is buried there. Of course, that is his country, I thought. The land he died for. Which is not my land. And now never will be. That greedy land has pulled us apart, and now it has taken him away from me forever. The handkerchief was soaked. Once I had let the tears flow, I was unable to stop.

His children. I would never carry his children. That certainty struck a new hole in my heart. We will never be able to form a family.

Ustad Yacoub suggested we would say the *Kaddish* for him, as it should offer us comfort in times of loss. Obediently I followed him in the prayer, but it brought

me nothing but words. Words, no warmth, no comfort. "May his great name be raised and held holy in the world he created to his wish. May his Kingdom be present in your life and in your days, and in the life of the entire family of Israel, quickly and soon…"
Is there any comfort? I have no more tears for the pain of the loss.
The room that I have had for myself since Asenath's departure, is empty and cold. The candle by which I am writing, is nearly gone.
Why did I keep him waiting until it was too late? If I had joined him, perhaps he would have been more careful, and this wouldn't have happened. It is my fault. Why did I not give him what he asked for?

6 STRUGGLE IN SULAYMANIYA

The people crowd around Zara in droves. Demonstrators are waving their flags. Rolled-up banners tower above the crowd. People are pushing and pulling, as up ahead the procession has come to a standstill and the mass of the crowd can only become more condensed.
They are in front of the offices of the largest Kurdish political party, the KDP, in Salim Street, the main street of Sulaymaniya. Slogans are shouted.
"Out with Barzani!"
"Out with the corrupt government!"
"After the Arab Spring it is time for a Kurdish Spring!"
The crowd lunges and pushes forward. They are mainly young people. Some of them Zara knows from the university. They push and pull. The crowd wants to push forward even if it cannot.

The atmosphere of a happy protest has vanished. The crowd has transformed into a large, angry animal. A caged animal.

The sun is hiding behind the clouds. Far ahead of her, Zara suddenly sees movement. What is happening there? Have they broken through the barrier? The crowd pushes forward. She hears glass breaking. Demonstrators are throwing rocks. She sees them flying, above the heads of the people. This is going very wrong. She wants to leave, but she is stuck in the swarm of people. Frightened, she grabs hold of Soran's coat as she is about to be separated from him. He pulls her back next to him.

Sirens are wailing. Then she hears loud noises. At first, she isn't sure, but then it becomes undeniably clear: it is gunfire. People are yelling, screaming.

"Shit," Soran swears. "Run!"

He takes her hand and pulls her along. They run, where the crowd allows them to. Around them, people are darting off in every direction. Away from the gunfire, that still is going on. A bullet lands just in front of them. Zara screams. They take a sharp turn and run in the other direction. And again. When they reach the park, they can go no further. A frightened Zara holds tightly onto Soran's hand. She cannot risk being separated from him.

People are yelling, shouting. They trip, fall and get back up. Small groups are moving forward, turn and once again fall apart. In front of them Zara sees that the safety police are charging at a large group of youths, some with their faces hidden behind Kurdish scarves. Shocked they turn around. It

is too close. Let's get out of here! Desperately they try to find a way out of the crowd.
Running past, she sees a child in a red sweater fall. Bystanders try to help him up – he must get out of there! – but he is not moving.
She stops. Suddenly her fear is no longer important. Soran pulls her arm.
"No, stop." She is out of breath. "A child."
He sees what she is pointing at. Seconds later he is bent down over the boy. Zara kneels beside him. Is he still breathing? Where has he been hit? Soran examines him with experienced fingers.
She is desperately aware of the battle that is taking place just behind them. And that they are in no way safe here. More than she sees them, she is aware of the countless running feet that pass by. From time to time someone bumps up against them. There is still the sound of stray shots.

It had all seemed so simple this morning, when Soran suggested that they take part in the demonstration. The youth of Sulaymaniya had been called on by text messages and Facebook to follow the example of Egypt and elsewhere in the Arabic world, and to demonstrate against the Kurdish government. Under the slogan that it is time for a Kurdish Spring.
Many fellow students had announced that they were going to take part in the protest. Out of concern about their future, as there are not enough jobs and if you are not affiliated with one of the political parties, it is nearly

impossible to find work. Corruption is getting worse, and while some Kurds are getting wealthier all the time, many others are growing poorer due to the ever-rising prices. Why is there still no electricity throughout the day, and are there problems with the water. What is the government actually doing for the citizens?

It was a clear, cold February morning. When they had left with their group of friends, it felt almost like they were going on a picnic. It was an outing. The privilege to be able to stand up for what they believed in – that is what they were discussing amongst themselves. How good that felt – even more so since their generation was the first to be able to do this in Iraq.

Security police and the army were present in masse. They were posted throughout the city, with shields, batons and weapons. It did not dampen the fun. The organizers had called for a peaceful demonstration, following the example of Tahrir Square in Cairo. We will do what they did, was the message, we are going to demonstrate, and not fight with the police.

Initially that seemed to be successful. The demonstration had ended on Saray Square in the city centre, when a group headed towards the KDP office. Because to all of them, the problems were mainly due to the KDP and the Barzani family, that had been in power for years. Zara and Soran had gone along without thinking too much about it.

The old animosity had immediately reared its ugly head. In Sulaymaniya you were either for the number two political party, the PUK, or the party for change Gorran, or for even one of the Islamic movements. President Barzani's KDP was from the Kurdish capital Erbil, from the traders' town Duhok – from the enemy. The battle that the parties had fought out in the civil war of the Nineties, is never far from the collective memory of the city.

Soran gets up and looks around.
"We must get him to the hospital, he is losing too much blood."
"Where has he been hit?"
"In his chest. I cannot apply any pressure to the wound. We must get him out of here."
Soran looks desperately at the people who are racing by. He speaks to a man, but he walks on. Another man helps him to move the child. While shots can still be heard, they carry him away from the scene. Zara sees the trail of blood they are leaving behind.
Afterwards, she barely knows how they managed it. They find a car with a driver willing to help them. At the hospital hundreds of people are waiting for news. Dozens have been wounded. The child receives priority. Soran stays with him. And then Zara is back on the street. The sun is gone. She is shivering from the cold and the tension. Groups of people are in front of the hospital. The atmosphere is grim.
"They are fascists!" she hears. "A corrupt gang!"
"How many wounded are there?" she asks a man with a blue bulletproof vest. Press, it says in big white letters. He has a camera in his hand and a heavy bag on his shoulder.
"More than forty," he says, answering Zara's question. "But there will be more. The guards fired off so many shots…"
"Why did they?"

She wants desperately to understand what has happened. What launched the violence she has just witnessed?
"The demonstrators tried to storm the KDP headquarters."
She shakes her head in disappointment. He does not know either.
"I was there. That is not what happened. Someone started throwing rocks, windows broke. And then the first shots rang out."
"Interesting," the photographer says. "What are you doing here? Are you injured?"
She tells him about the boy. He could not be more than twelve years old. What is a child of that age doing at a demonstration? Then she remembers the atmosphere at the beginning of the afternoon. It was an excursion. Not only for her and her friends, but also for kids like the boy. An excursion that has gone very wrong. She shivers and wraps her shawl more tightly around her.
"Where is the boy?" the photographer asks.
He turns away to look for him. On the way to the news of the day. That she was part of. In a flash she remembers the fear, the agony of getting away. She shivers again.
She turns around and hails a cab. It takes a detour to reach the house of her aunt and uncle. Now that she is finally sitting, she finds that she is unable to stop shaking. Hurry up, she silently commands the driver. I cannot take anymore. I badly need to go home.
When he stops in front of the door, with trembling fingers, she hands him the five thousand dinars that he demands. She lacks the energy to argue about the price, even though he is taking advantage from the misery of others. The front

door is calling her. Behind it she will be safe. She runs the distance between the taxi and the house. Blinded by her tears, she struggles with the key. Then her aunt opens the door.
"Child, there you are, finally! I was beginning to get worried!"
Like a little girl, she crawls into Aunt Lana's arms, who strokes and pats her on the back with little hushing words. Zara is not ashamed of anything. The tears do not cease. But the shivering slowly starts to lessen.
Later, sitting on the couch and giving her account of the day to her aunt and uncle, the tears flow once more when she starts to talk about the boy. "I don't think that he will survive," she sobs. "Who could possibly shoot at a child?"
"Kurds shooting at Kurds," Uncle Ibrahim grumbles. "Is this where we have now ended up? A new civil war?"
Her telephone interrupts them. It is Soran. She fears his news.
"Is he okay, Soran?"
It stays quiet. Zara hears sirens in the background. He is still at the hospital.
She hears Soran sigh. "There was nothing that they could do for him. He had lost too much blood. I am leaving here now and am coming to you, janakam."
Zara stares at her phone. "They have killed a child today," she then says. Suddenly she is exhausted.
"This will not be the end of it," her uncle predicts, "this cannot happen without there being repercussions."
Their silence is one of defeat, only broken by the beep of a text message.

"Tomorrow 11 o'clock Saray Square. Come all to protest against the murderers and thieves," she reads aloud. "Well, I don't think so. I had more than my fair share today."
"You are right, child, it is too dangerous," her aunt says.
"Is this the Arab Spring in Kurdistan? Can't they even let the people hold peaceful demonstrations?" her uncle asks.
"These were mainly young people, right?"
She nods. "Students, youths, the unemployed…"
"I predict that the political parties will now become involved," he says. "And then it will become the opposition movement against the governing parties."
Zara gets up. "You know what, uncle? I don't want to have anything more to do with it. If they are going to kill one another, I do not want to be there."

In the room at her aunt and uncle's home she has been using since she is studying in Sulaymaniya, Zara takes the journal and settles behind the desk. She shoves the book about Marx out of the way and places it on top of the one about the Kurdish national movement.
In the journal she searches for the passage that she thought about suddenly on her way up the stairs.
There has been unrest for months. (…) The prices have gone up, the wages have gone down, and there is a shortage of work – while the landowners simply keep getting wealthier. Strikes in the oil industry for higher wages have led to riots, where the military had to intervene and left at least ten people dead.
This is more than sixty years ago, and still as accurate as back then. Only, now there is an elected government, and

they have a democratic state. And still, the rich are getting richer, and the military takes action if the civilians protest. And people die.

Rahila did not experience it first-hand, though. Zara did. She sighs. Her studies have never been as confrontational as today. She suddenly wishes she had chosen a more practical course of study, as Soran has done. She could have become a pharmacist, or a dentist. But instead she chose to investigate the political processes; she wanted to make the world a better place.

The image of the bleeding little boy creeps back in and refuses to be blocked out.

Zara sighs impatiently. She wants to be rid of the images. She picks up the journal and returns to the place where her bookmark finds itself. Rahila has lost Azam. He died for his convictions, Zara realizes. For that child today, it was all just a game. Maybe that is why she is unable to think about little else.

And when Azam died, Rahila felt guilty because she had not kept her promise. She found her own life more important than a shared one with Azam. A thought hits her: what if Soran had been wounded today? That would have been very possible, she thinks dismayed. How guilty I would have felt...

Soran was right. I was too preoccupied with myself. And Rahila's journal shows just what that can lead to. I need to share more things with him. Starting with the journal.

She knows how difficult it will be. Soran will certainly not have the same feelings about the journal as she does, and not feel the kinship she has. She puts the book to one side and stretches out on the bed.

Soran was a hero today. She thinks of his seriousness, his state of mind, when he was examining the child. And he has not even finished his studies yet. She is so proud of him. A doctor in heart and soul, just like his father. Can that run in the family? That is not an unusual occurrence in Kurdistan; there are entire families of doctors and lawyers, as those professions go over from father to son.

What would have been the child's future? Impatiently, Zara tries to push him out again. She forces herself to think of Rahila. Her father was a teacher, and so was she - and at a time that it was not a usual occurrence for women.

She picks up the journal once again and flips to the passage that she wants to reread.

Will there ever be offspring who will read my words, and will then know what the life of a Jewish woman in Iraqi Kurdistan was like in the Forties? I like that thought. Perhaps I can stimulate a granddaughter in this way, to choose for herself and to head down a path that leads to knowledge, respect and self-respect.

Did Rahila have children? She certainly must have married. Instead of reaching a family member, Rahila's story has fallen into the hands of a stranger. Could that be why Zara is feels so gripped by the story?

Her eyes focus yet again on the last sentence: "...to choose for herself and to head down a path that..." Is choosing for a marriage with Soran choosing for herself? She will become the wife of a doctor, what does that say about her? What is she going to do after her studies, the usual job with the government? Or will she follow in her father's footsteps and go into politics? She would like that, but with which party? And would Soran allow it? He has become so possessive since the engagement. He wants to decide what is good for her or not. Who she sees, where she goes. If she would allow it, he would even choose her clothes. Has he changed? Or does she have only herself to thank for this? Is he reacting to her urge for independence, to do and discover things on her own?

She puts the book away again. Too many questions. Is that what a shocking experience such as what happened today, congers up? If there is one thing that today has shown her, it is just how unpredictable life can be. And at the same time far too short to do things you really do not want to. She turns over in bed. With great difficulty she sends her tired head back to the moment when she first skied down the mountain in Penjwin. Finally, last weekend. It was only just possible, the snow was getting too hard, Carlos said. But it was so perfect.

The snow. The crackling, white snow.

She wakes with a start from a knock on the door. Her aunt cautiously sticks her head around it. Soran is downstairs. Just let him come upstairs, Zara thinks sleepily. Suddenly she is wide awake and rebellious. Unbelievable, we are engaged, aren't we? And still we are not allowed to be alone together... not even on a day like today!

She is going to say something about it; she is not going to take it anymore. She bolts down the stairs, two steps at a time. In the room the words stick in her throat. The urge is gone, the anger forgotten. The blood on Soran's jeans

brings the images back. The quiet little boy. His red sweater. The bullets right in front of her feet.
She throws herself in Soran's arms. He pulls her up tight.
"What a mess, janakam, what a mess," he mumbles into her hair.
Next to her on the couch, he recounts the hours in the hospital in a sombre tone. How difficult it was to stop the bleeding. That the doctors were afraid to operate. That they did not have any blood for the child because he had an unusual blood type. And that no one from his family was there to give blood.
"Do they know who his parents are?" Zara's aunt asks.
"Luckily he had a cell phone in his pocket. I called his mother."
His face cringes. The poor mother, Zara thinks. And poor Soran. How terrible it must have been to have had to phone her with such an awful message. She imagines what it was like to speak to the crying woman. She strokes Soran's hand.
"She arrived too late," he says quietly.
He takes a deep breath and reaches for the glass of water that her aunt has set down next to him.
If only we were alone, and I could hold him, Zara thinks, once again angry at the world. She lays a comforting hand on his leg, covering the blood stains.
"You did what you could, goshawistakam."
While she speaks the words, she doubts that they will offer any comfort. She knows that he feels like he should have done more, then perhaps the child might not have died.

Her aunt and uncle join in; how wonderful it was what Soran had done, and that there were not many people who would follow his example. "People today only live for themselves," her aunt sighs.

"Did you receive a text about tomorrow too?" Soran asks, in an oblivious attempt to change the subject.

Zara nods. "But I am not going. I want to go to Penjwin."

"Me too. I have picked up the car. We leave as soon as you are ready."

Zara's aunt protests. "It is already dark. You really shouldn't be on the road now."

"We have to get out of town," Soran says. "There are rumours that they are going to arrest the demonstrators tonight."

Surprised, Zara looks up. Her aunt shrugs her shoulders. "There is so much gossip."

"They want to prevent the demonstration of tomorrow," Uncle Ibrahim thinks. "So you arrest the leaders. That is only logical."

"But you two are not leaders," her aunt persists.

"No, but there was no clear leadership. But I brought in that child. Just put on the news, you'll see that it is the lead story. We really should go."

Her aunt turns on the television, right in the middle of a report about the demonstration.

Zara has gotten up, but now she watches the screen hypnotized along with the others. That is where she was, just hours ago, she was part of that chaos. It looks even worse on the outside looking in, than when you are actually in the middle of it.

The footage changes over to the hospital. To the people waiting outside. And then suddenly the picture is there. Of the child with the red sweater, shot, bleeding to death on the street.

"Someone took that picture with their cell phone before we found him," Soran says, his voice sounds all raspy suddenly. "And left him to die."

Now he gets up too. "Zara jaan, get your bag. Come on, we are leaving."

They drive to Penjwin in silence. Zara looks at Soran, as he steers his old Toyota over the dark roads. The highway changes into a two-lane unlit road. She sees his concentrated look, completely focussed on the process of driving.

"I was proud of you today, Soran," she says.

He rejects the words with a small gesture. "I wasn't able to save him."

"You aren't a doctor yet, how can you demand that of yourself?"

In the light of the dashboard she sees his bitter smile. "In a few months, I will be working in a hospital, you know that. If I am unable to do it now, how will I be able to then?"

"Could someone else have saved him? They were shooting at us, Soran. There was no ambulance, no stretcher. You had no bandages, no equipment. No blood to give him. What do you expect?"

He grumbles something she cannot understand, and she does not ask. The silence returns.

They pass snow-covered slopes. Ploughed snow lies on the roadside. Inevitably Zara's thoughts keep going back to the events of the day. Could they really be looking for us, she wonders. Then they will be able to find us easily enough in Penjwin, won't they? Or was the rumour only spread to scare us?

"It will be terrible tomorrow." Soran's thoughts seem to mirror hers. "With so much police and the military, and after the dead and wounded of today, tomorrow will only lead to riots. It is a good thing we will not be a part of that."

"Will they close the university?"

"There is a good chance of that, don't you think?"

Soran slows down for the Penjwin checkpoint, and rolls down his window. The cold night air flows into the car. Zara tightens her coat around her.

In the light from the dashboard, she sees the blood stains on Soran's trousers.

What explanation do you give for that? What kind of world is this that we have ended up in, what has changed since this morning?

"*Bashi, brakam,*" greets Soran.

The guard waves them through. Luckily, he has not seen the blood.

Soran stops in front of her house and bends towards her for a kiss. As she closes the car door, she realizes that she will once again have to recount the entire story. Her parents will want to know everything. And yet all she wants to do, is sleep. She wants it all to vanish into oblivion, not to have to remember what has happened, and what has changed.

Zara clicks the light back on. She cannot sleep. Her brain is too busy with the images of the day. It stays dark; the power has gone again. Even the generator is not working. She reaches for the book reading light that she has bought for this kind of situation.

If sleep cannot bring oblivion, then perhaps Rahila's journal will.

May 21, 1947

Two months have passed. Two empty months. I did not realize before just how big a role Azam played in my life. He was always somewhere in the back of my mind. As my finance in Palestine, as the future father of my children. As the future pulling at me – and how often had I not postponed it.

And at the same time, that was the reason why I was working so hard – to get a reprieve for my journey to Palestine. From a life with him. How double it all was. Through my own stupidity, my postponement turned into a total cancelation.

After the *shive*, the week of complete mourning, I went back to work. I faithfully say my prayers. They bring order, as they should. But no comfort. Over and over again, I keep seeing how my Azam must have died. His group had fought from an impossible position against the superiority of the British. They were surprised by them, and did not have anyone to offer back up or cover. A number of Brits were injured, as Azam and his comrades kept on shooting until they no longer could. They had no choice, and knew that all too well.

What could he have been thinking about, in those last minutes? Certainly not only about the enemy, and how he should use his last bullets wisely. I can only hope that he had some positive thoughts about me, even if I don't deserve them.

They buried his body where he died. In a village close to Haifa. Perhaps, one day I will visit his grave.

Ustad Yacoub tries to distract me. He has asked me once more to take part in the debates with the Talmud students.

On our weekly evening together, we play tawla in silence or we talk about our students. I cannot share the pain of Azam's death with him. I miss Asenath, I miss ima and even abba. With them I would be able to talk about this great loss.

I now know the true meaning of mourning and sorrow. The colour has left my life. I mourn the love that I lost. And the promise that died with him.

I remember the deep disappointment, when after my return from Al Qosh, I announced that I would be moving to Mosul. Could I not stay closer? Was there no school in Kirkuk where I could go, he had suggested. Then at least we would be able to see one another on a regular basis.

If only I had done that. Who knows, how things would have turned out? I am unable to rid myself of the feeling of guilt. The feeling that if I had only followed him to Palestine, he would have been more careful, and he might still be alive.

And if you do not come, I will come and get you. This sentence from his last letter haunts me. He would have come to get me, of that I am certain. Is that not what I had been waiting on all along?

The missing is indescribable. The void is so immense. There is no prayer that can help me.

It becomes easier, Asenath's mother promises me. She says that the sadness lessens, and the pain becomes more bearable. That time heals all wounds. I want to believe her, but I cannot. The only thing that helps is working. And perhaps the purring of the kitten, a surprise gift of Asenath's mother. The small white kitten just turned up at our doorstep, she says, but I do not believe it. She has arranged that for me, to offer a bit of distraction. The small animal demands attention and warmth, and when she is on my lap purring, it gives me a great deal of comfort. More than all the prayers put together.

How cynical fate is, that Azam was not allowed to live to see the British hand their mandate over Palestine back to the United Nations. That means his struggle was indeed not in vain. And only after the British have killed him, they accept that their presence in Palestine is useless. If only they had seen that before, he might have lived.

A few days ago, a special commission of eleven countries was formed, to find a solution for Palestine.

In August it must present its report to the United Nations. Arab countries have boycotted the commission, as they deemed it to be a Zionistic conspiracy. They close their eyes to the reality that Jews have been going to Palestine for years, have built settlements and have established themselves there. Azam started a new life there, and along with him thousands of others. Do they not have the right to a piece of land to call their own?

Apparently, the Jews in Palestine must disappear – leave, head into the sea, vanish into nothingness. Even helping to come up with a possible solution for a problem that has grown more acute in the past ten to fifteen years, is unthinkable for the leaders of our lands, Iraq included. Azam would have found this to be unbearable. He and his consorts created a status quo that is being ignored. My faith in a peaceful solution diminishes with each passing day.

Even the leader of the Shiites is taking part in the smear campaign. He has declared a fatwa that prohibits the sale of land to Jews in all of the Arab countries. As a result, the atmosphere in Iraq is becoming even more hostile. Now you can even be cursed at in the streets simply because you are Jewish.

The other side of all this, is that it has become nearly impossible to leave our own country! If I now wanted to go to Palestine, I would be forced to come up with 1,500 dinars, to serve as a guarantee for my return to Iraq. That is a huge sum of money, that I would not know how to raise. A lost amount, because I wouldn't be coming back. And the government knows this. It meant as a milking cow, to milk the wealthy Jews in Baghdad and Basra.

But Azam would certainly have found a solution for this. After all that waiting, he wouldn't have allowed any sum of money to keep us apart. I read this sentences, and once more cannot hold back my tears. There will be no reunion.

This journal is becoming ever more a chronicle of our suffering. Look at the new rule. This is applicable for all Jews who want to travel abroad, even businessmen and the sick must first seem to find 1,500 dinars. Virtually no one is still able to go abroad for medical treatment. "The fate of the Jews in Muslim countries is dependent on the development in Palestine," the Iraqi minister of Foreign Affairs said. In reality, we have become hostages in our own country.

I did not follow Azam. Now that door has closed. Would I still want to go? I don't think so. Without Azam, there is not a single reason for me to want to settle in Palestine. Even more, I hate the land that took my man from me.

There have not been any letters for months now, not even from Asenath, who always wrote faithfully. No doubt she has had her first child by now. They say that mail from Palestine is being intercepted and read, and that the contents will be used against us. I only hope that she has decided not to endanger her family, and that nothing has happened to her.

November 18, 1947
The situation is worsening. After the United Nations Commission for Palestine came up with a split advice in August, the number of incidents against Jews has only risen. A majority in the commission wants Palestine to be divided into an Arab and a Jewish state with Jerusalem falling under international control, while a minority wants a neutral, federal state which would unite both states. Whichever way you look at it, the Jewish state has been born. This month, the United Nations must decide on this proposal, but the Arab League is already furious – and so are the Arab masses, to use one of Sasson's terms. His warning is echoing in my ears: when the masses speak, it is dangerous for the Jews.
Here in Mosul, it has become a dangerous adventure to find yourself outside of the Jewlakan. You take the risk of being cursed at, or yelled after. "Jew, get out!" is one of the friendlier comments spit out at you. I have even heard of an elderly Jewish man who was pelted with tomatoes on the market. Some merchants no longer sell to Jews. Some people even refuse to speak to us. I hate this new situation. Iraq is my country, Mosul is where I live. Who decides whether I am welcome here or not? The atmosphere on the streets frightens me. But what can we do? Staying inside is not an option.

I keep telling myself that Mosul is a city where we have lived together with Muslims, Christians and Yazidi's for centuries. Here a Jewish king has ruled, and after that a Christian one, and only after, the Muslims came into power. Our communities have always lived alongside and with one another. We meet in the teahouses and at weddings, parties and funerals. Neighbours have looked after each other, bringing one another food over the holidays. There were also marriages between the faiths. You would think that a centuries old way of life could not be so easily erased. But I am afraid that the poison from outside will eventually destroy our unity.

That same poison also possesses our administrators. The anti-Zionist League has been disbanded and is now forbidden. The reasoning behind this is just as cynical as it is unimaginable: it is believed to be a Zionistic club. The leaders have been arrested because "in reality, they support Zionism, and in doing so are undermining the stability in Iraq". What an unbelievable distortion of the facts! Sasson left the organization exactly because he was getting threats from the Zionists – and he wasn't the only one.

I am too restless to stay indoors, and went to the grave of Jonah, on the other side of the river in the older part of Nineveh. I had made it a kind of educational project, and I visited the grave each time with different students from the yeshivah.

While I stood by the grave between the women who were begging Jonah to open their wombs and the give them healthy children, I begged the prophet to open the eyes and ears of my fellow countrymen, and to let us live in peace. Jonah's tomb is located in the Yunes mosque, which was built later on the site where he died. Unfortunately, an Islamic cemetery is no longer a safe place for a Jewish woman accompanied by yeshiva students who tend to draw attention to themselves with their black suits and religious hair styles. When after our last visit on our way back to the Jewlakan we were followed by a group of young Muslims, I was forced to put a stop to the visits.

They were part of my self-chosen assignment, to make the loss of Azam bearable. I do not want to continue being so depressed, so without any joy of life. That is why in the summer, with the approval of ustad Yacoub, I set up a class to teach young women to read, write and learn mathematics. I am so very proud that most of them, after intensive lessons, could not only read a bit of Arabic, but even write some too.

After five months, I noticed that the sharp edges of the sadness were wearing away – Asenath's mother has been right. I can now think of Azam without falling into a deep abyss, and without my heart nearly bursting from the pain. But I miss him still. Unlike I ever missed him when he was alive.

I turned twenty-two this summer. An unmarried woman of twenty-two. One who does not even have a fiancé, or the prospect of a marriage. That is considered a problem. When I was in Penjwin this summer, ima also brought up the subject. She acknowledged that no one can ever take Azam's place, but pointed out to me I do not have much time left. At twenty-two, one is considered to be an old maid.

It is too soon, I said. I should have been Azam's bride. I miss him every day. Could she give me another year? She nodded. For who would want an educated woman of twenty-two? She would need more time to find someone anyway.

The idea that someone will take Azam's place is painful, but perhaps it is for the best. I cannot simply keep burying myself in my work so that I cannot feel the absence.

In September, when we have started a new school year, I noticed there were fewer children present than we had expected. At least five families must have left, I concluded. People are allowing themselves to be chased away by the hostile atmosphere. I find that to be a terrible thought. During our weekly evening with arak, water pipe and a game of tawla in the visitor's room, I asked ustad Yacoub how the families managed to get out of the country. I could not believe that they had managed somehow to get the needed 1,500 dinars per person. The Kurds have smuggle routes across the Tigris to Syria or through the mountains to Iran, he answered. He says that it costs a lot less than what the government is demanding. What happens to their possessions, I wondered. He explained to me that selling is not possible, because that would make the departure plans obvious. And for that reason, the synagogue makes sure that the empty houses are guarded.

I concluded we won't have the manpower, if many more leave. He sighed, and predicted that it can only get worse. He asks himself too, how long we will still be able to keep the school open. Alarmed, I looked at him. The UN-commission's advice is only leading to misery, he said. When the British eventually leave Palestine, the Zionists can claim their own state. He predicts that the Iraqis will vent their anger about that on us.

I petted the cat in my lap, and concluded that it has become too difficult to make plans. What if we close the school, and things turn out not to be so bad after all. He shook his head. Nothing will be easy, he said. And many members of our community have also come to that conclusion. They are exploring the possibilities to leave, or try to buy the protection of influential Muslims. Did I know that Salha had decided to marry a Muslim?

David's sister Salha, daughter of a respected merchant and one of the richest Jews in Mosul, marrying a non-Jew? My thoughts went immediately to my grandmother, who had also done that. And how it had resulted in bringing shame to the family. Ustad Yacoub must have seen the disbelief on my face. He said she had come to ask his advice, as a Muslim boy had asked for her hand. Her parents were pushing her to marry him, and to convert to Islam. For her safety, because the family is seen as connected to Zionism. Not only because David is in Palestine, but because their father has supported the Zionist movement financially, as he also supports the synagogue and the school.

He admitted this will have repercussions for us too. We can keep claiming that we are Iraqi Jews, and not Zionists, he said, but the connections between the two are everywhere, and are becoming ever more obvious. His daughter is in Palestine, my fiancé died there. Our most important financer, who is the father of ustad Yacoub's son-in-law in Palestine, subsidizes Zionistic activities too.

I took a drink of my arak so that with its taste I might wash the sense of fear out of my mouth. The threat is getting closer and closer.

I asked him what he had advised Salha. To get married and to convert to Islam, he said. But still to hold onto the Sabbath's day of rest, one of our most important rules. I concluded she would stay Jewish that way. He pulled on the pipe, and looked at me thoughtfully from above the plume of smoke. He asked what I could expect from a hakham. He had to think of her best interests, but at the same time he could not allow our faith to be renounced. Her children will after all be Jewish, even if she marries a Muslim. He hopes she can come back into the lap of faith, when the calm returns here once more.

Converting for your own safety – but that is still a conversion. To leave Judaism? The faith is your great certainty. What remains, once you leave that behind? I asked ustad Yacoub that question. He quickly reassured me. It was only a precautionary matter. If your heart remains loyal to the faith, then you are not truly converted, he assured me. But surely people will notice if someone only converts in name? That is very dangerous. He answered that she has to be very careful, and hide her true intentions. I pointed out that she will stand out, if she does not make a fire on the Sabbath, but he said that her future husband is rich. They will have servants to make the fire.

Salha's future husband is the son of an agha, a Kurdish landowner from outside of Mosul, who has had ties with the Jewish community for years. He is one of the aghas that we pay for our safety. Her parents hope that his influence will insure their safety too, but ustad Yacoub doubts it. Too many people know of their background, he said. We were silent, each of us lost in our own thoughts. It showed just how close this hit home for me too. For the outside world I too have Zionistic ties. Through Azam, and the school.

I tried to convince myself that things had not yet reached that stage. More urgent now, was the situation of the school. If it closed, what would I do? I asked ustad Yacoub about his plans, and managed thus to extract yet another sigh. He did not know. We can only take things a day at a time, he said, and react to what is happening around us. Happily, no synagogues or schools have been attacked yet, but that could happen without warning.

What would be a reason to close? I asked pushing for an answer. If we were no longer able to guarantee the children's safety, he answered resolutely. Or if the government orders us to close. I suggested moving the work to a house, where it could go unnoticed. He nodded silently. That was possible, of course. But was that a risk that we were willing to take?

Everything has become uncertain. Our safe little world no longer exists.

November 29, 1947

When I arrived at the school, Mustafa and Saman were standing outside talking. It was still early; none of the children were yet inside. They greeted me politely.

Both of the teachers here, while it was Jahal's day to teach? They saw that I was surprised.

Mustafa said that today the United Nations would be deciding about Palestine. I told them I was well aware of it. But where was Jalal? They looked at each other. Mustafa answered that he was not coming today. And that they did not want to leave me and the children alone.

Finally, I understood. Jalal was expecting riots today, because of the announcement in New York. He did not want to become a victim of that. My teachers had discussed the situation amongst themselves, and this was the outcome.

I was touched. My Arab and Kurdish educators both felt responsible for our Jewish school. Had my prayers at Jonah's grave been heard after all...? But if they were expecting unrest, was it wise to keep the school open today? Wouldn't we be putting the children at risk? I suggested to just send them back home again.

Mustafa pointed out that there would just be an empty school then. That could be looted, I thought, finishing his sentence in my head. And there are enough other places that need guarding, ustad Yacoub would have his hands full.

The teachers knew all too well how difficult it had been to collect the school supplies we had, now that an innocent Jewish school is seen as an instrument of Zionism. That was a dilemma. Because if something would happen and the children were here, then they would be in danger. Yet we would never be able to guard the school with only the three of us. The teachers admitted they thought the children really wouldn't be attacked. I reminded him that even old, defenceless men got pelted with tomatoes.

If we lose all the materials, or if the school is set on fire, how can we still teach? Saman wondered. In his words resonated the fear of losing his job, along with his salary. His concern was not solely for the school. I knew that with his salary he supported a large family.

I said we needed to be clever. The men looked at me, wondering what I meant. I explained that neither of the solutions was acceptable. An empty school with the three of us as guards would not work. A full school with children as hostages must be avoided at all costs.

We had to make sure that we cease to be a possible target, I said, and I saw Saman's mood change. He understood where my thoughts were leading me: the school had to lose its Jewish image. How could we change it into a Kurdish school? The Kurds are a minority in Mosul, that is mainly Arab, but in any case, not a controversial minority such as the Jews. As Kurds we would be safe.

I knew that it would be a bit odd: a Kurdish school in the middle of the Jewlakan. But we had to do something... Even if it were only to give birth to the notion that there was a Kurdish connection, even that could help. Saman was completely taken by the idea. Then we needed Kurdish clothing, he said enthusiastically. That should not prove to be too difficult, as many Jewish families celebrate the Kurdish holidays alongside their neighbours, covering themselves in traditional Kurdish clothing.

The idea grew. We would make it a Kurdish Day, of maybe even an entire week. We would send the children home to let them change clothes, and we would teach them today in Kurdish. Mustafa wanted to teach them Kurdish songs, and in the afternoon the national anthem.

Shalom and his sister Sara came in hand in hand, and walked to their seats. I waited until the teachers had filled the classroom, as on any normal school day. After Micha came running in as the last one, I clapped my hands and it became quiet. I told them about our special Kurdish week. That we were celebrating because we are all part of Iraq: We Jews along with the Christians, the Arabs and the Kurds.

The children looked at me wide eyed. As they must have heard something at home about the chance of unrest, I was surprised to see that no one had kept their child home today. When I told the children to go home and to come back in their Kurdish clothing, they became very excited. A party, and then at school! Cheerfully they ran out.

While the teachers also went home to put on their Kurdish outfits, I waited in an empty school. When the class was once again complete, then I would go and change too, but now I needed to be there in case any mothers might come wanting an explanation.

I looked around the classroom where our three groups receive their daily lessons. The school benches stood neatly in rows. The November sun shone through the high windows and reflected off of the clean, white walls. Our schoolbooks were already stacked up and ready for the day. I looked through the stacks and took out the Hebrew books. I put them away in the cupboard. I wiped the blackboard clean so that the remnants of yesterday's Torah lesson were no longer visible.

Not all clues that this is a Jewish school allow themselves to be so easily removed. The Hebrew verse on top of the wall for example. I stared at it. If the classroom had filled with children in Kurdish party clothes, it would not be so noticeable, I hoped. But what would we do tonight, when they had gone home and the empty school became an easy target? I sighed. Why had I not thought about this sooner, so that I could have discussed it with the teachers and ustad Yacoub? I know the answer: because I always push problems and decision making aside, as I had done with my marriage to Azam too. It is high time that I change this habit.

David's sister Salha came in, with her youngest sister in a festive Kurdish dress. The upcoming marriage did her good – she looked radiant. She said she understood what I was trying to do, and that her mother sent me her dear greetings. She suggested sleeping here tonight with some families, and again I mentioned the dilemma of whether or not you should put children at risk. Then she suggested asking our Kurdish neighbours in the Jewlakan for help. There are many Kurds who do not agree with the anti-Jewish policy, she said.

When everyone had returned and Saman and Mustafa started with the lessons, I left with Salha. Once outside I reminded her of her engagement and asked if I could congratulate her. She smiled. Of course, she said, Zagros was a nice man. When she said nothing more, I left it at that. This was neither the time nor the place to discuss something of such a sensitive nature.

Once outside the Jewlakan, Salha walked determined towards a house, where we were led into the visitor's room. The man of the house appeared. Salha and he were talking in *Kermanji*, a Kurdish dialect that I can understand, after five years in Mosul, but have not learned to speak well as I have too little direct contact with Kurds. I let Salha do the talking. After the usual niceties, exchanging information about the health of Salha's family and that of her fiancé Zagros, she explained the problem at hand. That we needed his help. That he would be providing us with a great service, if a few of his men could keep watch over the school.

Much to my surprise, the deal was made in no time. The lord of the household mentioned the names of men who would come tonight, and he promised that he would see to it that there would be protection on the coming nights as well. While his wife quietly set down some tea for us, he asked how much we would be paying. Clearly, Salha had expected this question. She named a figure, the man asked for more, and they came to an agreement somewhere in the middle. She promised her fiancé would take care of the payment.

Once outside, I expressed my amazement at how easily it all had transpired. She explained with a smile that the man is an uncle of her fiancé, whom she knew we can trust. He knows that Zagros would never forgive him, were he to abandon his new family in their time of need.

The candle which lights my paper is nearly burned up. It is time that I replace it, for tonight there will be no sleep. For more than an hour now, there has been the sound of angry voices outside and a thumping on the doors, but no one is opening them. Groups of men are going through the Jewlakan. The authorities have sent soldiers to maintain order, but that doesn't prevent the chants of "Jews get out!" and "Palestine is for the Palestinian people!" being heard loud and clear throughout the neighbourhood.

Buildings are being stoned. I hear shots, screams, and running feet. Breaking glass. A door that slams shut. The cat is meowing nervously. I try to keep the fear at bay, but with little success. What can I do? It is good, that the Kurds are protecting the school. I know that the students in the yeshivah are keeping watch there, and ustad Yacoub and a handful of believers are at the synagogue. I can only hope that trouble will pass by this house. Together with Asenath's mother, I listen in silence to the sounds outside. From time to time we try to comfort one another and calm down the cat.

It will be a long night, because the United Nations has just passed Resolution 181. That gives the British a minimum of two months to withdraw their troops from Palestine, after which an independent Jewish and

Arab state will be realized. The division of Palestine seems to be fact now, just as the arrival of a Jewish state. Azam has posthumously gotten his wish. But it is impossible to simply enjoy the fact that the Jews are getting their own state. Because the anger of the Iraqis is turning against us.

Now that the future has started for Eretz Israel, it has ended for Jews in Iraq. I can no longer deny this fact.

7 STORMY WEATHER

December 15, 1947

My sombre words of a month ago stare back at me. The ink has blurred from my tears. I was so afraid that night, and how I missed Azam!

The calm did not return for three long days. Although some empty houses were looted, the school and the synagogue were barely damaged, apart from a few broken windows. The cemetery was the hardest hit, as tombstones were struck and shattered.

We had been prepared for the worst. I had even decided to go back to Penjwin, because the school cannot possibly remain open under these circumstances. And then, things calmed back down. We cleared the broken glass, repaired the damage. We even quietly celebrated Chanukah, the festival that brings light to dark days.

And now, the hate is no longer directed against us, but mainly towards the government. Because Baghdad is in negotiations with the British about an extension of their mandate in Iraq. People want to be rid of the British and their army. In Palestine, those same British troops were responsible for Azam's death. For Iraqis, they are the colonists' soldiers. But I cannot deny that here in Mosul, we owe our lives to them. It is thanks to them, that we did not become the victims of mass murder in the Jewlakan.

It is still not calm here, but it is no longer about us. Thousands of people have taken to the streets to demand work and higher wages, and political liberties. It seems that the Communist Party, which had gone underground, is behind it. It wants to be rid of the monarchy, because that has always taken the side of the landowners and the rich. Of course, the rich are often Jews, and at the same time Jews play a role in the Communist Party.

And yet it isn't easy to wash away the bitter taste after what happened last month. The atmosphere outside of the Jewlakan remains hostile. We just are not the centre of the hate for the moment.

The unrest was a warning. There is much more stormy weather on the horizon. Because along with other Arabic combatants, Iraqi volunteers are off to Palestine to fight against the Jews. And because of reports that the fighting has been heavy, I can fully understand how the mothers of the soldiers look at us. Their sons are fighting against the Jews. If they perish – and some will – the hatred against us Iraqi Jews will only grow.

The world has been divided into two camps: you are either with the Jews in Palestine, or against them. To make clear where he stood, our Hakham Bashi in Baghdad, chief rabbi Sassoon Kadoori, has had to give a statement in support of the Arab fighters, rejecting Zionism. A rabbi that rejects the Jewish state that has been promised to us for centuries – how can he explain that from his faith?

The school is open again. The rhythm of the week is back. But we know all too well, that it is just the calm before the storm. When Saman asked me what we are going to do next time, I had no answer. He said we should not allow ourselves to be taken by surprise again. I promised to ask ustad Yacoub if we could hire the same Kurdish guards. But I fear that a few Kurds will not be enough to save the school from a next outburst of hatred against us Jews. Because that grows with time.

January 29, 1948
Today, after a month of unrest, we have a new government. The unrest was even given a name: Wathbah, the leap. It should have been a leap forward, a leap towards democracy. That is why many Jews joined in the protests. By doing so, we avoided being a target.

The anger was directed towards the renewed Iraqi mandate with the British. The troops remain; the British keep two military bases with air strips. Should they choose to, they can fly in extra troops.

Students played an important role in the protests, pushed by the communists and other underground groups. They took to the streets, and were beaten and shot. The army even brought tanks onto the streets. Last week in Baghdad, on one day there were between three and four hundred dead and wounded. Premier Salih al-Jabr escaped the country after that.

This morning I heard that the king has appointed a Shiite clergyman as prime minister. Mohammed al-Sadr is known for to his role in riots against the government in the twenties. The king probably thinks that he will be able to convince the protesters to go home. And if they do, it will all start over once again for us. I will indeed inquire about the guards for the school.

February 25, 1948

Sasson looked like he was one of the children in the class that had dressed up for the Purim feast, covered in mud as he was when he came in. I was just telling them about the smart Queen Esther. They were hanging on my every word, and did not even notice him. He motioned for me to continue and found a seat in the back. I ended the story saying that thanks to the clever queen, our people could be saved.

Shalom, dressed as a doctor, raised his hand. Who was going to save us now, he asked? Children miss nothing. And definitely not the crisis that the adults are trying to hide from them. I answered that God takes care of us. As Queen Esther was able to prevent the murder of our people, so was God able to help our people escape to Egypt.

When I asked who remembers how that happened, the children allowed themselves to be distracted easily. Micha, in his shepherd's costume, told us how Moses parted the Red Sea. He portrayed it using his imitation staff. Sara, the angel, joined in telling the story about how the bread had fallen from the heavens, during the long trip through the desert.

Later, Sasson repeating my words and asked if I really believe that God will care for us. He had washed himself and changed clothes. In the visitor's room, we listened to the heavy rain outside. I poured us both an arak. I knew I could no longer answer that with an unconditional "yes." Azam's death has changed me, in combination with the hostile atmosphere around us.

Thoughtfully I stroked the cat. Eventually I answered that if you no longer have faith in anything, life will become very bleak. He looked at me inquiringly. What else could I say, he said, as I was an expert in the Torah and must pass my knowledge onto our youth. But did I really believe that we could survive this? I confided in him that I am sombre. No one is going to save us, I said. If we want to survive, we will have to fight for it ourselves.

He drank his arak in silence. Then he asked what I was still doing here. If this was how I felt, how could I continue my work? I must be doubting all those stories in the Torah. Thoughtfully, I said that they are stories. They form the base for what we are. That is what I do, I said: I teach the children what their base is, their identity. He repeated his question. What was I still doing here?

He was right, and I knew it. But I wasn't yet ready for the next step. Faith no longer gives me any certainty. The only certainty that I still have, is my life in Mosul, with its order and regularity. And the fact that I am needed here, a responsibility that weighs heavily on me.

I have a role here, I said. This has become my family. And I asked him what else I was supposed to do. When Sasson did not answer, I told him that ima thinks that I should get married. But what man would want a twenty-two-year-old Torah teacher as a wife, who can barely cook?

And even drinks arak too, he smiled, refilling our glasses. He suggested it would be safer if I were to return to Penjwin. If the British pull out of Palestine in May, there will be consequences for the Jews here. And Mosul is not exactly friendly towards us anymore, he said. No more than Sulaymaniya. When I asked him if that was why he was here, Sasson answered that he needed a place where he could be invisible for a while.

In the middle of the sentence Ustad Yacoub came into the room. He brought the cold in from the rainy night, and walked straight over to the oil heater. Greedily, he reached for the glass that I poured for him. After he offered him our house as his home, he asked why my brother no longer feels safe in Sulaymaniya.

Sasson sighed. Because they have started arresting the Jews that have been politically active, he said. The government says that the communists could never have organized last months' protests without Jewish support. We supposedly financed them. Ustad Yacoub asked if the government has any evidence. The fact that so many Jews were also demonstrating has rubbed the government the wrong way, Sasson said. They have simply looked for a stick to beat the dog.

The past week, a number of his friends have been arrested. People who were active with him in the anti-Zionist League. I remembered that Sasson's best friend Kawa was also involved in the League. He is a Muslim, they leave him alone, Sasson said. A Muslim is naturally anti-Zionist, Sasson said scornfully; a Jew only claims that, in order to be able to help the Zionists.

We asked him why he thought they were on your heels, and Sasson said that he is on the list of active members. One after the other, everyone on the list is ending up behind bars.

A stay in an Iraqi prison is not something to be recommended. They are notorious for their filthy, small cells, the poor treatment of the prisoners, the abuse and the torture. It can take years to be released. Sasson needed help. We had to keep him out of a cell, one way or another. He should go into hiding, the old man concluded. He said he would not allow him to put us in danger here – even if he would be safe here. This was not a good place. There had already been arrests in the Jewlakan. We were being watched closely. If they were working through that list, then they would find him here in Mosul just as easily. Sasson thought he could remain unnoticed in the yeshivah, but I pointed out to him that he is a little old to be a student. And that he cannot grow prayer curls so easily. Ustad Yacoub thought that it would be exactly where they will look for him, because he is my brother.

The government is almost forcing one to flee to Palestine, Sasson said angrily. Even if one has no connections to the Jewish state, and loves one's country. Ultimately that seems to be the only safe place.

The cat jumped from my lap, stretched itself and went to meow at the door. I walked followed her to the kitchen to get something to eat to go with the arak. How to help Sasson?

The cat rubbed up against my leg. I bent down to give her some milk. I understood why Sasson had not gone to Kawa, since he was also on the list – but such a solution would have been best. Becoming Kurdish, becoming Muslim, merging with a community that is not being persecuted. I placed the plates of bread on a tray.

Becoming a Muslim. Salha's solution. Would that work for Sasson? I realize that only six months ago, this would have been unthinkable. Then Judaism still was everything for me. Now I know that survival is most important. You have to make compromises. It can even mean converting to another faith.

Inside, the topic of conversation had shifted to the expected British withdraw from Palestine in May. Interrupting the conversation, I said I might know a solution. The same as for Salha.

Sasson looked at me questioningly. Ustad Yacoub nodded in agreement, when I said Sasson needed a new identity. A Muslim identity, so that he no longer would draw attention.

My words were drowned in the sound of pounding on the door. We looked at each other in distress. Night time visitors usually meant nothing good, but this could only be the police. I ran into the kitchen, taking Sasson with me, opened the door to the spacious cellar and pushed him in. The cat ran in too. I stared after her for a split second, then closed the door and turned the lock. The key I hung back on the usual hook.

Alarmed, Asenath's mother came from upstairs in her nightclothes. In the visitor's room, I shoved an empty arak glass into her hands, the other disappeared in the pocket of my wide skirt. No one would think that a second glass could be mine. I searched for other signs of Sasson's presence. His travel bag, his dirty clothes. With a shock I realized that they had to be somewhere in the house. I heard ustad Yacoub talking to someone at the door. How could I make it upstairs unnoticed?

The policeman stepped into the room. I was relieved to see that it was the neighbourhood chief Jasin. Ustad Yacoub sent him a few kilos of sugar each week, to be sure of his favours. In these difficult times, the amount was even increased. He wouldn't like to lose this supplement to his meagre salary. The policeman greeted Asenath's mother and me politely. He was looking for Sasson, and wanted to know exactly when he left and where to. I said he was only here to pick up some books. And that he had been gone for a while, as he had an appointment in a teahouse outside of the Jewlakan.

The policeman looked around the room. Apparently, he was reassured by what he saw. He asked ustad Yacoub to let him know if Sasson came back, as he had to come to the station for questioning. I wanted to know what my brother had done. The policeman said he was sought for political activities against the government, and then walked out of the room towards a sound that I too had heard. Couldn't Sasson remain quiet in the cellar?

Jasin walked to the kitchen, apologizing to Asenath's mother for entering her domain. He felt on the door of the cellar. My heart skipped a beat. A loud cry rose up from behind the door. With a smile that was meant to mask my beating heart, I said that the cat must have slipped inside when I was taking out food for the hakham. I took the key from the hook and opened the door. The cat hurried past me with an offended meow and a puffy tail. What had frightened her so badly?

The policeman looked at me and then to Asenath's mother, and then around the kitchen, where there was nothing that revealed Sasson's presence. Could she offer Jasin something, the old woman asked politely. An arak, a couple of mezze? He could keep her husband company, now that he was here? Jasin smiled and accepted the offer. He must have thought that he could then wait for Sasson. Asenath's mother picked up a clean arak glass.

In the hallway I spied Sasson's muddy shoes. Had Jasin seen them? If so then he knew that Sasson was still in the house. And if he hadn't, then he would certainly see them when he left. I was left in doubt. If I hid them, it would work against us if he had indeed seen them. If I left them… Better to not move them, I then decided, as that could only draw attention to them. Jasin couldn't stay here forever. How could we get Sasson out of the house afterwards, and where would he be safe? Because Jasin would certainly return, and then with reinforcements to search the house.

There was a courtyard, but no back door. There was no other option than to get him out by way of the front door in the still of the night. Or over the flat roof. From the kitchen I stared at the rain that was covering the courtyard. And then, where? The yeshivah, the school and the synagogue were out of the question. The house of David's wealthy father too – that is where the Zionist connection lies, after all. I checked in my mind other acquaintances off and rejected them one after the other. Suddenly I remembered Zagros's uncle, where Salha and I had gone for help. Could I find the place again? In the dark?

The cat sat waiting at the cellar door. She would betray us, if Jasin saw her there! But Jasin did not need the cat. Even before I could chase her away, I heard him walking out of the visitor's room and heading towards the cellar door.

It had to be opened and he wanted a lamp. Ignoring the order was not an option. I said a quick prayer that Sasson had hidden himself well behind the bags, and with great fear followed Jasin down the basement stairs. The cat shot past us and disappeared in the dark. The light of the oil lamp shone past the supplies and over the bags at the far end. Jasin walked to the bags and looked them over. My heart nearly stopped, but there wasn't a living soul to be seen. If Sasson was here, he had really hidden himself well.

The policeman started to pull on the bags, until he had created a passage. Then I saw what he was looking for.

In the light of the lamp I could see the shine of a copper ring in the floor. We all stared at the hatch. The cat sniffed along its edges.

Where this was leading, he asked harshly. This was the first time I had ever seen the hatch, I said honestly. Perhaps to the street, to avoid having to carry the heavy bags through the house? He nodded, and concluded that my brother had gotten away. Without shoes or a coat in the cold wet night, I thought. But luckily, he had gotten away.

Now I understood what had happened. We had heard the hatch fall close behind him. That is what had frightened the cat so badly. Relieved I took a breath, but I decided to maintain the deception. Sounding offended, I said to Jasin that my brother was in a teahouse, and he would find him there.

The police officer angrily stomped up the stairs. Ustad Yacoub led him once again into the visitor's room. From behind the half-open door I could follow what was going on.

The policeman dropped down again onto the cushions. Their relationship had always been a good one, he said, reaching for the arak bottle. Ustad Yacoub nodded. He would double the number of kilos, he calmly said. Twice a month, Jasin demanded. He emptied his glass with one gulp. Then he would go and order his colleagues to search the teahouses for an escaped traitor. Before he headed back out into the rain, Jasin took a silent glance at Sasson's muddy shoes. That look said it all: on bare feet he wouldn't get far.

We were silent when the door finally closed. Once we were back in the room, I asked where the hatch led. Ustad Yacoub smiled. For all the other houses into the street. For us to the synagogue, he said. So Sasson was safe for the time being. I breathed a sigh of relief. The old man explained that the tunnel had once been dug to offer believers a way out from our house of prayer. And that there was yet another, that led outside of the Jewlakan.

March 3, 1948

When I was straightening up the books at the end of the day, Salha came in. I was happy to see her, as I had been waiting for news for days.

He had gotten married the day before yesterday, she said. With the daughter of one of Zagros' uncles. They were living with him, in a village along the way to Erbil. His new name is Yusuf.

Sasson was safe.

It would be better not to have any contact, she said. She would give me no further details. And I really must start using her new name, and call her Sazgar.In the same hurried manner, she asked me for a book, the reason for her visit. I grabbed an Arabic book of poems. She was again by the door. We would have no more contact for now, she said. And I should leave Mosul, it would not be safe here for me either.

THE JEWISH BRIDE

I thought guiltily about the risks Salha had taken only to reassure me. The police had not yet ceased their search for Sasson. A few days ago, they had searched the house, along with the yeshivah and the synagogue. Ustad Yacoub had been questioned for hours at the police station about the role of the synagogue in the departure of the Jews to Palestine. About his financers. And about all his followers; who is Zionist, who is planning to leave?

Sasson's arrival has put us all in danger.

Our situation is getting worse, because of the reports about the deaths of Iraqi volunteers in Palestine. Especially, since the commander of the Arabic forces was killed near Jerusalem, the anti-Semitic outbursts have greatly increased. In Baghdad, the protesters are even chanting "Death to the Jews!" The difference between Jews and Zionists seems only to exist in our minds and hearts. For Iraqis, it has not been a reality any more for quite some time.

Salha was right. I must leave Mosul. It is better for ustad Yacoub if I were to disappear out of his life, then there would be no more connection with my brother.

Nowroz is coming in a few weeks, and then it is customary to go to Penjwin. Then no one would find it odd that I left Mosul. But that would mean that I would be deserting the school and ustad Yacoub. Without saying goodbye to the children, or to the teachers. That I find very hard. Mosul has become my home.

What would I do in Penjwin? Sasson at least has a new life. Perhaps he is working as a farmer, perhaps he can establish a weaving mill. He has a new faith and a new family. I can't even go back to my old life. In Penjwin I would be looking after ima and abba. Taking over abba's school under the current circumstances, seems not very probable. With all the restrictions being put on Jews, the school will no doubt soon be closed. Maybe the same will be true for the school in Mosul. Yes, then I would have no more reason to stay.

I took the short route home from school. Despite the beautiful spring day, it was quiet in the Jewlakan, since most of the people prefer to stay safely indoors. More and more homes are empty, because the residents have chosen the illegal way out of the country, instead of waiting to see what will happen to us.

Once at home, I found ustad Yacoub asleep in the visitor's room. The old man looked fragile.

Asenath's mother said that he had been at the police station again all morning. That they are accusing him of Zionism. They want to be rid of us, she sighed. They are trying to bully us away.

Ustad Yacoub stood in the doorway. They will not succeed, he said. This was his city, his country. We were brought here 2,800 years ago against our will, and now they would not be rid of us so easily. The old man who only moments before had seemed so fragile, now strangely radiated a new sense of strength. A nap could not have caused this change.

We will go on until we no longer can, he said combatively. And I too, surely? Hesitantly, I said that I wanted to go to Penjwin for Nowroz.
I should not allow myself to be chased away. He needed me here. We should show our backbone. The school would remain open, as long as there are children to teach.
Had not he said before that we might have to close the school to ensure the safety of the children? What had they done to him at the police station, that has resulted in his newly-found combativeness? I pointed out that for the police, I was the sister of a traitor. That perhaps it would be safer if I left.
He looked sternly at me from under his bushy eyebrows. He could not forbid me to leave, but me destiny was here. He wanted me to take over part of the Talmud lessons in the yeshivah. Because there was no way he would even consider giving them what they wanted, to forget about our long history here and to leave.
I bowed my head. It was if my sentence had been pronounced. Going against him was not an option. But I am afraid. What is going to happen to us? Deep in my heart, I really want to go home, to the quiet and safety of Penjwin. But I owe ustad Yacoub too much. I have no other choice but to stay.

April 2, 1948

Iraq is sending troops to Palestine. The news has touched me deeply, because now it is no longer just about volunteers driven by their faith and convictions fighting against our Jewish countrymen. The government is now sending our soldiers to Palestine. To fight against Azam's comrades, against David and Asenath and their children. Iraqis fighting against Iraqi Jews – on the orders of the government. Where do our loyalties lie? With our daughter, son or brother in Palestine, or with our Iraqi military? How can you be forced to choose?

Since November, a civil war has been going on in Palestine. Arab volunteers are attacking Jewish fighters and villages. But the other way around too: we have just heard about a bloodbath in an Arab village outside of Jerusalem, by the hands of our Jewish fighters. They reportedly killed hundreds of Arabs – including women and children. The incident has put everything on edge. The expectation is that the after the departure of the British, the Zionists will occupy the part of Palestine assigned to them by the United Nations.

That is why the Palestinian Defence League is preparing for a large-scale intervention and Arab countries have sent troops to Jordan. Our government feels obliged to take part. Prime Minister Mohammed al-Sadr must be happy, that the attention has been drawn away from the demands for higher wages and more political freedoms.

Ten to twelve-thousand of our Iraqi boys will in the coming days be leaving for Jordan. Now it is official: Iraq is fighting against the establishment of Eretz Israel. The Jewlakan is buzzing with the news. What can we do to prove that we are on the Iraqi side?

This can only turn against us. Why would you only fight the Jews in Palestine, when you have thousands of these traitors in your own country... I am afraid, and my fear seems more and more justified. But we must not allow ourselves to be led by fear, as ustad Yacoub has always said – as Azam would have said. We must prepare ourselves. After the 15th of May we must be able to continue with our lives here, no matter what happens in Palestine after the British mandate has expired.

May 12, 1948

I did not see the door open. Before I had realized what was happening, five young men were already in our classroom. Two of them had clubs, one was even waving a knife. Mustafa, who was teaching today, was just as surprised as I was. He asked them politely how we could help them. I admired his calm reaction.

Some of the children stood up, a few started to cry. I told them to sit down and said that nothing was going to happen. I knew better. I broke out in a cold sweat. Out of the corner of my eye, I saw Shalom slip out. I had correctly judged his fearless nature when I gave him his role. And now I could only hope that he would do what we have told him to.

One of the men began to swear at us. We were filthy Jews, we were teaching the kids Zionism. And those filthy Zionists were stealing their land. The Germans should have killed all of us. One of the girls started to cry. Another begged for her mother. How I could calm them down, and not reveal my own shock and fear, I did not know.

Mustafa asked the men to consider that these were just children. I could see that he was having difficulty in staying calm. The man with the knife yelled that the Jews were stealing all their money. It was our fault that their children were hungry. We, filthy dirty Jews, should go back where we came from! Mustafa calmly pointed out that we were only teaching the children maths and languages here.

One of the men held up a Hebrew book. Zionism was what we were teaching! That was Hebrew and one of the oldest languages of Iraq, Mustafa said. He continued in his efforts to bring them back to a reality that had disappeared since they had entered. The man threw the book on the floor. It was dangerous propaganda! Micha ran forward and to save the book from the floor. These were our books!

He would cut him to bits, the man with the knife threatened. Micha jumped back, his eyes wide open in fear and holding the book in front of him as a means of protection. The knife fell at Micha's feet. The raised arm was being pulled back. I recognized a student from the yeshivah. Another was fighting with one of the men with the clubs. Luckily, Shalom had found them.

I chased the children to the door, but a man armed with a club jumped in front of me. I was a filthy woman, and I was not going anywhere! The man raised his club. As if he had been launched from a catapult, Micha stormed towards the man, still holding the book in front of him. The man should not touch his ustada! The hard book hit the man full in his belly. He doubled over. The club fell loudly to the floor.

Micha stood frozen. I grabbed his hand and ran out the door. Outside, the children were staring at the school as frightened lambs. I had to shout at them to get them to leave.

From every direction, men now came running. Yeshivah students, men from the synagogue, neighbours. Micha pulled himself loose to run back inside with the men. Luckily one of them stopped him. The child cried that he should help the teacher and tried once again to pull free. I caught him. He had done enough, I told him. The students would take over.

Together we stood gasping in front of the school. Suddenly, I felt exhausted and beaten. It had happened. What we had feared, not daring to believe, but what we had more or less prepared for, had happened. The hatred had now turned to the children.

Mustafa joined us, gasping for air and reporting that it was almost under control inside. Where was the police? The police were in no hurry to save Jews, I determined. For them, Jews no longer are part of the Iraqi community, now that the government has so clearly taken a stance against us.

Micha was hanging on Mustafa's arm, who praised him: he had saved the ustada! I was reminded of the book, the doubled-over attacker. Despite the situation, I burst out laughing. Hesitantly Mustafa and Micha laughed along.

Leisurely, three police officers came around the corner. In the school, we motioned. Five attackers. Inside, the students had tied the men together and formed a ring around them. One of them kept screaming. One of the officers asked what had happened. When Mustafa described it to him in a few words, the officers barely seemed interested. Clubs and knives, in a school, Mustafa repeated once again. No one was hurt, were they? he was told.

We looked at one another. I asked if it was normal, that grown men come and threaten children. Were the police not meant to protect Iraqi citizens from that kind of violence? With a dirty look towards me, one of the officers pushed the men outside. The other two lazily followed.

Mustafa said with dismay that they would simply release them again at the police station. The police are no longer here for our safety, one of the yeshivah students said. Jews have become outlaws in Iraq.

I couldn't get his words out of my head. They kept echoing, while we had an emergency meeting at the synagogue. The group that had gathered there, was not large; the community has already thinned out significantly.
I was the only woman there; these kinds of gatherings are typically male-oriented. It was already unheard of that I could be present, but being able to speak was not an option. The men were talking all at the same time. They want to be rid of us, but they do not want us to have our own state. Where do they expect us to go? one of the men asked. Another answered that we Jews stand for everything that is going wrong in Iraq, so we have to go. That they have never forgiven us for our support of the British.
People seem to think that the British have favoured us, yet another said. That we get the good jobs and they get nothing. The British go, we go too. They are accusing us of everything our brothers are doing in Palestine, I heard someone else say. They see all of us as Zionists. For them we are no longer Iraqis.
It only quieted down when ustad Yacoub started to speak. He pointed out that in a few days, the British would withdraw from Palestine. That we all knew that then the Zionists would declare their own state. The repercussions of that were for us. That what we

experienced today, was only a taste of what was to come. An agreeing rumble arose.

He said that God has decided to once again test the Jewish people. When the time is right, he will show us the way to safety, as he also led us out of Egypt. A silence fell.

There could have been deaths today, said one of the believers. Even our children are no longer safe. Another man added that the Iraqis are capable of anything. Didn't we remember how the military here in Kurdistan had murdered thousands of Christians? That was only fifteen years ago.

That was a revolt; the Christians wanted autonomy, answered ustad Yacoub calmly. We only want our rights as civilians in Iraq. God is with us in the battle, as he was with the Jews in Egypt.

One of the men felt that the Iraqis want to be rid of us. That there is no one left anymore to protect us from criminals and thugs. He was supported by the others. Bribing the police was no longer of any use. They took our gifts, but no longer helped us. And without protection we could not survive.

Ustad Yacoub's voice brought immediate silence. He said that we had two choices: leave everything behind and leave with our tails between our legs, or hold out, defend ourselves as best as we can, and stay. Our people have had to make these kinds of decisions before, he said. If we stay, that is because Iraq is our country. We are Iraqis, for many centuries now. We have seen the Assyrians disappear, just like the Romans, the Mongols, and the Turks. We have seen Islam come. And nothing has been able to chase us out, he said.

The men listened in silence. The choice was theirs, he said. They could leave everything behind and begin a penniless life in an unknown land. Or stay, and defend what we have built up here. He looked at the men, one at a time and said that his choice was made. That God would help us get through this challenge. That he needed guards for the Torah rolls, for the synagogue. That the yeshivah students could look after themselves, and that the school would be moved to a home.

No one said anything. Ustad Yacoub frowned and looked at the men. If we had the money, he would hire guards, he said. But due to the actions of the government, our source of funds had dried up. So, he was looking for volunteers.

The father of David and Salha rose. He would pay the guards for the synagogue, he said. If we had a few armed Kurdish men on watch, that would work even better.

I saw the effect of his announcement. The wealthy merchant who had paid for Zionism, is staying. His son is in Palestine, his daughter has been married off to a Muslim. He is not choosing for Palestine. He is staying. I admired him, and not only because he had managed to tip the scales in ustad Yacoub's favour.

This man was not about to have himself forced into making a split decision. He knew what he wanted. If only I could do that, if only I was so determined.

The law expert had also gotten up. He had a room in his house that was big enough for the school, where we could move tomorrow. The butcher would send his sons along to make sure that no one would be able to cause any trouble there. Ustad Yacoub smiled satisfied. Then it was decided.

No one asked me anything. Everyone assumed that I will continue at the new school. That I will stay. But God, I am so afraid. All the challenges that ustad Yacoub was talking about - I know them like I know the Torah and the Talmud. But this is for real. Perhaps I am not so brave. Or perhaps our men are fools, allowing themselves to be convinced to do something, that in reality does not serve their best interests. Perhaps they can do little else than follow their rabbi.

Today in the synagogue I smelled fear. The scent does not suit me at all. There are only a few of us. Our adversaries have the weight of the upper hand. We have no weapons, they do. This is an impossible battle. What will we do at night when the Jewlakan is under attack, and we are sitting in our houses – trapped? This time there will be no British soldiers to fight off the attackers.

Ustad Yacoub's drive frightens me. He has decided to die for our cause, if he must. He is an old man. How much time does he have left in his life? But the children, young people, their parents – they still have a lifetime before them. Can he put them in danger this way? What would Azam think of it? I wished that Sasson was here to talk to. If only I had gone to Penjwin for Nowroz. There the Jews live much closer together with their neighbours; there the anti-Semitic hate will be less. Mosul suddenly feels like a prison.

May 15, 1948
The Jewish state is a fact. Almost immediately after the declaration of it, Iraqi troops crossed the border between Jordan and Palestine. Everyone sat glued to the radio to hear the latest news, including us in the Jewlakan. The Arab troops already stand eye to eye with the Zionist fighters. For us this news can only be bad. Whoever loses, we will be affected.
The new state has immediately been recognized by the United States and the Soviet Union. The Arab countries are furious. Hear, the secretary-general of the Arab League predicting a "pan-Arab jihad" against Israel, and "a destructive war comparable to the blood baths of the Mongols and the crusaders."
In Iraq, the government tries desperately to prevent riots. The radio reports that a state of emergency has been announced. Military courts have been established, political parties are forbidden from meeting, and trade unions have been dismantled. Apparently, many arrests have been made, especially amongst communists.

It is eerily quiet in the streets. Everyone stays home. We are all prepared for the worst. I passionately hope that we are mistaken, and that the violence never comes.

8 OUT OF SIGHT

"Turn the TV on! Now!"
Soran's tone leaves little room for discussion. Zara runs down the stairs to the living room and grabs the remote. She zaps to the news station of one of the major parties. The camera shows a blackened building. Then a man comes into view who accuses the government of arson.
Zara recognizes the building. "Soran, have they burned the Nalia television station? They only started broadcasting a few days ago!"
The new station is the first independent one in Kurdistan, and was established and funded by a successful businessman in Sulaymaniya. Soran tells her what he knows: the television station was attacked during the night by armed men dressed in black who set the building alight. It is thought to be an act of retribution for being the only one to broadcast images of the attack on the KDP-headquarters in Sulaymaniya, now three days ago.

Could the government be behind it? Zara cannot believe it. Arresting students because they are demonstrating is one thing. But torching a television station is totally something else.

"The owner said that he had received numerous threats by phone from high-ranking political figures," Soran says. The television shows a pair of black boots, and trails of blood. The news channel reports that one or more of the attackers must have been wounded.

Zara drops down onto the couch. If this can happen to an established organization, a television station no less, what awaits her and Soran when they discover that they tried to save the child?

The child in the red sweater has become the symbol of the demonstrations. The past days, his photo has gone viral. And the protests are continuing; this morning she received yet another text message to join in the protests.

"Soran, they will know where to find us," she says. Her voice quivers.

He laughs. "Do not worry yourself about that, goshawistakam. They do not know who we are."

"But we helped the boy! You were with him in the hospital! Didn't you have to give a name there?"

He laughs once again. "I am not crazy, dearest. I gave the name of an acquaintance. They will not find us."

"And the mother? You spoke with the mother! Then you surely must have used your own name."

"Zara, the woman has other things on her mind than to remember that I phoned her. Do not worry."

Zara wishes that she could think about it as reasonably as he seems to be able to. But the feeling of impending doom is not easily pushed aside.

At breakfast, her father had even talked about his concern. He said that the police had been put on a state of alert in Penjwin, in case the unrest would blow over from Sulaymaniya. Extra controls have been put in at the Erbil checkpoint, to prevent protestors from slipping in and causing problems in the capital.

Demonstrating is a constitutional right. Our land has changed into a police state, Zara thinks.

The telephone buzzes again.

Zara reads Banu's name on the lightened screen, and sighs. She is not in the mood for cheerful chatter. It will no doubt be about Banu's upcoming wedding. About the dress, or the hairdresser, or choosing the music for the evening of the wedding.

For a moment the buzzing stops, then starts once again. Banu really wants to speak to her. It must be urgent.

"I will be over shortly to pick you up, so we can go to Sulaymaniya," she says as soon as Zara answers.

Sulaymaniya? No way I will consider going there.

"Banu, sorry janakam, but I am not going. What are you going to do?"

"Order the gifts for the guests. But you must come. You have to help me choose."

"I can't. Because of the demonstrations."

"What has that got to do with you? You have to come!"

"Soran and I were there, when they attacked the KDP headquarters."

"Yes, you told me that. So what?"

"They are looking for me. I have heard that they are arresting students who were there."

"Yes, those who were throwing stones and fighting with the police. You didn't do that, did you?"

Zara stares at the screen, where the item about the fire is being repeated.

"Zara, why would they be looking for you? What is this for nonsense?"

Perhaps Banu is right. Perhaps they are only arresting the troublemakers. Perhaps Soran is right and she shouldn't worry. In any case, it is a risk she is not willing to take.

"I am really not going with you, Banu. It doesn't feel right. Maybe in a few days."

"But we aren't going anywhere near to where the demonstrations are."

"Sorry. No."

Zara returns to Rahila's diary, that she had left lying on the bed when Soran called. It distracts her from the threat and her fear, which at the same time give her a strange feeling of connection with Rahila. She is shocked by the hatred for the Jews, that seems to be growing with each page she turns. Was it that bad all over Iraq? And what role did the deployment of Iraqi troops to Palestine play?

Ten to twelve-thousand of our Iraqi boys will in the coming days be leaving for Jordan. Now it is official: Iraq is fighting against the establishment of Eretz Israel. The Jewlakan is buzzing with the news. What can we do to prove that we are on the Iraqi side? This can only turn against us. Why would

you only fight the Jews in Palestine, when you have thousands of these traitors in your own country...
Zara knows from her studies that Iraqi soldiers were fighting in Palestine at the time of the establishment of the state of Israel, but that somewhat abstract knowledge has taken on a new light and meaning through Rahila's journal. Why did the Iraqi government send troops in the first place? It is not as if Palestine is right next door. Why would you get mixed up in a war that is not your own?
She puts the book away, goes down the stairs, and crawls behind the computer. Soon, her notes fill the paper. The Arab League decided on war. Egypt, Jordan, Syria, Lebanon, Saudi Arabia and Iraq all sent troops. Initially Iraq sent three thousand men; these forces were increased to 10,000 and later even to 18,000 men. Perhaps that was not many, compared to the 40,000 that Egypt supplied, but it was the first time that Iraq had ever sent troops abroad before. But why? Sending forces costs money, and would have been an expensive operation for a state that was buckling under the pressure of the economic depression, protests and riots. What was the effect of the establishment of the state of Israel for Iraq - considering that Iraq did not even share a border with the new state?
Zara keeps changing her search options, but a satisfactory answer cannot be found. Should she phone one of her professors? Perhaps she can focus her dissertation on this. She finds it odd, that Rahila has not asked the same question: why send troops to Palestine? The masses wanted it, and the mood was anti-Jew; for Rahila that must have seemed like sufficient cause. Zara has read how nationalists

organized hunger strikes, strikes and protests, to force the Iraqi government to send troops. All well and good, but why had the cabinet allowed itself to be forced into that situation? What good could come from it?

She grabs the phone. Her professor answers straight away. "That's so good of you, Zara, that you are continuing your studies, while the university is closed," he says.

The university is closed? Zara is right back in the present.

"Have many students been arrested?" she asks nervously.

"I have only heard that a few trouble makers were picked up, why do you ask?"

"I was there," she said, as if that explained everything.

"I am assuming that you were not throwing stones."

"There were no further arrests?"

"Not that I know of, Zara. But now that the university is closed, I don't hear everything."

Zara senses that for him the topic is a finished one and remains silent.

"Back to your question. The Arab countries used the intervention in Palestine in 1948 to bring order to the affairs in their own countries. Because there was ever-increasing resistance to the regimes."

Zara listens intently. On the one hand, the Arab nationalism was being used to forge a unity against a common enemy – the Jews. On the other hand, in all Arab countries a state of emergency was announced, to silence the opposition.

Rahila could not have thought of that, Zara knows. She was right in the middle of it. She was the victim of a policy that demonized an entire group of the population. A policy that was mainly about power. Politicians used the chastising of one group against another, to strengthen their own position.

"It is an interesting subject, Zara. You can make a connection with what happened later on in Yugoslavia, perhaps including Rwanda as well. Once the university is back open, we should discuss the best way to approach this. In the meantime, you could conduct some further research."

Silently she writes down the book titles the professor mentions.

"I think that you might have to go to Erbil," he then says, "now that the university is closed."

She stares at the fading light of her cell phone's screen, while she contemplates the next step. Erbil is far from the unrest. It is in the other part of Kurdistan, which is not under control of the PUK, like Sulaymaniya. And because it is KDP territory, it is safe, and no one will be searching for her.

But who does she know there? Who can she stay with? Then she remembers: her mother has a former school friend there. Aunt Awat will be glad to have her.

"Look," the resident of the house points out. In the corner of the dark room, Zara can just make out the shape of a low door. The man then motions behind the cupboard on the other side of the room. "Here is another one just like it. And at the neighbour's place it is the same."

"These doors connected all the houses of the Jewlakan."

"Exactly. That way people could escape unseen, if the need presented itself."

Zara stares at the door, which is not even a metre high and no more than a half metre wide. A way out, created by people who no longer felt safe in their own country. The doors have no function anymore, since the houses in the Jewish neighbourhood of Erbil have been taken over by Muslims and Turkmen.

The door no longer has a handle. Zara is reminded of the hatch in the basement of ustad Yacoub's basement, and the tunnel to the synagogue. Could young men like Sasson have used this, to escape from the police or other pursuers? Or were the doors only used by the women, to visit one another? Or by lovers?

"Zara?" Yunes yanks her out of her contemplations. Aunt Awat has sent her son along, because she feels that Zara should not be wandering around the Jewlakan on her own. Yet she advised her to visit the neighbourhood, because of her occupation with the Iraqi history. But the 16-year-old Yunes clearly does not feel comfortable in these surroundings.

They are standing in the primitive living room, where time seems to have stood still. This is most likely how it also was all those many years ago: bare floors, the mattresses and blankets for the night stored away in the cupboard, women in pyjamas and long Kurdish dresses lounging around on the thin mattresses and cushions that line the wall.

The Jewlakan is located around the corner from Erbil's busy bazaar. Many houses are in a poor state of repair. Some have partially collapsed. Many roofs are covered with blue plastic as protection against the rain. The narrow streets have an open sewer in the middle, from which the stone

covers have largely disappeared. Zara nearly stepped into one when she was busy admiring the old facades.
It is a neighbourhood in decline. Yet it still manages to radiate the pride of the Jewlakan from times gone by, when the best houses of the city could be found here. Houses with a second level, with beautifully decorated doors and window frames. You have to look closely, but then the past manages to show itself, despite the wear and tear of time. The man takes them up to the flat roof, by way of uneven steps where through the holes in the cement the original stones can still be seen. He points out over the neighbourhood before them. There, Muslims are living, and there, Turkmen. And there, that house, an old woman lived with her son, a Ben-Jew.
Zara follows his finger, while she tries to understand the title. "A what?"
"She was the daughter of Jews. But she became Muslim. She lived there her entire life."
An original resident of the Jewlakan? A Jewish woman who had seen first-hand how everyone left here? Someone just like Rahila! Or more like Salha, who also had converted to the Islam. How very much she would like to talk to her!
"She passed away last year," the man said, putting a damper on her excitement. "But her son still lives in the neighbourhood."
"Can I find him?"
"Of course, everyone knows him. Karwan, the son of Hanna. He has an electronics shop."

Zara stares out over the neighbourhood, and tries to imagine what it must have been like to live here. Do the current inhabitants even realize what past lies hidden?
"Most of the houses are still in owned by the original occupants, who now live in Israel or America," the man says. "We pay our rent to the government, which then deposits it in a special fund."
"And what happens to it then?"
The man shrugs his shoulders. "Maybe it is sent to Israel? Here, we see little effect. No maintenance work has been done in years. Parts of the neighbourhood have already been torn down, and I have heard of plans to build a shopping centre on that corner over there."
"Can they do that, if the owners refuse?"
"The problem is, that not all of the addresses of the owners are known."
"And the owner of your house?"
"Yes, him I know. He was here."
Another link with the past, Zara thinks.
The man looks closely at her, to make sure that she is hanging on his every word.
"It was just after the liberation..."
"In 2003?"
"Yes, that must have been it. An American came to the neighbourhood. He had a map, which he used while walking around and eventually he turned out to be looking for our house."
"A map?"
"Yes, he had a map of the neighbourhood, with all of the streets and houses on it. And on our house stood a cross."

"Wow," Yunes says, having up till now listened in silence. "And inside he looked further, with another map. The floor had to be opened."
"They had buried something, before they left," Zara says, nodding excitedly.
She knows what is coming, and this story is even more beautiful than her own. This is the story of a treasure hunter. She imagines it: the departing Jews burying their property and then drawing a map to record the place. Many years later, the last member from that generation dies, and a son or a grandson finds the map. And he then travels to Iraq, to dig up the treasure.
Her parents only had a key, of which they did not know what it was for. No map, no clues. How many similar treasures could there still be buried, waiting to be discovered?
"Did you see what he dug up?"
The man looks away and shakes his head. Zara is certain of the fact that he was there, when the earth revealed its treasures. He would have received his share, but does not want to talk about that. Could that be, because the Jews are still a controversial subject?
"What a story," Yunes sighs.
"And are you still in contact with the man?"
Once again, the almost guilty denial that tells Zara that he is not willing to reveal the truth.
"You must not speak of this to anyone," the man urges. "I work for the municipality, and I do not want them to find out about this."

When she silently nods, he adds: "Don't misunderstand me; I have nothing against the Jews. The man that came here was very nice. But the people gossip."
"How long have you lived here?"
"My parents took over the house from the Jews in 1951. I was born here."
Here, no one had intentionally destroyed the neighbourhood, as Saddam had done in Penjwin, Zara thinks. The damage that has been done here is the result of misunderstanding and a lack of interest, and is therefore more limited.
The man once again motions towards the city at their feet, and talks about how he has seen it change. Old houses and neighbourhoods that were levelled, and made way for modern homes and shops.
Wouldn't he perhaps prefer a more modern house, Zara wonders, instead of one with a leaky roof and a broken sewer?
He nods. "But new homes are expensive, and moving also costs money. I cannot afford that. I hope that the day will come when the government will help me."
He is waiting for the government's decision to destroy this last part of the old Erbil for the construction of yet another shopping mall, and to buy him out, Zara understands.
"Do your neighbours think the same way?"
He nods. "The environment is no longer healthy. In the summer we have many pests, even poisonous scorpions. We have problems with the water. It really stinks here when it is hot."

THE JEWISH BRIDE

Zara looks again. If she tries not to look at the present through the eyes of the past, then all she sees are ruins. Broken roofs, walls, open sewers. The proud Jewish neighbourhood has been transformed into an impoverished one, that the government no longer cares for.
Sombrely she follows Yunes down the uneven steps.
The Jews were not only pestered out of Iraq, their very existence is threatened with being wiped out once and for all, she thinks. Before long, no one will remember what role they played here.

The driver steers the car through the steep streets of Al Qosh. On this sunny winter's day, the centuries-old mountain village looks beautiful. Reconstructed homes stand next to ruins. In passing, Zara curiously peeks into the courtyards. Unheard of, those open gates; for Muslims, this private life is always carefully hidden away. Often, curtains are even hung behind the gates to shield all views.
It is cleaning time; Zara sees women scrubbing and sweeping, and cleaning the courtyard and the street with the garden hose. Through the ditch in the middle of the street the water streams to the lower parts of the town, as it must have done for centuries.
Yet another place, where time has stood still. According to Aunt Awat, that is because Al Qosh has always had many communists, for which reason Saddam Hussein did everything he could to punish the town. A lack of jobs and money, prison sentences – where people can just manage to survive, they are unable to tear down houses and build new ones.

Only in recent years, with the money also the cement blocks entered, but most of the homes are still built from sandstone and mud. A part is inhabited, and another has partially collapsed and become overgrown with weeds. Only the churches have been well maintained.

Zara wonders how much has changed here, since Rahila came to visit the grave of Nahum. That was the main reason why she wanted to come along, when her aunt said that she had to go to Al Qosh for her work to catalogue the influx of Christian refugees from Mosul. Zara would never have made the three-hour journey from Erbil on her own.

They found the refugees in the Monastery of Our Lady, located just outside of town. Ten families from Mosul had found refuge in two shared rooms.

Zara and her aunt stepped into a courtyard filled with children playing and men talking. Inside, the women and old men sat between piles of mattresses and around a kerosene heater. Chairs were emptied, and Zara and her aunt had to accept the sweet tea offered them. Especially amongst the poor, hospitality is an obligation, Zara realized. When Aunt Awat asked about the situation in Mosul, Zara listened silently to the stories about threats, kidnappings and murder. She was told that when under threat, the Christians from Mosul usually fled to Al Qosh and the surrounding villages on the Nineveh plains. They would find a safe haven in the monasteries or with families, and when the calm returned, went back home. Although the Christian city is not part of the Kurdish region, it is safe because the area is under Kurdish control and protection.

THE JEWISH BRIDE

The tension in Mosul has worsened since the occupation of a church in Baghdad, where recently nearly sixty followers were killed. Radical Muslims maintain a regime of terror, which especially targets Christians in Mosul. They are being abducted and if no ransom is paid, murdered. Or they are shot on the streets.

Jamal, a tall man sitting uncomfortably on a low stool, was one of their victims.

"Armed men came for me in my shop," Jamal started his story.

Now the men had come in to drink tea too, and the room had become crowded and hot. All attention focused on Jamal. Were they hearing his story for the very first time, Zara wondered. Had they become so numbed by the violence, that they no longer even asked about each other's experiences?

"They blindfolded me, and took me away. We had to pay forty thousand dollars, otherwise they would kill me. We managed to raise twenty thousand dollars. And I talked and talked, and finally they let me go."

"Who were they, the kidnappers?" asked Zara's aunt.

"I do not know. Radical Sunni's are not our only enemy. We also have gangs from the rest of the country, that are taking advantage of the poor security situation. For these criminals, abductions are a source of income."

"How were you treated?"

"They threatened me the entire time. Showed me videos of men whose throats were being slit. Horrible images."

Quiet blanketed the room; everyone was listening breathlessly to the story.

"That was what would happen to me, they said."
Jamal looked as if he was reliving it all over again, pulling his long legs up closer, as if he was cold in the hot room.
He did not want to experience this ever again, he said. He had fled as soon as he was released. "Even the neighbours said that it would be better if I left."
He had found shelter in Al Qosh. And it was here, that he wanted to get started again as a housepainter, and open a paint shop.
"Happily, the church is helping me now," he said, with a grateful smile towards the priest who stood in the doorway listening.
Aunt Awat smiled at him encouragingly, and made a notation of his information. She asked who else had decided not to go back.
"We are waiting for a visa for Germany," a young woman said, who was holding a baby on her lap. Like her, most of those present wanted to remain in Al Qosh only until they could travel on to Europe or America. Zara's aunt made notes and promised to help.
"And what are you going to do for the people who do want to return to Mosul?" asked a heavy-set man, who introduced himself as Adib.
"Why would you want to go back?" A young man with spiky hair grabbed demonstratively at the cross around his neck. "Most of the churches are closed, and we can no longer practice our faith!"
Adib raised a calming hand. "You are right, habibi. But I do not have the money to sit and wait. And there is no work for me in Al Qosh."

"My son now travels every day by bus to the university in Mosul," a man with a beard said. "That is a long ride, and a risky one. We are going back for him."
His son, who was sitting next to him, added: "The situation is better on the campus. In town, one does not know when and where bombs will go off, the mortars will rain down or when the kidnappers will find you."
Aunt Awat bowed her head over her notebook. "We offer help to displaced persons. I must find out if I can do anything for you." She sounded apologetic.
"Then you are better off staying here," the boy with the spiky hair concluded.
"I want to go home. I had to leave everything behind," Adib kept his stance.
A fat matron took the floor. "Just like you, we had to leave like thieves in the night. But this time we are not going back. It's the third time that we have been forced to flee."
Other women voiced their support. Adib stood up and silently walked out.
When Aunt Awat and Zara joined the priest in his office, he began to talk about those who wanted to return to Mosul. His desk was covered with papers. "We are unable to handle the stream of the displaced, Awat Khan. You know that every year, the number of residents here more than doubles as a result of the recurring violence in Mosul. You have to help the people who want to return too. For us, that is just as important as the help for those who choose to stay."
"My organization helps displaced persons. They wouldn't be if they returned," Zara's aunt said sternly.

The priest sighed, and straightened his back. "You know how many people we have lost. From the one-and-a-half million Christians we had in Iraq in 2003, a third is gone. Every month, at least twenty to thirty families are going abroad. In Mosul, only ten thousand of us are left, from the original 180,000. Our community is growing ever smaller. We are no longer able to make a fist. We have become vulnerable. Let us then help those who have enough courage to stay."

Aunt Awat kept up her sternly look. "The church is not particularly poor. It is your duty to help them."

"If they leave, they no longer are our responsibility. And in Mosul, the church has gone underground after the murder of our bishop. They can no longer count on it," the priest protested.

"Father Antoine, it is your problem how you help them. It is not our responsibility. We have limited options and clear rules." Aunt Awat smiled to soften her words. "On the other hand, we would like to help you with the care for this group of displaced persons. I have registered seven families, is that all of them?"

They bend over the list, reading it together.

Zara left them to it and walked into the church.

A large statue of Maria dominated the entrance. Icons of the saints looked down at her from the walls. Large flowers decorated the altar. Flowers in February? Zara looked more closely. They were plastic.

She inhaled the odour of the wax used to polish the pews and of the incense burned during the mass. She felt like a stranger there; Penjwin had no church and she had never visited the one in Sulaymaniya.

The stories of the refugees from Mosul had reminded her of the persecution of the Jews in Rahila's journal. Are the Christians the new Jews of Iraq, she wondered. Will they too all be gone one day, without even as much as a collective memory of who they were?

On the hard church pew, she categorized the differences. Unlike back in the forties, the violence in the church in Baghdad had caused an outcry. Even in Kurdistan, people had protested, with the Kurdish prime minister supporting them. The Iraqi government had sent the military to guard the churches.

She remembered the words of the spokesman for the Kurdish government: "It is like genocide. This is about Iraqis, our people; we do not want to lose them. The perpetrators are the enemy of the Iraqi people." She had not been able to find similar statements about the fate of the Jews in the forties. And certainly not from any politician, or the government. They had continually called the Jews traitors and Zionists.

"Iraq is a tree with its roots in Christianity. If you chop away the roots, the tree will die" – a statement she found too beautiful to forget. Why had no one said something like that about the Jews, after a history of nearly 3,000 years in Iraq? Then again, it was not that exceptional. According to the books recommended by her professor, politicians in former Yugoslavia had accused the groups that they wanted to be rid of, of being dogs and apes. By dehumanizing them, they could turn their own people against them. The same thing happened in Rwanda, between Hutu's and Tutsi's. Racism, ethnocentrism, religious fanaticism – all were used at one time or another to turn groups against one another, and always for some political advantage.

She was jerked out from her thoughts by Jamal, the kidnapped man, who had come to sit next to her on the pew. When he saw that he had startled her, he apologized. Without being asked, Jamal started to tell her about plans for a Christian province, here on the Nineveh plains. The autonomous region would offer Christians protection, he said. "There is much support for this in Al Qosh."

Zara's interest was stirred. "But not so much elsewhere, I would think. Radical Muslims would certainly not support it, and I doubt if the Kurdish government would be very enthusiastic either."

"Yes, you are right; the Kurds demand the plains for their own. But we think that if we have our own region, people will be able to return from abroad."

It is a beautiful dream, she thought cynically, but without political support doomed to fail. And the politicians do not see the advantages in it. They only see the danger of a further division in Iraq, and a limitation of their power. And have the dreamers forgotten about the bloodbath in the thirties, when the Iraqi army killed three thousand Christians because they had demanded more rights? It had even been the Kurds that had carried it out, following orders from the government in Baghdad.

"We think that in about five years, it can be a reality," Jamal maintained.

Zara did not want to speak out against him, and just nodded in silence. If you knew, how many problems the struggle for an own state had generated for the Jews, how could you even think that Christians in Iraq will get it offered on a platter?

"God gave us this land," Jamal continued. "We see it as ours, just like the Jews saw Israel as their country. Iraq will become the richest country in the world, and people must return to become a part of that."

Stunned she stared at him. "But how can you say that, if you know what happened to the Iraqi Jews?"

"They have their own land. Why then not we?"

"Don't you know how much misery there was, when the state of Israel was declared? How the Jews here were suddenly no longer considered to be Iraqi, but seen as Zionists and traitors?"

Jamal nodded. "Yes, but now they manage well in their own state, don't they?"

Zara swallowed impatiently. How could she explain to this man what she meant? That the process claimed so many victims, that you would have to ask yourself if you really wanted it. That the establishment of a Christian state, or even a province, could be like Pandora's Box being opened. He would not be able to understand it, she decided. Or even want to understand it.

Silently she walked out of the church with Jamal, back to the sunny and busy courtyard. Her eyes were pulled towards the mountains, where she could just make out the outline of a monastery. Jamal saw her staring. It was the monastery of the hermits, he said. It used to be quite a climb, but now there was a road you could get up there in a matter of minutes.

Zara remembered Rahila's story about the hours-long trek to the mountains with the Torah rolls, and the view of the Nineveh plains she described. That must be there; the place had changed from Jewish to Christian.

"It is beautiful there," Jamal interrupted her thoughts, "and so quiet, so peaceful. But I do miss Mosul. That is such a special city, with so much history…"

Zara swallowed her irritation about their earlier conversation. Of course, he wanted a place where he and his could all feel safe, she told herself. How long had the Kurds not fought for it!

"Mosul," she said slowly, tasting the name. The city where Rahila lived. "It's a pity that I cannot go there because it is so unsafe. But do you know anything about the former Jewish quarters there?"

Jamal looked at her surprised.

"That is where I lived," he said, laughing. "My parents took our house over from the Jews. It still has the Lion of Judea above the door."

Zara was delighted about the coincidence. "How is the neighbourhood holding up?"

What Jamal described sounded much like the Jewlakan in Erbil, but worse. Dilapidated, much garbage and many health problems.

"Do you know if the synagogue and the Jewish school still exist?"

Jamal looked at her for a few moments. "Are you Jewish?"

Laughing, Zara shook her head. "I am studying political science, and am investigating the departure of the Jews from Iraq in the fifties."

From visiting American soldiers, whom he had worked for as a translator, he had heard that remains of synagogues and schools had been found. But he himself only knew, where one former Jewish school must have been located. "People are living there now, even though it no longer has a roof," he said, almost apologetically.

Zara was gripped by the idea that she might be able to find Rahila's school in Mosul. That she could find her shadow. She sighed. Mosul was a no-go. No one would go with her; the checkpoints would never let her pass without an armed escort.

"Synagogues? Plural?" she asked.

Jamal nodded. "Have you seen the one here in Al Qosh yet?"

Rahila's story. So close by.

And here they are now, standing in front of a shabby metal gate with an old padlock. Over the walls, the ruins can be seen of a fairly good-sized building.

"What a mess," Aunt Awat says. "Not much left of it, eh?"

Jamal walks up with an old man, whose hand trembles when he puts the key in the lock. He got it from the rabbi, when he left in 1951, he tells them, as he walks ahead into the large courtyard.

"We were good friends, and I still miss him every day. When all the Jews had gone, he was the last to leave."

Zara barely hears the old man. She is extremely conscious of Rahila's shadow. There, between the arches of the outer wall, before the stairs to what must have been the women's bathroom – and also, on the courtyard that was filled with tents when Rahila was here.
As if in a dream, she slowly follows the others. She hears the children playing. A child's game can be heard throughout the courtyard: '*Ana mana lupana, wadzi amad charzana*'. She smells the bread that is being baked, and hears the clatter of pots and pans. Here is where Rahila met Asenath, a meeting that would forever change her life. Here she took her very first steps towards a new life, in search of knowledge.
The old man has now opened the wooden door of the prayer house. Carefully, she walks inside and down the uneven stairs. The roof is largely missing. Only in the middle, above the tomb's monument, it is fairly intact. The floor is made of uneven stones. Everywhere you look, stones and parts of the walls are lying about.
On the pillars by the entrance, lamps are hanging from which the glass is broken. In a rickety cupboard in the corner are a few oil lanterns, in another she sees candles and pieces of cloth.
"That sign there," the man points to a stone sign that has recently been cemented into a section where the roof is missing, "was stolen by criminals. I found it again though, and hung it back up."
She nods, her eyes fixed on the strange letters. So, this is Hebrew.

"I could not read it. Then, a few years ago, an American came here who could." The old man laughed out loud. "And he told me that I had hung it upside down!"

His laughter is contagious. Zara walks to the green ribbons that have been tied to the iron work around Nahum's grave. She looks at the old man inquisitively.

"You can make a wish," he says laconically.

She pushes the textile through the iron bars.

"We often get visitors," the old man says, "from all over the world. Sometimes the people will light a candle and pray."

The green piece of cloth is too small to make a good and strong knot.

I want to know what it is that is pulling me, what is connecting me to Rahila. It almost feels as if she has said it out loud. Startled, she looks over her shoulder towards her aunt. She is talking to Jamal.

"Now you must walk around the grave," the old man tells her.

Obediently, she moves forward.

"Seven times."

While she slowly walks around the grave that is covered with a green sheet, her eyes wander towards the dark corner in the back. She hears the reciting of prayers, the faint sounds of children's voices outside, she once again smells the fresh bread. Does she see movement in the corner? Is she seeing Rahila's father, sitting in the lotus position reading a book?

She stops. As if she has been nailed to the floor, she looks at the scene. Two young women in long Kurdish dresses slip out from the shadows. They kiss his hand, as they settle on the floor next to him. He listens to them, and answers. Then he lightly touches their heads – is he blessing them?

Zara realizes that her aunt is talking to her. And that she has goose bumps.

Is she imagining this? It is far too real for that; the images are engraved in her memory. She knows what she has seen. Here, Rahila's plan was born to go to Mosul, to study the Talmud, to become a teacher. Here is where one of the most important moments in her life took place.

"Zara, what is wrong with you?"

She realizes that her aunt has repeated the question, and rubs her arms.

"Is it cold here?" she asks.

Her aunt pushes her towards the direction of the door. Zara looks back; the corner is empty. Outside, the sun is casting shadows onto the courtyard. The afternoon is ending, they have to go back. The old man pulls the heavy wooden door closed behind him and turns the key.

As if she has just awoken, Zara's eyes now see the decay. The collapsed walls, the stones that are strewn over the courtyard. The grass and plants creeping over everything, covering it like a blanket.

"There was a Jewish delegation of American engineers, who came here with plans to renovate the synagogue," she hears the old man say.

"What has happened?" Aunt Awat asks.

"Nothing," he says sombrely. "If we have another winter with much rain, I am afraid that the roof will collapse onto the grave."

In the car on the way back, Zara gives her thoughts a free reign. What was it that she has seen? Is she becoming superstitious? Is her mother right, and has she become obsessed by the Jewish history?

But this is also the history of Iraq, it is part of the heritage of her country, she thinks, consoling herself. That is crumbling, and disappearing. The stones, but also the knowledge.

'Ana mana lupana, wadzi amad charzana' – how long ago is it that she has learned that children's rhyme, and when was the last time she has heard it? Where had it suddenly come from, today? She has not seen any children outside of the synagogue today. Of that she is certain.

Zara's aunt turns up the radio to listen to the news.

"Riots in Sulaymaniya have led to clashes between protestors and police. A number of people have been injured. At least five thousand people took part in today's protests. The Gorran opposition party has called for the dissolution of the parliament, and announces a vote of no confidence against the government. The unrest in Sulaymaniya has been going on for more than a week now."

"It is a good thing that you are here, Zara," her aunt says over the voice on the radio.

"To prevent the unrest from blowing over, the authorities have closed the University of Erbil until further notice," the news reader continues. "The safety police have arrested at least ten people at the Erbil checkpoint, who are believed to have had plans to bring the unrest to the capital."

"I wouldn't even have been able to get in anymore," Zara says shocked. "They would have arrested me too."

Her aunt looks over her shoulder at her, and turns down the volume.
"Why do you think so?"
"I was there, when things got out of hand at the KDP-headquarters."
Aunt Awat laughs. "And that is why they would arrest you? You better look out then, we will soon be at the Mosul checkpoint, the strictest of Erbil."
Her aunt thinks that she is exaggerating. But she did not experience what can happen to you in a police state. That during a protest you can be shot at, and that the police may arrest you for standing up for what you believe in.
The past week, nearly all the students from the group she had joined at the demonstration have been arrested, interrogated and threatened. Apart from Soran and Zara, because they are no longer in Sulaymaniya. But their names have been noted, because their friends were forced to reveal who else was there. One of Zara's friends had phoned her, crying and apologizing for this.
"But I was so afraid, Zara, for what they would do to me!"
She had reassured her; she would have done the same. She did not blame her in any way, but the thought that she is being sought made her even more nervous than she already was.
When the strong lights of the checkpoint come near, Zara feels her heart throbbing in her throat. If her name is noted here too, they will take her away.
"Basha brakam," the driver greets the guard, while he hands him the two identity cards. The guard looks,

comparing the pictures to their faces. Zara keeps her eyes fixated on a spot on the dashboard.

"Where are you coming from?"

"Duhok, brakam," the driver lies, without batting an eye. Never say you have been outside of the borders of the Kurdish region, because then the questions will start. The guard looks again at the cards. Zara holds her breath.

"Are you from Penjwin?" he asks Zara. And when she nods breathlessly: "Then what are you doing here?"

"Studying," her aunt answers before she can say anything. "She is studying at the best university of Kurdistan, here in Erbil."

The guard looks again at Zara's card.

"A wise decision, here at least we do not have any troublemakers," he says as he hands back their identity cards.

As the driver closes the window, Zara slowly takes a breath. "Is this the new Kurdistan?" her aunt says contemptuously, "if you are from another area, then you must be suspect?" Zara is silent, still in the grasp of her fear. So, this is how it feels, to be so afraid in your own country. When the authorities turn against you. That was how things were under Saddam, who persecuted the Kurds. And for Rahila and the Jews in the years of the Forties and the Fifties. Slowly she starts to breathe in and out, to try and calm her heartbeat. Stop it, she says to herself. You are becoming paranoid. Then things were far worse. Under Saddam, people vanished, and were tortured during questioning. The Jews had nearly everyone against them. It is not that bad. You would be questioned, and then released again. Soran was right: she has done nothing wrong. And she would be able to convince the police of that.

9 THE REPLACEMENT

June 30, 1948

Asenath's mother has not gotten up for days. She complains about being in much pain and barely eats. In a week, it looks as if she has lost many kilos. The doctor wanted to admit her to the hospital. She refused. He insisted. To be able to determine what was wrong, she had to go to the hospital to be examined. Her weak voice was barely audible when she said she would die here. The doctor tried to convince ustad Yacoub that she probably had many good years ahead, if only she would allow herself to be examined. He shook his head in failure. The doctor took his hat and left.

At night, ustad Yacoub and I take turns sitting at her bedside. The women in the neighbourhood take over during the day, and cook for us. We are worried, but do not talk about it. I cannot bear the thought of death coming for her.

Outside of the house, daily life has somewhat returned to normal, but we are not interested. Now everything revolves around Asenath's mother. Oddly enough, things remained relatively calm after the establishment of the state of Israel. At the same time, the atmosphere did not improve, and no one believes the peace is lasting. Everyone is nervous and touchy.

A week ago, we returned to our own classroom and in a few weeks, we close for the summer. I am looking forward to it, and at the same time I am loathing the thought of the gaping emptiness of the summer months. The lessons in the yeshivah will not fill it, unless ustad Yacoub has other tasks for me.

For now, all our attention is focused on Asenath's mother. If she speaks, it is almost always about the past. She tells us about her childhood, her parents, her many brothers and sisters, her life in a village outside of Mosul, and how that changed when ustad Yacoub had asked for her hand. He was already a hakham, and she was barely fifteen.

In the hours that I sat by her side, I have found out more than during all the years that I have lived under her roof. She was always very caring, but I have had few real conversations with her. I always had more contact with ustad Yacoub. Asenath's mother was always there, in the background. As a self-evident presence, who looked after ustad Yacoub, Asenath and myself. Of course, I knew that she missed her daughter, but we did not talk about it. I am ashamed now, that I was so preoccupied with myself.

On one of the evenings, she said rather unexpectedly that Asenath's birth was a miracle. I had to bend down to hear what she was saying, since her voice was so weak. Asenath was her only child to survive, she said. That is a pain I know too, even though through hearsay. Ima had also lost two children at birth.

Ten she had buried, she said softly. Six daughters and four sons. How can you possibly bear that: Ten times nine months of your life filled with hope, that yet again turned out to be in vain…

When Asenath came, she was really already too old, she said. She had given up hope. But Asenath lived, she grew, she stayed. She was a beautiful child, and very clever. A miracle. A gift from God. She fell silent to catch her breath.

Ustad Yacoub wanted to raise her as a son, she then said. That happens, in families where there are no sons. To hide the shame, one of the daughters is given a boy's name. She then goes through life as a boy. Until the age when her body betrays her. Then a marriage is arranged somewhere far away, and she suddenly must become accustomed to a life as a woman.

She had refused, the old woman said. When God had given her a daughter, he had a reason for it. Then Yacoub had remembered Asenath Barzani. Happily, her daughter was a good learner.

Asenath had come into the world with a mission. To have such an example when growing up, to continually hear as a child that your life was already planned out. It gave me a new insight into Asenath's life. It filled me with compassion.

I cooled the forehead of Asenath's mother with a damp cloth. Ustad Yacoub had been angry and very sad, when Asenath wanted to go to Palestine with David, she went on. She was to take his place. I do not remember that anger from ustad Yacoub at all. Asenath never told me about it, although we shared everything at the time. She said that he could not refuse David because of the money of his father.

Asenath wanted to go, away from Iraq, her mother said. She wanted a life. She had said that I could take her place. I could not believe my ears. Was this true? My friend had pushed me to the foreground, without discussing that with me first? She really had to do a lot of talking to convince her father, her mother said.

It felt like a betrayal. I always thought that Asenath and I shared everything. All those evenings in the dark bedroom, as we talked about our secrets together – now all of that has become a lie. I told Asenath my secrets, my most inner struggles. Her own she kept hidden from me. And the worst of all: behind my back she made decisions about my life.

The old woman was silent. The conversation was clearly wearing her out.

That Asenath was pregnant had been the decisive factor, she then said. Shocked I got up. How could she keep so much from me? Even her pregnancy she did not discuss with me! Were we really the girlfriends that I thought we were? I now understood her urgency to leave. We were not to know.

That child she had lost in Palestine, her mother then said. I kneeled again next to the old woman. She had decided to tell me everything, while she still could. I had to hold back my feelings and listen to her. I asked how she knew, as Asenath had never written to me. David wrote to his father, she said. She accepted a drink of water. I waited for more, but I soon saw from her breathing that she had fallen asleep.

I wanted to go outside to contemplate all the new knowledge, but I could not leave the old woman alone. I felt trapped in the house. Pacing back and forth in the guestroom, I realized just how betrayed I really felt. For me, Asenath was a girlfriend, or even the sister I had never had. I loved her – but she had been toying with me. And it was she, who had manipulated me into the position where I now found myself to be trapped in. It is not only betrayal. She has passed a cup of poison onto me.

I have looked at the last sentence, and eventually decided not to cross it out. For that is how it feels. If Asenath had not gone to Palestine, I would have long left Mosul. Perhaps I would have gone to Palestine, and had joined Azam. Maybe I would have gone back to Penjwin. Through her departure and her manipulations, my fate was now joined with that of ustad Yacoub.

Yet eventually, I came to understand what had driven her to do this. Of course, she did not want to become another Asenath Barzani. That was her father's dream, not hers. Perhaps it was hers too as a child, but when she grew up, she wanted a normal life with a husband and children, as all other women. That was something her father would never have allowed. She was supposed to lead the yeshivah and the school.

She thought that he would let her go to Palestine with David. And when he refused, she became pregnant. For she knew, he would never be able to live with the shame of it. How desperate she must have been! And still, she never revealed any of it. How could she keep quiet? Did she think that I would have snitched on her to her father?

I tried to imagine it. Perhaps she was right. It is too painful to admit, but somehow I had become more of his daughter than she had ever been.

The discovery casts a new light on the past. I remember how she had refused to take over part of the Torah lessons. She said she was not ready for that yet, while she had a great lead on me. She also maintained her distance, when it came to teaching the very youngest, while I had been doing that already in Penjwin. At the time I thought that she had legitimate reasons, but in reality, they were tiny proofs of resistance. She no longer wanted to follow in her father's footsteps.

When did things go wrong between us? When I had come to live in Mosul, we soon were best friends. She must at one point have realized, that I could take over from her, that she could use me to free herself. She must have planned it all. She passed a life onto me that she no longer wanted for herself. Did she never feel guilty about doing that?

July 21, 1948

Today we buried Asenath's mother. After the men had returned, I went to her grave to pray. Only then did the tears come, and only then could I allow myself to feel the pain of this loss.

I miss her, even though she never stood beside me as ustad Yacoub has done. The house is empty without her. Always, she was there in the background, or she would come shuffling in on her black felt slippers. And always, she had something for us to eat; no matter what time you happened to come in. She was also the one who gave me the kitten, when she saw how lonely I was after Azam's death. She was a caring person, and so righteous. That word comes to mind, when I think of our talk about Asenath. She knew that Asenath had used me to get her own freedom. She felt that I had the right to know. Because I was loyal, while her daughter had abandoned all of us. I am grateful to her for telling me, no matter how painful the truth is.

Asenath, in the distant Palestine, does not know that her mother has died. We cannot send her a message, because all the mail is now being intercepted. Many Jewish homes have been searched, and the residents arrested based on their exchange of letters with family and friends in Palestine, now known as 'contact with the Zionist enemy'. You can get a jail sentence of two years for it, or buy this off with a sizeable sum, but not many people have so much money.

We have had to bury Azam's letters, in case they come looking here too. They now are in a box under the ground. I am sad that his words no longer can comfort me. Even this journal I must also hide away, just as when I was a child.

Asenath's mother did not want to be a part of it anymore. I am starting to believe more and more, that she died because she did not have the courage to withstand the wave of hate that has hit us. She could not go against the wishes of her husband, who had sworn to go down fighting.

The night before she died, she seemed to be a bit better. I was even able to feed her some soft fruit, until she refused the spoon. I should go back to Penjwin, she said to me. I tried to disagree. She touched my hand to silence me. Ustad Yacoub should call on her niece Rivka; she could care for him, she said.

My eyes teared up, when I realized what was happening. She was nearing the end of her life and getting closure.

My duty was not here, she said. I should go home, and make sure I was safe. I looked at her old, spotted hand in mine. I did not have to fulfil Asenath's task, she pressed on. I had my own.

I did not want her to see my tears, but I could not hide them. Her hand slipped out of mine. The lucid moment had passed. She closed her eyes, and once again the sleep took over. She was not to awaken again.

August 10, 1948

My intention to return to Penjwin has yet to be realized. I cannot bring myself to confront ustad Yacoub with it. The death of his wife has affected him greatly. Despite the delicious food that Rivka makes for us, he has lost a great deal of weight. It breaks my heart to see him this way. His step has slowed, and he is dragging his feet. Often, he is so lost in thought that he does not even realize that you are there.

The community is sharing in his grief. David's father often comes by for an hour in the evenings to talk, just like other men from the synagogue and an occasional former student.

In the yeshivah, he continues to leave more of the work to me. Without him noticing, I have chosen one of the students to help me. Moshe has already taken over the Torah lessons. I am busy making myself replaceable. I am trying to follow the advice of Asenath's mother. I must leave Mosul; I must go and lead my own life. I must not feel obligated to stay here because I have the feeling that I am irreplaceable. I remind myself of this every day, and slowly I am starting to believe it myself. I have thought about it for a long time, but I have now finally understood why I have postponed making the decision for so long. Breaking with the life here, means breaking with the faith and my role in spreading it. I recognize the fact, that the faith I have immersed myself in, has hardly brought me what I expected. What has started after Azam's death, can no longer be stopped. I must recognize and accept, that faith to me now is nothing more than words and stories. That I must look elsewhere for the feeling, the emotion and the warmth. And that I can no longer in all honesty give lessons about the most important aspects of our faith, because I am not able to pass on my knowledge to others in a positive manner anymore.

I have decided to return to Penjwin. If I do not do that in the coming months, it will not happen. I must leave before the new school year begins. And that is just a month away, so time is short. The teachers can take over a large part of my duties. For the Arabic, a new teacher must be found. It is high time that I make agreements with ustad Yacoub. But I am hesitant. I know how much pain this will cause him. And he is so fragile at the moment.

The situation around us has not improved either. During the past months, many Jews have lost their jobs, often without them being told why. But everyone knows. Jewish bankers in Baghdad are no longer permitted to do business with foreign banks. To prevent the banks from supporting the Zionists, they say. The state of emergency that has been declared, has led to a wave of arrests. Many people who had participated in the last year's protests, have been arrested – and amongst them are many Jews. Not only political activists, but also others – happily, no one that we know well.

They are brought before the military court. Against a verdict there, no appeal is possible. So many arrests have been made, that a special camp had to be established in the desert. How terrible the conditions must be: in tents without any protection from the heat of more than fifty degrees and more, and all that under military control.

The arrest of a well-known Jewish businessman from Basra caused an outcry. Shafiq Ades is alleged to have sold military material to the Zionists. Old British material that he had sold to someone in Italy, has recently turned up in Palestine. The strange thing is that his business partners involved in this transaction, were not affected. They were all Muslim. At least another forty businessmen were arrested for doing business with the Soviet-Union – a year ago, when Iraq still had a trade agreement with the Russians. And here too, the other, non-Jewish business associates are left alone. Rumours have it, that a number of Jews have managed to buy their freedom for 10,000 pounds per person. That is a tremendous amount of money.

Zionism is now officially forbidden, and all activities to promote it have become illegal. The fine for leaving Iraq has doubled to 3,000 pounds. It has been said that this money, and the money being paid to avoid imprisonment, is going directly to the Ministry of Defence's coffers for the fight in Palestine. I find that to be rather cynical, since in that way the Jews in Iraq are paying for the fight against Zionism.

How things are in Palestine, we do not actually know. Following initial reports about large victories, it has been relatively quiet for a while. From time to time we receive a message that someone has been killed, but nothing about the current course of the battle.

The exodus to Palestine seems to have ceased. Perhaps because people do not want to go to a land at war, or perhaps the costs for being exempted have become too high. Maybe there are no longer people left in Iraq, who are willing to burn their bridges and start a new life in Palestine.

August 15, 1948

Tonight, I finally told ustad Yacoub about my intentions. He did not want to believe it at first. He asked when I would be coming back from Penjwin. I knew that it would be difficult, and fell back on what I had rehearsed. That I would not be coming back. He looked at me wondering, and suggested that I was concerned about the gossip because his wife was no longer here. I smiled about the fact that the first thing he thought of was the reactions of others - on the fact that an unmarried man and woman were living together under one roof. I said that was the least of my worries.

Why did I want to leave then, he asked. What had they done to me? I had work and shelter. My destiny was here. I said that I wanted to pick up on my own life again. He was adamant that my life was here. He was not going to let me go just like that. A few weeks ago, I might have been happy about that, but now it feels like he is bolting the door to my prison cell.

That was Asenath's life, I said, not mine. I had come here to learn, to garner as much knowledge as I could, and then leave again. And instead of doing that, I had stayed for six years.

The call for prayers from the mosque just outside of the Jewlakan, forced us into silence. We did not want to raise our voices. The setting sun cast the courtyard into a soft yellow glow. For many minutes, ustad Yacoub stared at the growing shadows. When the imam finally ceased the call, the long silence continued for a while.

Why, he asked, especially now that he needed me...? To hear him pleading like that, made me feel egoistic and ungrateful. I swallowed hard, and spoke to myself sternly: do not let him talk you out of it. I expressed my gratitude for everything he had offered me. Without him, I would never have been able to achieve this. My voice trembled. I straightened my back and told myself again to be strong.

I told him, how I had made myself replaceable. He listened, and sighed deeply. That was all possible, he said, but he thought that I would take over his work from him. Who must do that now? I remained silent. He could not expect an answer from me.

What was I going to do in Penjwin? Lead my father's school? I had outgrown that! He was right, and yet again he was not.

I answered that I might find work at a state school. But that was not the point. I had outgrown Mosul too, I said. I had learned what I wanted to learn, and I did not want to live here for the rest of my life. There was a life for me on the outside. And not here, he had finally seemed to realize.

Here, is Asenath's life, I said. She was to follow in his footsteps, not I. He said things turned out differently, as I knew. And it was an honourable calling. But not mine, I maintained. What had changed? He thought that we decided on this a long time ago.

I did not want to cause him any pain, but it was becoming obvious that I would not be able to convince him without revealing the truth. I said that I stepped into Asenath's calling, because he had asked me to. Not because it fitted me, or because it was something I really wanted. Because of that, I had lost the love of my life, and I was at the age of twenty-three still unmarried. I did not want to lose my entire life. If that was what it was, then we could look for a suitable husband? Someone, who would allow me not to have to do the housework. I heard the relief in his voice; the problem was solvable.

I looked at him in disbelief: how could he so easily ignore my pain? I said that I neither was Asenath Barzani. That I could not take his place. He sighed, and begged me to stay for a few more years. And not to leave now that we were under so much pressure. The irritation about the fact that he kept pushing, only served to feed my resistance. He was not listening to me. Everything else was more important than my wishes.

I answered him that he was fighting a battle here that was not mine. That I did not believe, that this was a test from God. That I saw only victims, and was afraid that there would be fatalities. That I no longer wanted to be a part of that. I shocked myself with my hard words, and the manner in which I dared to speak out against him. He had forced me to put into words just how far away he had pushed me from him.

Much to my surprise, he was not shocked, just sad. Had I lost my faith? He interpreted my silence for what it was. Through his doing? I could not do that: blame him for such a complicated process. It was through growing knowledge and insight, I said. I refused to discuss that now. He pressed me. He said he wanted to understand.

I was fighting a battle with myself. Now we had landed in a place I didn't want to be: at my deepest doubts that I could barely even share with Sasson. He had a right to know. After all, he was my mentor. And I quietly hoped that he would understand.

After Azam's death, it was difficult to find comfort in the prayers, or in the stories about how our people, time and again, had survived so much adversity, I began cautiously. I told him how I mainly saw just rules. For the prayers, for the cleansing, for remembrance, for celebrations… I looked him right in the eye, to make sure that he was listening to me. Our days are laid out in prayers and prohibitions, our years in celebrations and remembrances, I said. The past decides our future. But where are the people, I asked him. Where is the love, the comfort, the sadness, the life?

That doubt we all encountered sometime, he said softly. It was something that I could overcome. His answer came too quickly. He could not even allow himself to feel with me, to answer to the life's questions I am struggling with. Perhaps he was not even capable of doing that. Or perhaps he could not allow his own doubts to gain any ground. Had it ever been any different, I wondered. Had I allowed myself to be played by him? Had I felt touched because I was needed, even important? Was it ever even about me? That was how it had been for Asenath too. Perhaps that is why, I have been able to forgive some part of her actions.

I shook my head with certainty. Perhaps I did not want to overcome, I said. He was silent for a long time. The twilight had passed into darkness. When I got up to light the lamp, he stopped me.

I had no idea, how much he was going to miss me, he said. I do, I thought, I do have a very good notion of that.

September 1, 1948

Ima took the pan from the fire. I would burn the onions that way! She was teaching me how to cook, with mixed results. As a girl I had learned how to bake – bread, cookies, other sweets. But anything further than cleaning and chopping vegetables, I had never gotten to. Now she thinks that I should be able to prepare a meal, if I still want to have a chance to marry. My soup and chicken and rice are edible, but the more complicated dishes have not withstood the test. I am convinced, my talents lies elsewhere, but ima does not want to hear of it. One can learn anything, is her motto. I was only partially listening to her explanation about onions which must become translucent, as I had heard the door and quick footsteps heading towards the kitchen. Melka came in. Since her marriage to my brother, the kitchen was actually her domain. She was sweaty and agitated, as if she had been running.

They had been in the cemetery tonight! she exclaimed. Ima and I exchanged glances of understanding. It was bad news. Ima tried to calm down Melka by offering her some water, and led her to the bench in the shadow of the courtyard.

Her father's headstone was shattered, Melka said in between two gulps. She wiped her eyes with the hem of her skirt. Her father had passed away a few months ago. She had gone there to look after the grave. Was only the stone on her father's grave broken? I asked, afraid of the answer. One stone was vandalism, many was hatred. She shook her head violently. Nearly all the stones were broken.

Ima sat down next to her. Must they now also destroy our graves, she sighed. Wasn't it enough, that they were arresting and jailing us? The hatred of Jews had reached Penjwin. After only two weeks, it had managed to find me here, in this normally so peaceful village.

Inside, Melka's youngest started to cry. She took the mug and walked towards the sound. In silence, ima and I let the news sink in. I thought of Mosul, and I felt the fear creep back in that I had managed to cast off since my return to Penjwin.

Who could be behind it? I said, thinking aloud. Ima shrugged her shoulders. What difference did it make? It had happened. We didn't want it to be the neighbours, I protested. That was true, she agreed. But they would not have done this. She was right, of course. We have lived together for so many years. Why would our Muslim neighbours suddenly turn on us?

I wanted to see the damage with my own eyes. I left ima alone with the burnt onions, and hurried to the cemetery at the foot of the hill. My sisters who had died so young, were buried there, my grandparents, and Uncle Masrour who had died last year. But also, the grandparents of my grandparents – with the exception of abba's father, who was buried in Baghdad. The cemetery reflects the centuries-old history of the five original Jewish families, who had given their name to Penjwin.

The shock was immense. It was far worse than I could have imagined. The debris laid spread out over the paths and the graves. Nearly all the headstones with their beautifully formed Hebrew letters had been smashed – but only after someone had poured a few cans of red paint over the graves. The perpetrator – or perpetrators, as it looked to be the work of a number of people – wanted their message to be heard loud and clear. If they had been able to, they would have gladly used blood instead of paint.

The sadness of so much hatred overwhelmed me. I remembered, how we came here to pray with ima. And how she had taught us, that if you say the Kaddish, you can reach your forefathers. How those visits had always given me the feeling of being part of an ancient and special people.

The damage was irreplaceable. Centuries-old stones were destroyed. You can clear the debris, but you can never replace them. It was almost as if someone had tried to wipe away our history. In tears I ran from the cemetery. I could no longer bear it. Abba must know about this. I had to go to the synagogue.

I arrived out of breath. The news had already spread, and I was not the only one who thought that something needed to be done. When the first men had shown up, Abba and Shalom, who now teaches reading and writing, sent the students home. I was surprised to even find Yesula there, who had left his work at the gold smith.

In an effort not to attract attention, I sat in the back and dried my tears. I came in during a heated discussion, that did not allow itself to proceed calmly. Efforts by the maloum to bring some order, failed hopelessly.

We were under attack! I heard. This was the next step in their attempts to get rid of us! Now it was our dead, the next time our living! Someone else said that nothing was sacred anymore! Still someone else thought that we could not simply sit by and wait, until we would become victims ourselves.

The maloum tried to calm them. We gained nothing thinking of doomsday, he said. One of the followers answered that they wanted to be rid of us. The maloum asked to see things in perspective. The violation of our graves was a serious matter, but no one had threatened our lives.

I did not agree. The message was threatening enough. By destroying our past, our present was being attacked. From the sniffing and mumbling going on around me, I could tell that I was not alone in thinking this way.

The maloum continued, saying that we did not know who had caused the damage. The police thought that it must have been someone from the outside, as we have always lived here together in peace with the Muslim community. One of the followers exclaimed that we could not simply let this happen. Next, they would come and destroy our homes! someone else predicted. We had to do something, to prevent things from getting worse.

The maloum held up his hand. We could do little more than clean up and repair the damage, he said.

I remembered the meeting in Mosul, after the attack on the school. Ustad Yacoub had planned beforehand what was to happen, and had managed to get the community behind his plans. Our maloum had no idea, and not any kind of plan at all. My brother Yesula joined in the discussion. Who knew what would happen, if we did not clearly show that this was unacceptable, he said.

Abba had gotten up, and went to sit next to the maloum. I hoped that he did have a solution.

We should open a dialogue with the imams, he said. And ask them, to condemn this desecration of our graves in their Friday prayers, the maloum added immediately. There was a mumble of consent. We should invite our neighbours to come and talk to us about it, abba suggested. Again, the maloum added his comments, as if they had agreed to do this beforehand. We had lived together for so long, that this must be unacceptable for them too, he said. We could create a cleaning-up crew together with the mosque, abba added. The maloum said, that we should emphasize the unity we had this way. And if anyone had even the slightest idea of who might have done this, they should say so, abba said. The maloum would give those suggestions to the police. One of the followers asked why the police would do anything for us. His statement met approval. No one expected any help from the police.

The similarities with Mosul again became apparent. There, the police had done nothing, which left us feeling very vulnerable. Here, the same thing was happening. It frightened me.

We should convince the police that we were just as much Iraqi citizens as anyone, abba said when it had quietened down. And that we had the right to their protection, the maloum added. The follower maintained that we were on our own. First, they would aim their anger at our graves, then on us, he said. And the police only stood by, and watched.

We should strengthen the ties with the Muslim community, abba repeated. The maloum suggested to open a dialogue with our neighbours. Talk would solve nothing, they were told. For they saw us as Zionists, as the enemy. The government was setting the example by arresting the Jews, someone said. And by firing us.

We should make sure that our neighbours felt connected to us, abba kept to his discourse.

How did he want to do that, he was asked. They hated us! Abba said sternly that this was not true, and we should make sure that it would not get to that point. The hatred was everywhere, he was told. They were even destroying our graves! Abba told them to go and talk to their neighbours; they did not hate them. They hated the Zionists, because the government had imprinted that on them. Our neighbours saw us simply as Yacoub, Moshe and Sara - not as a Zionist. Once again, a mumbling of agreement could be heard. And that is what we must utilize, abba continued. We must strengthen the personal connections.

The maloum had little choice, than to sit by and watch how abba took over his role. Despite my concern, I was proud of him. If only he had been a maloum himself. Due to the superiority he showed, he would have been a good one.

How did abba suggest they would do that? a follower asked. Visit their sick, share food with your neighbours, let your children play together, abba said. Stop smoking during Ramadan, celebrate their holidays with them. Was that all?

What would greatly increase our security, abba added, would be if the dividing lines of our faiths would disappear, by relationships and marriages. A silence fell, that was then broken by shocked exclamations. Should our children marry their children? But then they would have to convert to the Islam! Someone said his wife would never agree to that.

Abba called for silence. He said that his own son had married a Muslim. A marriage would bring the bride's or groom's entire family to you, he said. In this way, we would become actually one community. I looked with concern at the maloum. Abba's idea was clearly not his.

Abba said that even if their children would marry, they could still remain Jewish in their hearts. He called their marriage a sacrifice, to offer our community safety. I was again reminded of ustad Yacoub. Eventually it all comes down to survival.

The maloum remained silent. I guessed he wondered if he could openly disagree with abba. He left him no choice, by saying that we must give the matter some thought, and discuss it in more detail. First, we were to establish a delegation to go to the imam. He asked the maloum for a suggestion.

When the kanishta had emptied out, only the maloum and abba remained. Impatiently, I waited in the courtyard until they were finished. I knew for sure that the maloum wanted to show his disapproval of abba's proposal, without me being a witness to it.

How different my life is, compared to in Mosul! Because I led the school, I could participate in the men's community. In actuality, I did not act like very much a woman. Here in Penjwin I am just abba's daughter, and I am supposed to behave like all women. I find that much more difficult than I had anticipated, and not only because to me, cooking is just as uninteresting as all of the women's talk about children and such.

In Penjwin, only the men go to the synagogue. Women pray at home. They are only welcome on certain holidays, and then only in the courtyard. Abba had explained to the community that I was a teacher of the Torah and had led a school in Mosul, and yet every time I walk into the synagogue, I once again feel unwelcome. They only accept me because abba wants them to and the maloum supports him in that.

When abba finally came outside, he silently walked towards the river. I had avoided my favourite place in Penjwin because of the memories it congers up, as even now I could feel Azam's presence. Even abba seemed to notice it. That I had not gone to join Azam in Palestine, he has never understood, he said, as we stood together staring at the water.

I was so surprised that he had not said anything about desecration of the graves, that I did not immediately have an answer. A request was made that I could not refuse, I said once I had organized my thoughts. I admitted, my life would have been very different if I had done it. And that I would always regret that.

Abba went to sit on a large rock, and looked at the circles the stones he threw created in the river. When I started to say something about what he had discussed inside, he interrupted me. He wanted to talk to me about my future, he said.

Shocked, because he did not want to discuss the crisis with me, I said sharply that I did not want to take over Shalom's duties at school. He smiled and said he knew. He let a silence fall. Sasson's friend Kawa had come here to visit him yesterday, he then said.

When he saw my surprise, he added that he came to talk about me. I only heard the implication of what he was saying: a marriage candidate had been found. I felt tears well up in my eyes. Abba saw my role in Penjwin only as a housewife. Of course, I had known when I left Mosul that I would have to step back. But not that I would no longer be able to play any active role in the community. And that on a day like today, my father would want to talk to me about marriage, and not about the ensuing crisis, I could never have imagined.

Abba was still talking. Kawa liked me very much, and he wanted to offer me safety in these difficult times. And through me, the family too. Abba wanted me to marry a Muslim. I swallowed, but the lump in my throat would not go. When Sasson married, it was a matter of survival, since he needed a new identity. And now I had to save the family.

Did I have a choice? Abba wanted to make sure that I would still get married, even though everyone thought that I was already too old. Kawa was nice enough, and who else would want me? What would Azam think of it, if he knew?

To marry a Muslim, I would have to convert. How could I, who was educated in Jewish religion and its laws, now become a Muslim? Had I then garnered all that knowledge for nothing? Of course, I would no longer be able to work as a teacher of the Torah. I did feel a bit betrayed. I tried to wipe away my tears, without abba seeing them.

There was another side to the story too, I realized. A positive one. I would no longer be confronted with the doubts I continued to have about my faith. Abba interpreted my silence as a rejection, and apparently, he had seen my tears. He said he would not ask this of me, if he did not think it was of great importance. I could save an entire family. And if his daughter married a Muslim, more fathers would consider the option too.

How is it possible that everyone is always calling on me to do something, I wonder. First ustad Yacoub who needed me, and now my father. Do they know that I will not refuse, that I cannot refuse? When I tried to react, abba interrupted me. He would completely understand if I did not like the idea. But he had something to tell me, that had put our situation on alert.

He took out a section of an Arabic newspaper from under his vest. The first thing I saw, was the picture of a hanged man.

I was overcome with a sense of dismay, when I read about the execution of Shafiq Ades, the rich Jewish businessman who supposedly had sold British military equipment to the Zionists. A few days ago, he was hung in front of his castle of a home in Basra, while an enthusiastic crowd loudly clapped and cheered.

Shocked, I saw that the newspaper had described what had happened to him as getting "what he deserved." Being a Jew, means being the enemy of the state, it said. I read the sentence out loud. Abba sighed. That about summed it up, he said. The Iraqis were being told that we Jews were the enemies of our own state. Ades was the wealthiest and most influential of us all. If even he could not save himself, who will? He was right. There is no more denial possible; the persecution and hatred of Jews is everywhere. Penjwin is a rather isolated village, but it cannot hide itself from the facts.

Shafiq Ades was one of the many Jews against whom a case had been made. Most of those who were arrested, were able to buy themselves free, but he could not. He was portrayed as a traitor of the people. And yet he had friends at the highest levels, and many of his business partners were Muslims.

But an execution, for a crime that was not even proven? And a public execution as well? The government surely knew what signal that is sending to the population?

This was inciting hatred against the Jews, I said. The Iraqi people were being stirred up against us. I asked what the government could possibly gain from this. Things were going badly in Palestine, abba said. Our boys were dying, the Zionists were winning ground. And we Jews were the scapegoats.

I stared at the horrible photo. If this could happen to a rich, influential Jew, then we were all fair game. There is not any solution for that. How could abba think that this kind of hostility can be fought with marriages and friendships? How could he be so mistaken?

He folded the newspaper back up again, and sighed once more. He said that he only knew that we have two options: leave, or try to guarantee our safety. He chose for the second option, because we have lived for generations in Kurdistan. And Kurdistan is no Baghdad or Basra.

I told him that when I left Mosul we had started throwing away everything that could be used to proof any kind of link between us and the Zionists in Israel. In Mosul too, we have lived together for some 2,800 years. There was once a king, who managed to convince his subjects to convert to Judaism. But even that past offered us no guarantee for our well-being.

In the silence, a bird began to sing. From the other side of the river it received an answer. Minutes passed, before abba answered. If I reasoned like that, there was no other option for us than to leave, he said. No, I thought, no. Everything in me was fighting that option. If I had wanted that, then the state of Israel would have become my land long ago, and perhaps Azam would still be alive.

Suddenly, everything became very clear. Up until now, everything in my life revolved around staying in Iraq. I do not want to leave my country. However much I must sacrifice, leaving is the absolute last option. So abba had been right. Staying here, meant taking precautions. And not only the nice, or commonly accepted ones. I could not avoid this.

I suggested that abba should let me talk to Kawa. I was well aware of the improperness of that suggestion; in a normal situation, a woman can only accept or reject if her father comes up with a marriage partner. But this was no normal situation. And besides that, I have long outgrown those worn-out rituals.

He did not move a muscle. I would be doing him a huge favour if I was to consider that marriage, he said. He would ask Kawa to come and visit us. No time soon, I will forget the sound of relief in his voice.

I have much to think about. Marrying Kawa in itself is not an idea that I am against. I like him, he would respect me. He knows my background; he knows what happened with Azam. To him, I could propose that I would like to keep working.

Exchanging one faith for another – that is something entirely different. The outside world knows me as someone who has studied in a yeshivah. And that is not something that you do just like that, and certainly not as a woman. That means, that at the very least you are an active follower. How believable is it when you then convert to another faith?

It does bother me though, that I will never be able to do anything more with my knowledge if I change over to the Islam. But let me be honest with myself: in reality that was already decided when I chose to leave Mosul. There, I garnered more knowledge then I had ever expected: next to the Jewish religion and laws, I know more about the world and the history of it than I ever would have, if I had stayed in Penjwin. That knowledge will certainly come in useful at some point.

It all sounds so reasonable. But my heart is not yet ready to accept, what is neatly organized in my mind. And the fear that I thought I had left behind in Mosul, has found me once more. Will I ever be able to shake it?

Kawa looked a little nervous when I greeted him in the guestroom. There, I noticed the arak bottle and glasses. Had abba left those there, of had he just put them out? It took a moment for me to understand, what he had intended. He wanted me to show Kawa the kind of life I was used to. So that he would know that he would be marrying a woman with a certain status who enjoys certain privileges.

Kawa did not seem surprised when he accepted a glass. In an effort not to completely scare him off, I let him open the conversation, as was the acceptable way. He asked about Sasson, and I told him that we had not had any news from him since his marriage. That we in fact had broken off the contact for his safety. He nodded, and cleared his throat. My safety and that of my parents were important for him, he said. I turned the glass around in my hands, and held back the impulse to make it easier for him. He said he thought it terrible how the government was trying to blame the Jews for all. How Jews suddenly appeared no longer to be Iraqis. He did not know how we could change that tide.

I nodded.

He continued. How he had talked to abba about the problems. How he looked upon abba's proposal to strengthen the ties between the Jews and Muslims in Iraq. Until I no longer could maintain myself. I asked him gently, if the reasoning behind his marriage proposal was only of a political nature? Passionately he denied that. I did know...

When he did not finish his sentence, I said softly that I only knew him, me and Sasson had some very nice conversations. He swallowed. Then he looked right at me. If I had not already been engaged, he would have asked for my hand then. Why did I think that he still had not married? Stunned I listened to him. I suddenly felt very shy.

He had never been able to find anyone who called up the same feelings in him as I do, he added. When he heard that Azam had been killed, he was sad for me. But not for himself. He said that many times, he had been on the verge of coming to Mosul. If he only had.

Everything would have been so different. I was almost angry with him.

He felt like he had to give me time to mourn, he said, and to decide what I wanted to do with my life. No man has ever spoken to me in such a way before. Everyone makes demands, asks me to do things, asks me for support and help. Only Kawa did not, he waited for me. I looked at him, and saw to my great surprise that his eyes were green.

It would have been better if he had not waited so long, I said then. He asked if it had been too long then. I wondered by myself what would have weighed heavier, the call from ustad Yacoub, or a proposal from Kawa? I know myself; I know how I acted when I was with Azam. But I have learned my lesson, would I really have kept Kawa waiting? I told him honestly, I did not know. But that in the meantime, I had become a teacher in the Jewish faith. Did that seem to be an objection?

He said he would not ask me to forget my faith. Only to convert for the outside world, since that is needed in order to get married. Because he wants to share his life with me. His words warmed me. But they did not take away all my doubts. Was he not afraid, that people would become suspicious, I asked, when someone with my background converted? He smiled. I should not worry, he said, as he would not allow that my motives be brought into doubt. This is what I came back from

Mosul for, I realized. Someone who accepts me for who I am, who will take care of and protect me.

It was as if the sunlight had suddenly come shining through the thick walls. I pointed out to Kawa that I cannot cook, and that I am a disaster in the kitchen. He said it was not important. What was important for him, was that I was a special woman. I could feel that I was blushing. Had anyone ever said anything like that to me before?

Kawa said he knows that I would like to give lessons in Arabic. We were going to look for a job for me in Sulaymaniya. And when the children were to arrive, we could hire a maid. He has thought of everything. I saw his questioning, uncertain look, and my heart seemed to burst from happiness. This was a dream. He smiled, when I said that, his eyes fixed on mine. My heart was beating far too fast. Is it possible, that what there was between Azam and me, is repeating itself?

The rest of the conversation was about practical things. How an imam needed to be arranged, how the conversion would come about, when we would marry and where we would live. In Sulaymaniya, because there is his school and there is also apparently an educational job for me. And we will live with his parents, who moved there years ago. I would like his mother, he said. She is a great cook.

When I rose to tell abba about the outcome, Kawa took my hands in his. His kiss was a conformation, and a promise.

10 A BENJEW

Zara reached for the box of tissues, and blew her nose. That Rahila is going to be married after all!
The further she gets into the journal, the more connected she feels to her. Yet she never anticipated or foresaw, that she would convert. Zara even is a bit disappointed that she was not another Asenath Barzani after all. The concept of having a vocation interests her highly.
And then there is the fact that she is on the run – not only from the threat in Mosul, thinks Zara, but also from the responsibility to lead a community during difficult times. How she left the poor old hakham to fend for himself! Zara finds it to be unforgivable.
Zara's visit to the Jewlakan, yesterday, has fallen under a new light, now that she knows Rahila converted to Islam. She had met the son there of the converted Jewess, the *Benjew*. She realizes that title must also have been used for Rahila.

The conversation was disappointing. The son had said that he knew little about his mother's past. She had converted to the Islam, and had given her children nothing of her Jewish heritage. She had wiped out the past.

Her son felt he was a Muslim. He was close to his mother, but for him his Jewish heritage played no role, he said. He continually emphasized how much the Jews and the Kurds had in common in the Forties. That Jews went unnoticed. That they wore the same clothes, women the same jewellery, that they spoke Kurdish.

The reason behind his mother's conversion remained vague. She was in love with a Muslim boy, the son had said, and had married against the wishes of her parents. Whether her conversion had anything to do with the threat of anti-Semitism, he did not know. And why her best friend had followed suit, also remained unclear. And yet the conversions did take place at the height of the hatred against the Jews, in 1948.

Zara wondered how Rahila had managed after her conversion. Had she too chosen to hide so much of her past from her children?

Or was the son in Erbil just afraid that the world would turn against him, if he were to admit that he was no ordinary Muslim, as a Jewish mother inevitably makes you a Jew too... The negative atmosphere has never really left. Kurdistan is part of Iraq, and its neighbours are Arabs who see Israel as the enemy. No place to be openly proud of Jewish roots.

Even more, the son had told Zara that a Jew that had converted to Islam, was highly respected. He had taken an

important step, by consciously choosing for the better faith. Life began anew after the conversion.
But in this way, much knowledge was lost about the life of Jews in Iraqi Kurdistan.
Zara takes out the picture of the Jewish bride, which she now knows is Rahila's grandmother. From whose life she knows little more than that she followed her heart. That was controversial, because the Jews in Kurdistan tried to marry within the group.
"You did not see the girls from the Jewlakan outside much," Kak Azad had said to her, last night. He is a government advisor, referred to her by her professor. "They visited one another by way of the inner doors between the houses."
The head of an influential family in Erbil had spent his youth in the centuries-old citadel, and was still able to remember and tell much about that time. Erbil's citadel is the oldest occupied location in the region. Now the houses are left crumbling, but back in the Forties and Fifties, this was the heart of the city. Jews were living here as well. Here, was the first school of Erbil; a Jewish one.
The Jews there were more open than those in the Jewlakan, Kak Azad explained. The citadel had its own synagogue, "where I played as a child. But nothing is left of it."
Apparently, a rift had grown between the liberal and more conservative Jews, who both had their own house of worship. The synagogue in the Jewish quarter is mostly gone too, as she has seen during her walks through the area. A family now lives there between the old walls, which origins are only visible from the arches that are still standing.

Kak Azad had received her in the guestroom of the family home, with the portraits of his forefathers on the walls. Proudly, he talked about the role his grandfather had played in the Kurdish political past, and his father's in the resistance against Saddam Hussein.

Zara had looked at the pictures with great interest, and wondered if she would ever see such tangible evidence of the Jewish history in Kurdistan. It was then, that she had decided to frame the picture of Rahila's grandparents, and hang it in her room.

When she asked Kak Azad about the rights of the property owners in the Jewlakan, he surprised her. "No one wanted to buy their houses when the Jews had to leave, as here in Erbil, people have lived together for centuries," he said. "That is why the municipality confiscated them."

"So, the residents rent their houses from the city. What happens to the rent?"

"That is deposited into a frozen bank account."

"Does the money go to the original owners?"

Kak Azad had looked at her thoughtfully. "I do not know. But because it is frozen, I do not think that anyone has access to it."

"So that is why nothing is repaired anymore?"

"The residents themselves are too poor to pay for that on their own."

Zara thought about the ruins in the neighbourhood and the advancing city renovation. How long would it be, before the last tangible memories disappeared?

"What is left then, from the 2,800 years that the Jews were here," she asked her host.

He took some time to think about that. "We should thank them for many of our dishes. Because of their history of fleeing and famine, the Jews were always afraid of hunger. That is why they dried their food for the winter. We still do that today."

Was that all, Zara wondered. Dishes, habits. That seems hard to believe from a folk that had lived here for so long.

"Not much, eh?" Kak Azad had said, reading her mind. "The Jews did not really mix. They preferred, that their women not married to Muslims, because then they were lost for the faith. And the Jewish girls were very beautiful."

In silence they drank their tea.

"You know, many Jews did not want to leave, back in 1948," Kak Azad then said. "But they were forced to."

That was about power, and economical gain, he said. When the Jews left, Muslims stepped into the void. Bankers were needed, currency brokers, gold sellers, merchants.

"But how did the Iraqi government benefit from sending troops to Palestine? I do not see the advantages of such an expensive operation during an economic crisis."

This was one of Zara's main questions.

"Yes, Palestine... have you noticed that it was not even a subject of discussion during the Arab spring? In the demonstrations in Egypt and Tunisia, I did not hear a single slogan about the Palestinians. The same in Libya and Syria."

Zara was confused about the sudden change of topic.

"For forty years, the Arab governments have used the lie about Palestine to keep their people busy, by way of exporting their own crisis. Distract the people, create a crisis elsewhere and you can do as you like. Now the regimes fall,

people wake up to what is happening. That is why the Palestinians have disappeared from the political agendas."
"So that is what it is all about? That is why Iraq sent troops to fight against Israel?" Zara was almost disappointed. "Is that all?"
"Even Saddam Hussein did it." Kak Azad sounded very certain about what he was saying. "Did you ever hear anyone in Iraq discuss the case of the Palestinians after his fall?"
Zara nodded, as she remembered how Saddam had generously rewarded whole Palestinian families for the death of a father or a son in the battle for Palestine. Palestinians who lived in Iraq had money and food, while the Iraqi people suffered from international embargos. After Saddam's demise, the anger of the Iraqi people had turned against them.
"The Iraqis discovered that the Palestinians were used as a cover. That they had been fooled by the government. Actually, ever since 1948, after the establishment of the state of Israel. Did you know, that they had even discussed an exchange: the Iraqi Jews to Palestine, for the same number of Palestinians who could take their place in Iraq?"
Zara shook her head. "Why? How could Iraq possibly benefit from that?"
"It would have at most gotten a hundred thousand new citizens, who would have felt obliged to support the regime. The plan was part of the rousing of public indignation, to distract citizens from what the government could or would not resolve."

THE JEWISH BRIDE

Is it really that simple, Zara wonders while she flips through her notes. The Jews in Iraq, and actually also elsewhere in the Middle-East, have become the victim of a power game. Kak Azad as right: could what happened to the Palestinians after 2003, not be compared to what befell the Jews in Iraq? Those were hated because of the protection they enjoyed from the British and the Iraqi king, while the Palestinians were protected by hated regimes like Saddam's and those which disappeared in the Arab Spring.

"You know," Kak Azad had told her, "that when the Iraqi troops returned from Palestine, they had nothing but compliments for the Jewish fighters. About their bravery, their commitment."

Of course, Zara thinks, they knew what they were fighting for: for their own state.

And many Kurds understand that all too well, Kak Azad had said. "People here looked up to the Jews. Their state was seen as the example for our own Kurdish state."

That would explain, why people could not differentiate between a Jew and a Zionist. How could you be a Jew and not support the Jewish state of Israel – when as a Kurd you could not possibly be against the establishment of a Kurdish state.

Zara breathes a sigh of relief. Finally, she has found the base for her dissertation. The Iraqi government had used Zionism to present Jews as the enemies of Iraq, even though they had done nothing wrong. Years later, Saddam did the same thing with the Kurds: they too became enemies of the state. Detaining Kurdish fighters was explainable: the Kurdish state they were fighting for, was part of Iraq. Their struggle was a threat to the unity of the state of Iraq. But the Jewish state did not even share a border with Iraq. Zionism was made illegal while it formed no direct threat for the state of Iraq. That policy was part of a bigger plan. Because by declaring the state of emergency in 1948, the government found tools to stand up to communists and dissidents. And in doing so, it could render all of its opponents harmless. She browses through Rahila's journal. Sasson had understood, she now remembers.

...how the people are being played. That the Arab League only exists to create a joint Arabic struggle – against Zionism. To keep the population occupied, so it does not realize how uninformed and poor it is being kept. The masses speak out with actions, he said, and that could be very dangerous for us Jews.

Nowhere is the effect of the policy as clear as the moment when the most influential Jew was hung in Basra.

Abba sighed. That about summed it up, he said. The Iraqis were being told that we Jews were the enemies of our own state.

The worsening situation had created a schism in the Jewish community in Iraq, between the Jews who felt Iraqi, and others for whom being a Jew meant that they supported Israel.

It was partially a conflict of generations. Zara has discovered that in Baghdad in 1947, an underground Jewish movement had been set up. It met in basements, spoke about Zionism and practiced using weapons. The members were furious about the discrimination of Jews. Youth for the Redemption was preparing for the moment that it might have to protect the Jews in a subsequent revolt by the general population. The youths felt more Jewish than Iraqi. That is why, they also became active in human trafficking to Israel. The older generation did not want to know. They viewed these hot heads as a threat for the Jews in Iraq. The Jewish leadership in Baghdad had determined that the Jews would be better served by supporting the Arab fight in Palestine. Some of the Baghdadi Jews even gave money to the Iraqi volunteers who fought against the Zionists.

Jews supported the fight against the state of Israel and its Jewish combatants. They would do just about everything to be able to stay in Iraq, Zara thinks to herself. Just like Rahila. The phone rings. Banu. She is happy with the distraction.

"And, when is the marriage?"

"Zara, you better sit down."

She sounds serious. Zara's cheerfulness makes way for concern. Has something happened to her parents?

"Soran was arrested this morning in Sulaymaniya."

Shocked, Zara drops down onto the bed. No! Soran. Arrested!

"What was he doing in Sulaymaniya? He knew that they were arresting students!" She curses loudly.

"Take it easy, Zara. He apparently needed to speak to someone, and then was arrested near Saray Square."

"When? How long have they had him?"

"Since yesterday afternoon. I heard it from someone who saw it happen, and then started making calls."

Zara pushes the images away from her mind of Soran being pushed to the ground by the police.

"Zara, are you still there?"

She swallows. "Yes... was that during the demonstration?"
"Yes, he was walking nearby, the fool. An easy target."
Soran, who apparently was headed for the bazaar, had taken the shortest route along the corner of the square. Where the riot police and security forces stand ready to take action, as the protesters are following the example of those in Cairo and have set up tents in Saray Square, where they hold wakes at night.
"They have arrested other people there too, during the past days," Banu is continuing. "They question them, and let them go after a few hours."
The words are ringing through her head. A few hours. Questioning. The image of a torture chamber does not allow itself to be easily pushed aside. No, she tells herself, that was under Saddam, and we are now living in 2011. Beatings, threats, assaults perhaps – but torture, they surely no longer do that? She sighs, and makes an effort to sound normal.
"Do you know whom they are arresting, Banu?"
"Students, hayatem. And journalists. And I know that they all were freed after a few hours."
Her tone in calming.
Zara is shaking, her hands are cold, but she has to know. "How were they treated?"
Banu is clearly hesitating. "The journalists have said that they were beaten and threatened," she then says.
Would Soran keep quiet about the protest at the KDP building, Zara wonders with great concern. Could he do that, even while being beaten? And what, if he talks about

the child that was shot to death? What will they then do to him?

She wants to leave Erbil. She wants to be with her family and friends; she must be there if Soran needs her. Maybe she can visit him in prison. She is already on her feet, next to the bed, driven by unrest and worry.

"I must..."

"You must do absolutely nothing Zara," Banu says sternly. "You stay right where you are, because then, nothing can happen to you. You cannot do anything here for Soran."

"But I cannot just sit here waiting until..."

"Yes, that is exactly what you are going to do. You wait right there, until he is released. Otherwise, I would not have phoned you."

Banu has never talked to her like that before.

The words have effect, and Zara drops back down onto the bed.

"But..." she says, her voice trembling, "how can I just sit here, while he is being mistreated by the police?"

"What could you do for him here, then?"

Defeated she pushes her books away over the bedspread. Banu is right.

"You go now to your aunt and tell her what has happened. And as soon as I hear anything more, I will call you. OK?"

Zara nods automatically.

"OK?" Banu repeats.

Slowly a tear rolls down her cheek.

"I am afraid of what they are doing to him, Banu."

"Yes..." Banu sighs. "Can you try, and think positive? He is being questioned, that we know for sure. The rest is all pure speculation."
She is right again, but this time that has no effect.
Zara feels both powerless and guilty at the same time. Because when was the last time that she even spoke to Soran? If she had shown a bit more interest, then she would have known what he was up to, and could have warned him not to go to Sulaymaniya...
With a quick knock, Aunt Awat opens the door. Zara has no time to wonder how she knows, because her aunt is already holding her in her arms.
"Child, child."
The phone falls to the floor, and starts to ring.
"Come," Aunt Awat says, "everyone will be calling you now. Just leave it. We are going downstairs, and will come up with a plan. We must make a few calls to the right people."

The tears come as soon as her head hits the pillow. For hours now, she has been able to hold them back, but here, in the loneliness of her room, the dam bursts. And with the tears come the images of Soran in a cold, dark cell, lying on the concrete floor, bleeding and broken. No matter what her aunt says, or how she has tried to convince her that the phone calls she made will work and he will be one of the first to be released in the morning – Zara does not believe it.
Soran will break, he will say that he did everything he could to save the child that has come to be the symbol of the demonstrations, and they will then see him as one of the

troublemakers. And then, they will certainly not let him go. No, they will beat and kick him, and maybe even torture him, in order to get more names. Zara knows this for sure. Just as she is sure, that it is her fault. If she had not been so busy with herself, and not so consumed by the journal – if she had made more time for Soran, then this most likely would not have happened. Then, they would have been together, then, he would have never made that dangerous journey across the square, then, he would not now be in custody.

She reaches again for the tissue box.

"Soran is a grown man, and almost a doctor, who is responsible for the lives of others," she remembers Aunt Awat saying. "He can look out for himself, Zara. There is nothing that you can do for him."

Zara blows her nose. Her aunt is right, of course. Soran makes his own choices. But the fact remains, that she did not keep her promise to him. She had not given him the time and attention that he deserved, as her fiancé. As the man she is going to marry. That she will change, once she gets back to Penjwin, she promises him from a distance. But for now, she cannot go there. Her aunt said that Banu was right. Erbil is safer – especially now with Soran under arrest. If he breaks, then he will give them her name too.

No, she doesn't want to think about that.

Again, the image of a bloody Soran in the small cell crowds her mind.

Zara reaches once more for the journal. That will at least offer her some distraction.

October 3, 1948

My life has changed completely in just a month's time. From being an unmarried Jewish woman in the village of Penjwin, I have been transformed into a married Muslim woman living in the city of Sulaymaniya. The difference could not be greater. The process of change has sometimes left me nearly breathless, and the time to write about it has been non-existent. And besides, I now have a husband with whom I can share everything.

I realize now, how much I have missed, these past years. Gaining knowledge is a lonely way to pass the time.

It was surprisingly easy to become a Muslim. I went to visit the imam, who had me repeat that there was no God other than Allah and that Mohammed is his prophet. Maybe it was so simple because I told him that I had read the Koran before? I did not have to choose a new name, because Rahilah is also known in the Koran. Our marriage too was a simple occasion: with two witnesses and in front of the same imam, we signed a marriage contract.

I was hung with gold. That is what Kawa gave me as part of the marriage contract. And abba insisted that we have a big party in Penjwin. Because only then, would our marriage be a fact.

The day before the party, ima and Melka had organized a henna-evening for the women from the neighbourhood, with much music and dance. My hands remained orange for many weeks. The entire village came out for the party. Kawa and I did not want to sit on the podium and watch everyone else dancing; we spent the better part of the evening on the dance floor. The village certainly gossiped about that for weeks.

Because it was too late to travel back to Kawa's parent's home in Sulaymaniya, my parents had prepared the visitor's room for us. They say, that the marriage night is the most important night in the life of a woman. We were tired, and fell asleep as we lay close to one another. That was not how it was supposed to go, but I was so happy that Kawa had not forced anything on me. To be honest, I was quite nervous about what was supposed to happen, after all the whispered stories about pain and the loss of blood.

I woke early, and lay for a while looking at the man who has promised to make me happy. Then I remembered, that they were waiting for the sheet that would bear the markings of the end of my virginity, and the nerves came back. That turned out to be unnecessary. When Kawa awoke, he took me in his arms. It took some getting used to, but now we are both enjoying it, each time anew. Why has no one ever talked about that; all the whisperings were about pain and never about the pleasure.

I am feeling a bit conflicted with what I have been taught. A woman in our faith must cleanse herself the evening before the Sabbath in the *mikve*, after which her husband sleeps with her. In Penjwin, the women use a special place for this on the banks of the river. But I can now no longer go to the mikve, since I am a Muslim. And we sleep together far more often than just that one time a week.

Also after their time of the month, Jewish women are to wash themselves in the mikve; another rule that I am now unable to fulfil. I try to hold to the rule by staying away from Kawa during my unclean days – even if he does not agree with this.

There are many more of these kinds of rules. Kawa's mother of course does not have a kosher kitchen. She has no reason to keep meat and dairy products separate. And I eat whatever is being served, so I am daily disobeying our rules regarding food. Should I feel guilty about that? Then I would no longer be able to eat…

The month of the feast of Yom Kippur, the Tabernacles feast and the Rejoicing of the Torah passed by unnoticed. How can you fast or celebrate, if no one else around you does – as those feasts belong to a religion that is no longer yours?

I try to keep up with my daily prayers, but even that is often impossible because the order of my days has changed so drastically. I am after all no longer alone, and my husband and my in-laws determine how my day will be, except for my time at work.

I teach Arabic at a state school in Sulaymaniya, the only one where girls also are taught. I am very happy.

And I am not even the only female teacher there. Yanar, who comes from Baghdad, teaches mathematics. Because we work on Saturdays, I cannot observe the day of rest for the Sabbath. Our day off is Friday. It felt very strange the first time, but it just takes some getting used to. What else can I do, except say the Sabbath prayers for myself? Abba most likely did not foresee this, when he promoted mixed marriages with the thought that we would be able to hold onto our Judaism. Happily, I am not expected to pray five times a day as a Muslim. No one needs to know that I use the Friday prayers, in the privacy of our bedroom, for prayers that I know so much better.

In the beginning, I felt guilty. The prayers, the rules, the holidays, the days of remembrance – not only did they decide the scheme of things, they were an obligation. I hope that God will not be angry with me, as long as I do my best to keep the spirit of our faith alive. And without anyone realizing it, I continue to worship the God of Israel, who led us out of Egypt and gave is his Word and Laws.

Sometimes, I long to be able to ask abba for advice, or ustad Yacoub. Travel has become easier, now that it is possible by automobile. But I work six days a week, and the journey would take several hours. And although recently a telephone line has been connected to our house, no one in Penjwin has a telephone, or in the Jewlakan in Mosul. So, I must somehow seem to manage without their advice.

The fact that I have been hired at the school, is completely thanks to the fact that I am married to Kawa and that I have become a Muslim. Because the anti-Jewish policies are continuing. At the start of this school year, all the state schools in Iraq have informed the Jewish students that they are no longer able to guarantee their safety. Many parents found it to be too great of a risk. Our school only has two Jewish sisters left.

I fear the consequences of this in the long term. Because if the Jewish children become solely dependent on the Jewish schools and yeshivahs, then the high-ranking positions in society will no longer be within their reach. For that, they must follow the education offered by the state schools and universities from the age of twelve.

Because Kawa and his father read the Arab newspapers and listen to the radio, news now reaches me far sooner than before. Such as news about the war in the Palestine. The past week, the Arab troops have suffered heavy losses. The Zionists have gained much ground.

Because of the conflict, many more Arabs have been coming to Iraq from Palestine. In Penjwin, that is not noticeable, but here in Sulaymaniya it is. I have a strong suspicion that they play a major role in the further escalation of anti-Jewish sentiment.

When I walked through the bazaar a few days ago on the way back from school, I saw a man in an Arab *disjdasja*, who had gathered merchants and civilians around him. I also saw a few Jewish merchants.

The stranger had climbed on top of a vegetable crate, and towered above the rest. He held up a large key. That was the key to his house in Haifa, he said. Now, Jews were living there. He spoke of Zionistic murderers that had driven thousands of Muslims from their homes. I paused there, curious to hear what he had to say and moreover, how the people of Sulaymaniya would react.

He spoke of the day that Jews in the village of Dayr Yasin, located outside of Jerusalem, had murdered 250 Arab men, women and children. And every day, 'the Jewish dogs' kill even more, he said. That was months ago! one of the bystanders said. Another one said that here, they had no problems with our Jews. I was touched when he spoke of 'our Jews.' Those beloved Jews are helping the Zionists to fight the Arabic armies, the stranger said. Because of their actions, Arab blood was flowing in Palestine. Iraqi soldiers were dying in a battle financed by Iraqi Jews, he said.

He is lying, someone else called from the crowd. Our Jews are our friends, he said. A few people had turned and walked away, but others remained and listened. The stranger shouted that half of those Jewish friends were in prison, because they were helping the Zionists. What kind of friends were they? The listeners became restless, and started talking amongst themselves. One

of the merchants laid a protective arm on the shoulder of a Jewish colleague. Get out with your lies! he yelled.
The stranger hardly seemed to hear him. He brought us the truth, he said. These so-called Jewish friends were Zionists that would turn against us, and kill us and our families. Just like they were doing in Palestine. One of the merchants, a big man in Kurdish attire, went and stood before the Arab. He was clearly an influential man. Sternly he asked the stranger who had invited him. He answered that he came from afar to announce the truth. The merchant told him that we were not interested in his words. His colleagues supported him. This is not Palestine! could be heard, and: We have lived together for centuries!
The merchant said to the man that we did not come from behind the mountains, and that we had better things to do than to listen to his provocative talk. As if a signal had been given, the men turned and left, or walked back to their stands. In no time at all, the man stood alone in the middle of the market. Passers-by walked around him in a wide berth. The stranger stepped from the crate, and rearranged his black-and-white chequered *keffiye*.
I fear that this incident will not prevent him from repeating his performance elsewhere. A number of times, the *mukhtar* has asked him to leave, but just as many times he will be able to spout his poison without any resistance. The problem is that he has the blessing of the Iraqi government.

More important still, is that the arrests are continuing, and that many Jews are losing their jobs. These days, the ministries have received the order to fire all the Jews, and those working for the railroads and in the harbours, are losing their jobs too. Young, recently graduated Jewish doctors no longer receive a work permit from the Ministry of Health, and even the permits from experienced physicians are not being renewed. The results of that for the health care system will be enormous, because many of the best doctors are Jewish. If they are unable to perform their profession, people will become reliant on second-class doctors. Does nobody realize that things are really getting out of hand?

How long will it be, before the Iraqis turn en masse against my people, fired up by the lies and half-truths they are being fed on nearly a daily basis – that will eventually affect them too?

December 10, 1948

There is life under my heart! After weeks of being sick each and every morning, Kawa's mother is now certain that I am with child.

Kawa is very happy, and knows for sure that we will be having a son. I miss my mother and her wisdoms. I know little about pregnancies and births. What must I do, to make sure that everything goes well? Nothing, Kawa's mother says, just eat well and get plenty of sleep. I know that in the Jewish traditions, there are numerous habits, amulets and remedies to ensure that the child will be safe and healthy. I am not even allowed to think about it, because our son will be a Muslim, no Jew. For the Iraqi law at least – in our faith the child inherits the religion of the mother.

In the past weeks, five women from the Jewlakan of Sulaymaniya have married Muslims, including one to the son of an agha. I have heard that it is also happening in Penjwin. Abba's plan is being put into action, my example is being followed. I hope that it helps, so that our communities here in Kurdistan can escape the retaliations from the rest of Iraq. But I wonder. Especially after a recent incident in Zakho. It is remarkable that it happened there, as Zakho has been called the Jerusalem of Kurdistan, because it is home to one of the largest Jewish communities here.

A group of Jewish rafters was arrested on the charge of Zionism. The group was headed over the Habor-river with a cargo of wood, but were stranded due to bad weather. The story is that they danced to keep warm, as they could not make a fire because of the Sabbath. They sang a traditional dance song, which mentions the word 'Israel' several times. I can see them doing it, in a circle, with in the front a man waiving a handkerchief, 'hey, hey, hey' and 'Israel, Israel,' like it is done at weddings. The song is about our past, not about the Zionist Eretz Israel. But the non-Jews who were present, reported the event to the police. The entire group was arrested and transferred to Mosul.

Even the local agha, who had always protected the Jews, could do nothing for them. Zionism now stands equal to treason.

The hatred has hit very close to home. Apparently, you can end up in jail if anyone simply has a grudge against you. I now understand why abba was pushing for good relationships between the communities. Perhaps you can thus prevent someone having evil intentions. But on the other hand, when it has reached that point, those relationships accomplish nothing. Once you are in the hands of the police, then the law must take its course. And that law now is aimed almost entirely against the Jews.

Just look at the decision, that all the properties of Jews who left Iraq will be confiscated, if they do not quickly come up with a date for their return. That means that everyone who went to Israel leaving behind their house, their land and all their other possessions, has in fact lost everything. Yet many Jews had no other choice, than to flee like thieves in the night, because otherwise they would have been accused of Zionism. You ask yourself how non-Jew Iraqis would react, if the government were to confiscate all of their belongings, only because they had gone abroad. They would not accept it.

In contrast, I only know of one case when a Jew has openly spoken out against what is happening to us. That was Senator Manahem Daniel, who made a fiery plea reminding everyone of the role the Jews have played in the development of our country. I have great admiration for the way he dared to speak out against the discrimination and extortion that Jews have been confronted with. Jews must be treated as the constitution demands, namely as equal citizens, as he stated to the Ministry of Justice.

Daniel is the only Jewish member of the Iraqi senate, and enjoys great respect for his age of 74. His speech seems to have opened a few hearts, and there were even some promising signals that Jews would be treated better. Since then, the reports of arrests and harassments in Baghdad have decreased somewhat. Some Jewish businessmen have apparently resumed their activities, reopened their shops, and there is talk of a slight improvement in the situation.

May 25, 1949

My son is growing under my heart, and kicks passionately. The birth will take place during the Ramadan, so I have roughly another month to go, but my belly seems too big. I hope that I can hold on until the end of the school year.

Fatima, who last week joined our group of converted Muslim women, predicted that I was having twins. She speaks from experience, as her twins are now a year old. I hope that she is wrong. I cannot burden Kawa's mother with two babies; if it is really twins, I will have to stop working.

Since the beginning of this year, I have had regular meetings with women who just like me have given up Judaism to marry a Muslim. I search for fellow sufferers, to talk about my new Muslim identity and the conflicts it brings with my Jewish faith. I found that I have little to complain about. Fatma for example, has to help her mother-in-law with the cooking, and in doing so must forget about all of the customs and habits in the kosher kitchen. She complained, that if she cuts the veins out of the meat, she gets comments about wasting costly meat. She cannot get used to the way her husband likes yoghurt with his meat. She also had to make the fire and cook on the Sabbath. In the beginning, she made all kinds of excuses so that she wouldn't have to. Then she offered her mother-in-law that she would cook on the Friday, if she could then be relieved of household chores on Saturdays.

Our group is now made up of six women, but I hear about other conversions every week, so we will likely be getting some new members. It is something like a homecoming; we all have the same problems, no matter how different our backgrounds are. I am the only one who has been to school, as most can neither read nor write. They have asked me to teach them; which would then be an excellent excuse for our afternoons together.

Kalsoom, who does not live with her in-laws, has solved the problem of celebrating the Sabbath by cooking all the Sabbath dishes just like the Jewish women on Friday night, keeping them warm and serving them to her husband on the Sabbath. He has obliged, as she is an excellent cook. Hafsa has proposed to her husband to include the main Jewish holidays like Yom Kippur, Shavuot and Pesach in their family traditions, which he agreed to, with the stipulation that she not advertise the fact to others. Most of us are able to hold onto much of our Jewishness, if we do not bring attention to it.

But then there is the question of the language. We all speak our Targum, and now live in an environment where Kurdish is spoken. Hafsa and Kalsoom want to teach their children Targum. I too would like to teach my son our language, but is that safe? Wouldn't that draw too much attention on us?

And that brought us to the matter of how much of our faith we can pass onto our children? I have not yet figured this out. Kawa agrees that our children must know their background, but they will be living in an Islamic environment. Won't the Jewish knowledge get in the way? Would it not be a burden, in a world where Jews no longer play any significant role? From the women in our little group I have the most knowledge, and that question preoccupies me more than it does them. With them, it is more about traditions and habits, and they do not seem to realize that too is a means of expressing their faith.

I am happy about our gatherings, where I get support and advice and can blow off steam, when it all becomes too much. Kawa is sweet and caring, and his mother has accepted me whole heartedly, but I still do not feel completely at home in my new life. And I know that the old life will never completely disappear, no matter what happens to the Jews in Iraq.

There is a new wave of anti-Zionism coming over us, now that it has been decided Iraqi troops will be withdrawn from Palestine. It is of course our fault that our boys have suffered such great losses. And along with the troops, the Arab refugees come too. We now have a few thousand of them in Iraq. I have heard that there are plans to place them in the homes of Jews who have left for Israel. There has also been the suggestion made, that the Jewish clubs and schools in Baghdad must be made available for their reception. These Arabs have started to play a role in education, thus indoctrinating the Iraqi youth with anti-Zionist propaganda. There must be a relationship to the fact that more Jews again want to leave.

On the other side, the new government has a more moderate policy in relation to the Jews, which means that people now are more willing to talk and think about joining their family in Israel. Underground groups are again active arranging the journeys.

When I was in Penjwin for Nowroz, Yesula was also preparing to leave. The plans are already set. Shalom will then be able to marry and move in with abba and ima. This plan seems to suit everybody. Yesula has always been interested in Zionism, but like Uncle

Nasim he never took the step. He seems once again inspired by our uncle, who appears to be active in the underground movement, now that he is in Baghdad so often and cousin Moshe is running the shop in Sulaymaniya.

Yesula told me he wanted to help build Eretz Israel, because it was the Jewish homeland for all of us. For us Jews, living in an Arab world is becoming more and more difficult, he said. Israel is by far no longer just the place for the survivors of the war in Europe.

I asked him to look for Azam's grave, once he's got settled. He looked at me in surprise: I left him waiting, then married a goj and now I wanted him to visit his grave?

I do not expect my brother to understand what Azam meant to me, and why I have made the choices that he never would make. I simply nodded.

He pointed to my belly, and said he hoped that at least I would raise my child as a Jew. Yesula has never agreed to abba's call for mixed marriages. He saw my marriage to Kawa mainly as a solution to get a husband for his old maid of a sister. Once again, I greatly miss Sasson, who always understood me so much better.

I made no attempt to explain to Yesula why his demand was impossible. I answered him that my son will be a Jew in a Muslim family. He nodded in satisfaction.

June 27, 1949

Ibrahim was born last week. A big, healthy baby, and happily he was alone. His arrival has completely changed my life. Everything now revolves around him. Feeding him, changing him, rocking him when he cries, and calming him when he has cramps. Kawa is enormously blessed with his son. Our happiness is nearly perfect.

October 10, 1949

Uncle Nasim has been arrested in Baghdad, during a police action to shut down the underground Zionist movement.

Late in the summer, the police, who were searching for communists, stumbled across a group of Zionists. The leaders of this movement were able to escape to Iran. Those who were caught, betrayed their comrades and in the subsequent large-scale operation that followed there were some fifty arrests. Uncle Nasim was one of them.

We are starting to notice, that the stories about our misadventures have reached the rest of the world. In America and Europe, reports are made about Jewish arrestees being badly treated in Iraq. American newspapers are reporting on "Iraqi Terror," where thousands of Jews are being tortured in special concentration camps. The government denies that, and I can in all honesty not imagine it; we surely would have heard something about it! In an effort to prove these reports wrong, contact has been allowed with the detainees, which is how we know about Uncle Nasim's fate. Cousin Moshe has been able to visit him in prison. The American reports have been the cause for much unrest in the Jewish community in Baghdad. Hundreds of women have gone to the office of the chief rabbi, to beg him to protest against the arrests. The dissatisfaction about rabbi Kadouri is mounting; he is said to do little for his people. As a protest, a Day of Fasting and Mourning was announced whereby all the Jewish shops, schools, clinics and banks were closed. Baghdad was virtually paralyzed for a day. Perhaps this will convince people how important Jews are, with their banks, merchants and doctors.

In September, Yesula was able to leave by way of Iran for Israel, just in time before the arrests. He let us know, that the entire family withstood the journey well, and that they were waiting in a temporary camp until they have a house designated to them.

I have had little time to write in the past months. Ibrahim is an active child, who demands much attention. I went back to work in September, and when I am at home all my time and attention goes out to my son. I hear what is happening around me, but it does not affect me as it once did. The happiness of my family controls my life. Perhaps now this journal can finally come to an end. Because compared to misery, little can be written about happiness.

11 DEPARTURE

May 25, 1950

More than fifty thousand Iraqi Jews have registered for their emigration to Israel. It is so unbelievable, that I have picked up this notebook that I had nearly forgotten. In March, the government decided unexpectedly to implement a special law, which allows Jews to leave Iraq if they surrender their Iraqi nationality. The reason given, is that since lifting the state of emergency so many Jews have left illegally, that "it is not in the public interest to force people to stay in a country if they do not wish to do so." Through this law, Jews who left the country illegally, will also lose their Iraqi nationality if they do not return within two months.

The government had a kind of exchange in mind: for the Jews that leave, Arab refugees could then come in. They could move into the empty Jewish homes. The law will be in force for the period of one year. It is a complete turnaround: after the government spent years fighting Zionism and an Israeli state, they are now promoting the emigration to Israel. The ministers must be feeling pressured by the fact that since December, some four thousand Jews have left the country by illegal routes.

The actions against the underground Zionist movement seem to have had little to no effect. As Uncle Nasim and thirty-two other active members have been in custody since October, others have taken over their work. The fact that we have a new rabbi in Baghdad, who is a supporter of the emigration to Israel, most likely also has contributed to the increase in the number of illegal departures.

Those who thought that people would be happy with a legal solution, were disappointed, as there was little interest for it in the beginning. When I spoke to abba about it in Penjwin in March, he anticipated that only a few thousand people would take advantage of the opportunity. Only the people who were already planning to join their children or family, and who otherwise would have left by illegal routes.

He said he was not at all considering following Yesula to Israel. He had asked them repeatedly, but ima also has no desire to go. Let the poorer people go, abba said, for them Israel means an improvement. For our family it barely does.

Kawa thought that most of the people who had wanted to go and join their children, have already done so. I noted that since the cancellation of the state of emergency, the situation has improved. And above all, the government cannot want to be rid of all the Jews, Kawa said, as they control the Iraqi economy, with their banks and trade.

Early April everything changed. On the last day of the Pesach, Abu Nawas Street in Baghdad was crowded. Many Jews stayed out until late. That night, around nine thirty, a bomb went off in a café, where Jews for the first time in eight days were eating regular bread, instead of the matzoth, the unleavened bread of the Pesach. Four visitors were seriously injured. The police announced shortly afterwards that they had arrested three Jews in connection to the attacks.

With that, the fear is alive again. Jews are under attack, and are even being given the blame for it. No one believes that Jews in Iraq will be able to have a normal life ever again.

The result was a run on those synagogues where civil servants had their temporary offices to register those who wanted to leave. Between the beginning of April and now, some fifty thousand people have registered. That is a little under half of all the Jews in Iraq. If that continues, there will not be any Jews left here at all.

Even abba seems to have changed his mind. He is now thinking of registering as well – while just two months ago, he had definitively refused any thought of departure – this man who tried everything to keep us in Iraq. If everyone left, he would no longer have any students, he said through the telephone that Kawa had installed in my parental home. The neighbours were leaving, the butcher, the baker, my uncles. Soon the Jewlakan would be empty.

I pleaded with him, to just wait and see what happen a little longer. Perhaps they are just saying that they are going, but will not really leave. But I don't even believe that myself. Whoever registers, has, according to the official documents, fifteen days before they lose their Iraqi nationality. Then any return is no longer possible.

October 4, 1950
Sasson has moved to Sulaymaniya with his family. I am happy with his arrival, because I was afraid that there would be no one left, who shared my Jewish history, with the exception of my group of converted friends. The past months, thousands of Jews have left. They sold their belongings, and were transported to Baghdad by trucks. By way of Cyprus they flew to their final destination. It is said that around a hundred thousand Jews have registered to leave. How many will be left?

The Jewlakan in Penjwin has changed. Muslims have bought the homes. The same has happened here in Sulaymaniya too. The Jewish neighbourhood is now a mixed one. Still missing are the mosques, but they will certainly come, I think.

The last time I had seen Sasson was in Mosul, when I went there this summer to visit ustad Yacoub. I was worried about the old hakham. When I did not find him in the yeshivah or synagogue, I knew something was wrong.

At his home, I was welcomed by Rivka, who was still looking after him. Ustad Yacoub was lying on the pillows in the visitor's room. He had difficulty in getting up, then gave me a fatherly hug. He asked about my health and that of my husband and son, and about the school where I was teaching. I had gotten the life that I had left everything behind for, he concluded. I heard the pain behind that observation, and imagined what his life was now like, with an emptying Jewlakan and worsening health. I felt sorry for him.

He said his community has shrunk by half. And the school was changed completely, now teaching modern Hebrew and English, to prepare the children for their new lives in Israel.

I asked about the yeshivah. He said he would close it, as soon as the last students had left for Israel. Everyone had registered. Even if I had not left, my work in Mosul would have ended. We looked at each other sombrely. I wondered if anyone would be left. He shook his head. The regulation will still be running for another four months. He expected that we would have a total of about 40,000 Jews left in Iraq, and then mostly in Baghdad, because that is where most of the wealthy Jews lived. He compared it to pulling on the loose thread in a rug. It unravels. Why would you stay when the butcher, the baker, the weaver, the goldsmith and your family have all left, and when the schools have closed too? Our community was completely dislocated, he said.

Ustad Yacoub thinks that the incident with the rafters in Zakho has especially caused much damage, since it compromised the trust in the community. Most of the rafters are now serving long prison sentences for a crime that none of us understands. If you no longer are permitted to sing or dance as we have done for centuries, what is left?

I could see that the conversation was tiring for him. He had aged more in two years than you would expect. The life without Asenath's mother, with a changing Jewlakan, with far fewer friends around him – it all had left its scars.

I asked him about his plans. He shook his head. How could I ask that? He and I were the last Jews in Iraq. His place was here. Here is where he was born, and it is here he would die. Even later on, when all of the faithful had left? I asked. He thought only a few would stay behind. The elderly, who like him did not want to be replanted. For them, he would remain to be the hakham.

For how long, I wondered. Rivka told me that the old man could only manage it to the synagogue with the help of one of the students. But he refuses to see a doctor. Even without the doctor's advice, I know what is wrong. Life is slipping as sand through his fingers. His resistance against leaving has been ignored. He has lost his function in the Jewlakan in Mosul. His life's work is being destroyed, right before his very eyes.

When the hakham was resting, a messenger came. I was summoned to come to Zagros, the Kurdish husband of Salha. His father, the agha, had recently died, and he had taken over his affairs, Rivka told me. I get into the backseat of the automobile Zagros had sent. He must be doing well. More and more of the rich bought one of these. We rode to the family home. Inside Salha took me in her arms. She asked about Ibrahim, and why I had not brought him along? We exchanged the latest news. About her two children, her husband, her life outside the Jewlakan.

Her father was considering taking advantage of the scheme, she then said. I looked at her in amazement. He supported Zionism, but had turned just as fiercely against the departure of Iraqis to Israel as ustad Yacoub. I thought about abba, whom I haven't heard talking about a departure for months now. She told me he thinks that those who stay behind, will have a very difficult time. That he was busy transferring his businesses to Zagros. She thought that he would register soon. When I asked her about her own plans, she smiled. Just like you, she said. Her life is here. Her husband, her children.

Aren't they the most important in life, a familiar voice said from by the door. I turned around in surprise. My brother took me in his arms. He was coming to Sulaymaniya, he announced without much ado. I was happy to hear that. Finally, someone who is coming closer, instead of leaving for a distant, strange land. But was it safe enough? Sasson said that the old accusations are forgotten, now that he is a Muslim. He is going to establish himself as a weaver. As so many are leaving, there will be a demand for good craftsmen, he said.

January 30, 1951

Abba has registered himself, ima, Shalom and Benjamin for departure. They are leaving Iraq, they are leaving Penjwin, they are leaving me.

The bombing of a synagogue in Baghdad, has put everything and everyone back on alert. The bomb was detonated, when Jewish families were registering there for the departure scheme. A child was killed, and dozens more were injured. It is being said that the Zionists are behind the attack, in an effort to frighten people and lure them to Israel. People are registering in droves to leave.

I was completely devastated, when abba phoned me to announce his plans. Kawa told me to go there, to take a few days off from school, and go and talk to them. Perhaps I could change their minds. Sasson, as concerned as I was, decided to join me. It was a difficult journey, as the roads were impossible for cars due to the snow. The last bit we had to travel as in the old days, by horse and wagon.

Ima took me in her arms, excited about my new pregnancy. Abba was sombre and distant, quite consumed with the decision he felt was being forced upon him. Ima brought us to the visitor's room, that was comfortably warm thanks to the oil heater. That place has so many memories for me. While ima served us a meal, we listened to what abba had to say.

He showed concern about how Jews will be able to survive in Iraq. He said the Jewlakan will become a mixed quarter. Mosques will be built; the Jewish life will disappear. I mentioned to him that he is the one who has promoted the mixing of the people, but he shook his head. He thought that if we were to live closer together, we would be safe. He had never wanted the Jewlakan to disappear altogether.

Sasson asked if he thought not to be able to live in a mixed neighbourhood. Abba said that his life is connected to the synagogue, to the Torah school. Will there still be enough followers, enough children? Abba saw no other life for himself in Iraq, than the life he knew, I realized.

And would we still be allowed to practice our own faith? he asked himself out loud. Sasson did not see the problem. What kind of threat would a small group of Jews pose? The smaller our group becomes, the more vulnerable we would be, abba answered. When I asked him what he was planning to do in Israel, he pointed out that there will be enough children that need to learn about the Torah.

We fell silent. The decision seemed to be irreversible. Was there nothing that could convince abba to stay? I asked softly. He remained silent, and simply shook his head.

Sasson made another attempt. He spoke about the role that abba had to play in Penjwin. How his departure would pull the last holdouts over the line, and the Jewlakan would be emptied. Abba waved that off. Even if he stayed, this was destiny. It would not allow itself to be stopped.

We could not convince him. Two days after our return to Sulaymaniya, he reported his planned departure and signed the *Tasqueet* agreement. My children will grow up without their grandparents.

March 21, 1951

Even Nowroz is different from other years. Spring is late, and it is too cold for the usual picnic in the mountains. The dancing in the streets cannot tempt me this time, even if my growing belly would allow it. It is not a time for celebrations.

It is the last Nowroz with abba and ima. We are trying to keep the sadness far from us, but are failing miserably. The latest news is not helping. The government has accepted a new law, which freezes all the property and assets of the Jews who have registered to leave. It is so unfair: the tens of thousands who have already left could sell their homes, and take care of their affairs. My family is only allowed to take a mere fifty dinars out of the country.

Abba has asked Sasson to take over the house. He refused, because the business in Sulaymaniya is just starting to do well. In Penjwin he would have to start all over again. Then Abba made the same offer to Kawa and me. I had not counted on this, but if none of us takes over the house, it would be confiscated. Did I really want to return to Penjwin? Would there be work for me here?

No longer living with my in-laws. It has both pros and cons. Who would cook then, and who would look after the children when I would be at work? Kawa said we could find someone to do that. He thought it was a good idea, having a house of their own. But then we would be living as Muslims in the Jewlakan, I pointed out. He said that we would not be the only ones, and he was right: even the old Jewish sanctuary and the garden around it have been sold to a wealthy Muslim. The Jewlakan is emptying out. If we come to live here, then it will be among the Muslims and perhaps a few Jews who stayed behind.

He could start his own school, Kawa said dreamingly. Then I understood it. Kawa saw a future for himself in Penjwin. A new challenge.

I have to get used to the idea. Coming back to my hometown, to live as a Muslim in the house where I was born as a Jew. And leaving my life in Sulaymaniya.

October 6, 1951

The trucks drove into Penjwin this morning.

It is a sad day that ends weeks of uncertainty. My family is leaving. Abba, ima, Shalom and Benjamin got into the first vehicle. Each with a suitcase and some hand luggage. They must leave their belongings behind, in the house where Kawa and I moved in last week. We are going to renovate it and build a second floor with a slanted roof, so that we have enough space for our young family.

And eventually, once I am done writing, I will hide this journal, with the Sabbath silver and the other possessions that I am keeping safe for abba and ima. For when they come back – or for the lucky finder, after my death.

The entire village had come out. Kawa and I walked with them, to the trucks. Ibrahim holding his hand, Mariyam in my arms. I am happy that ima has at least been able to see her granddaughter, and can take the image of her to the distant Israel.

We cried, when the trucks left. Everyone. Even the new residents of the Jewlakan. Together we cried for saying goodbye to our loved ones and friends. But mostly for the end of an era.

Jesaja says: They, who were banned to Assyria or driven to Egypt, shall return and bow before God, on the holy mountain in Jerusalem. His prophecy has been realized.

The book lands onto the floor.
What a fool I am, Zara thinks to herself. Then she says it again aloud, listening to her voice in the quiet room. To see if it is real, that she is not dreaming or has gone mad. She grabs a piece of paper.
My house. Arrow: Rahila's house.
Rahila and Kawa, she writes. An arrow*: Kawa = grandfather Ibrahim. Arrow: Uncle. Mariyam. Arrow: daykem*
Blind I am, blind. All the time I felt so connected to Rahila, not realizing that she is my very own grandmother. That is why I felt such a bond with her! Of course! That is why I want to understand it, why I must continually learn more about it! That is why I am unable to stop, as if it is a kind of addiction. It is my own background. Rahila has buried the book, I was to find it. For me. She wanted me to know. I am her granddaughter.
She picks up the book from the floor. Opens it and stares at the words on the first page. The words that she could not read. Because they were in Aramaic, she now knows.
It is as if lightening has struck.
My God, I am Jewish.
If Rahila is my grandmother, and her daughter Mariyam is my mother, then I am Jewish. Because that is passed on by the lineage of the mother. Not just Kurdish, but Jewish. Why has daykem never said anything about this? Not even, when we dug up the treasure, or when they saw me behind the computer searching for the background of it? She must have known. Didn't she? She must have known what

grandfather's key was for. When we found the treasure, she wasn't really that surprised, now that I think about it. She must have known that her mother was Jewish. Or had grandfather decided that it would be safer if she did not know about her Jewish roots? As many of the other Benjews in Kurdistan had done with their children?
"Gosh. I am a Benjew."
She grimaces.
She walks to the mirror. Could you see it? Critically she looks at herself. A normal face. That nose? Hmmm….
Then she remembered the yellowing picture.
My great-great-grandmother. My Jewish grandmother.
She compares her face in the mirror with the one in the picture. The nose, the mouth, the shape of the face.
"Wow," she says to her reflection. "She could be my sister."
It is true. The mirror doesn't lie.
She drops back down onto the bed, the picture in her hands.
Why has daykem never told us this? Why didn't she want me to know? Perhaps, because being Jewish in Kurdistan is still viewed with negativity, or could there be another reason?
Soran. He knows nothing of this. How can I tell him? How will he react? Will he still want to marry me, now that I am Jewish? A Jewish bride?
Soran.
With a shock she remembers. Soran, in the prison. In the interrogation room. Her fiancé, which she keeps forgetting every time when she dives back into the journal. Once again, she is ashamed for not giving him the attention he

deserves. But her aunt says that he will be released in the morning, she reminders herself, in an effort to try and remain calm. She sighs. Soran is suddenly so far away. What is happening to her, is so big. Her life has suddenly changed drastically. Everything has come to be in a different light. He will no doubt land on his feet.

If only she could share it with someone. Banu. How would she react? She grabs her cell phone, has already found Banu's number, but lowers it again. She must first talk with daykem. That must happen, before anything else. She must understand it. She zaps to her mother's number, but then clicks it away impatiently. This is too big. This cannot be done over the phone.

She throws the phone onto the bed. Hurriedly, she puts the clothes that are laying scattered throughout the room in her backpack. The picture goes back into the journal. Some books that no longer fit in the pack, go separately in a plastic bag.

What will Aunt Awat think, when she comes home and realizes that Zara is gone? Calling her is no option, because then she will only try to stop her. Leave a note then?

I will phone her when I am in the taxi, Zara decides.

The checkpoints, she thinks then. Panic grips her heart. How will I manage to get through?

For a moment she pauses undecidedly with her backpack in her hand in the middle of the room.

But I have to go home. I must speak to daykem. It must go well at the checkpoints. Why would they be looking for me? But if Soran has given my name, and they then arrest me? What will happen then?

No, he hasn't talked. That is why he is still being held, she suddenly knows for sure. Because he refuses to cooperate. She must at least give it a chance, and just play the dumb but attractive little woman, if the security officers become difficult. That usually works well enough...

She looks around the room. The evidence of the week-long visit is nearly wiped out.

The most important week of my life. Who could have predicted that?

I am not just a Kurd. I am a Jew. In me, centuries of Jews live on.

Suddenly, she smiles. Life is truly interesting.

"Where did you come from, all of a sudden?" Zara's mother is sitting at the kitchen table. Her knife is left hanging in the air above a half-peeled potato. Zara sets her backpack down by the door, without uttering a word.

"Did you come alone? Did Awat let you go?"

Zara puts down the plastic bag, next to the backpack.

"Did you have any problems at the checkpoints?"

She looks at her mother. Sees in her the resemblance with the woman in the picture. She rubs her arms. How do you begin to talk about something so big?

"Why are you just standing there? What is wrong? Is it something with Soran?"

In the taxi she had decided that she would start about Rahila – but her mother doesn't know that she has found the book. Maybe she doesn't even know that there is a journal.

"Zara are you sick, is that why you came back? What is wrong, girl? Did something happen on the way here?"
Her voice begins to sound concerned. The knife has fallen onto the table.
Zara drops down onto one of the kitchen chairs. "We are Jewish, dayke," she blurts out.
On her mother's face she sees relief is taking the place of surprise. Then she laughs a mocking laugh. "Who has tried to convince you of this, daughter?"
Zara looks at her seriously. "Dayke, stop it, you know that it is true."
"Where ever did you get that idea?" Her mother's look is stern, almost cold. "Oh, wait a minute. You thought that because we have found a Jewish treasure under the house, that somehow makes us Jews? That is nonsense, Zara. That treasure is from the previous residents of our house."
"From your mother, from Rahila. She buried it herself when she came to live here with grandfather Kawa."
"She buried the treasure of the previous residents, Zara." She sounds impatient, almost angry. "Who has told you all of this, and why do you believe it?"
Zara looks at her mother and wonders. Why does she keep denying it? Does she really not know?
"The previous residents were your grandparents, dayke," she said confronting her. "When they went to Israel, their daughter Rahila stayed here. She had married a Muslim, but she was Jewish."
Her mother, who had gotten up, sits back down.
"What are you saying Zara? How did you come up with this? My mother was a Jew? You act, as if you knew her

personally! But I barely knew her myself! Where are you getting all of this from?"

Zara is barely listening. She hears only the tone of indignation. Why is her mother so angry? Was it supposed to remain a secret?

"Why have you kept this from us, dayke? Why were we not allowed to know our true background? And why are we not allowed to know our family in Israel?"

Her mother looks at her, clearly stunned. "Family in Israel?" she repeats.

"Rahila's brothers went to Israel."

"Zara, what is this? What are you talking about? I don't have any uncles."

"Dayke, do you really not know this? Or are you just pretending not to?"

"My dear, why would I deny it, if it was true? Your grandfather told me that the treasure belonged to the previous owners. And not there was any family connection. Whatever gave you this idea; what makes you so certain?"

"I found Rahila's journal."

Her mother stares at her. Behind her dark, inquisitive eyes Zara can almost see the wheels in her mind turning.

"Show me."

When Zara puts the journal on the table, her mother wipes her hands off on her apron.

"So, this is what you have been busy with, these past months."

Carefully she picks it up and opens it. "Rahila, Jozua's daughter. June 1, 1941," she reads slowly.

Zara is silent. She waits. She sees her mother turning the pages, stopping here and there to read. Minutes pass by in silence.

"The journal of my mother," she says, her voice trembling. She strokes the red fabric on the cover, as Zara too has done so often during the past weeks. Zara has to keep herself from yanking the book out of her hands. For weeks now, it has been her most prized possession. Now she must share it.

Daykem has more right to it than I do, she kept telling herself. Rahila is her mother. But she wrote it for her granddaughter, and that is me.

"You have read all of it?"

Zara nods. "Only at the end did I realize who she was."

"Tell me what she wrote. I cannot wait until I have read all of it."

Where to start? "She describes why the Jews left in the fifties, about the hatred against the Jews, the Zionism, the threats."

Her mother nods impatiently. "But who was she, Zara?"

"She was a rabbi who lost the love of her life, and then her faith too."

"Tell me Zara, tell me. A rabbi? Can a woman be a rabbi?"

"No, dayke, actually not," she says as she begins to tell the story of her grandmother's life. Her mother interrupts her repeatedly when she does not understand something, or wants other information, or to proclaim her amazement.

"That your grandfather never told us that my mother was a rabbi," her mother said with a sigh once Zara was finished. "You really had no idea?"

Her mother caresses the red cover again. "He wanted to protect us, Ibrahim and me. Being Jewish was dangerous; in the sixties once again, Jews were being executed in Baghdad."

"But here in Kurdistan, it was different," Zara protests. "Mala Mustafa Barzani even went to Israel to visit his childhood friend from their hometown of Barzan. President Barzani has been there too. It seems that there continue to be good contacts between the Barzani's and Israel. And it is said, that their security officials have been trained by the Israelis."

"Your grandfather must have thought that it was better this way," her mother maintains. She slides the book back over to Zara. "Keep this in a safe place. I want to read it, but not now."

Zara looks at her mother in astonishment. She does not understand. Not read it now? Wouldn't you want to know everything, if you had just found out that the mother you barely knew, had written about her entire life! "But it is your mother!"

"Let me get used to the idea, Zara. And maybe you shouldn't discuss it with anyone else."

How can you be quiet about such big news, Zara wonders, somewhat bewildered.

"It is better for your father's job, if no one knows about this."

Zara looks dismayed at her mother. She discovers that she is Jewish, and does not think about the consequences for herself, but only of those for her husband.

But this is too big, to keep quiet. Zara cannot do that.

"Soran must be told."
"Yes, you are right about that, janakam. Shouldn't you phone, to see if he has been released?"
For the umpteenth time today, Zara feels guilty.
"Aunt Awat thinks that her phone calls will not have any effect until tomorrow morning," she said somewhat apologetically. "But perhaps she is wrong. I am going to make some calls."

Penjwin is different today. Is it the colours? Or is it because spring is on the way, with a sun that causes the fresh grass to smell of the season?
Zara walks through the streets of her city, on her way to the house of Soran's parents. She feels somewhat out of place, as if the city no longer is hers. As if the man from the vegetable shop and the policeman she greets, have roles in a play she plays no longer a part in. She is unable to put her finger exactly on where this feeling comes from. With her new knowledge, Penjwin is still just as much her hometown as before, the place where she has grown up, where she learned to walk and speak, where she has gone to school and where she became engaged. And even more importantly: it is the ground of her new forefathers. The history of her Jewish family is played out here.
She tries to shake the feeling, and to bring her thoughts back to Soran and what must be done for him, but then she is suddenly standing in the middle of lush, green plants. Without realizing it, she has walked to the place where the synagogue must have been. The river from that time has been changed to a mere stream, as a result of the dams

which were built upstream. There are new buildings along the riverbanks, but her feet have brought Zara to a path between the buildings that leads down to the river. I must have played here as a child, she thinks vaguely. Why am I here?

That flat rock there, is that where Rahila had sat so often? Where she was with Azam, when she told him that she would not be going with him to Israel? With her father, when he had asked her to marry Kawa?

Zara sits down on the stone. Her grandmother had experienced her defining moments here. She came here, whenever she had to make difficult decisions. Zara tries to imagine the fast-moving river from back then. She must overlook all the plastic water bottles and cans lying around. Green plants cover the banks, trees cast their long shadows. It must have been stunningly beautiful. The low sun has cast its golden glow over everything. A bird begins to sing. Zara turns her face towards the sun and listens. With eyes closed she takes deep breaths of mountain air.

A hand rests on her shoulder. Surprised she looks up. There is no one there.

Her heart skips a beat. Shaken she looks around her. Nothing is moving. No one can be seen.

She has imagined it. She takes a deep breath, and once again turns her face to the setting sun. In silence she listens to the bird. The calm returns once more, and with that her thoughts come too.

What will Soran say, when he hears what she has found out? Why is she so worried about it? What is the uneasy feeling, that she is walking around with; what does it have

to do with him? Can she really expect him to share her fascination of the Jewish heritage of Iraq? He knows nothing about the journal, and everything she needs to tell him about her Jewish heritage, might shock him.
He will not like it at all, of that she is suddenly very certain. Just as Azam did not like the fact that Rahila went to Mosul to study, and that she built a career there. Because that excluded him. Rahila was brighter than he was, and through her studies, that fact quickly became obvious to everyone.
That is not the case with us, she thinks. But Soran envisions a caring role for me in our marriage. My career is far inferior to his. If I want to work, it must fit his busy lifestyle.
And my new past will exclude him, she knows without a doubt. He cannot relate to it. At the very most, he will have negative feelings about it, due to the way the world around them views Jews.
She thinks of her mother, who foresees a problem if the party discovers that Zara's father is married to a Jew. And therefore, tries to deny the fact.
I cannot do that, Zara thinks, if Soran wants me to deny my heritage, then...
Yes, what then?
She sighs. Then I cannot marry him.
Something in her rebels: this is too absolute. Is it so important then? I have only just found out? How can I make a decision, just like that?
A breeze glides along her arm. Zara looks at the goose bumps that come up as a result. She feels no panic, not even surprise anymore.

This is a magical place, just like the synagogue of Al Qosh. Here my family lives on.
That is why I am here, Zara suddenly realizes. This is important. I must realize that I am not alone, that I am a part of something much greater than I ever knew about before.
And that everything is different, from this moment on.

When she finally reaches Soran's house, it is already dark. With the sun, all the warmth of the spring day disappeared. Zara shivers in her thin blouse, and is happy when she steps into the warm kitchen. There, she runs into a wall of sound. The house is buzzing from the activity.
Soran's mother stands laughing with a woman Zara does not know. She fills the glasses on the tray with strong tea.
"...happily listened to her," she says.
"If Hero Khan gives an order, then they have to," the young woman laughs. "I am happy that I was able to do something."
It takes Zara less than a second to make the connection between the activities in the house, the many automobiles in the street, and the order that the Iraqi first lady Hero Khan is said to have given. Could it be true, she thinks surprised, which is immediately followed by: Why do I not know about anything?
"Soran is free?"
The women look up in surprise.
"Zara! Where were you? We could not reach you?"
Soran's mother puts down the teapot and takes Zara in her arms. "He was brought home half an hour ago." And with a

soft voice, only meant for her ears: "He had a hard time. They were very rough with him."
Soran's mother pushes her towards the door. "He will be happy to see you."
On the way to the living room, Zara glances at her watch. She stops abruptly when she sees the time, and looks again. It is seven o'clock. More than two hours ago, she left for Soran's house. Had she spent all that time by the river? Never! What has happened to her? It has been dark and cold now for a while, so why did she not notice this? And why did her cell phone not work?
She takes it out of her pocket. It is off, she sees in her amazement. She never turns the thing off; normally she only turns off the sound when needed. That is odd. Is the battery empty? She turns the phone back on and walks into the filled room.
When she sees Soran, the phone makes its welcome tune. Distracted she puts it back into her pocket, her eyes focused on Soran's swollen face. He has a black eye; his cheek is red, and his lip swollen. There are blood stains on his wrinkled shirt and pants. Yes, they were without a doubt rough on him.
From the doorway, she watches how he talks to his brother, and a friend. And registers with a distant precision the absence of happiness in seeing him, or of shock because of his injuries. There is no urge to run to him and hold him tight. No great relief that he is back; that he is no longer in that cell she feared so much.
What has happened to her?

Soran notices her. His eyes greedily take in her face; his mouth forms a smile that immediately disappears in a grimace of pain.

Zara forces her feet into action. Soran takes her in his arms. She kisses his one almost unscathed cheek and smells his sweat and dirt from a night and a day spent in a filthy place.

"I did not betray you," he says in her hair.

She knows what he is not saying: others I did. "I know," she says softly.

"Hold me tight; it was so cold in that cell."

Zara tries to pull herself out of her state of indifference. This is her fiancé! She must be happy that he has come back to her in one piece! But the spontaneity is missing; she is acting as she thinks that she would normally act.

But nothing is normal. Soran's body up against hers in a full room – that is unheard of, as you are not to show the love you feel to others. And yet it does nothing for her. She is not even embarrassed. Where is the warmth, the excitement to be so close to him?

She holds onto Soran, because she knows he needs warmth. Not only because of the cold that has crawled into his bones. Even more still, to get over his self-hatred, the repugnance he has for himself because he has lost the battle against his fear – because they have won.

She realizes very clearly that Soran needs her more than she needs him. But maybe that is how it has always been, and only now is more acute.

When Soran's mother comes in with the tea, she is almost relieved that she must let go of him.

"I tried to call you on the way here, but your phone was off," he says reproachfully.
"Battery, I think," she says, happy with the everyday subject of conversation. "Maybe I need a new one."
"I needed to hear your voice..."
The arrival of Zara's parents makes any further conversation impossible. Soran grabs her hand. When other friends walk in, he firmly holds unto it. She must remind herself that this is not odd; she is the fiancée of this young man who everyone has come to congratulate on his release. But what is being said seems to not to register.
Why does she feel so strange? Is it because she knows, that everything is different now? That her roots are different from most of the people around her? That she doesn't belong here?
Stop it, she says to herself. Snap out of this mood. Soran is back. You were worried about him. They have beaten him. You are here, now. Come on.
The room slowly empties out.
"I want to take a shower," Soran says.
"The doctor is still coming," his mother says. "He must have a look at your face."
Soran grimaces. "And the rest? I am covered in bruises, dayke."
She is visibly shocked. "Should we take you to the emergency room?"
He shakes his head, all of a sudden, he looks very tired. "I just want a hot shower."
"Let him be," Zara says softly. "The doctor will prefer a clean patient."

Gratefully he squeezes her hand.
She watches him, as he walks out of the room. He is limping with one leg, she notices.
Soran is back, but Zara is gone, she thinks. I am not the same anymore. Everything is different. How can we go on? Can we still?
The doctor enters the room. Zara looks on, as Soran's mother accompanies him to the sofa and gives him tea. They talk a bit together. It is as if she is watching them from a distance. Once again, she tries to shake off the strange mood. Has she sat too long in the cold by the river? Is she coming down with something?
What happened by the river? What was the hand on her shoulder? What happened to her phone and with the time? What happened to her?
She jumps from a hand on her arm.
"Sorry I scared you," her mother says gently. "Good, that he is free again, eh?"
Automatically she nods.
"You must let it be for now, Zara," her mother says to her so softly, that no one else could hear. "He needs you. He has a right to you."
Zara nods again. Of course. Her mother is right.
"Concentrate on him," her mother says encouragingly.
"I know, dayke," she says. "I will try."
She knows that it sounds lame, and far too disconnected. There is something missing, something is wrong. Can it be that she has landed in another phase, without the current phase being closed? What a thought – how did she come up with that?

Stop it Zara, she says to herself.

Then she thinks of Rahila, and her feelings of guilt when she heard that Azam had been killed. Her regret, that she was not with him. Her conviction that everything would have been different, if only she had made other decisions.

You do not want that, she knows. Learn from her. Do what is necessary. For Soran, but also for yourself.

"They have really worked him over," she says. "He will not have an easy time."

Her mother nods. "Your place is with him now."

12 KINDRED SPIRITS

"There," Yousef says pointing, "is where the fields must have been." Where he is pointing to, are now houses. Behind it, Sulaymaniya stretches out in the direction of the mountains.
"The Jewlakan was in fact on the outskirts of the city," Zara concludes.
"Many inhabitants had a piece of land that they grew crops on. The neighbourhood was made up of no more than twenty or maybe thirty houses, all built around the synagogue."
She turns around again to look at the building. Above the door is a sign, that states that the mosque dates from 1958. During her walk through the neighbourhood, that date had caught her attention. This must have been the synagogue, which changed into a mosque a few years after the departure of the Jews. The bottom half of the building is certainly old enough for that, and on top of it more recently a new level was built from concrete blocks.

She had taken her scarf from her purse, covered her hair, and had gone inside. It was quiet in the mosque. She was alone. Not even the imam was there.

In the back of the prayer room, she had sat down on the thick carpet and let the atmosphere sink in. High, small windows let the sunlight in, that striped across the carpet. Nothing served as a reminder of the previous function of the building. Only perhaps the women's gallery. Zara was unable to see, if that was part of the later addition to the building. The past fifty years of service as a mosque, had left more marks than anything from before, she determined disappointed.

When she got up to leave, a young man walked out from the shadows of the gallery. Surprised that she had not noticed his presence before, she answered his greeting. He walked with her to the door.

When she asked him about the history of the mosque, he had nodded enthusiastically.

"This is the old synagogue of the Jewlakan."

At the doorway, they both had stepped into their shoes. Zara noticed that the courtyard looked more authentic than the rest.

"Look, that must have been the mikve, the bathroom for the women," she pointed out, excited that she still could recognize something.

Yousef had looked at her inquiringly. "How do you know that?" he asked. "I am Yousef, and I come here often, but I have never seen you here before."

Zara put her scarf back into her bag. She hesitated. This young man came here often, but did not look like a radical Muslim. How would he react? Should she be honest?
He saw her hesitation.
"Me too," he said with a wide grin.
"What?"
Somewhat taken by surprise, Zara took a step backwards towards the gate.
He had raised an imploring hand.
"My grandfather was Jewish, I meant."
Yes, of course. He had added things up, and had then recognized her as someone who shared the same fate, Zara realized.
There must be many more young people like myself, she thought, who have Jewish roots, and want to know more about their background.
"When did you discover it?" she asked, barely able to hide her excitement.
He laughed out loud. "I have known for a long time. My grandfather was an important man in Sulaymaniya, and there is even a square named after him. And you?"
Zara told him about her Jewish grandmother, who had lived in Sulaymaniya. As they talked, they walked outside.
Yousef said that he had been born in England, but that his parents had recently returned to Sulaymaniya. And that since that time, he had been searching for the history of his Jewish family. And that he had received much help from the elderly, who had lived together along with the Jews.

Now, at the edge of the Jewlakan, they exchange the information they have discovered thus far, both excited to have met someone with the same interest.

Zara notices, how the pressure of the week of maintaining silence about something she was so passionate about, had fallen away. Finally, there is someone she can talk to about it!

Soran had been busy licking his wounds over the past days. He had relived the moments of threat and fear again and again, and was having nightmares.

That was not a situation to bother him with her stories and emotions. She had listened to him, had encouraged him to talk, and then when there was nothing left to be said, she had simply kept him company during the pained silences.

Her mother has not uttered another word about the journal; it is as if their conversation has never taken place. Only with the greatest of difficulty, Zara has managed to swallow her many questions.

Why is her mother reacting in this way? She must have also made the connections at some point? She must have looked at certain occurrences in her youth from a different point of view? Zara keeps thinking about the regret that Rahila had about her children growing up without their grandparents. How was that for her mother?

Zara hopes that the moment will come, when they will be able to discuss it. And especially, that they will be able to share this great discovery, and together decide what they will do with this newfound knowledge.

Yousef pulls her out of her contemplation. "My grandfather drank himself to death, you know," he says, with his eyes facing the mountains behind the city.

"Really?" Zara says, shocked, "that is terrible."

Yousef sombrely nods. "It was a long time ago. I never knew him."

The silence between them is broken by a scooter racing past.

"Perhaps we should look for a quieter spot to talk," Zara proposes. Her curiosity is aroused. And the meeting is too special to simply just say goodbye. She wants to stretch the time a bit longer.

Yousef knows of a hamburger place where they can drink coffee. On the way, there they point out to each other the original elements of the houses that once have stood in the Jewlakan. This is a very different neighbourhood than the one in Erbil; here there will not be any connecting doors, Zara thinks. Yousef confirms that, when she asks him about it.

"Following the departure of the Jews, the houses here were confiscated and were then rented out by the government to Muslims," Yousef explains. "With the exception of some homes that had been given to good friends, or where converted Jews lived. Do you know how those houses were called?"

Zara looks at him questioning.

"These are the houses of those, who lost the Iraqi nationality," he says solemnly.

"As if with that, they could make people forget the Jews!" Zara sniffs dismayed.

A door has been left open, and they are treated to a glimpse of the courtyard, filled with an array of green plants and flowers. "Can you imagine, having to leave everything behind," Zara says.

"I have heard, those two weeks before the exodus, the neighbourhood was just like one big bazaar. Everyone was selling their things on the street," Yousef tells her. "Later, it became known that some had buried money and their possessions."

Zara nods. "My grandparents too. That is how I found my grandmother's journal."

Yousef lets her go first into the little restaurant. The place is empty, it is still early. They find a table in the back. Yousef goes to the counter to order their drinks.

"Do you think many people have buried their things?" Zara says, thinking out loud as he returns with the steamy, sweet Nescafé.

"That is what is said," he agrees. "But I have often wondered why you would do that."

"Because they could take very little with them," Zara says. "Just a little money, and some clothes. People tried to hide jewellery in home-baked breads, but were caught."

"Then why wouldn't you just give it away? There are so many stories about friendships with the Muslims. I think that they buried it because they counted on coming back one day."

Zara thinks back to Rahila's last sentences. She wanted to keep the stuff for her parents. *For when they come back – or for the honest finder, after my death.*

"Maybe you are right," she says. "That is why the rabbi from the synagogue in Al Qosh gave the key to his Muslim friend: it was only temporary, he would be coming back."

"Wasn't it also, about them wanting to bury the past?" he asks, after pondering on the subject for a moment.

Zara looks at him in surprise; why she has not thought of it herself? Of course. Rahila had every reason to want to bury the past, and that is just what she had done. In fact, she had already begun with this task when she converted and married Kawa, disappointed as she was in the faith. She had buried her Jewish identity all together.

Being Jewish was dangerous. That is why, Kawa had not told his children anything about it. That is why Zara's mother wants nothing to do with it. For her, the past should have remained buried.

She tells Yousef about her visit to the Benjew in the Jewlakan in Erbil, and her feeling that he and his mother had also wiped out their Jewish past.

"And then we come along, and dredge it all back up," he says.

"Don't we have a right to our past then?"

Yousef nods thoughtfully. "But they too to their denial of it, Zara. They had every reason for that."

The restaurant begins to fill up with students from the neighbourhood. And then it empties out again. Yousef and Zara notice little of it, as they are both so enthralled in their stories.

"My grandfather did not want to leave, because he felt Kurdish," Yousef says, picking back up from an earlier conversation. "But he landed in a depression, when everyone left. His entire surroundings changed, because there were no friends or acquaintances left. He started to drink, and within a few short years, he was dead."

Zara is silent; she doesn't know how to react. Yousef does not seem to notice.

"The Kurdish sheik that lived next to them, immediately let his gaze fall on the widow, my grandmother. He promised to look well after her money, if she married him. How could she know that she would lose all her rights? She wanted protection, so she married the sheik and became a Muslim. Just like her daughters. One of them is my mother."

"And he spent all of the money?"

"Yes, you can say that again. Because my grandpa was very wealthy. Years later, when my mother was almost married herself, the city was putting in a road where their house used to be. When they were digging, they found two chests full of old coins, that my grandfather had obviously buried at some point."

"Wow, that is really a buried treasure. Did your grandma get them?"

"No, even though they knew who the money belonged to, they didn't give it back."

Zara shakes her head. Her parents were right, when they wanted to keep the digging up of the treasure a secret. Otherwise the city would have confiscated it too.

As Zara looks at her watch, she is shocked to see the afternoon is almost gone. She knows that she must hurry up, so that Aunt Lana will not become worried. Then Yousef asks: "Have you found your family in Israel yet?"

Zara looks up from the text she wants to type for her aunt. Concerned she looks around, to make sure that no one else heard what he said. The two men at a nearby table seem to be deeply engaged in a conversation. "Ssst...," she demands nervously. "Not so loud. No, it seems I must have a few uncles there, but I have no idea on how to find them."
Yousef grins. "Don't be paranoid. The Kurdish leaders have as the only ones in the region friends in Israel, and are not afraid to make that known. Kurdish Jews have come back here, and converted Jews have been to visit in Israel. Why should I not be able to say that aloud?"
"Have been to visit?" Zara repeats, keeping her eyes focussed on the men just to be sure.
"Yes, don't you know that? My family has also been to visit here too."
Zara's attention has now returned completely. "And you? Have you been there?"
Yousef nods. "I have aunts and uncles there, and many cousins."
"How was it?"
Greedily she listens to Yousef's account of his visit to Israel, about the modern ways of the land, about the emotional reunion with his family.
"Wow," Zara says, "I want to go too."
She tries to remember the names of Rahila's brothers. Sasson, she knows right away, but he stayed here. He had been converted too. Benjamin was the youngest. What were the other brothers called... But Sasson stayed here! Then I must be able to find him, she thinks.
"What is it?" Yousef asks when he sees her excitement.

She tells him that her great-uncle Sasson had converted and lived in Sulaymaniya, that he worked in the textile industry and had his own business.

"Then we will find him," he says, having clearly been infected by her excitement, "and your family in Israel too."

"How then?" she asks as her phone peeps. Soran sends a message asking if he can speak to her at her aunt's house. "I have to go," she says while she answers him 'in half an hour'.

"When can I see you again? You must give me all of the information about the uncles, so that we can search for them." He stretches out his arm and lays his hand flat on the table. "Zara?" She recognizes the gesture as an attempt to make contact in a society where men and women are not supposed to touch one another in public. "When will I see you again?" he asks persistently.

Zara lays her hand next to his.

What has happened, is so very special, she thinks. Why must I dash off, must I really allow myself to be lived by Soran? He can surely wait for five minutes longer.

"Give me your telephone number, Yousef." And while she calls his number so that he has hers too she says: "I am so happy that I ran into you. I could not talk to anyone about it, and I thought that I would burst. Thank you."

He shyly smiles. "We will meet again soon."

She gets up. "Zara?" Yousef asks with some urgency, when she reaches for her coat and bag. "Don't tell anyone about this, how we met one another. No one will understand."

She nods. He is right. This is too much of a coincidence, and too bizarre. Two Jews who meet one another in a mosque. With a smile, she places a hand on her heart. "Promised."

Above her, the stars are high in the sky. Despite there being no moon, Zara can still see the outline of the mountains around her. From time to time, something rustles in the grass, and in the distance, she hears a car. But everything else is silent. A gentle breeze brings the coolness from the mountains.

Soran's head weighs heavily on her shoulder. His breathing is slow and regular. Has he fallen asleep? She stays silent not to wake him, even though she has lost nearly all the feeling in her arm, and she is starting to get cold. He has after all not slept for days now.

How long will she still be able to hold him off? The evenings they spend together at their dark private place in the mountains above the city, are starting to look more and more like a fight. Without a word being spoken, except her repeated "No, Soran." As a doctor, he should know how risky it is what he wants. But how do you discuss something like that? Zara wrestles with it.

She understands his thoughts: in a few weeks they will be married. So why should they wait?

I do not want to get pregnant. There is still so much, that I want to do before I will be ready to have children.

How many other couples have had the same struggle, under this same starry sky, Zara wonders. This part of the mountain is known in the local community as "blow job mountain" due to the large number of unmarried couples that meet one another here.

How many children would have been conceived here? Just as one is expected to marry before turning 24, women are then also to have their first child within a year. Not that much has changed since Rahila's time, Zara thinks.

Could ask him to buy condoms, she wonders. She hesitates; posing that question is the same, as letting him know that she wants to have sex. A girl should not do that, unless she wants to be seen as a slut. Would Soran look at this any differently than other Kurdish men? Zara doubts it.

She cannot get the pill, which is only given to married couples, and only on prescription. No doctor would see any reason to give her this; she is healthy and there is no medical reason not to have children. Despite the jump forward that Kurdistan has experienced on an economical level, discussing sex is still seen as a taboo. There is no sex education, and the subject of 'reproduction' is skipped in biology class. That Zara knows far more than many other young Kurdish women, is due to the information she received from Aunt Awat, who has lived in Germany for many years. Last year, she had given her a book, and answered all her questions. "Don't tell your mother," she had warned her. Without her, she probably would have let Soran have his way. With all of its consequences.

What time could it be now? Should she wake Soran? Aunt Lana wants her to be home before eleven, from her movie night with friends. Zara lays a hand on Soran's forehead. "No, no, don't do it..." he mumbles. The nightmare has found him once again.

Should I look to get help for him, Zara asks herself concerned. She has read, that people who are active in the resistance and have every reason to hate the government, generally are psychologically better off after torture, than someone who is innocent. Soran clearly is part of the latter category.
"Soran, wake up," she says softly, as she strokes his cheek. His mumbling now starts to sound panicky. "I don't know anything," she is able to make out.
He does not want to talk about what they have done to him. He complains mainly about how unfair it is. He did not throw any rocks; he tried to save a life. He should not be treated this way. He has said this a few times: if they make these kinds of mistakes, what kind of government do we have? Who can you still trust?
Only when Zara rolls him from her shoulder and shakes him, does Soran finally wake up. Somewhat bewildered, he is still in the grasp of the dream. He shivers as Zara pulls him up against her. She shushes him as a child, until he loosens himself from her arms. His trembling hands stroke through his hair. "They did not want to believe me," he says.
Zara sighs. "Perhaps we should make an appointment with doctor Barham."
"I don't want a doctor."
Despite everything Zara has to smile. "Doctor Barham, the prime minister," she said explaining.
"What? With Barham Saleh? Why?"
"I think that they owe you an apology. Barham is, as the prime minister, ultimately responsible. And that can be arranged via my father and the party, I think."

"How will I be any better off then?"
Zara helps him up and folds up the blanket. "You have a right to an apology. They have made mistakes and must admit to them. They cannot treat someone who tried to save a life in this way. That cannot happen. And absolutely not, when you were only doing what is to be expected from a doctor."
Soran has stopped trembling. He takes the blanket from her. "Maybe you are right."
He is too proud to admit that he longs for an apology, Zara thinks. But if it would help him to get to grips with what has happened to him, why not?
"I shall ask my father to make an appointment for us."
In silence they drive back down. Zara realizes that the long silences between them have greatly multiplied. Soran is especially preoccupied with his arrest, and she has still not seen an opportunity to tell him about her Jewish grandmother. Because everything revolves around him. It is as if there is nothing else left to talk about. She sighs. If only they could pick up where they had left off. The daily regime of the university would do Soran good.
"When do you think the university will open again?" she asks, in an attempt to break the prolonged silence.
"I am going to work in the hospital," Soran says.
"Oh? Were you able to get an internship?"
"No, I got a job."
"Why didn't you say anything?"
"I only just found out, Zara."
She sighs once again. She remembers he wanted to get one a few months ago, but he did not tell her that he was

actually working on it. Why he does not discuss something as important as this with her? Perhaps he was still too taken by his own suffering, and he thought that she knew about it, she tells herself.

"Congratulations." She can hear how lame it sounds. "That is better than sitting at home."

"But you don't like the idea."

Zara knows, that even if she objects, she will not be able to get rid of that impression. She shrugs her shoulders. She is not in the mood for this.

"It is not, as if you have helped me very much," Soran continues.

Zara remains silent. Where is this going to?

"Your father could have at least helped me to get a good job."

"Did you ask him?" Zara automatically defends her father. She will not allow him to be accused just like that.

"No, but couldn't you at least have put in a good word for me?"

Zara sighs. She squeezes her hands together, to keep from responding. Anything she would say now, would come across the wrong way. It is hard to keep silent, because Soran's implications put their relationship in another light. Had he expected to get a good job by way of her father? Is she just a leg up for his own success?

For minutes they ride along in silence. When he stops in front of her aunt's house, Soran says: "Why are you acting like this, Zara? Can't you even grant me this? Why do I get so little support from you?"

She explodes. The entire week everything has been about him, and she has tried her very best to stand beside him, and in doing so putting herself and her own needs off. She does not deserve this. "That is ridiculous Soran, and you know that! Everything is about you, and that is all we talk about anymore! And if there is something important, you don't even discuss it with me!"

He looks at her, and frowns. "You weren't even here when I got picked up. Why did you need to go to Erbil anyway? Do you have someone there?"

"I didn't feel safe anymore in Penjwin, and you know that." The direction the conversation is taking, only makes her even angrier.

"Who do you have in Erbil?" he hammers on.

"I am not in the mood for this anymore Soran. Forget about it." She opens the door. "Find someone else, to listen to your complaining and your jealous fabrications."

She slams the door shut. With three steps she is at the door, and luckily her key slides easily into the lock. In the dark hallway she leans against the wall, to hold back her tears and calm her breathing.

What have I said? Did I mean it? Do I really want to end it? Her aunt exits the living room. "Was that Soran? Why didn't you ask him in?"

Aunt Lena isn't crazy. She knew all along she was not with her friends. "You shouldn't be arguing, janakam. The boy is having a difficult time. Give him a little space."

Is she starting too? Dismayed, Zara shakes her head. "I have a headache, auntie. I am going to bed," she says, as she walks up the stairs.

"Take some paracetamol," her aunt says, calling after her. In her room, the self-pity comes, and the tears. Thanks, but no thanks. Everyone is against her. Then follows the realization of what she has done. In a matter of a few words, she has dumped Soran. Where had that come from? She stares at her mobile. Would Banu still be awake? But would she understand? She only shows her full understanding for Soran.

It is warm in the room, and there is no government electricity. The generator power is insufficient for the air conditioning. She pushes open the window, to let in the cool evening air.

She must talk to someone. Her finger stops at Yousef's number. No, she cannot burden him with this. And especially not at this hour. With a sigh she puts her phone away. There is no one; she must do this on her own. She gets undressed and lies on the bed in her underwear.

The very thought, that she could have someone else! Unbelievable! Soran must have come up with that delusional idea when he was in jail, when he had the time to think about everything. When he still had the time to worry about her. And now he is using that, to keep himself from having to think about the time in jail, Zara understands. What has happened to him, is getting in the way of everything, she tells herself. That is what she must work on first. Helping him to get apologies for what happened would help. After that, things would surely go better between us.

She thinks about all the others, who share in Soran's experience. She has read somewhere that post-traumatic stress is the number one illness of the Iraqi population. At the time, she could hardly believe it. Soran's reaction to a day in jail has opened her eyes.

How many people are around in Kurdistan, who have experienced far worse things? Because Saddam's Baath regime arrested so many Kurds, tortured so many people. How many people bear similar scars, and what affect does that have on their behaviour?

She gets up to put on her pyjamas. The night air is cool, but she does not want to close the window. She leans against the window sill, and stares at the silent houses. There is hardly any light left. Further up, a generator is humming. Soran. She sighs and thinks: Maybe I should not have gotten engaged to him. Perhaps we do not fit together well after all. I cannot efface myself for him. And he is unable to give me the attention that I need.

Back in the bed, she realizes once again that he will have great difficulty in accepting her Jewish background. Soran does not want to be different from everyone else. Marrying a Jew will affect his status, and on the way people will look at him. That is something that he would want to avoid at all costs.

He will tell me to forget about it, to hide it. Can I do that? Do I want to? For him?

And then she remembers the matter of the job, that she should have helped him get, by way of her father. Is that why he got engaged to her? She just does not want to believe it. It knocks the footing out from under their relationship. It changes everything that has happened up until now. It cannot be true. She surely would have noticed that?

Zara throws the covers off. She is sweaty. Has the window fallen shut? No, it is still wide open. Once again, she leans up against the window sill. The moon light shines on the quiet, dark houses. The coolness calms her.

She clicks the light back on, and takes a book from her bookcase. It is better to put an end to the churning thoughts. After reading the first sentences a couple of times, the book finally get her in its grip.

In the middle of the night, Zara wakes with a start. Uncle Ibrahim. Daykem's older brother. Would he know about it?

The book that had helped her to fall asleep, falls onto the floor. Zara sits up straight in bed. Why had she not thought about this before? She is living under his roof, and sees him nearly every day. He is Rahila's son; he has seen the departure of his family to Israel. How old would he have been then, around three perhaps? Would he remember that now, some sixty years later?

Zara is wide awake. Her heart drums an excited beat. She grabs her cell phone to see what time it is, but then the call for the first prayers of the day reverberates through the open window: "It is better to pray than to sleep." It must be around three thirty. Far too early to disturb her uncle.

If Uncle Ibrahim knows, why has he never said anything about it? Is he ashamed of his heritage? Or has grandfather frightened him so badly as a small child, that he has repressed all knowledge? She sighs. Sleep will come no longer, now that these new questions have come on top of all the others.

She fishes for the book on the floor. And changes her mind. Maybe she can find something about her Jewish family on the internet, as Yousef had suggested. When her laptop comes to life, she sees an email from Yousef. Excitedly, she clicks it open. It is very short.

I have found family of yours, in Sulaymaniya. Call me. Zara stares at the words. Her eyes shoot upwards. Time sent? 03:30. She smiles. Yousef cannot sleep either.

She goes to Facebook. "Tell me everything," she orders him in a message.

The response comes immediately. "Call me."

The man was standing by the gate in front of the house, where by phone he had directed the taxi. Zara looks at him, longing for confirmation. Is that Ayub? This handsome, slim man in his forties, with shiny shortly clipped black hair? With eyes like those of a hawk, and a strong nose? This man looks nothing like her, she concludes disappointed.

When the man sees the car, a wide grin comes across his face. Zara now experiences a flash of familiarity. Who else laughs like that? Is it Uncle Ibrahim, or her brother Himen? The man opens her door, and takes her in his arms almost before she has gotten out. "I had nearly given up all hope," he says.

He holds her at an arm's length. Does she see tears in his eyes?

"Rahila's granddaughter. Finally. I think that you look a bit like her too."

Zara lets it all happen to her. The man has now taken her by the hand, and is leading her through the gate inside. Yousef can do nothing but follow them. They walk through the bare hallway to the nice room, where French couches stand along the walls and light-yellow curtains are draped before the windows. On the floor lay thick carpets.

A woman enters with a tray full of small cups of sweet coffee. Two girls follow her curiously. Zara smiles, and they shyly smile back.

Are these my little cousins?

The oldest is around eight, and helps her mother scoot the little tables into place and to divide up the cups. The youngest, that Zara guesses to be around five years old, goes to her father, who strokes her raven-black hair while she leans up against him.

"Look Zara, this is Zara," he says laughing. "Named after my grandmother. Just like you."

Stunned, Zara looks at him. Suddenly, the questions that are all competing to be asked first, somehow merge together into that one, that is more of a conclusion than a question. It is out before she realizes it.

"But then my mother knows about it?"

Ayub coughs, stricken by the question where he can only guess the answer.

"Your mother is Mariyam, Rahila's only daughter. Rahila is your grandmother. I am the youngest son of Sasson, her brother. Their mother was called Sara. Same name. Coincidence?"

"No," Zara shakes her head, "that cannot possibly be a coincidence. But why has there then not been any contact between you and us?"
"My father did not go back to Penjwin anymore, after my Aunt Rahila, your grandmother, had died."
"But he was good friends with my grandfather, wasn't he?"
As Ayub looks at her wonderingly, Zara realizes that he knows nothing about the journal. She reveals her find. He looks at her in stunned silence. Then the questions come. Which Zara happily answers. About Rahila's youth, her time in Mosul, about the departure of the family to Israel, and even what she knows about Ayubs father.
"So, he was politically active!" he says surprised. "He never told us about that, but that's no wonder, when you hear about how he had to go underground."
The oldest daughter begins to take away the cups, following instructions from her mother.
"Oh," Ayub says apologetically, "how terrible. I have not yet introduced you to my wife Nasrin and Hanan, our oldest."
Zara nods and smiles, consumed by the question that have not yet been answered.
"If I had not found the journal, I never would have met you," she says. "Why did grandfather break the contact?"
Ayub sighs. "Iraq was a difficult place for the Jews. Only after the fall of Saddam, things started opening up a bit for us, but even now, at my job, I cannot be honest about being a Jew. Your grandfather wanted to protect you."
"By wiping out the past?" Zara asks sharply.
"I understand that you are upset. But he only wanted what was best for you. And your grandmother would have agreed

with him. They did not talk about it at home, unlike us. They did not rest on the Sabbath, like we did."

"Rahila was a female rabbi. How could she possibly have sworn off the faith so completely?"

"She did just that, Zara. Very consciously too. And not just the faith, everything. The complete Judaism. Very differently from my father. Perhaps he was less cautious. He made sure we knew, and held onto our language."

"You still speak Targum? Fantastic!" Yousef says. He has been listening intently.

"With whom?" Zara asks.

Ayub smiles. "Here at home, amongst ourselves, and with my brother and sister and their children. With my cousins in Israel. And of course, up until the time of their passing with my parents too. Even my wife has learned to speak it."

Zara is almost unable to process all the information. There is more family. And Ayub has contact with the family in Israel. There is an entire family that she does not know: uncles, aunts and cousins.

Ayub explains that Aramean has become a sort of secret language within the family, and complains that their language is borrowing more and more Kurdish words, since the group speaking it is too small. But Zara is too excited to listen to him carefully.

"What happened to the family in Israel?" she interrupts him. "The journal stops when they leave," she says apologizing, as he leaves an unfinished sentence hanging in the air and looks at her wonderingly.

Ayub slowly nods. "Of course, you are right. That first." He sighs. "It is no happy story, Zara. They had a very difficult time. My grandmother Sara died from being homesick." Nasrin comes in with a tray full of glasses of tea. Ayub explains that the first years in Israel were difficult for all the Jews from Iraq, but especially for the Kurdish ones, because their level was so low. Some of them went to work on the land, or found work as craftsmen and traders. Just like most of them, Rahila's parents had great difficulty in adjusting to the new country and new ways of life. Her mother was unable to learn but a few words of Hebrew, and became isolated. Rahila's father spent much time in the synagogue. "Neither of them is still alive. Yesula, my eldest uncle, died while serving in the Israeli army. Shalom became a teacher, but he too died, in the Six-Day War. Benjamin is a rabbi. He has three children."

"And Melka and the children?"

Ayub shakes his head. "You know more about the family than we do."

"Yesula's wife," Zara explains.

"I know that Shalom's wife and children live at Benjamin's place. But I have never heard anything of Melka. Perhaps she is remarried, and the contact got cut?"

"Do you have any pictures?"

Nasrin nods, and walks out of the room. "Not from the family in Israel, because we have never met them," Ayub says.

Zara is surprised. "Then how do you know all of this?"

"Nowadays, you have Facebook and the Internet," he says with a smile. "But before that, I have once gone with my

THE JEWISH BRIDE

father to Turkey to phone them. That was shortly after the *raparin*, in 1991. My father was crying on the telephone when he spoke to Benjamin. He did not yet know, that all the others had died."

In the silence that falls, Zara stares at the melted sugar at the bottom of her tea glass. She searches for words, but can find none. His sadness is her sadness too – but then in a different way. The family that she thought she had, has been swallowed up by time.

Ayub coughs. "After that, we too tried to go to Israel. My mother wanted very much to do that. And my father realized, that that there was no longer any life here for us." He picks up a stack of pictures that Nasrin has just brought in, and hands one to Zara. A sturdy woman stares sternly at her from the picture; no grey lock in her black hair betrays her age. Zara sees the resemblance with her son and granddaughters. Ayubs resembles his mother, not Sasson.

"My father remarried in the early sixties. I think his first wife died during childbirth, but that was something, that was never discussed. My mother came from Rania, and that is where I was born and where we have lived for a long time."

"She is Jewish," Zara concludes.

Ayub nods. "My parents chose to be Jewish. We had a double life. My mother cooked Jewish food. Saturdays, on the Sabbath, we ate no meat, and we did not make a fire. We celebrated the Sabbath. She held onto the Jewish holidays. We did not fast during Ramadan. We spoke Aramean. But for the outside world, we were Kurdish Muslims."

He explains, that in Rania many descendants were living of Jews who had converted to Islam. After Kurdistan became more or less autonomous in 1991, the Islamic parties got the upper hand in this Kurdish town on the border with Iran. "They believed that they would earn a place in paradise if they killed us. That is why, we wanted to leave." And they were not the only ones. After the fall of Saddam, Kurdish Jews had been able to contact family in Israel. As a result, in 1994, a new exodus of Kurdish Jews to Israel began, with the first group being made up of some fifty people from the town of Kaladze.

"My Uncle Benjamin heard about that in Israel. He knew how many Jews still were living in Rania, and he informed the Israeli authorities about us."

Then things went fast. At the end of April in 1994, a group of 285 Jews left Rania.

"They drove to Zakho, crossed the border and went to Diyarbakir with an escort from the Turkish police. From there, they were flown with a special plane to Jerusalem. A huge celebration was organised when they arrived." He falls silent for a moment. "I heard about it on Radio Monte Carlo."

Zara was distraught. "You were not with them? Your parents were?"

Ayub reaches for the glass of water. Zara sees his struggle to control his emotions, but Yousef seems to miss that.

"Someone else went in your place," he said excitedly. "I have heard about that before."

Ayub has a drink and takes a deep breath. "We were told, that we would go with a second group. But we soon discovered that our places had been sold, and that they had been taken by non-Jews."

"What!" Zara exclaimed.

"It was at the time of the embargo against Iraq," Yousef said, taking over. "Kurdistan was being hit doubly hard, because Saddam was boycotting us, on top of the international embargo. Many Kurds were poor, and people needed money."

"Large amounts were involved." Ayub had regained his composure. "They paid nearly seven thousand dollars for our places. That was a lot of money at the time."

"And did the second group go?"

"No. I can still see the face of my father when he heard the news. He started to sweat, he was devastated. But he didn't leave it at that. I wrote a three-page letter for him, that went to Israel."

As a result, part of the group of emigrants from Rania was placed under house arrest, and following an investigation, a number of them were deported. The letter also caused problems for others in the group, after which the contact with the family in Israel cooled considerably. "Because our family was the whistle blower. In the beginning, we still had a lot of contact with them, when we hoped that a second group would still go. But then we got told: you have to do it on your own."

"That was the end of the dream," Zara realized, full of compassion for her deceased uncle.

"No, not yet. Not for my father. He sold everything: house, belongings, everything. We travelled to Turkey, to tell our story to the Israeli embassy in Istanbul. It was an expensive trip, in a difficult time. Because in Kurdistan there was a civil war raging, and the day we arrived in Istanbul, was the day when the Israeli Prime Minister Rabin was assassinated. No one had time or attention for us. Eventually, we returned home, empty handed."

Broken, they came back to Kurdistan; both financially and emotionally bankrupt. "We went to live in Sulaymaniya, which seemed safer than Rania. My mother passed away a year later." Zara mumbles her sympathies, but Ayub ignores it. "For father, the desire to go to Israel became an obsession. He made a second attempt to get into contact with the Israeli embassy in Turkey. He had to travel across the mountains, to cross the border. A difficult journey, that proved to be too much for him. He died on the way."

Zara watches how he grabs the water bottle once again. Sasson's son. How much misery has come out of staying Jewish for this family! And yet, he embraces it still.

"When he died, we were devastated. He was going to open the door for us to the Promised Land. When he died, we had lost the key."

In the heavy silence, Ayub picks up the pictures once more. While he is looking through them, his wife comes back into the room and they exchanged a few words. Zara tries to understand what is being said, but fails. So that is what Targum sounds like.

Ayub puts some pictures on the table. He points out: his father, Sasson. Before 1996, and after. The disappointment had accelerated the aging process, Zara can see clearly. Another old picture shows Sasson with Rahila and Kawa. All three posing for the camera. This is the first picture that

Zara sees of her grandmother, as at home, everything that serves as a remembrance of her has disappeared. With a shock, she sees that Ayub is right: she does look like her. Rahila is smiling at the photographer, the men look more serious. Zara recognizes the courtyard of the demolished house. There are blooming potted plants; it must be in the summer. She turns the picture over. Someone has written "1958" on the back. Not long after this, Rahila must have taken ill and died.

"Could I perhaps borrow this to scan it," she asks hesitantly. Ayub looks at her wonderingly. "Have they even destroyed the photographs?"

"I only have a picture of Rahila's grandmother, which was in the journal. But at home, we have none. I never thought anything of it. Until now."

Ayub shakes his head. "That Kawa wanted to protect you, I understand. But this goes too far."

"I have great difficulty in understanding it. Daykem denies knowing anything about it."

"She was still very young, when your grandmother passed away. Maybe she really did not know."

"And then she names me after her Jewish grandmother...?"

"It could be a coincidence," Ayub says, but Zara can hear that he is not convinced of that either. What could have happened, that would cause her mother to go to such lengths to deny her background? How can Zara convince her to talk about it?

She can feel her discontent growing. She has a right to know her past!

Ayub distracts her with a picture of him with his parents, brother and sister. He points.
"Leah lives in Rania, is married and has three children. She works for the party. My brother Yahja is a rich businessman, and an active Muslim. He even had a mosque built where he regularly goes himself."
Yousef joins in the conversation. "I have noticed that many Benjews have become very strict Muslims. Often, the neighbourhood knows them as hadji, because they have made the journey to Mecca. Can you explain that?"
Ayub smiles. "I am but a simple Army officer, no expert. I only know, that the converted are often more strict in the rules. They are searching for something to cling to, I think."
Nasrin sticks her head through the door. The aroma of meat fills the room, and Zara realizes that she is hungry.
"Who wants to wash their hands?" Ayub asks.
In the kitchen, the sofra on the floor is filled with numerous steaming bowls. Rice, chicken, sauce. Nasrin hands Zara a sweet-smelling sauce made from apricots. "This is tershana, and Ayub's mother taught me to make it. Just a little different from what the Kurds call qaisi. And the chicken, with almonds and raisins, that is really Jewish."
"We still eat many Jewish dishes," Ayub tells them, while he spoons some sauce unto his rice. "The legacy of my mother."
This is what I am missing, Zara thinks, while she heartily enjoys the food, and is generous with her compliments for the cook. When she is offered cooking lessons, she accepts them laughingly. It won't happen anyway. Because if she ever does end up getting married…

THE JEWISH BRIDE

Soran. Yesterday's discussion.

The memory rushes back in. Zara becomes flustered by it. What has she done? The entire day, there has been no contact. Not even the usual morning text, which she skipped, and Soran also sent nothing.

Is this how it goes, she wonders, is this how we will break up? Are we really finished with one another then? And is that what I want?

She is glad when Ayub asks about her brothers, and her studies, and pushes Soran away to a remote corner of her brain. Only afterwards, she will realize that she has not even mentioned him; and that the fact she is engaged has therefore played no role in the conversation.

Ayub shows to be interested in her dissertation on the deployment of Iraqi troops in Palestine and the massive exodus of the Jews in the Fifties. "Courageous," he says, complimenting her. "You do take on a taboo."

"We must bring back that knowledge. The Jewish heritage belongs to all of us," she says.

She allows Nasrin to spoon some more rice onto her plate, and pulls the apricot sauce towards her. "I am eating far too much. This is divine."

Ayub puts down his spoon, and leans against the wall. "Maybe I should warn you," he says contemplating. Yousef nods approvingly. "The negative feelings are still there, Zara. People ask me: Why don't you go back? As if I don't belong here, as if Iraq is not the land where I was born. They see us Jews still as being inferior. The social control is intense, and they do not accept us. For that reason, at my work they do not know that I am Jewish. And for the same reason, we can only marry within the family."

Zara looks at Nasrin. "I am a second cousin of his mother," she tells her.

"There is almost no one in Kurdistan, who openly dares to show that they are a Jew." Yousef said, joining the conversation once again. "I have tried to talk about it, but got all kinds of nasty reactions."

"Surely, it can't be that all that bad? There are all kinds of stories about the cooperation with Israel, and many people have compared the formation of a Kurdish state to that of Israel."

"Tell her about Rania," Nasrin says.

Ayub gets up to wash his hands. "Shall we do that with the tea?"

Back in the sitting room, Zara realises with a shock how fast the evening is progressing.

"I will take you home," Ayub promises her, when he catches her looking at the clock. "But let me tell you something more first. Because radical Muslims are getting more influence here too. They hate us Jews."

While the tea glasses are being passed out once again, he tells her about Rania in 1994, soon after the group of Jews had left for Israel.

"I stood listening to a speech by a member of the Islamic party of the spiritual leader Ali Bapir, who at the time enjoyed much power in Rania. I asked, myself but out loud, why the Islamists caused so many problems. 'You must keep your mouth shut, because we know what you are,'

someone next to me said in a threatening manner. I wanted to fight him, but some people came between us."
The incident led to a fatwa, Ayub says, issued against him by the leader of the Islamic party.
"I worked for the PUK, and there was a political struggle going on between the two parties. I discovered that there was a real plan in place to kill me."
"Was that about your politics, or about being a Jew?" Zara asked.
"They were targeting me because I am a Jew. That was what it was about. Against a random PUK member, they would never have announced a fatwa." Soon after that he was walking down the street with a friend. "He saw, that there were armed men waiting on a rooftop. Luckily, we were able to get away unharmed. I immediately reported it to an officer of the PUK. They had a grenade fired, at the spot where the men lay in wait for me."
"Wow," Yousef says. Zara shivers.
"I have never been so close to death before," Ayub says with a deep sigh. "But enough about that. The hour of horror is over. I am taking you home."

The front door opens as the car stops in front of her aunt's house. Am I too late, Zara wonders concerned. A glance at her watch reassures her, it is not eleven yet.
As she gets out, her uncle opens the gate. It clicks in her head. Uncle Ibrahim, the son of Rahila. The cousin of Ayub. Zara bends down back into the car. "It might be a good idea for you, to meet my Uncle Ibrahim."

Ayub is already next to the car. His hand outstretched, he walks towards Zara's uncle. "We are cousins," he says. And as Uncle Ibrahim stares at him in silence: "I am the son of Sasson, your mother's brother."

As Zara's uncle grabs the hand, the look on his face is one of confusion. "But didn't he go to Israel?"

Something explodes in Zara's head. Her uncle knows. Then her mother must know too. And everyone has kept silent. It is a conspiracy.

Her uncle has taken Ayub into the house. Zara stares after them longingly. Can she walk with them?

The car is still running. Yousef turns the key, and hands it to Zara. She realizes that she is happy that he was there, tonight. That she is not alone during her search, and in the process of dealing with the results of it. "Thank you," she says. Suddenly she is in no hurry to follow the men anymore. So much has been happening to her.

"Now, we are going to look for your family in Israel," Yousef says.

Zara makes a gesture of refusal. "Sorry Yousef, I need to work through all of this first. And find out why everyone has been silent about it."

Yousef puts a hand on her arm. "Take your time. I know how overwhelming this is. I will see you tomorrow."

"Tomorrow?"

"Yes, tea in our own café outside of the Jewlakan. Four o'clock?"

Zara looks at his back, as he walks away in search of a taxi to take him home. In a short time, he has become one of her best friends. What she can share with no one else, she can with him. Only not her doubts about Soran. Those she cannot share at all.

On her way inside, she takes her phone from her pocket. No missed calls, no text messages. No Soran, no Banu. And she should be coming up with news about her postponed marriage!

Is that my old life, and have I now started a new one?

Zara is not quite sure if that is a pleasant thought.

"Zara!" The call comes from the sitting room. All eyes turn to her when she enters. Her uncle motions for her to come, and sit next to him on the couch. "Ayub says that you have my mother's diary."

Zara nods. She is still out of breath. There is so much happening all at once. "Would you like to see it?"

In her room upstairs, she takes a deep breath. Finally, alone for a moment. With loving fingers, she strokes the book. More and more she is realizing just how very special it is. That Rahila's diary is not just a voice from the past, but that it also passes along knowledge to the current generation. Knowledge that was very nearly lost all together. She picks it up, and hesitates. She is on the verge of handing the book over. The men want to read it. Can she bear to be separated from it?

It is not mine. Rahila wrote as to not forget. For all of us. And I am not the only one, who has to pass along that knowledge.

She listens to her own strict words, and holds the book up tightly to her chest. She can ask to have it back. She can even offer to have it copied.

Ayub has gone to sit next to Uncle Ibrahim, as he takes the book from her. Zara sees his cautious fingers, which open the book on the cover page. He bends forward, his fingers following the letters while he mumbles the words.
"What does it say?" Zara asks excitedly.
Ayub smiles. "She has dedicated the book to you, Zara."
Stunned, Zara falls silent.
"To my granddaughter who will keep our story alive, where it has become too dangerous for us," Ayub says. "That is what it says."
Now Zara is quieter still.
How can Rahila possibly have known? That she would find the journal? Or better still: how did she know that there would be a granddaughter?

13 RECONCILIATION

Zara knows it for sure: she will never forget the look on her mother's face.
First there is amazement, then dismay, then anger.
"Zara, go to your room!" she commands.
Zara looks at the men for support, but doesn't move.
Ayub holds out his hand. "I am Ayub, your cousin, the son of your Uncle Sasson."
Zara's mother ignores the outstretched hand. "I know who you are," she says, her voice cold and distant. "Ibrahim, how could you…"
"Mariyam, give us the chance to explain, why we are here," Uncle Ibrahim says interrupting her.
"I know why you are here. That damned diary!"
Zara looks at her mother with increasing amazement. She is embarrassed for her verbal attack; she is ashamed that she does not invite her guests in. What a theatre! Awkwardly, they are standing in the courtyard in front of the house.

From the open gate, everyone can see what is going on. Zara can no longer bear it.

"Come inside, gentlemen," she says, as she tries to avoid her mother's look of rage. "They took me home, dayke, then they surely deserve at least a cup of tea?"

While talking, she steps out of her shoes and into her slippers, walking past her mother into the house. She's happy to note that the men follow her.

In the sitting room, her mother drops down onto the couch, and motions for the men to sit. She seems to have given up on her resistance. Zara slips into the kitchen. Her hope that there is a pot of tea ready and waiting on the fire, is dashed. She will have to make one herself. Maybe it is better that she is not in the room for now, she thinks.

She is anxious to hear what is going on. Unfortunately, the sounds from the sitting room do not carry over into the kitchen very well. She fills the kettle, and sets the teapot ready. Then she walks with four glasses of cold drinking water in the direction of the room.

"Your attempt to go to Israel, has brought us into huge problems," she hears her mother say.

Zara remains standing by the door.

"That was never the intention of my father. You know how good the relationship was with your father."

"What happened?" Uncle Ibrahim asks. "This is the first time, I hear anything about this."

"You were in Erbil for the party at the time," her mother answered. "Someone from the city government discovered the family relationship with Sasson. They came to the house, and asked for our identity cards."

"Really?"

"You don't make something like that up, do you?"

Zara can hear a hostility in her mother's voice, that she never heard before. Why ever is it so important for her to hide her Jewish background? "Our ID's of course say that we are Muslim. Then they asked if we were related to you, since they couldn't tell that from the ID. And if we wanted to leave for Israel too. Father denied both adamantly."

The tray gets heavy in Zara's hands. She uses a foot to kick open the door and can just manage to keep the glasses from sliding off the tray. The conversation is stopped. They all are looking at her. They know that she has been listening. Zara feels her cheeks burning as she hands out the glasses, and shoves side tables in place.

"Did things remain calm after that?" Uncle Ibrahim says, breaking the silence.

As her mother casts a glance towards Zara, he says irritated, "Stop this, will you, Mariyam. That child knows more than all of us put together. And she has a right to know this too."

"No, because then she will blab about it. She wants to go public with it, announce it," her mother says angrily.

"What is wrong with that?" Zara challenges her, not wanting to remain the topic of discussion.

Uncle Ibrahim raises an authoritative arm. "Not now, please."

"Were you not going to make some tea for us?" Ayub asks with a demonstrative nod towards the kitchen door. Zara feels as if she is being treated like a child. Angrily, she heads back into the kitchen.

"What happened?" Uncle Ibrahim asks before she has even left the room.

"Mahmoud knew nothing about daykem's background. After that visit, I had to tell him."

Her father didn't know anything about it? Her parents were married without him ever knowing anything about her Jewish background? Zara listens in awe.

"So that was a crisis," Uncle Ibrahim concludes dryly.

"He took the news well," her mother says. "Happily."

"But...?"

"One of the party leaders found out. The story circulated throughout the department. Mahmoud was running for the position of chairman of the department in Penjwin. He lost."

Zara suddenly understands her mother's negative reaction, when she first saw the journal. It had happened once before. Zara's father's political career had already suffered from the fact that he was apparently married to a Jew.

"The problem is, Ayub, is that your father was so stubborn. He did not want to adapt. He had to be Jewish. Without thinking about the rest of the family!"

"That was his choice," Uncle Ibrahim says calmly, before Ayub gets a chance to respond. "But Mahmoud is deputy mayor now, isn't he? It no longer plays any role?"

Zara's mother sighs. "Happily, politics has a short memory, and it has long since been forgotten. And that must stay that way. I want him to become mayor. He deserves it."

Zara turns from the door with a sigh. Her mother is right. Her father's career must not be damaged, only because his daughter insists on coming out about her Jewish background.

Her hands prepare the tea, and search for cups and saucers, but her head is busy with the consequences of what she has heard.

I must remain silent about it. Yousef was right. But will I be able to do that? I would like to shout it from the rooftops! But why is that?

She stares at the golden edge of the tea glass in her hands. Because I now know that I am different? No longer one of the many? Special? Because I am proud of my Jewish heritage? But why should I be proud? If Rahila herself has completely distanced herself from it? And if daykem is so ashamed about it?

She hears her name being called. Inside, she slides the tray with the hot teapot and glasses onto the table next to her mother, who begins to pour them almost automatically.

"Dayke, you do not need to worry. I will keep quiet. Of course, *bawkm* must become mayor. If not, it will not because of me."

She serves the tea around. "You see," Uncle Ibrahim says, as he pulls her onto the couch. "Zara is not a child anymore, Mariyam."

Her mother shakes her head. "She can act without thinking."

"We were young once too," Uncle Ibrahim said smiling as he puts a hand on Zara's shoulder.

Only last night, he had told her how his father, Grandpa Kawa, had told him from the time he was very young, never to talk about their Jewish history. "If you hear that at such a young age, and it is repeated over and over, then you will start to believe for yourself that it is dangerous. And something really bad," he had said.

But why was there such a big difference between Rahila and Sasson, Zara had wanted to know. Why had the one banned anything and everything connected to Judaism, while the other choose to lead a secret Jewish life? "On our side of the family, there have always been ties to the government," Uncle Ibrahim said. "Your grandmother and grandfather both worked in education. I went into politics, your father did too. For us, a Jewish background can cause problems. But Sasson had his own business. He had much more freedom."

"And when did the rift between grandfather and Uncle Sasson take place?"

Zara's uncle wasn't quite sure. "I think that it happened around the time that he remarried, with a Benjew. I can only remember that he no longer came."

"But didn't you find that a bit odd?"

"Yes of course, but your grandfather said that they had moved. Had left the country, even."

"And grandfather and Uncle Sasson never saw one another again?"

"I do not think so, Zara. Your grandfather thought that any contact was too dangerous."

"So, you didn't know that Sasson lived here?"

"No, and this is the first time that I have seen Ayub, and that I hear that I have another nephew and a niece. Thanks to you. That's good work, girl."

The men had laughed together. Zara's ears had glowed from the compliment.

"Our story is not unique in our family, uncle," she said. She had taken the picture of her great-great-grandmother from in the journal and handed it to Ibrahim. "This is grandma's grandmother."

"You look like her, and not just a little bit either," Ayub said, who had been listening to the conversation in silence. "If you were to put on those clothes, no one would know the difference."

Zara had thought of that herself.

"Rahila's grandmother married a Muslim, against the wishes of the family."

"Through the centuries, Jews have never allowed their daughters to marry outside of the faith," Ayub remarked. Zara nodded. "She was crazy about the man, who was a poet and a writer. But he did not convert to Judaism, and they found themselves no longer a part of the community. That is why they moved from Penjwin to Sulaymaniya. They had three children. Rahila's father, and two other sons."

The two men listened with great interest. "So, there is even more family?"

"When Rahila's grandmother died, the father took the two youngest sons back to Baghdad. But the eldest, Rahila's father, stayed behind. He became a teacher at the Jewish school."

"We have family in Baghdad," Ayud concluded.

"The two sons had nothing with Judaism. They were successful businessmen, when Rahila wrote her diary."

"You mean that the rift between Sasson and Rahila wasn't unique, because there was one too from a generation before, between Rahila's father and his brothers," Ayub concluded.

"But then there was contact," Zara said.

"Does she give the names of the brothers in Baghdad?" Zara paged through the journal and searched for the paragraphs about her great-great grandmother. "No," she determined with disappointment. "No names. That trail is a dead end from here. She does mentions an Uncle Nasim, a brother of Rahila's mother, who knew the two brothers. He has gone to Israel too."

Ayub shook his head. "Don't know him."

A silence had fallen, as the three of them were looking at the picture. "Secrets run in the family," Ayub had remarked. "The two sons hid their Jewish past, when they went to live in Baghdad."

"Yes, and Rahila's dad tried to hide his Muslim father, when he wanted to become a rabbi," Zara added. "But he was unsuccessful, because that was obvious from his birth certificate."

"So, he never became a rabbi," Uncle Ibrahim said. "Painful for him."

"That a family with rabbis and great educators such as Rahila can fall apart in such a way," Ayub said to them.

"And could leave the faith like this," Zara added.

Shortly before Ayub went home, he had asked to meet Zara's mother. Zara had agreed that all three of them would go to Penjwin this morning.

Daykem is right, sometimes I do not think before I act, Zara thinks while casting a glance on her mother, who sits somewhat uncomfortably discussing this and that with her uncle.

I could have prevented this by calling her. How stupid of me.

"Dayke, I am sorry," she says, when there is a moment of silence in the conversation. "We should not have just dropped all of this on you. Sorry."

She looks at her in surprise. Uncle Ibrahim gives her an approving pat on her hand. She is gathering courage; now she must go on. "Dayke, did you know that history in our family keeps repeating itself? Bawkm missed a job with the party because his mother was Jewish. Grandma's father could not become a rabbi, because his father was a non-Jew."

The men nod and mumble in agreement. Her mother remains silent, but her look seems somewhat less cold than before.

"Dayke," Zara says pleadingly, "We can talk about it amongst ourselves, can't we? We do not have to deny it completely? Ayub is in the Army, and there they know nothing about it either. That is possible, isn't it?"

"Every contact brings people on the trail," her mother says. Her voice is once again as hard as steel. Zara doesn't know her like this.

"You do not want me here," Ayub determines as he gets up. Uncle Ibrahim pushes him back down onto the couch.

"You are here now, if there is evil doing coming, it will then be too late. Mariyam, it is our past. And that of our children. And Zara is right, there is much which we can learn from it."
Zara's mother sighs and looks at her hands. "I don't want nothing to do with it."
"But dayke, you were happy when we found the treasure," Zara remembers. "And you were interested when I could tell you that it was Sabbath silver. I have even polished it!"
Uncle Ibrahim looks from Zara towards her mother. "A treasure? Was there more than the diary?"
Zara walks to the display cupboard. She takes the seven-armed candlestick and hands it to Ayub. He gentle takes hold of it.
"It isn't going to break, you know," Zara laughs.
"This candlestick is very special for us Jews," Ayub says, while looking at it from all sides. "This is a menorah, which stands for the union between Moses and God."
Zara walks back to the cupboard. Uninvited, both men follow her.
"Oh," Ayub exclaims, while he takes a cup from the silver tray in the cupboard, "there is also a Sabbath set. What a beauty!"
"Do you celebrate the Sabbath?"
They had not noticed that Zara's mother has joined them. Surprised by her question, Ayub only nods.
She takes the candlestick and the barrel that both belong to the set. "You must take this home, Ayub. Then at least it will be used."
Zara turns around astonished. Where does this sudden change in attitude come from?

Ayub doesn't seem to notice. He is staring with delight into the cupboard. "Is that...." he said, pointing at the red satin box. "Did you find a Torah?"

"It is empty," Zara's mother says, taking the box. "Pity, eh?" Together they bend over the box. "They must have taken the roll by itself to Israel, so it was less noticeable," Ayub says.

He strokes the satin, looking at the silver decorations carefully. "I only know this from pictures on the Internet," he confesses.

"We too," Zara laughs, "and only after we had taken it from the cloths on our kitchen table."

Then she remembers her mother's delight, at the moment of the discovery, and her visible disappointment when the box was empty. She knew what it was, that they had found. She even knew what the pointer was for. How could that be, if she wants to know nothing about her Jewish heritage? Zara is anxious to ask her, but this is not the time. She looks how her mother takes the items one at a time. How gently she handles them, with honour and respect. Every item is commented on, its purpose is discussed, and the state which it is in.

Nothing is right about her story, Zara thinks. She knew what a Torah was; she knew about the treasure, she named me after her Jewish grandmother. Daykem has always known she was Jewish. And in actuality, it interests her intensely, she can see that now, and you could see it too when she asked me about my investigation.

But why then all this hostility? Only because bawkm's career might be at risk? She is pulled from her thoughts as Ayub nudges her.

"Where were you? We are talking about your treasure hunting," he says smiling. "Tell us."

"The workers thought it was a hatch, but it was a kind of safe," she begins.

The two men listen excitedly to her story.

"And at her engagement she wore jewellery from the treasure," her mother says finishing the story.

Ah. Painfully Zara lands back in the present.

Soran. What is she going to do with him?

Ayub looks at her. "Congratulations," he says, without showing his amazement that she has not even mentioned this yesterday.

She is grateful to him for that. She does not want to talk about Soran, and would prefer not even to think about him. Because then, she will have to make a decision.

"Did you know, that I have found the old synagogue in Sulaymaniya?"

Her attempt to change the topic of discussion is successful. The conversation goes from the mosque that used to be a synagogue, to the Penjwin of the past, to the Jewlakan, to the old house, and eventually to the new one which should be completed soon.

The afternoon progresses. Zara's mother is so absorbed in the conversation that she, much to Zara's surprise, has not even given any thought to the preparations of the evening meal. Zara has, according to the rules of hospitality, made coffee and then once again tea.

THE JEWISH BRIDE

Then Ayub asks her to show her mother the picture. The one of Rahila, together with Sasson and Kawa. Zara's mother nods when she sees it, and then walks out of the room without uttering a word. She comes back with a flat box, which she sets down in front of Zara with an almost solemn gesture.

"It is not much, but your uncle is right. You have a right to it."

Zara knows that all eyes are on her. With trembling hands, she takes the lid from the box. What will be inside? Photographs? Letters?

On top is a yellowed picture of her grandmother as a young woman. Her dark eyes stare sternly at Zara, her mouth is in a Mona Lisa-smile. Even the way she has folded her hands in her lap, is a reminder of the way Da Vinci immortalized Mona Lisa.

Her dark hair is braided in the cap that she is wearing. Her tight vest is edged in lace and worn over a shirt of white lace, and over her shoulder a silk cape is draped. Her earrings are her only jewellery.

Zara sighs, overwhelmed with emotions. Rahila is beautiful, mysterious and at the same time she radiates strength and self-awareness. No wonder that she had almost become a rabbi.

"A Jewish bride," Ibrahim says. "Could this be her wedding picture?"

Zara turns the picture over. The back is bare.

When she picks up the picture, another one comes into view. A young man laughs whilst looking into the camera, his dark curls escaping playfully from a kippah. "Azam," Zara

knows for sure, even though there is not a single notation on the picture. "What a hunk. No wonder that grandma didn't want to let him go."
This causes the group to laugh heartily.
"What a bustle, here!"
No one has heard Zara's father come in. He looks surprised. Zara's mother greets him smilingly and introduces Ayub. The surprised look does not leave his face.
"Your nephew?" he says, looking from Ayub to Ibrahim. "Does Ibrahim have a son that I don't know about?"
Zara sees her mother's uneasy smile, and asks herself how much she has told him. Somewhat ill-at-ease, she puts the pictures back in the box, and closes the lid.
Awkwardly, Ayub tries to salvage the situation. "My father is Sasson, Kak Mahmoud. The Sasson that wanted to go to Israel."
Zara can tell from the look on her father's face that he knows exactly who this is about. But he is too much of a politician to show that. He motions for the men to sit down. Zara hurries to the kitchen, to get him a glass of water. Her mobile vibrates in her pocket. Banu. She has not spoken to her in a long time. Zara hesitates. She really wants to talk to her friend, but this is not the time. But she cannot simply ignore her, since she would then only phone again. Her fingers fly over the keys. "Banu, I cannot talk now. I will call you later, alright?"
Then she stares at the phone in her hands. What has happened to her? Her best friend knows nothing about the most important discovery in her life. And she knows nothing

about her doubts over Soran. And she is unable to discuss
either with her, as she will not be able to understand.
She sighs, and fills the water glass. When she comes back
into the room, her father is at the drinks cupboard.
"Arak?" he asks, "or whisky?" He sends her back for glasses.
"It looks like we have something to celebrate."
Now, all the eyes are focussed on him. What does he mean?
Isn't he angry? Have I been mistaken? Zara wonders.
Her father extends the tension by pouring everyone a drink.
"Mariyam, arak?"
To Zara's great surprise she nods. She has never seen her
mother drink before. Then Zara too gets a glass of the
milky-white drink. Just as Rahila got her first glass from her
father, she thinks. But Rahila was Jewish... And in this house
we are not recognized as being Jewish. Muslims are not
meant to drink.
"Bawke, what are you doing?" Zara can stay quiet no longer.
Her father raises his glass in a toast. "I want to celebrate
that in this house the past has finally been accepted. What
the discovery of the treasure wasn't able to accomplish, and
not even Zara, when she showed Mariyam the diary, has
happened today, thanks to Ayub and Ibrahim."
Her mother blinks. Then a wide smile appears on her face.
She raises her glass while she looks her husband into the
eyes.
"To our communal past," Ayub toasts.
"To our shared future," Uncle Ibrahim says. "And to Zara,
who was not able to keep silent."

Zara feels her eyes filling up. Is this really happening? And because of her? As she raises her glass, she feels a lone tear roll down her cheek.

"To Rahila, my extraordinary grandmother. Who entrusted me, to reveal the past."

"I need ten thousand dollars."

Soran says it thoughtfully, as he pulls blades of grass from the ground. Zara looks at the pile that has formed and remains silent. She tries to think what he needs the money for.

"They say that the route via Greece no longer works. That many people are sent back. I do not want that: paying so much, and still ending up right back here."

Ah, Soran wants to go to Europe. The dream of many young Kurds has taken him.

"Why?"

Soran looks at her surprised, as if he had not expected her to say anything.

He came to get her for their evening in the mountain, as if nothing had happened. Had told her in the car all the latest family news, and went on about their mutual friends. Zara had played along, and did not touch on their argument from the previous week, and the fact that they had not spoken to one another since. At their regular spot, they had spread out the blanket. The usual struggle was absent. Soran was not interested, it seemed.

This was the last time, of this she was certain. And he knew it too.

"I want to leave here, of course. What do we have here to look forward to, in this mess?"

"You can still go this week to see doctor Barham. An appointment is being made for you on Thursday or Friday, when he is in Sulaymaniya," Zara says.

Soran does not seem to have heard her. "What should I do in a country where you are arrested simply for taking part in a demonstration? Where they threaten and abuse you... And then the mess in the hospital. There is no system, it is not about the people. Only about the money."

Zara listens to the litany she has heard so often before. But it is different. This time he is really going to do it. Yet another certainty.

"They have given me a chance. I now have a reason to get asylum." Soran smiles. "The idiots did not think of that, when they were burning holes in me with their cigarettes. And when they beat me black and blue. Now I can prove, that I have a political reason to flee."

Zara notices, that she isn't even surprised about the turn around that Soran has made since last week. From a victim, he has become a political refugee. Still a victim, but one who has managed to turn his suffering into something positive.

"But you have nothing to prove any of it," she remarks to him. "Your bruises have long since faded."

Soran sweeps the pile of grass blades away in one swoop. "Did you really think that I am so stupid?" He looks at her contemptuously. "I have photographed everything. Every spot. And the pictures are safely in cyberspace. They will accept me, with so much evidence."

"Soran, Kurds from Iraq are being sent back from Europe one at a time. You need a story. A very good story about political persecution. And you are not even a member of any political party."

He snorts. "You underestimate me. But I already knew that. I have a membership card from Gorran, with a date starting a year ago."

Zara listens more to the tone, than to his words. The tone of distance, of repulsion.

Why did he come to get her, why has he broken the silence between them? What is the point of it all, if he feels about her in this way?

"So, you are leaving," she says in a business-like way.

"The story is watertight. I was arrested and tortured because I had taken part in a demonstration as a member of the opposition. If I do not leave, they will know where to find me again. And my chances of ever finding a job as a doctor will have vanished. Beautiful, isn't it?"

Except that it is nonsense, Zara thinks. Our relations with the party are strong enough to prevent that.

"Where are you going to go, then?" she asks.

"Yes, that is the question. All the escape routes have become expensive. That is why you must help me."

Zara laughs cynically. "What can I do for you? Roll out the red carpet?"

Soran laughs along with her. "Yes, you put that well," he then says seriously. "You are going to roll out my red carpet."

She looks at him, and wonders what he is talking about. Where is that tone coming from? What does he mean? The answer comes like a flash of light. He knows. But he cannot possibly know. Can he? Only if Banu has made a slip of the tongue. Or even intentionally told him.

She suddenly feels very cold. Yousef was right, she should have kept quiet, even to Banu. But when she had spoken to her at the end of last week, it had just happened. How could she not share her secret with her? Even if Banu was not able to understand it. "Because your grandmother on your mother's side of the family is Jewish, then that makes you Jewish too?" she had asked a few times, full of misunderstanding. And to eventually add: "But you don't have to go along with it? You can just ignore it? Your parents are Muslims, so you are one too?"

Zara had seen her simple reasoning, but not felt it. Since she has known the story about her heritage, she has felt different. Why? Because the God of the Jews had declared them to be the chosen people? But she had no connection to the religion, she knew far too little for that.

She had attempted to reason with it, but got no further than the special connection she feels towards her grandmother. And the feeling of coming home she had when meeting Ayub, and her special friendship with Yousef. She feels more connected to them than she ever would to her old world. Even though it sounded ridiculous.

But how do you explain something like that? And then to someone like Banu, who expected that a woman was to find happiness in marriage and children? Who would never use her studies to work, who despite the topics of her studies had little to no vision on what was going on in the rest of the world?

Disappointed she had taken the discussion back to safer subjects. To the breaking down of the tent city on Saray Square, and the massive intervention of police and military which had brought an end to nearly two months of protests. And to Banu's marriage, which once again had to be postponed, now that the date of the exams had been shifted so they could make up for the lost time due to the protests.

When she said goodbye, Zara had made her promise not to tell anyone what they had discussed. Something Banu had solemnly promised. But there was something in the way she said goodbye, that was less spontaneous and warm than before.

I am imagining it, Zara had told herself. You have changed, she has not.

But now, Zara is suddenly reminded of something that Ayub has said. People look down upon us; they see us as being inferior. He had even said that people thought Jews were dirty.

She notices that Soran has started building a new mountain of blades of grass.

He wouldn't dare to, she thinks. Could there be something left from what they had?

"Shall we go back now?" she asks.

"You haven't answered my question," Soran says.

Zara gets up. "I have no red carpet for you, Soran jaan. I cannot help you."

She sees he is hesitating.

"With your help, we will not need the ten thousand dollars," he then says.

Once again it is the tone that she hears first, long before the words are spoken. She hears something pleading, but also something of dependence. Then she hears the "we."
"Spill it out, kid," she says.
He motions towards the blanket. Reluctantly she crouches down on a corner.
"We can go to Israel together."
"How did you ever come up with that idea?" Zara says, playing her amazement, as she has no plans of making this easy on him.
Soran stares once again to the mountain of grass. Zara waits to see how he will end his internal fight. Will he tell her what he has heard from Banu?
"That diary. It is your grandmother, isn't it? That is your ticket to Israel, isn't it?"
Zara makes no effort to deny it.
"Who says that I want to go to Israel?"
His answer is honest and hard. "But that is what all Jews want, isn't it? To Jerusalem, to their promised land?"
Zara's breathing stopped. It was as if she was hearing Rahila's words. All those years later, and still the same prejudices.
"We can marry, and then you can ask to return to Israel. Right?"
Zara is not even surprised about all the steps they have passed over tonight. The argument has not been resolved. She has not told him about her extraordinary week, about the sudden changes in her life. Soran has stepped over all of that, and she did not raise any protest. In a week's time, a

marriage to Soran has become nearly unimaginable. And going anywhere with him as well.
But it is especially the word "return" that strikes her. As if she no longer belongs here, now that it seems she is Jewish. As if Kurdistan no longer is her homeland. She again thinks of Rahila. They are taking away my country and I do not even know the alternative.
"Right?" Soran repeats, when he feels her silence lasts too long.
Zara gets up and walks to the car. "Will you take me home, or are you going to let me walk?" she asks, as she opens the door.
Soran looks surprised. Then he gets up and grabs a corner of the blanket. Without making any effort to fold it up, he tosses it onto the backseat.
"But it is possible, isn't it, janakam?" he continues while turning the car onto the road.
Zara fights against the urge to tell him that she is no longer his janakam. That it is over. But she is too tired for that. She does not want any battle, any accusations or emotions. The night candle method is better.
"I do not know, if I want to go to Israel," she says. "That is something that I must think carefully about."
"It seems to be a great country. Modern and progressive."
"That sounds like paradise," Zara remarks.
Her cynicism is lost on him. "It is really the very best option. You must think about it."
"Sure."

They drive back down mostly in silence. Now and then Soran makes a comment, but it falls in the vacuum of Zara's silence.
"Are you tired?" he then asks.
It is the first time in a long time, that he has shown any interest in how she feels. But it is too late, it has no effect anymore.
It is real. I have not imagined it. Everything revolves around him. How can I ever have fallen in love with this egoistical guy?
"Very tired," she says. "I have never been so tired before."
He glances over at her. "A good night's sleep will do you good."
You have no idea at all anymore, of what is good for me, Zara thinks.

The table is set with a white table cloth, and decorated with flowers from the garden and candles. There is home baked, braided bread on the table, and a bottle of wine. The Sabbath set is placed in the middle.
Hanan walks in with dishes that Nasrin has filled in the kitchen. There is rice, meat, sauces, chicken. And there are numerous salads.
"Have a seat," Nasrin says, as she carries in the last dish.
Shyly, Zara stands next to the table, gazing at the abundance of food. Only when Ayub motions to the place next to him, does she go and sit down. Nasrin nods to her warmly from across the table. Then she gets up, and lights the candles on the table one at a time, with matches from

the box in the Sabbath set. With a hand covering her eyes, she recites a text.

When all the candles are burning, Ayub pours the wine in the Sabbath cup. While standing he speaks solemn words that Zara does not understand.

When he sits back down, he explains that he has said the *Kiddush*, to bless the Sabbath. He drinks from the cup, and then hands it to Nasrin. After taking a sip, she hands it on to Zara. Carefully she tastes the wine. The taste is not bad; much better than the glass she has once drunk at a student party.

Then Nasrin begins a song, which is cheerfully sung along with much laughter.

Zara watches it all. She feels a bit uncomfortable, and a bit of an outsider. That is because of the strange rituals, she thinks. If only Yousef was here. He would know what to do.

Ayub gets up, and lays his hands on the heads of his daughters. When he speaks, Zara can only recognize the names Sarah, Rivka, Rachel and Leah. Then he lays a hand on her head, and repeats the words. It gives her a warm feeling.

"Those are our strongest women," Ayub says, "and we wish our daughters to have their strength."

Zara can only nod, as she has a lump in her throat.

This is my world. Here is where I belong.

Nasrin puts a dish invitingly in front of her. "You must try this fish."

"Do you always eat such an extended meal on Friday nights?"

Nasrin smiles, and shakes her head. "I overdid it a bit. But there is always too much, because tomorrow I do not cook. Then we eat what is left over."

"Nasrin is a good cook. She has that from her mother, you know."

Nasrin smiles at Ayub. "And all of our mothers before us. These are all family recipes."

"For us is the Sabbath meal the time to be with the family," Ayub says. "That was the same way for my parents, and at Nasrin's home too. We always had family over. It hasn't been that way for a long time. That is why we are so happy to have you here today."

A bit overwhelmed, Zara bows her head over her plate. The conversation around her is about the daily activities. The exams of Hanan, the school of little Zara.

"What are you going to do after your exams, have you decided yet?" Nasrin then asks her.

Zara shakes her head. "Actually, I would really like to get my masters, somewhere abroad, but that isn't an easy thing to arrange."

Ayub tells her about a Kurdish governmental program, in which graduates have the opportunity to do a master's study abroad. Zara realizes she does not know, because she had been consumed by the demonstrations and Rahila's journal.

"Perhaps you can study for a year in Israel," Ayub suggests.

"And then never be able to find a job here in Iraq?" Zara says, without a moment's hesitation.

"You could stay there, perhaps," Nasrin says softly.

Again, Zara thinks. Why do all these people want to get me to Israel?

"Iraq is my country," she says.

"Well, I know what I would do, if I were to get such a chance," Ayub says.

Zara is touched by the desire that can be heard in his words. "Do you still want to go away?"

Ayub looks at her curiously. "We are Jewish, Israel is our country. Of course, we want to go there. We say that every year, as we remember the exodus from Egypt and from slavery during Passover. Next year in Jerusalem, we say. Those are not only words."

Zara remembers the last sentence from the book of her grandmother:

They who were banned to Assyria or driven to Egypt, shall return and bow before God, on the holy mountain in Jerusalem.

"Why don't you go then?"

Ayub sighs. "I don't know how we could."

Zara looks at him in surprise. "It can't be that difficult, can it? Via Turkey? Isn't there an Israeli embassy there?"

"And then?"

Zara quickly swallows her answer. Of course, you can go there and report to them, but how do you prove you are Jewish? From Iraqi documents it cannot be seen, their entire family is registered as being Islamic. She nods. "Can't the family in Israel start the procedure on your behalf?"

Ayub shoves his plate away. "They do not dare to anymore, after the last disaster. And there is really no way for me to ask them. What if it was to fail, then I would end up losing my job."

He is afraid that the army will no longer trust him as a Jew, Zara understands. Then she sees what opportunities it would offer Ayub, if she were to go to Israel. She could become the bridge builder. Once again. She is unable to repress a deep sigh.

Ayub lays a hand on her arm. "No Zara, that is not why I brought it up. Don't get me wrong. I expect absolutely nothing from you. You must decide for yourself where you belong."

She looks at him gratefully.

"But I do want to show you what options are available to you. What do you know about Israel? About the life there? The Jewish lifestyle?"

"Nothing," she admits.

"If you choose, you must also know what it is you are choosing," Ayub repeats. "So, we are going to teach you about our ceremonies, and our rituals. OK?"

"Please," she nods.

Nasrin begins collecting the plates. "What time are we speaking to Ruth?" she asks.

Ayub looks at the clock on his cell phone. "Wow, is it that late already? I will put the Skype on; she will no doubt come online soon."

Zara helps Nasrin bringing dishes and plates to the kitchen. There, she is told that Ruth is a daughter of Uncle Benjamin, Rahila's younger brother in Israel.

"Every Friday night, we have contact with someone of the family in Israel," Ayub explains, while he installs the laptop between the flowers and the candles on the table. "Ruth wanted to speak to us, because she is planning to come for a visit."

Zara looks at him in amazement. "Visitors from Israel to Iraq? Is that even possible?"

"It has happened before," Ayub said neutrally.

Zara is not so easily put off. "But Iraq had no diplomatic ties with Israel."

"We live in Kurdistan, Zara."

"You mean that Israelis can visit us because of the good ties between the Barzani's and Israel?"

Ayub nods. "Official ties are not possible, because Kurdistan is part of the Arab region. But there are personal ties with President Barzani and his family, as you know. His personal guards were trained by Israel, and there are a number of Jewish advisors here."

"Really?"

"No one will ever confirm it, but around the Barzani's there are a number of Jews working."

"Do you know them, then?"

Ayub smiles but does not speak.

"No more secrets, we had agreed, Uncle Ayub," Zara presses with a smile.

Ayub puts a finger to his lips. "About some things we do not speak, Zara."

"But in a moment, we will be openly Skyping with Israel," she says in response.

Ayub shakes his head. "Enough, little terrier," he says friendly.

When the tea is on the table, there is an incoming call on Skype. Zara sees a face appear; a young, blonde woman looks into the room. She is wearing little make-up and her curly hair is well kempt. She is Western, Zara thinks. And blond. In our family? That is odd.

"That is Ruth," Ayub says. "Come and show yourself, Zara. Here, in front of the camera. After that I will turn off the video, so that we will have a better connection."

"Shabbat shalom," can be heard, "who do you have there with you, Ayub?"

"Shabbat shalom, Ruth. This is Zara, the lost sheep that has found us once again."

A hearty laugh can be heard. "As usual, you are speaking in riddles."

"She is our cousin from your Aunt Rahila's side. But we will tell you about that when you are here. How is the family?"

Zara listens intently to the conversation. Ruth talks about her parents and sisters that live in Haifa, about the operation that her mother had, about the renovation of the synagogue where her father works. And about her soccer team, where they continue to win game after game, and as a result are at the top of the national league.

"I found a soccer club in Sulaymaniya that also has women's soccer," she then says. "Can you get in touch with them for me, and see if they will invite me?"

Ayub looks at Zara. "I think that my brother knows the trainer," she remembers. "What do you want to do there, Ruth?"

"Oh, maybe take part in a training session." From the airy manner in which she says that, Zara understands that it is only an excuse to make her trip somewhat official.

"I will see what I can do. Just send me your information, OK?"

"I will send it to you by way of Ayub."

"And the rest of the arrangements?" Ayub asks. "You will be staying with us of course."

"The visa application is being handled by the office of the Kurdish president," Ruth says. "That contact you gave me has worked well, Ayub. But it isn't working with my passport. I have to arrange something else. They will be helping me with that."

Ayub nods and says nothing more about it. Zara longs to know more, but contains herself. The conversation switches to the conflict in Israel. The situation in the Gaza Strip has been turbulent for some months now. Ruth makes no big issue of it, there is nothing new, she says.

"Look, Uncle Ayub," Zara says as the computer has been switched off again, "here it is quiet and there it isn't. And yet you want to go to Israel. I really do not understand that."

Ayub smiles. "You heard how Ruth reacted. Remember when there were riots in Sulaymaniya? A kilometre away, no-one noticed nothing about it. And even more so in Erbil." Zara has to admit that it was true.

"The outside world also thinks that Kurdistan is unsafe, because there are bombs going off in Kirkuk and Baghdad. But we know better. That is how you should view Israel."

"Watch out, the paint is still wet," Zara's mother warns. Cautiously, Zara maintains her distance from the door. She steps over the rubble, and avoids buckets of paint, tools and ladders.

"Do you really think we will be able to move in next week?" she asks, somewhat critically.

Her mother is standing in the middle of the new sitting room. "There," she points, "is where the new couch and chairs are coming. There the television. And what do you think, should we hang the portrait of Rahila there, above the couch?"

Zara is lost for words. Her mother has not mentioned their past since the conversation with Uncle Ibrahim and Ayub.

"And the cupboard with the candlesticks and the other objects there?"

"That looks like a good spot," Zara says carefully. "Or there, against the wall, that would work too."

Her mother turns around, and considers the suggestion. "That is better. It will draw more attention over there."

Zara watches her, as she walks around the room. "Are you going to have her picture enlarged?" she asks.

Her mother nods. "I have already taken it to the photo shop. We will put a nice frame around it."

Zara can no longer pretend anything is normal. "What has happened, dayke? Why is Rahila suddenly allowed to be in our living room?"

Her mother smiles. "Because she is my mother, Zara. There is no longer a reason to keep her hidden."

Zara blinks. She doesn't understand. Rahila's portrait is allowed? And the rest? She follows her mother through the kitchen to the garden. Here trash and rubble from the construction are everywhere.

"When this is gone, we are going to make a garden with a lot of green and flowers," her mother says. "This will be beautiful Zara, you will see."

Zara nods, but the garden does not interest her in the least now.

"Dayke, why now?"

Her mother turns around. "I want to read the diary, Zara." Zara waits in silence. Her mother knows that she has copied the journal for Ayub, and has kept the original herself.

"My father thought that it was too dangerous to tell us about the past. But I want to know. My mother never would have wanted it to be kept so secret."

"If she wanted that, then she would have burned the diary," Zara says softly.

"Exactly. She wanted it to be found. So that the past could and would be discussed."

"And bawkm's career?"

"He wants to know too, Zara. He says that we should be proud of it. How many women have done what Rahila did? She was almost a rabbi; she ran a school... and all that, in those days!"

Zara nods. Her parents must have discussed the subject at great length. "Do you know why she died so young, dayke?" Zara is happy that she no longer has to remain silent about what has kept her occupied now for weeks. That she finally has somewhere to go with her questions.

Her mother shakes her head. "Perhaps she died during childbirth? In any case, her death controlled our lives. My father kept us close to him, and tried to keep us safe, because he couldn't bear to lose us too."

"That is why he was so adamant about burying the past," Zara suddenly realizes. "Maybe that is why he thought the rift with Sasson was necessary? Because he refused to deny his past?"

"Will we ever know? There are so many secrets in this family, Zara. My father has taken a lot of them to his grave."

Zara hesitates. Is this the moment?

"What happened to you, dayke," she asks softly.

Her mother smiled. "I was afraid of the past, Zara. My father had made us afraid of it. If you have been in denial of something for years, it is then difficult to admit it."

Zara nods, but still does not understand.

"My father planted many seeds of fear. Fear for the unknown, fear for being different, fear of what others thought and said. I think that he was afraid that we would want to go to Israel, just like Sasson and the rest of the family, if he were to be open about our heritage."

"And that he would lose you."

Zara's mother puts an arm around her. "I know that fear too, janakam. What are you going to do with being a Jew? Do you want to go to Israel? Are we going to lose you?"

Zara thinks about the conversation with Ayub. "I do not know, dayke. I want to find out where I belong."

Her mother pulls her up against her in an embrace. "And don't forget to talk to me about that, girl. I want to know, understand your reasons. I hope that you will choose for Kurdistan as Rahila did. But it is your life, janakam."

Zara allows herself to enjoy the hug. She has never heard her mother speak to her in this way before. So... mature. As if she is no longer the youngest.

"This house has a room for you."

"Thank you, dayke. I do know that."

"Then you will move with us next week?"

Zara hears the tension in the question. "Dayke, do not worry. I am not going to up and leave just like that. And our cousin Ruth is coming from Israel next month; she will need some place to stay, won't she?"

"Who?"

"The daughter of Uncle Benjamin. I talked to her on Skype at Ayub's house."

"How can that be, visitors from Israel," her mother says, full of disbelief.

Zara smiles. "I do not know that either, dayke, but she is really coming."

14 DECISIONS

It is hot on the parking lot. June has just started, but the summer heat is already here.
Erbil is much hotter than Sulaymaniya, Zara realizes. Our mountains really cool us. Here everything is flat, and the sun beats down on it.
The sweat runs down her back. Once again, she searches in vain for some shadow. Behind that bus perhaps... She takes a big gulp from the water bottle that has long lost its coolness.
"How late do they arrive? I am afraid that I am going to melt here."
"Don't nag, Zara," Ayub says, "be happy that we don't have a sandstorm today."
Zara grins, and tries once again to look against the sun to see the bus that brings the passengers from the arrival hall to the parking lot. Because the safety regulations are strict

throughout Iraq, both the arrival and departure halls are only accessible for passengers and personnel.

She is distracted by a large group of people standing a bit further up; a few families, from the looks of it. Children are running around laughing and yelling, despite the heat. She classifies the women with head scarves and long, black robes as Arabic Iraqis who have traded Baghdad for the safety of Kurdistan. They talk to a sheik, in a long, white dress and a chequered scarf over his head, from which he keeps throwing the corners backwards. He must feel hot too, she thinks. And the women... all that black clothing, and then in the full sun!

Ayub has followed her glances. "That group is waiting for the body of a sheik that passed away abroad, I think."

Iraq is the land of the departing, Zara thinks. And from those who seek their luck elsewhere, like Soran. But if they die, they still want to be buried here.

Soran has left a week ago for Turkey. To investigate the possibilities, as he called it, when they met one another at the graduation ceremony of the university. When she added it up, she found they had not seen or talked to one another for ten days already. Soran had apparently taken the hint, she thought as she saw him, surrounded by his classmates and friends.

Then the thought had then crossed her mind, that they somehow still must have the imam annul the engagement. Somewhat confused about the realization that she in her unconsciousness seems to have flipped a switch, she greeted Soran. For a change, she was grateful for the conservative Kurdish rules which did not allow men and women to kiss in public.

"That looks nice on you," he said, pointing to her long black toga and square hat.

"Well, you don't look so bad yourself," she had answered a bit too quickly.

"I do not like this red scarf at all." He touched the long scarf hanging over his toga with distaste. "The brown one you have is more of a classic."

An uneasy silence had fallen. Soran had broken it with the announcement that he was going to Turkey. She had only looked at him in wonder.

"You know, that I want to leave. I am going to see if there is work for me in Turkey. I have made appointments with two hospitals to come and talk."

Zara had nodded.

"If that doesn't work out, then I will search further," he said. Suddenly, Banu showed up from out of the crowd. "What are you searching for?"

She had greeted Banu warmly with kisses, happy to no longer be alone with Soran.

"It is going to be on Sunday of next week," Banu had then said, "and you can't stay away."

"Your wedding party? Of course, I will be there."

"I will still be in Turkey then, Banu. I do not think I will be there."

"You aren't coming together? What is going on?"

Zara directed her gaze to the ground. *We are no longer together, Banu. It is over. When will I be able to say that out loud?*

Soran too had not replied. Zara was grateful, that Banu had then dragged her along to their classmates.

I am going to bring Ruth along to Banu's wedding, Zara decides, just as she sees the bus arriving at the checkpoint. As the vehicle passes, she scans the windows. Is that her? That blond woman who is hanging on to one of the ceiling belts? Then her heart stops. Next to the woman is a man she would recognise anywhere.

In the manner that he bends towards her to listen, it is obvious that they know one another. How is that possible? Her heart is throbbing in her throat, as she walks with Ayub to the bus which is spitting out its passengers and their baggage. Soran helps Ruth carry a large bag from the bus.

"Ayub!" Ruth runs over, and hugs Ayub. Zara sees the looks that it attracts from the people around them, but especially the distorted face of Soran.

"Hello Soran, how are you?" Zara says. "I see that you have already made acquaintance with my cousin?" He looks at her in disbelief.

Ruth has let go of Ayub, and has now grasped Zara in a warm greeting. Two kisses land on her cheeks. "Zara, I am so happy to meet you! I am so excited!"

Soran stands by, somewhat uneasily. It appears Ruth has forgotten him. Zara has no desire to introduce him to Ayub. As what? Not as her fiancé! To avoid a conversation, she sets course for the car, past the family that is still waiting for their deceased relative. Ayub follows with Ruth, who is talking non-stop about the flight and her first impressions. Soran lags behind, with both of their suitcases.

"Oh, Soran!" Ruth calls out, when he puts the suitcase next to the car. "Sorry man, I am acting like a savage. These are my cousins Ayub and Zara. Guys, this is Soran; we met one another in Istanbul."

Ayub greets him with a handshake. "Where are you headed, Soran?"

Zara ignores him, as he is ignoring her too. If she had an inkling of doubt about their relationship, then this scene has certainly helped her with that delusion. Soran's eyes are hanging on Ruth. Zara might still be his fiancé, but he clearly has more interest in her cousin. And now she has to sit for three hours with him in the car!

Zara is happy, when Ruth pulls her to sit next to her on the back seat, and almost immediately begins to talk to her.

"You know one another?" she hears Ayub ask, while he steers the car through the busy traffic of the city.

"We met one another yesterday in Istanbul," Soran said. Zara knows almost for sure, that Ayub was not talking about Ruth.

"Soran has shown me the Blue Mosque and the Aya Sofia," Ruth interrupts her account, while she brushes her blond curls from her warm face. "And the best places to eat in the city."

"What a great coincidence that you met one another," Ayub says.

"We were staying in the same hotel," Soran answers, as he looks at Ruth from over his shoulder.

"He promised me that he was going to show me his beautiful country!" she says from the backseat, while she touches his shoulder.

Zara feels a wave of disappointment. She had looked forward to Ruth's arrival. She had hoped to find a friend, a soul mate. She had wanted to share her own special places with her, like the old synagogue and the Jewlakan of Erbil. But Soran has come between them, and so has what happened between them in Istanbul.

Are you jealous then, she wonders? But she absolutely no longer wants anything to do with Soran. Let Ruth have and keep him. Then she will be rid of him, once and for all.

And does the fact that they have had something together, stand in the way of a friendship with Ruth then? She speaks sternly to herself. You are not going to let him monopolize her too, are you? Come on!

She turns to Ruth. "You are lucky. Ayub is taking the route through the mountains; it is longer but much more beautiful."

Ruth nods, and is beaming. "I have so much to tell you, Zara!"

Will she start talking about Israel with Soran there, Zara wonders? Otherwise there is little else that they can talk about...

With a questioning look she motions towards Soran's back. Ruth barely shakes her head.

"Cyprus is so beautiful this time of year," she says. "You must come and visit me soon."

When they pass a checkpoint nearly an hour later, Zara has learned to listen between the lines, and now knows that Ruth has studied history, and that her sisters are married, and one to an American. She has questioned her about her successful soccer career, and her plans to meet with and possibly train female players in Sulaymaniya.

"My entire family has advised me not to take this trip, because it was said to be too dangerous," she laughs. "But if you can play soccer here, then it must be safe enough, no?"

"Ruth, your passport," Ayub says over his shoulder.

Zara motions for her to open her window, so that the guard can see who is sitting on the back seat. Ruth digs around in her large bag, and takes out a burgundy-red EU passport. Cyprus. Ah. Of course. How did she arrange that?

The guard flips through the new passport, finds the stamp from the visa, and hands it back without a comment. Ayub greets him, and drives on.

An hour later he stops again. "Tea with a view," he announces. Soran takes Ruth by the hand and leads her to the terrace that lies high atop a steep hill and offers a wide view of the area. He points towards the lake from Dokan, with in the distance the range of the Qandil Mountains.

"That is where the Kurdish fighters are located," he adds proudly.

"What a romantic idea," Ruth laughs.

Zara points to the other direction. "Look, that mountain there. That is called Sara, coincidently. What do you think that it looks like?"

Ruth strains her view. "It looks like a mountain...not like a Sara. I give up."

Zara points: a face, hands that are folded over a stomach, legs.

"Yes! I see it! An old man. Why does the mountain have a women's name?"

"Maybe, because this region has an old Christian and Jewish history?" Ayub says, as he joins them. "And in both, Sara was a strong woman."

Zara sips from the hot tea, her eyes on the mountain range. "Couldn't it be the other way around, Uncle Ayub," she says in contemplation. "In Kurdistan, many people are named after mountains, cities and rivers. Soran, for instance, is a place located close to the Iranian border. Perhaps the original Sara, Ibrahim's wife, was named after this mountain?"

All eyes are now focussed on her. "Interesting thought, Zara jaan," Ayub says.

"I don't believe that the birthplace of Sara is known," Ruth says. "She married in Ur with Ibrahim. In their time it was a two-day trek."

"In the neighbourhood, then," Zara said laughing.

When Ayub shows Ruth where the toilet is, Zara and Soran are alone for the first time.

"Are you going to see the imam?" Zara asks as soon as they are out of listening range.

Soran takes a drag from his cigarette, and looks past her to the blue surface of the lake.

"You should have told me the truth then."

Then. On the day of the engagement. Zara thinks about his doubts, and hers. But there was too much pushing her to go on with it, and too much that they both did not yet know.

"We both had our doubts, Soran. It is not too late."

She was surprised by her own calmness, her distance.

Ayub waves, and motions that he is going to the car. Soran snuffs out his cigarette. "I will put it in action."

THE JEWISH BRIDE

She watches, how he walks towards Ruth and how they laugh about something together. She tries to decide what she is feeling. You should feel something, when you have just broken your engagement!
Relief. She has just managed to escape, from that unhappy marriage. But there is also an emptiness, with the certainty that she will marry, gone.
Is it all negative? The world lies open for her, Zara reminds herself. Future, I am on my way.

The little stream glistens in between the green. In the summer heat, this must be one of the coolest places in Penjwin.
Zara points: that is where the synagogue must have been. That is where the women bathed. And there, the men would stand and talk with one another after the service.
Ruth nods, deeply impressed by it all. "This is one of the most magical places that I know," she then says.
Zara thinks of her first visit, after the horrible talk with her mother. The overwhelming sense of presence, of no longer being alone. Since then, she has come back many times.
"It is our past," she says softly. "Rahila's father had a school here. Your father learned to read and write here. Here you can meet our past." Zara goes and sits on the flat rock, and pats the spot next to her.
"Magical," Ruth says, after a long silence.
"You have felt it," Zara concludes.
Ruth looks at the goose bumps on her arms. "What is this, do you know?"

"I have the same thing, each time I am here. I think that it is the presence of my grandmother, and with her the generations of our family that have lived here. I feel that I am a part of it all."
"You say that beautifully."

Zara lets her thoughts go over the past weeks, in which she has been crisscrossing the country with Ruth. She has shown her the remains of the synagogue in Al Qosh, the Jewish quarter in Erbil and the one in Sulaymaniya too. Sometimes Yousef came along, who did not allow himself to be excluded because of this new friendship. Zara was always happy with his company. His accumulated Google knowledge ended up being very handy indeed. Ruth had looked at and photographed everything with an almost sacred seriousness.
"My roots," she had said, time after time whenever her camera clicked.
At the grave of Nahum in Al Qosh she had opened a small, blue can, lighting the candle that was inside. "For the remembrance of Rahila," she had said.
Zara had picked up the can with the Hebrew letters to read the text. "Memorial Candle," she read. "This candle burns for 24 hours?"
Ruth had nodded. "This is a way to remember our ancestors. It seemed fitting."
Zara had placed the can in the stone crevice that was filled with candle wax and the remains of candles. She knew, that it would be found, and that the next visitors would know that there had been people here from Israel. Officially,

something that is not possible, but in reality, something that does indeed happen.

Zara had lent her Rahila's journal. They had talked for hours about how the family had fallen apart. About their departure from Iraq. About the hatred for the Jews. About Jews being the chosen people of God.

"That has brought us much misery," Ruth remarked, on one of the evenings at Ayub's house. "Only in the past century, if you look no further back. The Holocaust, the struggle to establish our own state, the escape of the Jews from Europe and the forced departure from the Arab lands."

"But is has also given us our own state," Ayub had protested.

"That we will have to fight for and defend, to the bitter end. Where we are not allowed to feel safe for a moment," Ruth answered critically. "What kind of state is that?"

"It may not be perfect, but it is ours," Ayub maintained.

"That is true, and that is why I stay there. But the militarism - that is something that I feel bad about. And not because I had to do service myself, and now can be called to war any time."

Repeatedly, they had discussed how Ayub's wish to go to Israel could be realized. Ruth and Ayub had driven to Erbil to get a DNA test done, so that Ruth could start the procedure for a family reunification once she would have returned to Israel. The discussions with Ruth had convinced him that he needed to make a new attempt.

"I have the feeling that I belong there," he said. "And at the very least I owe it to my father, who gave his life trying to get there."

"Come along with us Zara, also do such a test," Ruth had suggested. "Then I can submit your application at the same time."

"Good idea!" Ayub had said. "You can go with us!"

Zara had laughed a bit, but had not taken them up on their offer. Ruth did not push the issue. But when a day later, they were standing together at the grave of Assenath Barzani, she had brought up the subject once more.

After having driven around for hours, they had finally managed to find the grave of Iraq's only female rabbi, in the centuries-old mountain town of Amedi. There was not much left but some overgrown rocks, in the middle of a city where little more was left from the past but a minaret and a gateway of thousands of years of age.

Leaning on a wall near the grave, Zara had wondered whether Rahila too had ever visited this place. It must have almost been a pilgrimage for her, and it surely would have been a very long trip in the time of horse and wagon.

"Why aren't you coming along with Ayub and Nasrin?" Ruth said interrupting her pondering. "You won't get a chance like this anymore."

Zara had looked over the grave to the mountains and valleys on the horizon, where the greens just managed to dominate the yellows of the sun-dried earth.

"Ruth, can you tell me what is so special about Israel, that I would abandon a stunningly beautiful country like this?"

Ruth had started a summation. "The nature, that is beautiful too. We have the land of milk and honey, you remember? And the fact, that there you will be living with other Jews."

"Here I live with other Kurds."
"You are mimicking your grandmother's comments," Ruth had said.
That had made Zara laugh. But she had to admit, that Rahila's decision had influenced her own.
"We have always lived together as Jews. We had our own neighbourhoods, our own communities. Here, that is gone. There, you will be able to celebrate the holidays. When you come to Israel, you will feel like you have come home."
"Maybe," Zara said laughing, "if only for the fact that you also have attacks and violence."
"The most important thing, has to be the freedom. You can say and do as you please. There is no censorship, no fear for revenge from politicians of militias. And don't forget, the universities there are much better. You will have far more career opportunities."
That was true, Zara had to admit. Her future in Kurdistan was an uncertain one; dependent on the master's study she was planning to do, and the function that the party would then offer her. And with that, it all was a bit less uncertain, since that party would be giving her a job. Her studies gave her the right to that, and her father's position served as a further guarantee. But that was not the future that Zara wanted for herself. She wanted it to be more exciting, more intellectual too.
Ruth had motioned towards the grave. "You could even study the faith, and follow the example of your grandmother, and this lady here."
Zara had laughed out loud. She, a Jewish scholar? Never!

"It is not such a crazy idea," Ruth continued. "It is all about the possibilities. Your future there, would be more interesting than here."

Everything always came back to the basic question. Does being Jewish, automatically mean that you must go to Israel? That Israel is the promised land, that your only real future is there? And not here, in Zara's country of birth? In the land she feels connected to, and far more so, than to Israel?

"We shall always be different here," Yousef had said, when she discussed it with him, in the garden on Salim Street where they met one another on a nearly a daily basis. The smell of sweet tobacco was dominant; around them the youth of Sulaymaniya were smoking the water pipe.

Zara looked around, and laughed, as they were the only table where no one was smoking. "Maybe that is fun," she had said. "Being just like everyone else, is also boring."

"If the mood stays as it is now, then yes. But you never know. Anti-Semitism is a continually recurring phenomenon."

"Would you want to go to that country?"

"Don't you have a problem with the fact that we cannot even openly talk about the Jewish state, here?" Yousef asked somewhat rebelliously. "Always the code words, the secret language. We will never be able to come out about our true heritage, here."

"But is that really enough of a reason to want to leave Kurdistan?"

He looked at her thoughtfully. "I don't know. I would like to go and have a look first. The last time, I was so young."

She had nodded. That idea she liked: first having a look, and then making a decision.

"Is that possible?"

"We can try."

A silence fell, in which Zara stared at the smokers while she considered the possibilities.

"May I ask you something?" Yousef then said. "Do you think that Soran is going to go back with Ruth?"

Zara looked at him in surprise. "Whatever gave you that idea?"

"I saw them together."

"Soran is a toy for Ruth," Zara said confidently. "He doesn't even know where she lives."

Yousef just shook his head.

"Now you aren't giving him credit, Zara jaan. Soran isn't a fool, even though you would think he was, for letting you go."

Zara did not want to talk to Yousef about her double feelings for Soran. She could not get used to seeing Soran with Ruth. It was painful, it was too soon. She tried to remind herself, that Soran had mainly started something with Ruth to have a way out of the country. And that this would not work. She would have a difficult time taking him to Cyprus, and there was no way he could go to Israel. But he could not know this. Because Ruth had most likely not told him, that she didn't live in Larnaca, but in Haifa. Yousef's question brought her too close to the painful realization that Soran had mainly wanted her, because as the daughter of a high-ranking party politician, she would help him rise up the social ladder.

But if he had eventually dropped her, because her Jewish background would make that impossible, what was then going on with Ruth? It would be nearly impossible for him not to know that she too was Jewish.

She shook that feeling off.

"Why don't we try to go to that place together for a week?" Yousef picked back up on their earlier conversation, as if nothing had been said since. "Just to have a look. So that we both at least will know what we are talking about."

Zara happily accepted the idea. "Maybe I can even study there."

They discussed how they would go about it, and where they needed to start.

"Make contact with the Swiss embassy," Yousef suggested.

"Do you think that they still operate as a mediator?"

Yousef picked up his Blackberry. Zara watched how he typed with quick fingers, and read the results. He is special, she thought. With him, she discussed everything that she used to talk to Banu about. Maybe he was the only one that she really trusted.

"Yes, it's the Swiss that we need," Yousef said. "I am going to try it there."

Zara nodded, and then changed her mind. "What if it works, won't we have a problem to return to Iraq?"

Yousef nodded. "That is what we must know for sure, eh, before we get started with it…"

Zara had asked Ayub the same question, when she visited him at home, later that night. Ayub had reacted surprised. "So, you are coming?"

"I would like to take a look, Ayub. A vacation, maybe studying for a year. But would I then still be able to start a career here with the party?"

He had laughed out loud, but when he saw that she was serious, he had shaken his head. "If you go, then there is no way back. The party will no longer trust you, I think. Or would not want to run the risk of being accused of bringing in an Israeli spy."

"But what will you yourself do, if you totally do not like life in Israel?"

"I don't expect that. But if that is the case, then I can perhaps go to America, or Europe."

"Do you think that I can go, and take a look? That vacation at the sea in Haifa, that Ruth has been trying to force on me this entire week?"

"Perhaps," Ayub had reluctantly suggested, "if you don't have a stamp in your passport, and don't post any pictures on Facebook? If you tell everyone that you are going to Cyprus?"

"Would Israel let me in?"

"That we would have to arrange too. Talk about it with Ruth."

Ruth. Where was she anyway? Zara had expected to see her at Ayub's house.

"Soran picked her up; he was going to show her Azmar."

The mountains above the city. Zara suddenly had a vision of Soran with Ruth on the blanket.

"They are really an item, eh?" Ayub had said. "You have not told me how you know him."

Zara hesitated. Should she tell him the truth? Then Ruth would hear that she had been messing around with Zara's fiancé. Because that visit to the imam had of course not happened yet. This was too embarrassing. "He comes from Penjwin," is all she said.

She had been worried about Banu's wedding. That Soran would come with Ruth, and it would then come out. How much the village would have to gossip about!

"Are you alone? Isn't Soran coming?" Banu said greeting her.

"Maybe he will still show up. Something urgent came up," she had answered, each time again when someone asked about him. Because going to the wedding of your girlfriend without your fiancé was strange. To her great relief, he had not shown up. That there would be talk was not so bad, as long as it wasn't about him and Ruth.

Of course, she had gotten questions about Ruth, whom the people in Penjwin had seen walking around. "My cousin from Europe," she had answered each time. "Yes, she thinks Kurdistan is great."

Zara's eyes kept getting pulled towards Banu, as she stood next to her new husband in her white wedding dress. That dress, where for she had been dragged from shop to shop. Because it had to be perfect. And it was. There she stood, on the podium with the two thrones, behind a row of fake flowers, as she had wanted. The radiant bride. Would she really be happy with her Mohammed? Would he give her enough freedom; would it really be enough for her to be playing the role as a wife, and later on as a mother?

Zara was supposed to have stood there, in a few months time. According to the planning, her wedding would have been held in the same hall. She felt a great sense of relief that it would not now happen. Yet at the same time, there was the sense of distance that kept coming over her. The feeling that she no longer belonged there.

Zara had joined the line of people waiting to congratulate the new couple, and had hugged her friend and wished her every happiness. Of course. Banu must be happy. But Zara knew that she would not be part of it, as their friendship had cooled since Banu had known about her background. This became painfully obvious on this evening.

She had met former classmates, had danced the folk dances with them, happily waving with the scarf as she got the chance to take the lead. But her heart wasn't in it.

How often had she not done this with Soran, who was a good dancer, and before that together with Banu? Who had found her Mohammed at such a wedding, and had seen him again at the next one, until her parents had contacted his and they had become engaged…. as it was supposed to happen.

That evening, Zara realized that they had now parted ways. And that it probably would have happened, even if she had not found Rahila's journal. That she was a free spirit, and that Banu needed the certainty of a traditional life.

While she sat at a table recovering from being overheated from the dancing, she was very aware of her being different. Yousef was right, she knew now. It can never be as it was.

It was at that time, that she had decided to visit Israel. Making a conscious decision, and never regretting it. Learning from Rahila's story, and making up her own mind. Not allowing herself to be lived by others.

Ruth touches her arm.
"You are very far away."
With a shock, Zara is back on the rock near the stream. She feels warm and happy, contended with the decisions she has made.
"I am coming on vacation to Haifa," she says.
"Yes!" Ruth takes her enthusiastically in her arms. "I will take care of the visa."
"With Yousef," Zara added laughing.
"Of course."
"Let us try to find a publisher for Rahila's diary. I want to give her story more notoriety."
Ruth looks at her. "Are you sure about that? What about the family, then?"
Zara thinks of her mother, who had devoured the diary in only a few days' time, and who could now talk about little else. And after that, she had given the book to Zara's older sister Bayan. She thinks of her Uncle Ibrahim, that has started a search for Jewish heritage in remote Kurdish villages.
"Once you know who you are, you can no longer push it away to it cannot be seen."
Ruth nods silently.
Zara stares at the spot in the green where she thinks the synagogue once stood. "I don't want the Jewish history of

Kurdistan to remain hidden any longer. I want to make it known. And I want to lobby, so that the few remains that there still are, will be protected and preserved."
Ruth still does not speak.
"We must no longer be silent. Our history is the history of Kurdistan. That history must find its way back into the books."
"You are sure about that? It is a taboo. You can get into trouble by doing that."
Zara only nods.
"It will turn your life upside down."
"That is what is needed."
Together they laugh aloud.
A soft warm breeze blows over Zara's arms, and moves her hair.
Yes, Rahila, my dear grandma, she says in silence. I have gotten the message. You can count on me.
Ruth grabs the camera.
"No," Zara says, and then she puts a commanding hand on her arm. "You mustn't photograph this. You must remember it. This must be a place you can come back to in your memories, for the times when you are lost and no longer know what to do."
Ruth looks at her wonderingly. Then she nods. "This is ours."
"Precisely. And that we share with no one else."

THE JEWISH BRIDE

EPILOGUE

I walked through Al Qosh with Tofi, in an attempt to locate the synagogue there. Once before, during a walk through the little Christian town under Khidher's lead, I had passed it far too quickly to be able to remember where exactly it is situated. As it was too hot, I let myself wearily drop down onto the step, in front of an old door. Tofi disappeared, and returned after a bit. He was very excited. 'We have found it; you are sitting in front of the entrance. Give me your camera.'
That must have been the moment, when my fascination for the centuries-old Jewish legacy of Iraqi Kurdistan began. Which led to a search for hidden stories, crumbling heritage and a nearly forgotten past, through which I have been led by a number of loved ones.
First and foremost, Khidher Domle, the Kurdish journalist with an impressive knowledge of his own land, who as a member of another minority, the Yezidi's, both fed and shared my fascination. Then Tofi and Sam (a.k.a. Mustafa

Al-Ani and Saman Penjwini) my 'adopted' sons, who accompanied me to places and people in our search for parts of the puzzle. Without Sam, Penjwin would not have played such a (justifiably) prominent role in the book, nor would I have ended up on the trail of the stories of Jews who had converted to Islam.

Kurda Daloye shared her family history with me even before we had become good friends. Ahmed Mufti brought me into contact with his erudite family and their history. Nazem Shekhani took me along to the Jewlakan of Erbil, where he had spent his youth, following the departure of the Jews. Yadgar Mahmoud helped me find the family, whose history bears a striking resemblance to that of Ayub.

Akram Jibouri stimulated me during the writing and editing, and helped me to keep believing in the book despite setbacks. Badran Habib helped me understand the current relationship between the Kurds and Israel. Benjamin and Whitney Kweskin supported me with their interest and questions. Shivan Fazil helped me to share my slowly accumulating knowledge during presentations in Kurdistan. Inez Polak was the critical reader whom I needed, to prevent me from making the mistakes a non-Jew might make; Lizan Hardi did the same for the Kurdish. Els Horst kept me from making errors in continuity. If there are still any errors or untruths which have slipped into this book, then I am completely accountable for them.

Pamela Williams was already working on the English translation of the manuscript when I was still finishing the Dutch edition, and stimulated me with valuable advice and comments.

I thank my Dutch publisher Jurgen Maas and his wife Annemarijke Stremmelaar for their trust and patience, especially when my journalistic life once more took precedence before the book, and for their valuable comments.

I owe many thanks to a group of friends and acquaintances who made financial contributions to allow me the possibility to write this book in peace, and to Sabina Gazic who made the website to organise that support.

I would also like to mention the excellent book by Ariel Sabar entitled 'My Father's Paradise', which inspired me in the writing of this book. The scene in which an Arabic activist speaks to the sellers on the market in Sulaymaniya is an adaptation of a similar incident in Sabar's book that is set for the most part in Zakho. Also for the incident with the rafts men, I am also indebted to him.

The characters in The Jewish bride are expressions of my fantasy, but most of the occurrences in this book are based on actual fact.

A Kurdish translation of the book by Miran Abraham was published in Sulaymaniya in August 2017, an Arabic translation is also on the way.

JUDIT NEURINK, BYBLOS, JULY 2014/ERBIL, FEBRUARY 2018

LIST OF TERMS

Abba – (Aramaic) father
Agha – literally: master. The landowner, in the countryside the one who protected the Jews
Aramaic – the language that the Jews speak in Iraq, which has a link to the language spoken by the Assyrian Christians in the region
Ayran – salty buttermilk
Arbil – Arabic name for Erbil
Bawke – (Kurdish) father, bawkm – my father
Bar mitzvah – the celebration, at thirteen years old, when the adult law becomes applicable for a boy
Barês – (Kurdish) the one deserving respect, barêsem – my respected
Bayani bash – (Kurdish) good morning
Benjew – (Kurdish) 'the root is Jewish', converted person of Jewish ancestry
Daykem – (Kurdish) my mother – dayke – spoken form for mother

Disjdasja – Arabic men's robe
Eretz Israel – the land of Israel
Farhud – pogrom against the Jews in Baghdad on June 1st and 2nd in 1941, literally: uprising
Goshawistakam – (Kurdish) my love
Goy – (Hebrew) a non-Jew – plural form: goyem
Hakham – rabbi (amongst Iraqi Jews)
Hakham Bashi – chief rabbi
Hayatem – Kurdish adaptation of hayati (Arabic): my life
Ima – (Aramaic) my mother
Janakam (Kurdish) my dear, (jaan means dear, also jana)
Jihad – holy war
Jewlakan – (Kurdish) Jewish neighbourhood
Kaddish – prayer for the death
Kak Azam, kaka – (Kurdish) Mister Azam, mister
Kafir – (Arabic) non-believer
Kanishta – (Targum) synagogue
Keffiye – chequered headscarf for men, is worn throughout the entire Middle East (also by the Jews), usually with an agal, a black band around the head
Kermanji and Sorani – the two most important Kurdish dialects in Iraqi Kurdistan
Kibutzim – Jewish corporation in Palestinian territories
Khalutz – Jewish pioneer movement in Iraq
Kharg and Rasafa – the two banks of the river Tigris in Baghdad. The Jewish neighbourhood was in Rasafa
Maloum – (Targum) rabbi
Mezze – collective word for a number of starters, of which hummus and baba ghanous are the most famous
Mikve – bath where Jewish women cleanse themselves

Mukhtar – neighbourhood chief
Naan – (Kurdish) flat bread that is baked by sticking it to the sides of the oven
Nowroz – Kurdish New Year (on March 21)
Peshmerga – (Kurdish) warrior for the Kurdish cause
Raparin – (Kurdish) uprising (most often used in referring to the events of March 1991)
Rosh Hashana – Jewish New Year, (in September/October) two days of reflection and prayer
Rosh Hodesh – New moon, the celebration of this is held in the synagogue
Shavout – Feast of Weeks in which receiving the Torah on Mount Sinai is remembered
Shive – week of mourning for family of a deceased
Sofra – a sheet used when sitting on the ground to eat, now often made of plastic or paper
Stikan – small Iraqi tea glass
Talmud – discussion of rabbis about the Jewish laws and ethics, largely written by Jews in Babylon
Tanna'it – female Talmud-teacher
Targum – the name used for Aramaic in Iraqi Kurdistan. Anshei Targum are the Jews, literally: the people of the Targum language
Tasqueet – The Iraqi law that gives Jews the right to renounce their Iraqi nationality, their birth certificates and leave all other goods to the state in return for a departure to Israel
Tawla – backgammon
Torah – First five books of the Jewish bible, the five law books of Moses, literally: doctrine, instruction

Ustad – (Arabic) mister, name for someone who is respected
Ustada – (Arabic) female teacher
Yallah – (Arabic) we are going!
Yallah dey – Kurdish adaptation of the Arabic yallah: we are going
Yapprach and kubba – Kurdish dishes that are also part of the Kurdish-Jewish kitchen
Yeshiva – Jewish (religious) school

LIST OF BOOKS

*The Jews of Kurdistan. Daily Life, Customs, Arts and Crafts.
By Ora Schwartz-Be'eri, published by the Israel Museum in Jerusalem
*The Jews of Kurdistan (Raphael Patai Series in Jewish Folklore and Anthropology)
By Eric Brauer (Author), Raphael Patai (Editor), published by Wayne State University Press
*Jewish Subjects and Their Tribal Chieftains in Kurdistan (Jewish Identities in a Changing World)
By Mordechai Zaken, published by Brill
*The Jews of Iraq. 3000 years of History and Culture
By Nissim Rejwan, published by Fons Vitae, Canada
*Iraqi Jews. A history of Mass Exodus
By Abbas Shiblak, published by Saqi in London
*From Baghdad to Jerusalem, the journey of an Iraqi Jew
By Mordechai Yerushalmi, originally published by Kotarot Publishing, Tel Aviv
*Full Circle, escape from Baghdad and the Return
By Saul Silas Fathi, published by the author
*Daughters of Iraq
By Revital Shiri-Horowitz, published by Horowitz Publishing

*When the grey beetles took over Baghdad
By Mona Yahia, published by Peter Halban, London
*Memories of Eden: A Journey Through Jewish Baghdad
By Violette Shamash, published by Forum Books Ltd
*Farewell, Babylon: Coming of Age in Jewish Baghdad
By Naim Kattan, published by Souvenir Press Ltd
*Last Days in Babylon: The Story of the Jews of Baghdad
By Marina Benjamin, published by Bloomsbury Publishing PLC
*The nightingale
By Morgana Gallaway, published by Kensington Publishing Corporation
*The Kurds, a nation on the way to statehood
By Jamal Jalal Abdulla, published by Author House UK
*Invisible Nation: How the Kurds' Quest for Statehood Is Shaping Iraq and the Middle East
By Quil Lawrence, published by Walker & Company
*My Father's Paradise: A Son's Search for His Jewish Past in Kurdish Iraq
By Ariel Sabar, published by Algonquin Books
*Kurdistan: In the Shadow of History
By Susan Meiselas, published by University Of Chicago Press

ABOUT THE AUTHOR

Judit Neurink (1957) is a journalist and author from the Netherlands, a specialist on the Middle East who has been living and working in the Kurdistan Region of Iraq since 2008. She set up a media center in Sulaymaniya (the Independent Media Centre in Kurdistan IMCK) to train journalists and teach politicians and police how to work with the media. Since leaving the center, she has worked for Dutch and Belgian newspapers, radio and TV as well as international media.

She has written seven books, all of them connected to the Middle East, and the most recent ones focusing on the Islamic group ISIS. 'The women of the Caliphate' gives a picture of women's lives inside ISIS held territory, both victims and women who married into or were recruited by ISIS. The latest is 'Women survive ISIS'.

She lives with her two Siamese cats between the capital of the Kurdistan Region, Erbil, and the Greek capital Athens.

Printed in Great Britain
by Amazon